HER
WRITHING
CROWN

HER
WRITHING
CROWN

L.A. RIEMENSCHNEIDER

PRESS

VULPINE

PRESS

Published by Vulpine Press in the United Kingdom in 2025

ISBN: 978-1-83919-683-6

www.vulpine-press.com

To all of the survivors searching for peace in the after.

I believe you.

I see you.

And it was never your fault.

With love: a fellow survivor.

National Sexual Assault Hotline (Confidential 24/7 Support):
1-800-656-4673

A Note from the Author

This book ventures through some triggering topics, and I want to provide readers the option to know in advance what will be talked about in the following pages.

Her Writhing Crown is an honest and raw retelling, loosely based on the Greek mythology of Medusa, and does contain some scenes that include sexual violence, abuse, and PTSD.

1

Beresford de Blasis, whose essence tasted of flickering midnight coals and wet pine trees, and was perched on the chipped railing adjacent to the blackjack table I occupied, was going to die tonight.

And I was to be the one to kill him.

He just didn't know it yet.

There was something frighteningly evocative about watching those who were on death's doorstep and were simply not aware.

Of course, Beresford would not die a permanent death.

No. Those were saved for the righteous.

And for those that hadn't royally pissed off The Collectress.

Perhaps the only thing worse than the final, imminent death that we would all face, was a death stranded in time.

Alive yet dead.

Breathing but not.

And that's what Beresford would face.

"I wouldn't do that if I were you," Rohesia tsked, her golden eyes glimmering with supernatural knowledge as she appeared to the left of me.

I scoffed, lowering my voice to a whisper. "The odds of drawing another high card are much lower than you might think."

At least I hoped.

Clutching the cards close to my chest, I tapped the table, motioning for the dealer to hand me a third card.

"If you say so." Rohesia shrugged, elevating one elegant eyebrow.

My skin tingled with anticipation as the red-haired man deftly placed the card face up on the table. Rohesia could sometimes see into the immediate future, but I had been raised by ruthless, card-mongering sisters. I knew when to hold 'em or fold 'em. At least that's what I liked to tell myself.

Slowly opening my eyes, I frowned.

A five of hearts put me over the goal of twenty-one points.

"I'm out," I sighed, tossing the dealer two gold doubloons. The dealer grinned, bidding me a good night with a nod.

"I hate to tell you I told you so..." Rohesia said with her singsong voice.

"Then don't," I grumbled.

I had always been a sore loser.

Rohesia wrapped her arm around mine as we wound through the sea of tables that offered games like poker, bridge, rummy, and similar pastimes.

Despite my numerous trips to this tavern, my eyes still widened and pink stained my cheeks as we hurried past a velvet crimson curtain. A particularly antsy bunch of customers, with eyes full of desire and longing, waited for their turn as sensual shadows danced across the curtain. I peeked out from beneath my lashes, curiously watching as the elongated shadow of a scantily clad patron straddled a customer who seemed to be dressed in the flowing, wispy swaths of fabric.

Dread claws past the thick bile gathering at the back of my throat and plummets into my stomach uneasily, like a block of forged, blazing hot steel, as the man's clothes continue to disappear.

The man's naked and sinewy form seemed to have captured the attention of multiple people behind the curtain, women and men alike. Greedy, shadowed hands began to trail down the man's broad chest, stopping only to tug at the belt tied to the worn leather trousers that hugged his thick thighs like a second skin.

Beads of sweat collect at the small of my back, as I stand there, watching in unmovable terror as groans of pleasure slink around the curtain and into my ears, before I have a chance to cover them with my clammy and shaky hands.

"Where'd he run off to now?" Rohesia voiced, her words dragging me out of my frozen stupor.

Unsteady breaths escape from my lungs, as the panic dwindles from Rohesia's sudden question and her warm, steady grasp on my shoulder.

She knows where I was trapped in the past.

And by whom.

That's why Rohesia was my best friend.

"I am safe, I am in control, I am present," I breathed in a hushed tone, repeating my mantra for the fifth time today.

Inhaling, my mind shifted to focus on the task at hand.

Beresford de Blasis was no longer leaning against the railing that was connected to a winding and perilous set of stairs. He had been there for the last hour, drunk off his rocker.

I muttered a curse.

There were only three options.

Two gave me hope.

And one filled me with dread.

The upstairs lounge or the latrine seemed reasonable. If I had drunk as much as Beresford, I would be holed up in the bathroom, puking until the sun rose. But he could also be wetting his whistle again in the exclusive lounge upstairs. Exotic alcohol was the main attraction of the elevated lounge, along with other sordid activities that were rumored to be available to high-paying clientele.

Or Beresford had turned in earlier than normal.

And that meant returning empty-handed to The Collectress. My back itched and burned at the thought.

Tenby informed me that Beresford visited the tavern every three days, like clockwork, and didn't leave until well after midnight. If his intel was mistaken, I would be forced to strangle the poor mage. A pity it would be, especially since I was growing strangely fond of his visits.

"I'll take the upstairs."

Nodding, I jogged over to the adjacent wall, entering the men's latrine. I gagged, and sucked in a sharp breath, the mix of stale, hard water and urine created an overpowering stench.

The dimly lit room was no bigger than a powder room. Chipped sea green paint and crude drawings were scattered across the walls. Two urinals and one toilet lined the east-facing wall. There were no dividing barriers separating the porcelain commodes, offering no place to hide.

An open pipe with rushing water served as a sink. No soap was on site. I made a mental note to stop shaking hands with all the customers that frequented the tavern's bathrooms.

A frosted window, no wider than my shoulders, occupied the space above the urinals and toilet, the glass jagged. Dark brown droplets stained the edges of the glass, suspiciously resembling dried blood.

Grunting, I propped my feet on the wall, whilst gripping the grime covered lock with my fingers. Trusting that my legs would give my body extra leverage to unlock the rusty windowsill, I attempted to open it.

It didn't budge.

Sweat beaded at my temples as I yanked at the cruddy lock a second time.

This window hadn't been pried open in years.

Leaving the latrine empty-handed, I could only hope that Rohesia had found Beresford. Before arriving in Iydara, over three and a half years ago, I might have prayed to the gods. And maybe they would have listened.

But that was before they had screwed me over.

I sat at a table by myself for over an hour, watching as Rohesia performed her dirty work on Beresford at the bar. She was sitting in the mortal's lap, laughing at his lame jokes as he flaunted his money around. I was certain that he did not earn enough income as a stable hand to buy the gluttonous number of drinks his gullet could consume.

Beresford had scampered back in just as we were fixing to leave. Rohesia said it was an act of grace from the gods. But I thought it was just impeccable timing with a smidgen of luck.

At half past ten, Rohesia and Beresford passed my table, the former giving me a haughty wink. I was forced to turn my grin into a scowl. We had performed this same routine a hundred times.

Rohesia would use her abilities on an unsuspecting mortal, encouraging them to share a bed with her for the night. No one would suspect that she was a mage.

Most of the mortals in Iydara laughed at the possibility of magic, because in their eyes, only the gods were worthy enough to possess such gifts as fortune telling and necromancy.

However, there were still whispers that slithered through the cracked walls of Iydaraian homes, creeping into the beds of mortals like a boogeyman with bloodied fangs and sunken eyes.

The murmurs talked of monsters with such physical traits.

But mages did not have fangs nor blackened eyes.

Though we were as close as sisters, we looked nothing alike. My wild, black and white curls were an odd contrast to Rohesia's caramel locks, wispy bangs framing her heart shaped face. The color contrasted beautifully with her fawn skin, while an even tan clung to my bronzed skin at the dawn of yet another brutal Iydaraian winter.

She was also at least half a foot taller than me and was slender with lean muscles. I had muscles, but I also liked to have my cake and eat it too.

Tattoos also covered most of Rohesia's arms, depicting magical scenes of forest animals running through various mountain landscapes. Her long legs were covered in whimsical tattoos depicting multilayered landscapes of animals, humans, and mages. Dozens of different earrings adorned her rounded ears.

Though not visible, I knew about the small, black heart tattoo that was on her ribs. No bigger than my thumbnail, I had a matching one on the top of my foot.

I silently wondered what would happen if humans realized that there were dozens of mystical beings living, and thriving, right beneath their noses.

Would they run or fight?

My money was on the latter.

Years ago, a group of foreign fortune tellers craving to earn a quick doubloon had been attacked by a mob of humans because of their magic. In Iydara, it was sinful to even breathe a whisper that someone besides a god or goddess could possess an ounce of magical power.

People had been killed for less.

The Collectress made sure when her secret reached the rumor mill, because it had in the past, that the offending party was killed. Because if her secret was proven to be true, then her perfectly crafted façade would crumble. And her mortal followers would surely die from shock, but not before murdering their leader in a spectacular show of blood and gore.

The last thing Iydara needed was another scandal. And if some nosy gossips were to discover that their darling leader was a dealer and collector of all things magical and forbidden, then Rohesia and I were screwed.

Because if she went down, we all did.

Swallowing the last of my ice water, I departed the tavern minutes after Rohesia and Beresford. The streets were relatively crowded for a winter's night. Hurried elbows jabbed into my rib cage and my toes were stepped on more than once. I silently wished for the thousandth time that I was a bit taller.

Though I wasn't in a rush, I didn't mind the pace. Blood heated my frozen cheeks as I withstood the swift pace the crowd had set. Our rendezvous spot was five blocks north from the tavern and I had already walked three of them.

The crowd began to dissipate as I crossed the deserted railroad tracks and entered the Northern Boundary of Iydara. There were four boundaries that made up the mortal continent of Iydara, the one I was now entering being poverty and disease ridden. Refugees often sought out this deserted boundary over the others, where they were less likely to be seen, beaten or robbed.

The Western Boundary, where the tavern was located, was known for money-spinning activities, such as gambling, brothels, illegal drugs and pool halls. It was almost as poverty ridden as the Northern slums, but the people that resided in the Western Boundary were… different.

Ruthless.

Many there wouldn't pass up the chance to slip a slinky hand into the pocket of an orphan and steal their meager coin to buy a foaming stein of bitter ale.

Where the Western Boundary was as shameless as a whorehouse on worship day, the Eastern Boundary was prestigious and exclusively accessible to only a handful of Iydaraians. Known to house only the most tasteful and wealthiest blacksmiths, florists, brewers, butchers, and temples that Iydara had to offer, the East was an unreachable dream to many.

Unreachable not because of lack of talent or determination, but because those who lived there were in The Collectress's pocket and kissed her derriere until it was rosy pink.

The Anghor Peaks occupied most of Iydara's Southern Boundary, extending onto Iydara's singular island in The Restless Sea, making the land unlivable for humans.

The outlying town of Kilmarn was located at the edge of Iydara's island, connected to the continent via a frozen land bridge. The rules and moral code of Iydara were inapplicable to the forgotten scrap of land, the people of Kilmarn living and abiding instead by a cruel and ferocious set of laws that did not apply to mortals.

Chills skittered down my spine as memories of fighting through haunted, barren forests and over ice packed slopes ambushed my mind. Not the premier place to raise a family, that's for certain.

Halfway down the alley that I walked through was a deserted wooden entryway with piles of overlooked boxes and broken bottles of liquor. A forgotten gate near the entryway opened up into an abandoned backyard. The rank stench was strong enough that only a few sewer rats lingered around the area.

The chirps of frantic birds filled the night air. They anxiously departed, flying out of massive holes in the fabric of the building, as I stumbled upon their forgotten home. Broken glass was scattered about the porch, causing rays of fractured moonlight to project shadows onto the moldy ceiling and walls.

As I stalked up the creaking stairs of the forgotten house, each step fueled by simmering rage, uninvited memories threatened to flood my mind for the second time that night.

I yanked open the back door, the icy handle biting into my skin like a blade. Intense loneliness greeted me as I strode inside.

Before meeting The Collectress, this run-down house was where I had lived for six long months. Summers in Iydara were just as brutal as the long winters. I was on the brink of dehydration and death when Rohesia found me and brought me to The Collectress.

I was grateful. I was.

The Collectress gave us shelter, training, and food in return for our services. But she was one of two people on this damn continent who knew my secret. And she took every chance to dangle this sword over my neck. With every mistake, every mishap, she threatened to expose me. Why she hadn't yet, I wasn't sure. But that was a mystery that was to never be solved. No matter how badly I ached to unravel it.

Footsteps came from behind me as I walked around the house. Hurrying up the stairs, I crouched behind a curtain filled with moth holes, holding my breath. Rohesia should know better than to be this early. I wasn't in position yet.

Only it wasn't Rohesia that walked through the entryway. No, it was more terrible than her being early.

"—WAS THE LOVELIEST FLIRT, MY LITTLE LADY LOVER," crooned a drunken beast of a man with a half empty bottle of whiskey in his hand.

Annoyance seared through my blood as I moved to cover my ears to tune out his horrid singing. I had partaken in my fair share of out of tune, drunken singing and knew the sober ones, such as myself, were the ones that suffered the most.

My irritation grew as he began to show off some seriously poor dance moves. Using his bottle as a dance partner, he twirled around the room, kicking up dust bunnies and clumps of mud from the floorboard

"WE USED TO LOVE SO WELL. I THOUGHT WE'D BE FOREVER, ME AND MY LADY LOVER. BUT ONE MIDNIGHT, ONE—" the man paused, letting out a loud belch. "S'cuse me."

His dark eyes were distant as he stumbled onto a dust-covered chair, propping up his feet on the edge of the coffee table.

"Where was I? Ah, yes, ONE MIDNIGHT WE WALKED TOO MUCH AND DRANK TOO MUCH. SHE GREW SO COOOOLD. MY LITTLE LADY LOVER."

I knew I should move, should demand that the man leave and never come back. Rohesia would want me to stone him. So would The Collectress.

But for some reason I chose not to. Maybe because it was kind of refreshing to see a man who towered at least a foot over me singing a drinking ballad whilst attempting to form a dance line with an empty bottle of liquor, without a care in the world.

"AND THEN IT HAPPENEEEED. OH NO! OH NO! SHE KISSED A CHICKEN. ALAS, A CHICKEN! MY LITTLE LADY LOVER KISSED A CHICKEN."

9

The man's singing resembled a wild boar's bellow.

Brash.

Unpleasant.

Slightly endearing in the sense that the first growl of a hydra pup is endearing and cute, but only for the first few moments before it swallows its prey in one glorious, glutinous chomp.

A loud snort escaped me as I envisioned a group of wild hydra pups frolicking through a field of wildflowers, while hunting down a frightened gazelle. I froze behind the curtain, certain that the man had heard me. Peeking out, I scrutinized his stocky form as he began to drool on the arm of the chair, appearing to have fallen into a drunken sleep. Relief calmed my racing heart.

I snuck around the room and hurried to the bedroom door, desperate to catch Rohesia before she came across this mess. She wouldn't be as nice to the man as I had been.

An airy giggle flitted through the broken windows from the street below as I placed my hand on the tarnished bronze knob that led downstairs.

Rohesia.

Cursing to myself, I looked at the drunkard who I should have kicked out, or stoned, minutes ago. The Collectress would be disappointed. Stoning two people had not been in tonight's plan.

Grabbing the man, I began to half drag and half carry him across the floor and into the closet. Sweat beaded my temple and my muscles ached as I moved the behemoth across the splintered floorboards.

"What exactly are you doing, lovely?"

I jumped back, dropping the man's legs as though they would burn me. My mouth fell open in absolute horror as his penetrating, inky blue eyes met mine. He didn't seem bothered that a strange woman was dragging him through an abandoned building. Instead, he seemed rather fascinated.

"By all means, carry on, I am quite interested to see where this may lead. Though I have never had a woman physically drag me into bed, I am very open to experimenting in the bedroom."

From the man's lilting brogue, he wasn't a native Iydaraian.

Sniffing the air gently, I was pleasantly surprised to find that his essence tasted and smelled of warm cinnamon and bitter orange. There was a hint of rotting flesh, mixed with a strange note that I was too tired to identify.

Mortal.

A wolfish smile emphasized his full mouth as he observed my antsy movements from beneath thick lashes. His shadowed hair was tightly coiled, and his complexion a deep, rich umber. The man's face was rather eye-catching, consisting of well-defined angles, fiery eyes, and arched eyebrows.

I couldn't help but chance a glance at his physical form as he placed one hand behind his head and the other on his lower stomach, giving me a glimpse of the taut muscles that were previously hidden beneath layers of clothing.

The man's eyes flickered in the low light, as if daring me to begin dragging him again.

Finally recovering, I snapped back with disgust. "Please. I wouldn't be caught dead rolling around in your bedsheets."

The sound of a heavy door closing downstairs served as my signal to get into position. With time running out, my ego was going to have to take a backseat for now. I had no option but to grab the man's legs and haul him into the closet.

The man simply watched me struggle with a smirk on his stupidly attractive face, not bothering to help me. When we finally reached the closet, I all but threw him into it.

"Do not make a sound. Or you will regret it," I threatened, my breath coming out in short pants.

11

The part of me that had viewed the drunkard's off-tune singing and dancing as refreshing was long gone. Because what I had to do next was far from amusing.

The mortal raised his hands in surrender and sat down in silent compliance. I hurriedly closed the door, my heart racing.

Stuffing the singing drunkard into the close quarters of the closet had been easy. Way too easy.

Before I had the chance to question the man in the closet any further, Rohesia and Beresford entered the room.

Beresford was even more drunk than he had been in the tavern. His eyes were glossy with intoxication and red lipstick was smeared across his thin lips.

"Come on, Beresford. It will be fun, I promise. Even the gods used to hunt for spirits," Rohesia teased, steering him to the corner of the room I occupied.

Earlier that day, Rohesia had performed an Erebus spell in the space where I silently stood using blackened soil from the island of Tabrn, forcing Beresford to see swirling dark shadows instead of a predator waiting for her next meal.

I took a steadying breath as they neared me, my hands sweaty with nervous anticipation.

A primal growl escaped my mouth as I released the hold on my magic. My back arched as the constant, daily pressure of holding back my true form gave way to immeasurable pleasure. The agonizing pain of fighting my natural form was similar to a mortal attempting to hold their breath for days on end.

Cruel.

Maddening.

And oh so arduous.

Beresford was still blissfully unaware of the monster standing feet from him. The monster buried deep in my soul would gladly take advantage of his blissful ignorance.

I felt a sharp pang of regret as I shifted to grab his clammy hand. Rohesia averted her eyes as I forced Beresford to shift his gaze to mine.

He blinked rapidly as he took in my jade reptilian eyes, their black pupils narrowed to a thin slit. His eyes remained overly bright and damp. It wasn't until Beresford's gaze traveled up to my head that he began to shake and beg for mercy.

My hair, once black with face framing white streaks, was gone. In place of the curled strands were white and black snakes, coiled and ready to attack. They hissed and spat at Beresford, craving violence and punishment.

I was a monster: one that fueled the nightmares of small children. No more than a chilling story that was to be told around a campfire.

"Where's The Collectress's money, Beresford?" I whispered, and the malicious female voice that spoke was not my own. My gorgon dwelled in the darkest part of myself, only coming out when I called.

The relationship I had with this monstrous part of myself was confusing at times like this. The constant fight between mortal and monster was exhausting. Especially when they both craved very different lives.

"I already paid her," Beresford insisted, his breathing becoming more and more shallow the longer he stared at the crown of snakes that writhed on my head.

Humans.

They were all liars, especially when it came to saving their own hides.

"That's not what we have on record," I told him simply.

His story changes with my words.

"I have it. I swear. I just need more time," Beresford countered, sweat collecting on his quivering top lip.

"Don't we all?" I snickered dryly, watching as one of my snakes wrapped her elegant body around Beresford's neck, tightening around his thin skin until he began to sputter and spit.

From the bulging file that The Collectress had on the man in front of me, it was safe to assume that Beresford had a serious gambling problem.

He had racked up a debt of over ten thousand doubloons in just the past month.

"But strange that you in particular should need more time," I tilt my head at him, the monster in me showing him no mercy, "when I have it on good authority that you were given plenty."

"No, I pr— Ouch!" he winced as Rohesia pinched his upper bicep.

"Now, now Beresford, I thought you told me you were an honest man. How can you expect me to wed a man who is not honest?" She slowly shook her head, her nose crinkled with feigned disappointment.

"Ok— Okay, I just need another day to give it to The Collectress. Please, I have it."

Rohesia loudly popped her gum, an edgy habit she had picked up since working for The Collectress. The pink, strawberry flavored gum was a stark contrast against her skin.

Beresford de Blasis dropped to his knees before me; his hands grasped together as he begged for mercy. If Beresford's fate was up to me, I would give him another month, show him the compassion he desired. Kindness that had never been shown to me.

Unfortunately, The Collectress had no mercy to be given.

"Then you know the price for repayment," I said sadly.

I placed a single finger under his chin, forcing him to look at me. He didn't fight, knowing that it would only drag out his misery. Part of me had to admire that.

Hazel eyes gazed into my green ones.

I inhaled deeply, tasting his essence once more.

Flickering midnight coals and wet pine trees, with a touch of rotting flesh. The essence of the shivering man came into focus as I released the hold on my gorgon. Focusing on the glowing saffron aura tinged with emerald flecks, I held onto its edges tightly, grasping the flowing veil between my hands.

I anticipated the essence to feel coarse and rough, similar to the material that clothed Iydara's middle class. But instead a thin layer of grease coated my hands, quietly informing me of Beresford's grisly schemes and questionable life choices.

My magic left me in a hot wave, rustling my clothes as an aura of silver light departed my body and crashed into Beresford's hunched form. Silver light swiftly encapsulated saffron, tearing and eating the glimmering form as my magic overpowered the man.

Like most victims, Beresford's eyes were the first body part to transform into stone. Rohesia and I watched in silence as my magic slowly spread, encasing every wrinkle, pockmark, and hair in stone.

Much like the grains of sand that were forever stuck in an hourglass, he became trapped in an endlessly cruel loop of stagnant time.

Once encased entirely, Beresford would be alive, but dead. His heart would slow to a single beat per minute, enough to keep him alive with magic.

His skin was no longer a healthy golden hue. No. It was the color of the mist covering the Anghor Peaks, a silent omen to anyone that attempted to cross the perilous mountain range.

Beresford's body would be but a whisper of the past, yet his mind would be fully intact. He would remember his lowly life before this eventful evening, but not the night itself.

And fortunately, he wouldn't remember who had stoned him. Nor who had led him here.

The Collectress was always careful, refusing to reveal my identity to protect herself from angry mobs of humans. It was a business transaction, one that I didn't mind.

And sadly, I needed her protection. Because if anyone found out who I was…then I would be worse off than Beresford.

Rohesia released her hand from his hard grasp, watching as I shifted back to my mortal form. "We really should perform these little stonings closer to home."

I exhaled, offering her a nod.

15

The Collectress's outlandish mansion in the center of Iydara would never be my home, like it was Rohesia's. My friend knew this, but it didn't stop her from trying to make it my home too.

A low noise came from across the room, coming from somewhere in the corner.

The closet.

Oh, gods.

I had a grown man hiding in my closet.

Normally, Rohesia would want to know all the explicit details of my encounter with such a handsome man. But if she became aware of his presence, then she would force me to transform him into a living statue as well.

"Roh—"

She raised a small, manicured hand, stopping me before I could ask my question. Bile rose in my throat as I feared she would insist that I return to The Collectress's mansion immediately.

She was my best friend. But she was also The Collectress's second in command. I knew deep down in my heart which one was more important to her.

I just didn't like to think about it too much.

"Just be back before midnight. You know how she gets when you're out too long." It was hard to miss the worry in her eyes. I had missed curfew one too many times.

And The Collectress thrived on punishing her employees.

A sigh of relief escaped from my lungs.

"You know you're the best, right?"

She gave me a small smile, the skin around her golden eyes crinkling, "Right back 'atcha."

Sighing, I gave her hand a quick squeeze.

Rohesia winked and I watched as she and the statue of Beresford disappeared into a cloud of white smoke. The sweet tang of Rohesia's magic stroked my nostrils.

Mages could transport to places they had visited, and the ability was a convenient necessity. Especially when we were far from The Collectress's mansion and needed to transport a newly made statue into her garden.

A deep, baritone voice filled the empty room, "That was an interesting show you put on there, lovely."

I bristled at the nickname, watching as the man dusted off his worn leather vest. It appeared that he had managed just fine while cramped in a drafty, damp closet in the middle of a particularly frigid Iydarian winter.

It was easy to remember how fragile humans were.

And it was even easier to overlook how resilient they were.

It wasn't something I should ever forget, I silently chided myself. They were ruthless and rapacious things and should never be underestimated.

"Finally sobered up?" I asked, averting my gaze. The holes in the ceiling had suddenly gotten a lot more interesting. My heart pounded rapidly in my chest, and I was thankful that he couldn't hear it.

This man made me nervous.

And humans never made me nervous.

It had to be the tiredness from today's stoning.

"Hardly."

I stared at the man, taking in his good looks and expensive but ragged vest with boredom.

A thick and heavy silence filled the room. The man wandered over to the spot where Beresford had met his final fate, examining the area. An impression of two weighty stone knees could be seen if you looked closely enough.

"What brings you here?" I asked the man, watching as he examined the area. He had a certain air of self-assurance about him, as if he knew more than he let on.

Surely, he had a legitimate reason for being in the Northern Boundary at nightfall. It was a dangerous place for humans to be once the sun kissed the horizon. Crime ran rampant here, The Collectress not caring for those that didn't bow to her and were forced to fend for themselves in the slums.

The gods didn't seem to care, either.

"An atrocious string of unlucky decisions."

A soft snort escaped me as I watched gray dust particles mix with the fresh snow that fell through the roof. Digging further into my fur lined jacket, I silently hoped that it wouldn't snow much.

I loathe the cold, which was strange considering how much I used to love it. But a lot has changed since my life in Kilmarn.

"Why did you kill him?" the man asked bluntly. It seemed like he wasn't one to beat around the bush or make small talk, and I appreciated that.

Small talk was for people without an imagination. It was for the boring and bland. I liked individuals with depth. People who spoke of the overstated emotions and experiences that lingered in the barbaric pits of their own tormented minds.

"I didn't exactly want him alive."

The man shrugged his broad shoulders, glancing around the dark room with obvious disinterest. "Fair enough."

"How is that fair?" I scoffed, surprised that the man hadn't run away with his tail tucked between his legs.

I was even more shocked at the sudden urge to argue with this man, as I should be thankful that he wasn't running to The Collectress or to the wardens. Though The Collectress had ordered the hit and the wardens, all non-mortal, were aware of her extracurricular activities, she would still bring terror down on me if she knew a mortal had witnessed a stoning.

"I'm sure you had your reasons, lovely," he answered.

Though it was a challenge to see clearly in the darkness, I didn't miss the man shrugging his shoulders dismissively.

I also didn't miss the nickname he had decided to bestow upon me. Though it was better than the nickname my ex had called me, because how could one ever live down a nickname like Deucey Usy? It still bothered me.

"If you call me that again, I'll throw you out that window, are we clea— What in the gods are you doing?"

I watched as the man looked out of one of the many second-story windows, choosing the one with the thin glass still intact.

"Looking at how high the drop is, see if it's worth it."

I scoffed, bewildered that he was cracking jokes.

Warning bells were sounding in my mind. My brain couldn't seem to decide which indiscretion was more shocking.

The fact that he was a simple human.

Or that he had witnessed forbidden magic and hadn't even blinked an eye.

Most of Iydara's mortals did not know that magic was as real and tangible as the soaring sequoias that grew in Marren's Grove. But there were still some who slipped through the cracks. Those who came from ancestors whose memories had survived being shattered and manipulated by the gods.

But most of those who did remember chose to willfully ignore the past, instead choosing to focus on a rose-colored world. In return for their discretion they were often rewarded handsomely by the gods.

Setting my shock and curiosity aside, I needed to stone him.

The man gazed down at me, his eyes such a dark blue that they appeared black. Backing me into the wall, his hands on either side of my face, he licked his lips and exhaled.

"You're seriously considering it, aren't you?" His breath was hot on my face, coming out in white puffs. I was rarely intimidated by humans, but this man sent shivers up and down my spine.

"Considering what?"

"Stoning me, as your partner called it."

My silence presented him with the answer.

19

The man's throat bobbed as he leaned in close, pressing his lips to my ear. "I dare you to."

During normal circumstances I did not favor being pressed into a wall, and certainly not by mortals with an arrogant disposition. Now, during a fragile and secretive situation that could change the course of my life, I was pissed by this man's hubris.

Shoving my knee into the mortal's groin, I watched with satisfaction as he fell to his knees, heaving for air. He attempted to stand, only to be pushed back down by the tip of my shiny, black heel.

The man's eyes flashed as he fell on his back.

"Do not tempt me," I laughed without humor, turning slowly. My long cloak scraped the ground as I began to step away.

While my hand was searching for one of the sharpened daggers that I kept tucked into the waistband of my pants, the man grabbed my ankle.

I crashed to the floor in a pile of tangled limbs and fabric next to the man. He was quick and agile for someone with a lifespan of only seventy years, I'd give him that.

My knife skittered across the splintered, dusty floor.

It became a desperate battle for domination.

The man quickly pinned me on my back, with one arm pressed into the planks of the floor, my other arm powerless behind me. I frantically attempted to free the arm I was lying against, desperate to reach the knife that was a mere foot from my grasp.

I let out a frustrated screech as he grabbed the knife in one swift movement. Dirt and fractured wood scratched my face as the man shoved my face into the disgusting, disintegrating floors.

"There's nowhere to run now, lovely," he said triumphantly, pressing the knife into the delicate skin of my neck. Warmth began to trickle down my skin. Again, I was impressed by this man's brazenness. Though, he was gravely wrong with me being trapped here with him.

I tried to hold back my laughter at the thought but was unsuccessful.

Flipping me over on my front, I watched as the man straddled me, his smile beginning to waiver at my insistent giggling.

"It seems that you bit off more than you can chew. Which makes you royally screwed. If only you knew. Or have you no clue?"

Dammit, I would make a wonderful poet.

He furrowed his brows in confusion and the pressure of the knife against my skin lessened. Doubt was beginning to hook her sharpened talons into his mind and provided the opening I needed.

"Know what?" he asked, his throat bobbing.

"I'm glad you asked."

Faster than any mortal could comprehend, I disarmed the man, pinning him on his back. My knees sat on either side of his hips as I pressed the blade to his throat, being sure to draw blood, as he had done moments ago to me.

Who needed friendship bracelets when you could have matching scars?

The man's eyes were dilated and wide as he stared at me, my snakes on full display. They wouldn't stone him unless I ordered them to, but their sudden presence seemed to have put the fear of the gods in the man. Making them appear and disappear was as easy as blinking, but it only became more difficult when I was simultaneously attempting to transform someone into a statue.

Despite both of our best efforts to appear unbothered by the violent struggle, as we both silently agreed that whoever was less winded held control of the situation, our bodies betrayed us with drops of sweat and ragged breaths.

A second trail of red blood appeared as I pressed the knife into his throat, hoping my actions would convey my message without having to use my words. He didn't seem to be too fazed by the knife at his throat.

As the beads of blood traced a path down his neck, almost imperceptible scars became highlighted. My knuckle brushed his skin in disbelief, now seeing and feeling the dozens of small scars on his neck.

Before my inquiring mind could distract me further, I increased the pressure of the weapon flush with his neck.

"Had my partner not left, you would be facing the same fate as the man I stoned. Nothing is funny about this. You should be dead."

"But here I breathe," he repeated, eyes dancing with internal humor.

"Is this a joke to you?"

The man continued to ignore the knife at his neck, as though it was a feather tickling him and not a steel apparatus designed for a quick and bloody death.

He tilted his head at me, fidgeting with a ring thoughtfully on his middle finger. "Nothing about this is a joke to me. I just don't see what the big deal is about me seeing you go all garter snake on Beresford de Blasis's ass. He had it coming."

My brows creased and I bit my lips in frustration. I was unsure if I should be offended that he referred to my lethal vipers as measly garter snakes. It also seemed that Beresford de Blasis had more enemies than just The Collectress.

"He might have, but no one can know about me. No one. Not your friends, not your wife, not even your children," I warned, my voice quivering.

A dark, demented part of me hoped he would tell someone. Just so I wouldn't feel so alone and weighed down by my secret. Or maybe so The Collectress would find out, fueling my own twisted sort of rebellion, despite knowing better.

He released a dark chuckle, one that skittered across my bones. "Seeing as I only have one out of those three things, it shouldn't be an issue. Scouts honor."

I began to lift myself from where I was still straddling the man. "Why not report me?"

He considered my question, shoving his hands into his pockets as he answered me, "Maybe I should ask you the same thing. Why not report a mortal knowing about magic? Surely someone as close to The Collectress as yourself would benefit from turning me in."

"Fair point," I agreed.

It was a strange balance that The Collectress had with the mortals of Iydara. Some knew about magic and were allowed to stay informed, but only if they were of use to The Collectress. The bounty above any given mortal's head that knew about magic was astronomical.

My boss would shower me with praise and gifts if I did indeed turn him in. But I had been defying The Collectress for years now and wasn't going to stop anytime soon. Refusing to turn him in added fuel to my secret rebellion.

I started to leave the room of shadows, his words ringing in my aching head. A loud sigh escaped his mouth and I turned on my heel, facing him once more.

"And maybe," he ran a hand over his head, seeming to be frustrated with his mortality, "maybe, I don't believe that the world is as black and white as it seems to be. Maybe it's a messy picture of silvery, ashy choices and consequences. Ones that change your path but never your fate."

"That's a rather positive outlook for a mortal."

"And you're a rather cranky immortal."

He wasn't wrong.

"What's your name?" He asked the question so quietly that I strained to hear him.

I lifted my gaze, meeting his cobalt eyes once more.

"What does it matter?"

"Mortal curiosity, I suppose." He was a strange man. The way he said his statement, like some kind of inside joke had me on edge.

But I didn't shy away from his question.

"Medusa. But my friends call me Usa," I replied, giving him a soft smile.

"I hope we meet again, Usa."

I frowned.

"Fighting with each other doesn't make you my friend."

The man released a low chuckle, winking at me in the low light. "Depends on where you're from."

At that, he gave me a smirk, nodding as he climbed out of the window and disappeared into the inky night.

It wasn't until I was a couple of miles away, in a different part of Iydara, that I realized I hadn't bothered to ask what his name was.

2

"What time did you return home last night?"

The question snapped my attention from the pork sausage I was currently demolishing to Casimar Daemarrel who sat across from me and Rohesia.

Casimar had been working for The Collectress long before Rohesia had. Born a mage, he had been banished from his coven at the ripe age of fourteen.

Banished was putting it nicely.

He was auctioned off to The Collectress for a whopping five doubloons. His coven accused him of being cursed and wanted nothing to do with him.

Damning evidence had proved that Casimar had regularly assaulted and violently taken advantage of mortal girls multiple times once he reached puberty.

The mage was a lanky thing, probably weighed no more than one hundred pounds dripping wet. I had at least seventy or eighty pounds on him.

Because of this, many people underestimated Casimar. But it wasn't Casimar's physical strength that gave him an advantage over most trained warriors.

His cruelty and intelligence were unmatched, making him one of the most feared warriors and Keepers in Iydara.

Thank the gods he had not been born with dunamis, a primal magic so malevolent and wild that not even Rohesia knew much about it. Rohesia often compared dunamis to a raging river, where her own magic was a steady creek. The only individual in Iydara with dunamis running through their veins was The Collectress.

The magic could be almost as powerful as that of the gods.

It could create portals out of nothing, conjure up deadly, striking weapons, and so, so much more.

There were whispers that the magic came directly from the blood of the gods. The same blood that was used to construct the island of Oernear, the land of mages, sprites, elves and other humanoid but magical beings. It was where Rohesia had been born.

Each of Enthlos' five islands had been constructed with a different bodily fluid from the gods.

Gross, I know.

Rohesia had attempted to explain the magical process in depth to me, but I hadn't been able to get past the fact that the very land we stood, breathed, and fornicated on was kept viable by bodily fluids of the gods.

Disturbingly, the *fluids* were necessary to keep the islands alive and flourishing and also acted as a reservoir of raw magic to those who could access it, such as mages.

Dunamis was thought to be tied directly to the blood of the gods, while the magic of mages was tied to the sand of the islands.

While the mage infested island of Oernear was built with blood, the vacation-esque island of Tabrn had been created with saliva. The luscious island served as an escape for the gods from the heavens and only a few mortals were allowed to visit.

Travel between any of Enthlos' islands was difficult and scarce. To enter the island, one needed the corresponding *fluid*, gross again, I know, in their possession. They only needed to sprinkle the liquid on the land to enter, but it was almost impossible to come by.

To enter Oernear you needed to sprinkle a few drops of blood from a god onto the expansive grassland. To stay in Tabrn, one needed the spit of a god or goddess. And so on and so forth.

To the southeast of Tabrn and Oernear was Ahtelah, the prison island for human and non-human beings, mainly demons, the gods deemed unfit for the other masses of floating land. It was no wonder the craggy land was built from the tears of the ones we worshipped.

Sweat built and sustained the southernmost island of Raas. The desolate territory was a breeding ground for monsters that the gods had banished from Iydara after The Siege of Insanity. The citizens of the island had been safely moved to Iydara, after pledging allegiance to the Iydaraian gods, of course.

Many boats had mysteriously vanished within ten miles of Raas' black, sandy beaches. It was an act of war against the gods to visit the island without permission, even if you did have a vial of their sweat handy.

Hey, I didn't judge.

And finally there was Iydara, the island that was intended to act as a safe haven for the children that worshiped the gods, and was formed from breast milk. After decades of disagreements, The Collectress had managed to convince the gods to open the island to Oernearians, stating that humans were incapable of governing themselves and needed someone with a magical background to keep the peace.

I almost agreed with her.

Most humans were already violent, selfish creatures of habit and mayhem. Discovering magic would only make humans turn into power hungry monsters like Beresford de Blasis. And the gods knew we didn't need any more of those wandering around Iydara.

A small, almost miniscule part of me felt bad for the mortals, wondering when the world had turned so predatory, or if it had always been that way and I had just been too ignorant to care.

I chewed my food thoughtfully, continuing to study Casimar with careful intent. The bland food sated my growling stomach but didn't do much to calm my racing mind.

With greasy blonde hair that was plastered to his forehead with sweat, sunken in eyes, and plaque covered teeth, Casimar caught the attention of a multitude of women. Just not for the reasons he had hoped.

When Rohesia had first started working for The Collectress, she quickly rose through the ranks. Within two years, she had taken over as The Collectress's second in command, leaving Casimar third and rather bitter.

"I returned before midnight." Wiping grease from my mouth with a napkin, I shrugged indifferently. I had actually gotten back a few minutes south of midnight, but Casimar didn't need to know that. And with The Collectress in his pocket, he ratted me out every chance he got.

"Are you sure about that?" Casimar asked, his eyes shining with a predatory gleam.

"Of course, Casi."

My saccharine tone and matching smile triggered his eyes to darken wickedly.

I had the feeling that Casimar knew I had been ten minutes late. He seemed to know everything about everyone. Probably because he didn't have anything better to do with his time. And there was that vendetta of his.

Casimar, Rohesia, Iva, and Zayd were all the Keepers of the boundaries of Iydara. Casimar had been the Southern Keeper for years, until Rohesia recently bumped him down from that position.

A Keeper's boundary said a lot about them.

For instance, Casimar was now the Keeper of the Northern boundary. The crummiest, sloppiest, and most spiteful boundary of them all. It told citizens that Casimar was unloyal, foolish, and not trustworthy. Now humans steered clear of him, even his own mages had begun to avoid him. Being demoted from the best boundary to the worst had been a major blow to his ego, putting me and Rohesia in the crossfire.

Placing my fork down, I met his black eyes again, resisting the urge to shove my utensil in his neck. I had thought about it more than once but didn't think it would be worth bloodying a utensil that I would then have to clean.

Quickly glancing at his white-knuckled grip on his butter knife, I smirked. It seemed that I wasn't the only one weighing the pros and cons of first-degree murder with a dining utensil.

He began to open his vulgar mouth, surely to protest the legitimacy of my story, when a deafening silence filled the room. This silence was too familiar and bone chilling.

My mouth clamped shut and became parched.

All of the mages that occupied the common room stood, while I remained seated. I wasn't allowed to stand in her presence. Instead, I clasped my hands in my lap and gazed down at the floor.

The sound of pointy stilettos hitting the floor would haunt my sleep for years to come.

"My Usa. You have upset me yet again." Her voice was an awful caress, causing my heart to lurch in my chest.

I bit my lip until I tasted blood.

Deafening footsteps filled the silence as she grew closer to the table I sat at. I didn't need to look up to know that Casimar was grinning.

The Collectress placed her slim hands on my shoulders, squeezing painfully. I fought the urge to slam my head back into her chest.

I knew what came next.

"As you were," she commanded, only she wasn't talking to me. The sounds of forks and spoons scraping against ceramic plates filled the air once more as I was hauled to my feet.

The Collectress's cold hands trailed down my body to grip my upper arms, hard enough to leave bruises. I didn't fight as she started to drag me to her chambers.

Rohesia looked on with worry, her gold eyes turning into flaming coals. Her jaw ticked as she played with her food. But she did nothing to stop what would come next.

The Collectress released her grasp on my arms once we stopped in front of the ornately decorated doors that would lead into her lavish chambers.

The marble door frame was engraved with depictions of The Siege of Insanity, when humans went to war with the mages of Enthlos and other magical creatures, battling to claim the lands we currently stood on.

Prometheus, a Titan and one hell of a trickster, created and forced the mortals to go to battle with mages, who were the Daughters and Sons of Hecate. Prometheus wanted to challenge Zeus for power but was too much of a coward to do it himself, sending the humans into a bloodbath.

Deciding to attack the followers of a close, personal friend of Zeus was a major mistake by the disgraced Titan.

The humans had lost.

But, Zeus had other plans than to just kill the remaining mortals off, despite the protests of the rest of his council. Legend says that the gods stole the humans from Prometheus because they wanted servants and followers who did not have magic running through their veins. They wanted compliance instead of obedience.

Though the mortals had been ripped of their memories of magic after the battle, they had gained the rolling hills of Iydara and the protection of the gods, specifically Zeus and Hecate, in return for their unrivaled devotion.

Understandably, this led to a tense relationship between Iydara and the other countries of Enthlos. I would be pretty pissed too if my people had been banished to a foreign land all because my gods had gifted my homeland to their new playthings.

These days, if humans courageously, and stupidly, decided to traverse to a different island without the gods, then they were practically signing their own death certificate.

A shiver snaked its way down my spine as I faced the door. Portraits of striking gods and goddesses were carved into the top of the door, depicting the bloody war, and served as a silent reminder to us who it was that truly reigned over our world.

I refused to pray to them anymore. They were dead to me.

As if sensing the disquiet that was building in my chest, The Collectress unlocked the door. I stared up at her brooding form, refusing to lower my gaze.

Jagged, puckered scars trailed down her forehead ending at the tip of her bird-like nose. The pink scars only made her features even more interesting and striking.

"Oh, Usa," The Collectress said sadly, voice clipped and face unreadable. She acted like I was the biggest disappointment of her life. But I knew she wouldn't be nearly as intimidating when I was released from her clutches.

One day, I told myself.

One day.

"Don't Usa me," I fired back, glancing at the clock that displayed half past ten. It had been stuck at that time for an entire year now.

I knew better than to talk back. But I couldn't help it. Even when I faced her wrath, which was more often than not, I refused to roll over and bow to her.

Despite The Collectress's chilly demeanor, her chambers were fairly inviting, with open facing windows pointed towards the gardens. An elaborately long mahogany table sat in the middle of the room, holding chairs for at least twenty people.

I warily sat in a chair to the right of The Collectress's plush, magenta throne-like chair. Which, of course, was at the head of the table.

"Do you realize how upset I am with you?" she asked, pouring herself a hot cup of unknown red liquid. My stomach clenched as I considered the different possibilities.

31

"I imagine extremely," I said dryly, taking in short, measured lungfuls of terse air. I wished she would just get on with it. She always insisted on baiting me, as if we were playing a game.

Ready to have my punishment over with, I splayed my hands out on the table, my chin pointed at the floor.

The Collectress angled her head at me with a casual refinement, glancing at me as though I was a puzzle yet to be solved. My patience was already running low after the conversation with Casimar. But The Collectress continued to stare at me, her black eyes dull.

My body jerked when she placed her glass down rather violently, muscles in my shoulders stiffening as she walked around the table, beginning to kindle a fire in the outlandish marble fireplace.

A dress of deep burgundy clung to her slim figure. The dress parted at her thighs, a single strip of fabric falling between her legs. Heavy, ruby encrusted jewels hung from her ears, complimenting the shining golden hue of her cropped, pin-straight hair. Heavy bangs sat on her forehead, seeming to be held in place by magic.

Never a strand out of place.

"I do not take breaking curfew lightly, as you know. But that is not why I have requested our meeting."

Part of me wanted to laugh.

She always acted like I had a say in these *meetings.*

The traumatized part of myself breathed a sigh of relief, though I was angry at Casimar for ratting me out yet again. I silently wondered why she had summoned me to her chambers if it wasn't to receive punishment for breaking curfew.

Confusion tore through me, followed by a sliver of hope. But that sliver of hope was quickly extinguished as I watched her place three iron brands into the fire.

"Lower your eyes," she demanded quietly, and I did so without a breath of hesitation.

I felt her gaze travel down my face and curvaceous frame. My cheeks and neck prickled from the heat of her intense stare.

For the first and surely not the last time that night, she yanked my hair.

Dragging me across the room, she shoved me against the window that faced the gardens. The cold glass bit into my cheek, and my head screamed in pain as it throbbed from her iron grasp.

"Do you see what I see?"

My neck was snapped back as I was forced to look into the gardens. The sun had begun to set, casting a warm glow over the statues and flowers. Snow only covered the ground, refusing to touch the humanoid statues. Even the weather knew that they were cursed.

Never to breathe again unless I, and only I, unstoned them.

Only the creator of a statue could unstone it; a failsafe created by the gods in case one good-hearted gorgon decided to free the souls of every statue in the land.

I turned my head to look at my employer.

"An obsessed and lonely woman? Probably with daddy issues?" I panted through gritted teeth, venom dripping from my lips.

I felt the blood drip down my face before my body could register the pain. Stars flitted across my vision as I stared up at the ceiling. Clenching my teeth, I attempted to focus on the spinning light fixtures.

The Collectress's muscled legs were taut as she stood above me. I watched as a phantom breeze danced with the thin strips of fabric that scarcely covered her long legs. From this angle, she resembled a malicious goddess.

"Let me correct myself, Collectress." I raised my hands, wiping blood from my lip in the same motion. "I acknowledge that making the mistake between daddy and mommy issues is undesirable for someone with your reputation. I just never would have pegged you as someone with the latter. Who would've thought? Thankfully, for you, I'll never make that mist—"

Agony pulsated through my spine as I was launched into the adjacent wall. Expensive paintings were knocked onto the ground, their frames breaking and splintering. The crystal chandelier shook as I fell into a crumbled pile of wood on the deeply stained floors.

"Two hundred and fifty-three statues have blessed my garden since I took pity upon you. This morning, there were only two hundred and fifty accounted for. Explain."

She walked around my crumpled form, waiting for an answer. I fought against the fear in my throat, refusing to bend.

"Maybe you have a thief with atrocious taste?" I chortled, choking on more blood as her stiletto connected with my nose.

A sickening crunch filled the air.

Draped across her shoulders and neck was a thick, velvet cloak. I silently wondered what would happen if it got a little too tight. Or what would occur if she just happened to accidentally fall on one of my hidden daggers.

One day I would make her pay.

That day just couldn't be today.

"Are you sure your goons counted right?" I said wryly, unable to stop myself. I walked a fine line when it came to The Collectress.

And I tested that line often.

But it wasn't my fault that the wardens were notorious for not using their heads, and half of them could not solve basic arithmetic problems.

A boundary Keeper ruled over a group of wardens, as well as two or three mages for each section of land. Wardens were the brawn that kept everyone in line, while mages were the brains that kept each boundary running.

Rohesia controlled the Southern and most important boundary, while Iva ran the illicit Western, Zayd ran the esteemed Eastern, and Casimar ran the unkempt Northern.

That left Central Iydara with the unwanted scraps of wardens that the Keepers deemed unfit for duty in the boundaries. Most of them came from Casimar's boundary.

I rested my head on the floor, the cool wood easing the headache forming at my temple. The room became tinged in pink as blood dripped into my eyes.

The Collectress's jaw ticked at my jab, leafing through what appeared to be a newspaper for Central Iydara. The front pages were filled with propositions of expanding the Eastern Boundary.

Again.

If they expanded the boundary any more, the Northern Boundary would almost cease to exist. But The Collectress only cared about creating more condos, hotels, and clubs for the wealthy citizens of Iydara.

But on the bright side, Casimar wouldn't be ruling over those wardens, mages, and citizens anymore. The Northern boundary citizens would be forced to move, and since the Southern boundary was off limits, they would be placed in the Western or Eastern boundary.

Which had to be better than the Northern.

A loud *clink* disrupted my errant thoughts.

The Collectress finished her drink, red liquid staining her pearly white teeth. She tossed the glass on the floor, pieces of mosaic crystal glittering in the dim light as it danced across the polished floors.

"You and I both know that only one gorgon can unstone the statues in my garden." She folded her arms across her chest, watching as I struggled to get up.

Terror pulsated through my body at her accusation, realizing just how serious this situation was. Unstoning someone? There had to be a mistake. Someone must've miscounted.

"I was in my quarters, Collectress. You know how I like to spend my off days. Sleeping. Eating. Rinse and repeat," I jested, hoping she couldn't hear the shaking of my voice.

There was a slight chance that someone had moved the statues. But the last time someone tried, they were launched into the sky by silver bolts of otherworldly lightning.

"I wish I could believe you, my Usa. I really do." Chills skittered down my spine as she leaned in close and hissed into my ear. "Unstone my statues again, and I will inform your sisters and mother of your whereabouts."

My stomach dropped. There was no fighting her on this.

She didn't believe me. And I couldn't risk her contacting my family. No. I would rather be branded again than face my bleak future with them.

The Collectress might torture, abuse, and loathe me, but she wouldn't kill me. My abilities were too important to her agenda.

My coven, on the other hand, definitely wanted me dead.

"Hurry now, I don't have all day. You know where to go."

Black spots burst across my vision as I sat up. Holding my chin high, I stood. Unsteadily, but still, I stood, and began the uncomfortable walk to the chair she had constructed for our meetings.

Unbuttoning my shirt, I straddled the chair, finding comfort in the cool material as I sat with my back exposed to The Collectress. I balled up my shirt, placing it in my mouth with shaking hands.

"Three more letters seem reasonable, don't you think?" The Collectress's voice was airy and light as she stood behind me.

My eyes stung as I gripped the front of the chair, hard enough that my nails dug into the plush stuffing. The most brandings I had received in one sitting had been two. And those had knocked me out for four days. I couldn't suppress the shudder that traveled from the base of my skull to my tailbone.

A moment later, I felt her cold hand on the back of my neck, clenching my dark, tightly curled hair in her fingers. She yanked it into a harsh updo, not wanting the strands to get in the way.

I took a steadying breath, silent tears threatening to spill over.

The room fell silent as The Collectress removed the first branding iron from the fire. The letter 'H' stared back at me.

The word 'PROPERTY' had been branded onto my back, letter by letter, in less than twelve months after my arrival.

'OF' was finished the day before Rohesia's birthday, five months ago.

'THE' would be finished today.

And the letter 'C' would begin the process of the final cursed word. When I left, I would have to find someone to remove the ugly brands from my body.

I didn't care if they had to tear my skin to shreds to do so.

My entire body jerked and fought as fiery pain rippled across the sensitive skin of my back. Rancid smoke wafted across the room and bile burned in the back of my throat as I smelled my own burning flesh.

Sweat streamed down my face as I bit down on the shirt stuffed into my mouth. If I bit down any harder, I would crack a tooth. Blackness crept at the edge of my vision, threatening to take me under. The swelling and itching began as The Collectress switched brands, grabbing the 'E' that was being licked by orange flames.

Strangled screams departed from my lips as she placed the brand into my spine. The ones on the spine always hurt the worst.

Always.

I was drenched in sweat, my body thrashing and trembling as she placed the third and final letter on my lower back. Darkness was coming fast. And this time, I didn't fight as she took me into her cold, forlorn embrace.

3

The heavy snowfall that covered the dirt roads of Iydara had turned into slush by dawn. Silvery sunlight fluttered through fluffy, white clouds, casting an ethereal glow over early morning pedestrians.

Grumbling to myself, I sharply turned the corner of an abandoned alleyway, and narrowly escaped the growing crowds of extravagantly dressed socialites.

The Eastern Boundary housed more people than the Center of Iydara by a few thousand, making for cramped streets and shops. Perfect for someone who wanted to disappear.

Vendors attempted to sell me frozen fruit pops, steaming hot chocolate, decorated candied apples, but they backed away when they saw the scowl and bruises on my face.

Normally, Rohesia and I would have gorged ourselves on hot chocolate and candied apples. But not today.

I soon found myself lost in the rush of festivities. Happy families with giggling children twisted and twirled on the ice-skating rink in the middle of the square. Mages with an affinity for water worked year-round to keep the ice impenetrable and pristine, unknown to the mortals of the land. Rohesia had always begged me to go skating with her and her mage friends.

I never had, though.

I told myself that it was because I was afraid of slicing an appendage open, which was partially true. But the real reason was because the other mages despised me. Rohesia tried to reassure me that they liked me, but not even she could stop the rumors and whispers of me being The

Collectress's harlot. If only my co-workers knew that our late-night meetings were filled with torture rather than pleasure.

I'm not sure they would care.

Soon, I found myself drawn to a quaint music studio on the south side of the busy square. Music had always held a special place in my heart, though I hadn't listened to much for the past few months. And when I did, it was often the same artists and vinyls I had heard hundreds of times.

Rohesia had postulated that it was a coping mechanism from trauma. That the familiarity of certain musicians, songs, or books helped me to feel in control of my uncontrollable life. I supposed there was some truth to her observation.

The doors opened to a musty shop with a handful of older patrons. Many of them were filing through dirty vinyls and books of aged music. A ghost of a smile tugged at the corner of my mouth as I recalled memories of Rohesia playing songs about cheating lovers in our shared room.

Her soft yet powerful voice could hold a magnificent tune. I always sounded like a tone-deaf puppy. She would laugh and pinch my cheeks and say that it was an endearing sound.

A bluesy song was playing on a turntable, projecting lyrics of forgotten loves and melodies of a lost time. People paid me no mind as I took a seat and watched a small gathering of young mages as they danced in the middle of the shop.

Unlike the dancing at the exclusive nightclubs in the Western Boundary, this dancing was smoother. More intimate. It called to me and made my heart ache all at once.

A hunched over man, a human waiter, brought me a warm mug of hot chocolate, topped with a wonderful amount of whipped cream and chocolate shavings. His burly, misshapen eyebrows raised in astonishment as I tipped him three silver doubloons. He thanked me and hurriedly ran behind the counter, smiling to himself at his good fortune.

The variances between mortals and mages were so slight that it was easy to confuse the two species. But once you were trained to see the differences, or the lack of them, it was hard to ignore.

Mages showed no signs of aging. Even if they did, it wouldn't matter since they could alter their appearances with a single thought. Casimar had once made the mistake of changing into Rohesia.

He thought that it would be a chance to get me to spill my secrets to him. And he had almost succeeded. Had it not been for his essence, I would have fallen for his trap.

Every living, breathing person, be that mortal or magically blessed, releases an essence. An essence was thought to be an extension of one's spirit. Sort of like an aura, but one that you could see, smell, and occasionally taste. Sometimes, if the bond was strong enough, I could see the person's memories.

The magic that flowed through my blood allowed me to physically touch someone's essence. It was how I could perform my stonings quickly and smoothly.

Casimar, like most male mages, smelled of freshly cut grass, mixed with a sharp tang of sea salt. Rohesia's essence reminded me of cocoa with hints of peppermint and rosemary.

And mortals…well most mortals smelled of death and whatever overpriced fragrance they enjoyed.

I winced in pain as I adjusted in my seat, reaching into my purse, careful not to brush the bandages on my back.

The Collectress had branded me over a week ago. Normally, it would take me but a few days to recover. But that was with only one, maybe two letters.

Rohesia and a mage named Naydeen had carried me back to my room. The Collectress forbade Rohesia, or anyone else, from using healing magic on my injuries. Since The Collectress had forced her hand, Rohesia had stayed by my side for days, changing my dressings and medicating my wounds with ointments made from varying plants and flowers.

Her birth coven was known for their healing tonics and ointments. Iydara received monthly shipments from Hecate's First Coven, allowing The Collectress to sell the coven's ointments to mortals at an overinflated price.

The profit margin was enough to pay for The Collectress's monthly meetings with the gods on the tropical island of Tabrn.

Rohesia never talked about her reasons for leaving Hecate's First Coven. And I never pushed her to talk about it. Just as she never pushed me to talk about my past at Kilmarn.

As fate would have it, the client we needed to stone today was a banished member of Hecate's First Coven. Rohesia didn't know him, and it didn't surprise me. The adolescent mage would have been in diapers when Rohesia had just started her work for The Collectress.

I sipped on my piping hot drink as I skimmed over the file The Collectress had given me the previous night, waiting for Rohesia to show up.

The mage's name was Philemon Farfose and he had been illegally transporting magical antiquities overseas. Normally, The Collectress wouldn't see Philemon as a threat, but she had evidence that those relics had been taken from her own personal collection.

The hot chocolate warming my insides turned to ice as I noticed The Collectress's specific notes.

Rohesia and I usually performed the interrogation, but not this time. The Collectress had left detailed notes to bring Philemon to her chambers as soon as we apprehended him. If she branded the ones that were loyal to her, I didn't want to know what she did to those that stole from her.

"Slouching isn't good for your bandages."

I rolled my eyes, not lifting them from the file as Rohesia took a seat next to me. "Yes, mother."

Snatching the file from my hands, Rohesia dropped a plate of baked goods on our table. I hurriedly grabbed a flaky croissant that Rohesia had brought me, devouring it in a few bites. I licked butter from my fingertips and watched Rohesia chew her bottom lip in concentration.

Sighing, I skimmed the file once more. Philemon's last place of employment was this music shop. It was our only lead. Even with the scarce amount of information, it shouldn't be a problem for Rohesia. She was like a bloodhound.

"I'll go ask the worker if he knew Philemon," she said. "Watch my back?"

"Always."

I smiled as I watched Rohesia saunter up to the counter, enchanting the worker with the sway of her hips and a beaming smile.

The shop seemed to grow louder as Rohesia questioned the man, the grins, and faint shared touches indicating that their conversation was going well.

Rohesia told me that the correct way to question someone was to have a simple conversation with them, instead of berating them with questions. Suspects also got defensive and closed off if you asked too many questions too quickly.

It was a delicate balance, one that Rohesia had mastered.

The pair continued to talk as a low buzzing filled the music shop, sounding like a nest of very aggravated hornets.

My temple began to ache as the noise soon became unbearable. It didn't seem to bother anyone else, even my partner. Flashes of fluorescent lights crowded my vision, turning the inside of the shop into an overstimulating nightmare.

I groaned in pain as lights continued to flash, though, again, no one seemed to notice.

Rohesia seemed to be handling the interrogation well, a strange, little voice told me. She wouldn't mind if I left.

Leaving the store seemed like a good idea, suddenly.

Crisp, bitter air gnawed at my face as I walked across the square, willing the flashing lights to stop.

Walk, the voice whispered.

Then the pain would stop.

And it finally did.

Frowning, I twisted, realizing I had walked a few blocks away and was standing outside an alleyway.

I turned away, anxious and confused, when something changed in the alley. It was a subtle change, like leaves falling quietly to the ground.

A nearly imperceptible buzz reverberated from the sidewalk.

Taking a measured step, I placed my hand on the hidden daggers in my waistbands. The alleyway was rather dark for mid-morning and the wind grew soft when I walked further down the passageway.

The world stilled.

A humanoid figure appeared at the end of the alleyway, so dark and shadowed that it was almost invisible to the eye. Its jerky and shuddering movements were all wrong. A horrid, gravelly moan left the creature. Hair on the back of my neck stood on end as I tentatively walked closer.

Sliding my daggers into my hands, I squinted as the creature emerged from the shadows. It was too big and misshapen to be human or mage.

If someone had taken my picture at that exact moment and sold it to an art gallery for an outrageous amount of money, the artist would have titled the photograph *Untainted and Impervious Terror*.

Because that's what I felt deep in my bones as Beresford de Blasis emerged from the inky shadows.

4

Fear was a peculiar thing. Too much of it and one could die from a racing heart. Too little and one could grow reckless and start acting as a god rather than a mortal.

I stared at Beresford, frozen into place, rooted to the cruddy sidewalk under my shoes. His eyes were gone. Black eye sockets roved my face, seeming to linger on my eyes, my nose, my mouth.

My heart.

My mouth hung open. Beresford tilted his head, and I watched in horror as pebbles fell out of his ears, tumbling to the ground and landing before my feet.

This man…no, this *creature* was both fascinating and chilling.

His skin was thick, veins no longer visible beneath his colorless complexion. He truly was a walking, breathing figurine. And that terrified me. The only glimpse of his human past were the strange, wispy strands of hair that peeked out from a layer of stone.

When a victim became stone, they stayed trapped in the position that they were last in as a mortal. They never moved. Whatever Beresford was now, it wasn't of my own creation. Instead, he had turned into something much more sinister.

"What happened to you?" I choked out, raising my weapons. Fear threatened to take over, but I forced myself to stay in control of my turbulent emotions.

Beresford only grumbled, his voice resembling rough gravel in a cement mixer. He pounded his fists into his skull with anger and dismay.

Cracks formed in his stonelike skin, growing and growing until chunks of it fell off, only to grow back minutes later.

I scanned the deserted alleyway behind me, careful to watch for any curious mortals. The last thing The Collectress needed was a riot at the discovery of magic. Those that did discover magic often had their memories wiped, and if that didn't hold, then they met me.

"Beresford!" I exclaimed, raising my voice. His black eyes seemed to lock on mine as I swallowed loudly.

Placing my daggers on the ground, I walked to him with my hands raised, my voice gentler than it had been moments ago.

"I'm not going to hurt you. No one's going to hurt you anymore." Shivers skated down the length of my back, a combination of the frigid breeze and overwhelming terror.

A step away from him, I touched his arm with a shaking hand. It was cold and gritty, unlike anything I'd ever felt before. My statues were smooth, but his skin was bumpy and coarse.

Gasping, I realized my mistake moments before he attacked.

I was thrown across the alley as Beresford swatted at me like I was nothing more than a pestering fly. My back seized up as the impact shook me to my core. I reached for my knives, only to remember I had placed them on the ground near his clunky feet.

Cursing myself, I watched in dismay as he grabbed them from the ground and squeezed them in his hands, reducing them to warped fragments of metal with his brute strength.

This was it. This was how I was going to die. Not at the hands of The Collectress or my mother and sisters, but by being ripped to shreds by this awful monster.

It seemed only fair as I had been the one to turn him into an immovable statue against his will. The gods had a funny sense of humor.

Without any back-up, any weapons, I wildly lunged for Beresford. He surged from the ground, crashing into me with a powerful leap, his arms of stone wrapping around my waist.

I kicked and screamed, not willing to give up.

Shudders rolled through my body as he pressed his mouth against me and scraped his sharp teeth against my neck. They weren't sharp enough to pierce my delicate skin, but still left a mark.

Long, gouged lines covered the ground beneath us, as I realized his feet were decorated with spikes of stone. The ground did nothing to dull the edges of the spikes, only acting as a whetstone and perfecting their lethal edge.

I thrashed and fought against the stone creature holding me against his chest, attempting to kill me, to no avail.

A wild and crazy idea tore through me as I struggled to keep breathing. My body went limp as my plan was implemented. I slowed my breathing.

I stopped fighting.

It went against my nature to give up, but I didn't have another choice.

The intense clutching stilled as Beresford dropped my body, muttering once again. With all the strength left in my body, I pulled on his massive arms, screaming in fury and horror.

His black eye sockets seemed to meet mine again as I called upon my gorgon, holding his vacant gaze. A thin film of stone began to form over his skin, trapping him once again in time, as my snakes hissed, and eyes shifted.

Crawling out from under his massive form, my eyes widened as Beresford de Blasis once again started to turn into an unyielding statue.

Winded and puffing, I limped over to a forgotten ax next to a pile of rotting lumber. Hands sweaty and sore, I held onto the ax for dear life, my knuckles turning white.

I tasted salt in my mouth as I licked my chapped lips, watching and waiting for the layer of new stone to grow thicker.

Only it didn't.

A horrible cracking sound filled my ears.

5

The stoning hadn't held.

That was my only thought as I launched myself at Beresford, fury tightening my belly. My rusted ax bounced off his hard skin, almost knocking me in the face.

My muscles throbbed as Beresford bellowed in annoyance, covering my face in viscid spit.

Dude could use a mint.

I bolted to the right, swiping at his legs in one smooth motion. This time, the ax scratched the skin of his calf, but the blade was chipped by the force of the attack.

Beresford sidestepped my next strike, grabbing the ax from my hands and breaking the wooden handle. He tossed the damaged weapon to the ground and charged at me.

I shifted onto the balls of my feet, waiting.

At the last second, I stumbled out of the way, only to land in a disgusting pile of decaying trash. A sticky substance covered my skin, and I gagged as Beresford suddenly spun on his heel and ran towards me.

Reaching for the forgotten ax, the fractured handle grazed my fingertips as I was pulled up into the air. The monster held me in his arms, lifting me above the ground, my face meeting his.

I wrenched my head back and slammed my forehead into his, stunning him. Blackness grazed my vision. A welt began to form under the thin skin of my forehead as I grabbed the ax, swinging it above my head.

Maybe the gods were still listening to my pleas after all, because Rohesia suddenly appeared from an alley to the right, and taking one look at the scene, she launched Beresford into the air with a powerful gust of wind.

That was all the time I needed.

Standing above the man turned monster, I slammed the ax head, blade first, into the comparatively tender flesh of his jugular.

One more whack and I could see his cement-like spine. Twisting growths had sprouted from his spinal cord; it was a wonder he had still been walking around.

Three more whacks and he was entirely decapitated.

I did not think, did not feel until his colorless blood pooled at my shoes. The blood he had spilled was the same color as his skin.

Ashen. Lifeless. Dull.

Dropping the ax, I breathlessly landed on the ground in a heap, stuffing my hands under my armpits. I laid my bruised head on my knees, slowly rocking as the world came back into focus.

Everything was muffled. Every sound. Every breath. Every order Rohesia yelled at her underlings.

What in god's name had just happened?

I had barely begun to process the events that had just unfolded when The Collectress emerged before me, grabbing my upper arm and pulling Rohesia towards her in a single motion. Two wardens appeared, one grabbing Beresford's decapitated head and the other grabbing his mutilated body.

Within seconds, we all landed in The Collectress's chambers.

"I will only ask this once. What in the *hell* happened out there?" The Collectress demanded, her tone chilling.

I—I didn't know.

But I refused to tell her that, deciding that biting my tongue would save my back from another branding.

The Collectress looked at me expectantly, reaching for a decanter of whiskey and three glasses.

Rohesia saved me from answering.

"Clearly, we stole your statues and forced them to attack us," she said wryly, pouring herself a drink, catching my eye. I could feel Rohesia's seething rage, directed at The Collectress and her lack of concern for my injuries, pulsating through the room.

I hadn't moved from my position on the floor. I wasn't sure that I could.

"Explain, Usa. Or I will tell your—"

Rohesia raised her hand, silencing The Collectress. To my surprise, The Collectress obeyed, although bad-temperedly, and sat down on her throne. As our boss waited, she outstretched her long legs over the jewel and gold encrusted armrest.

Cocoa and peppermint filled my senses as Rohesia laid on the floor with me, resting her chin on her arm. Her golden eyes scanned my face, taking in the lack of emotion and assessing my injuries.

Physically I was alive.

But mentally and emotionally I felt nothing.

"Hey."

I couldn't talk. I couldn't lift my head from the floor. It was too heavy. Too cold. It was all too *much*.

"I know how you must feel. I still remember my first real kill," Rohesia started, ignoring the muffled sigh from The Collectress.

Of course, she knew what was bothering me.

"I was a juvenile mage, on the verge of my tribulation. All these decades later and it still feels like yesterday. Most mage's tribulations happen at the age of eight, but being the daughter of the coven's leader came with certain…expectations. I completed my tribulation at the age of six."

Turning my head, I looked at her wide-eyed. I hadn't known.

"During the tribulation, you have to perform three tasks. One spell, one potion, and one crossing. I flew through the first two tasks with flying colors. But no one had mentioned the details of the last task. It's not like they could regardless, they were forbidden to talk about the events."

Her throat bobbed, eyes distant as she continued to talk.

"Anyway, I remember when I walked into the crossing, the third and final task was to transform from a mageling into a mage. It was in an open wildflower field, under the darkness of a lunar eclipse. There were twenty or so unconscious mortals laying in beds of wilted flowers. I wasn't scared. I knew that we were to help the deceased cross over to the Otherworld. Only no one told us that they were still alive.

"The final task was helping their souls cross over. But we were also the ones that had to kill them. To show our undying loyalty to Hecate's First Coven. A six-year-old, becoming a murderer? Can you imagine?"

I shook my head, sitting up.

"But I had to complete my tribulation. I would bring shame upon my family if I didn't. And so, I did it. I murdered an innocent mortal. I can still feel him thrash under my hold, gasping for air as I took it from him with my bare hands. Who was I to take an innocent life as though I was a god? But it was a balance that needed to be filled, to access the blessed sands and fall into my powers."

The blessed sands were the grains of sand that soaked up the blood, saliva, tears, sweat, and breast milk that the gods shed to keep the islands flourishing and alive.

Once a millennium the gods would come down with their offering and restore the magic. Without it, the islands would die and mages would be without power. Each offering would take place in the singular temple on each island.

I had seen the event once, and it was unlike anything I had ever witnessed.

As drops of Aphrodite's breast milk had landed on the gray sands of Iydara, the seemingly ordinary dirt had begun to glow with otherworldly light. Ribbons of gold stretched throughout the sands, spreading deep into the land like the outstretched fingers of someone falling to their demise. The ribbons moved with a will of their own, twirling with a dance just for the gods.

Not just anyone could access the power from the blessed sands that covered the grounds of the temples, though. As if the gods didn't already have a stronghold on our free will, you needed their *permission* to use the sands.

It made for a lot of ass kissing and politicking.

Every mage had different powers depending on which sand they stored in a small glass vial that was kept on their person at all times. The strength of the magic and gifts also depended on how gracious the gods' feelings were towards each particular mage.

Some favored and important mages, like Rohesia, were given access to more than one sand.

The sands of Oernear that were soaked with blood allowed the user access to divination magic and insight into sanctity. With that, certain mages could access the unknown, being the future paths or past memories.

Though it took only a singular grain of sand to complete most spells, a decree of balance needed to be maintained. With each sand of grain used and harnessed, the gods demanded something in return.

For the divination powers of Oernear, it was a dream the mage had once had.

For the natural magic of Tabrn, such as healing magic, light and shadow magic, or elemental magic, the user burned a lock of their hair.

Iydara was known for its psychic magic, like telepathy, psychokinesis, mind control and influence, given the mage sacrificed a memory to the gods.

Sacrificing a memory, dream, or hair was child's play compared to the islands of Ahtelah and Raas.

Conjuring magic from the demon prison island of Ahtelah granted the mage the capability to bring forth any form of creature, misplaced item, spirit, demon (unless they were trapped on the prison island, of course), deities and allowed them to do their bidding. Blessed sands of Ahtelah were rarely given out. Only the leaders of each island were said to have the sands in their possession.

The magic was dark and dirty, a sacrifice of the user's blood being the only item that would satisfy the gods. And sometimes that wasn't enough, and the mage was drained of all their blood and killed before harnessing the powers.

Raas was known for its black sands and life and death magic. Necromancy and death manipulation were the two abilities given to mages, in exchange for a piece of their soul. The gods were known to take one's kindness, empathy, a loved one's life, or even the user's free will.

It wasn't as if anyone besides the mages could harness the powers, though, given they need to have the god's blessing first and the proper training that took decades. And carrying a small vial of it everywhere you went seemed rather tedious.

But the gods loved chaos and control.

Perhaps that was why they forced children like Rohesia to become murderers at the age of six.

"I wanted to die that night, Usa. Gods, did I. But I decided that I would just *try*. Try to get up in the morning. Try to eat. Try to look at myself in the mirror. I tried and tried. And I've never stopped just trying. So, I'm asking you, please, just to try."

Try.

Breathing in for four seconds, I held it for seven seconds, then exhaled it for eight. Again and again until the crashing sound of my heartbeat in my ears turned into a soft lull.

I could try for Rohesia. For me. For the life I had taken.

Though I turned people into stone on the daily, I never truly killed them. Their hearts still thrummed, and their minds were still intact.

But I killed Beresford today.

And there was no bringing him back.

"Okay," I whispered.

Rohesia asked me to try, and so I did.

I relayed the past hour to them, as Rohesia gave me encouraging smiles and words of comfort, and as The Collectress stared at me with fire in her eyes.

I didn't include the part about why I had been drawn to the alleyway. Hearing voices seemed a tad ridiculous, even for those with magic humming through their blood.

"I didn't want to believe it."

"Believe what, Collectress?" I asked, clenching my hands around a glass filled with ice water.

Frown lines appeared on her forehead. "That there was another gorgon in Iydara."

Time stilled.

Another gorgon? No. There couldn't be. The only other gorgons I knew were hundreds of miles away, tucked away in the Anghor Peaks.

"I believe you're mistaken, Collectress. Only the gorgon that stoned a victim can release the curse. And I did *not* unstone Beresford de Blasis. Nor any of the other statues. And gorgons can't create those *creatures.*"

Without hesitation, she ignored me, instead looking at Rohesia, silent words spoken between the pair.

The Collectress nodded.

Rohesia faced me.

"There have been rumors, Usa. About a species of gorgon unlike anything we've ever seen. They can change their appearance, like mages. They can unstone any statue and even breathe life into man-made statues, forming monsters out of stone. They're more powerful than you or your coven. And there have been signs of them in Iydara for the past year, if not longer."

I swallowed, placing my head in my dirt-covered hands. I wasn't angry at Rohesia for not telling me sooner. The Collectress had her on a tight leash, even tighter than mine.

"The gorgon that is turning your statues into nearly unkillable creatures, known as golems, has yet to be seen or caught," Rohesia continued. "We don't know who is behind it yet. The wardens are currently working on it."

The wardens of Iydara are *working on it.*

Right.

I started to laugh but stopped as I glanced at Rohesia's ashen face. If the future of Iydara was in the hands of the wardens, then we were screwed.

Seeing the look on my face, The Collectress rolled her eyes, pressing her lips into a fine line before continuing to question me.

"What is it?"

I downed the shot of liquor that Rohesia had poured me, needing all the liquid courage I could have. The bitter liquid burned on the way down.

"I just think that maybe you should have an outside source investigate the incidents. An outside perspective would be good. Especially since the wardens can't tell a mage from their own ass."

The Collectress seemed to consider my words for a moment, before leaning across the table, her cleavage spilling out of her dress.

"But pray tell, dear Usa, *who* did you have in mind to investigate these incidents?"

I opened my mouth only to close it.

Heat flooded my cheeks as I realized that I knew none of the detectives or private investigators in Iydara. Even then, the ones that investigated crimes of a magical nature were unheard of. Only the wardens and The Collectress investigated such horrid crimes. It was a miracle that their solved case rate was above ten percent.

"That's what I thought. And seeing as this was the first attack in months, I believe the other gorgon is in hiding. As are the other statues that they unstoned. The wardens and I have it under control, Usa."

I began to protest, standing up from my chair, when The Collectress dismissed us with a single wave of her hand.

6

Sleep didn't come for me that night. Nor the next. I was running on fumes by the time another sleepless evening rolled around. Soft songs played from the record player in our room attempting, but failing, to distract me from my thoughts. Rohesia softly snored on the bunk below mine, sleep capturing her hours ago.

None of it made sense.

Not the missing statues.

Not the horrid golems, as Rohesia had called them.

Especially the lack of concern from The Collectress and the wardens.

Was it really possible that there could be a more powerful species of gorgons? I didn't think so. The gorgon coven I had been born into had been the only one of its kind. At least, that's what the gods and goddesses had told my family.

Doubt began to creep into my mind. Could the gods have lied? What could an all-powerful god possibly have to gain by concealing another species of gorgon from my people and the mages of Enthlos?

Rohesia had informed me that the beast hadn't been captured on any surveillance cameras yet.

And The Collectress's mansion had no surveillance cameras that I knew of. She didn't need them when she already held an entire city in the palm of her hand. No one dared to cross her.

I rolled over, the sound of my creaking mattress almost becoming louder than my tumultuous thoughts.

Wincing, I climbed down the ladder attached to the bunks, not bothering to be quiet. Rohesia could sleep like the dead. As if to prove my point, she tucked herself deeper under the covers and mumbled something about a cat dancing with a...banana?

Furrowing my brow, I held my breath to listen to her incoherent speech. Concentrating, I read her lips.

Yup.

Definitely a banana.

Silent laughter shook my shoulders for a few precious moments before unwanted, anxiety-riddled thoughts dug their filthy claws into the jagged crevices of my consciousness.

Who would want to steal the statues in the first place? And why? Those were the main questions that tumbled through my mind as I changed the scratched vinyl out for something more upbeat.

My feet and hands began to sweat at the thought of the one and only person I could see wanting an army of hard to kill monsters. Coincidentally she had been the one to birth me.

But I was also convinced that my mother would know if there was another species of gorgon. And if she did, she would have already killed them off, or at least attempted to. No one was supposed to be more powerful or blessed than her.

No one.

Not even her own daughter.

I learned that lesson three years ago, at the age of sixteen. And I will never forget it.

I resolved to ask Rohesia what evidence there was of another species of gorgons, besides the statues.

Footprints? Photographs?

Without any hard, concrete evidence, it felt as though The Collectress was leading us astray on purpose. It wouldn't be the first time she had done so.

My dark hair fell in curls over my shoulders as I dared to glance at my reflection in the mirror above our dresser. I was a murderer, but I still looked the same.

I had the same emerald eyes and midnight curls with white highlights around my face, same wide nose and hooded eyelids.

It was different when I stoned someone. They were mentally present, just immobile. They had a chance, however small, to be turned back into their old selves.

Death, on the other hand, was certain.

Final.

And that's what Beresford had faced because of me.

An ignorant, perhaps childish part of me had clung onto the notion that one day I would be able to free every person I had ever stoned. Freeing them from a lifetime of horrors. But I realized now that it would never be possible.

A blinding red light flashed overhead, casting an eerie glow around our room. The same light flashed on both mine and Rohesia's watches. I groaned as a loud alarm began to shriek at us.

As if tonight hadn't already been long enough.

The last drill had been over three months ago, so I shouldn't be surprised, seeing as they were recommended monthly. We were overdue.

Should we ever be attacked, we needed to be ready. Though I didn't know of anyone stupid enough to actually attack us. Not even my own mother.

Pulling on a pair of jeans, I hobbled over to Rohesia to shake her. I winced again. My body was still sore from my fight with Beresford, and I had some nasty bruises that not even the medications could heal.

"Roh. Get up. Drill."

She proceeded to groan into her pillow and kick her feet. I felt the same way. With sunrise only a few hours away, I really needed to catch up on sleep. But that possibility was long gone now. Drills took at least an hour, if not more.

Rohesia seemed on the verge of falling asleep again, drool pooling at the corner of her mouth, and I knew the perfect thing to wake her up.

Sitting on my knees next to her bed, I changed into my gorgon form, willing my snakes to be quiet. I had to contain my laughter as I watched a handful of snakes begin to slither their way under her blankets.

Rohesia's nose twitched as a rather friendly one began to crawl up her face and into her hair.

"Yumi, stop," she huffed, her hand batting at the reptile.

The movement only made my snake more determined to crawl up next to her and cuddle.

Her eyes slowly opened, and she shrieked loudly as she began hitting at the snakes. I rolled on the ground, clutching my stomach in amusement.

I heard a loud thwack as Rohesia rushed out of bed, only to hit her head on the edge of the bunk. It only made me chuckle harder. A soft snort escaped me as she looked around, taking in the flashing lights and sounds of the mansion waking.

"A drill? At this hour?" she groaned, pulling a wrinkled shirt off the ground and over her head.

"That's what I said!"

"Someone must've really pissed Halvard off."

I raised my hands innocently. "Not me this time."

"Yeah, this time," Rohesia snorted, grabbing her phone off the wooden desk.

We didn't rush as we readied ourselves for the drill. The Collectress was always late to them. She didn't control when the drills happened, it was the building inspector that was given free rein over them. I had a feeling he had them at this hour just to spite us.

"Don't think that just because you're still healing I won't get you back for that," Rohesia said, wrinkling her nose at my snakes.

"What? These poor girls? They only wanted to cuddle," I teased harmlessly. Most people were terrified of snakes and rightfully so, but my girls only hurt someone if I commanded them to.

Shoving her feet into combat boots, the laces worn and in need of cleaning, she mumbled to herself about how all snakes should die by fire. I might feel the same way if they weren't part of me.

Fully dressed and armed to the teeth, warm air flooded into our room as we opened the door.

Silence.

Something was wrong.

Rohesia and I shared a look at the flickering lights and blue-black darkness. The drill had started ten minutes ago, and no one else was anywhere to be found.

We were the only residents in the hallway. Normally, we all lined up to wait for instructions.

This was bad.

I unsheathed my sword from my back, watching as Rohesia formed balls of burning flames in her hands. We did a slow circle of the hallway, not finding a soul.

Passing door after door of vacant rooms was unnerving.

Shouts came from the foyer below the living quarters. Swords clashed and the smell of magic filled the air. As did a scent of something burning. What, though, I didn't know.

We froze at the scene that met our eyes in the foyer. Dozens of golems were attacking wardens, mages, and the other residents of the mansion. The double glass doors that led outside seemed to have been barricaded, only to be forced open by the army of golems.

Screams pierced the night.

More and more statues began to rush the room. They were the size of battering rams and seemed to attack anything that moved.

I couldn't spot The Collectress in the maze of fighting, shouting, and killing.

Casimar stopped in front of us, panting, soot covering his forehead. "How nice of the two of you to finally show up! Only fire and decapitation can stop them."

He gave me a once over, smirking at my lack of magic and my chipped sword. "Sorry, Ussie, better luck neck time."

Casimar seemed to know that I couldn't stone the golems. It wouldn't have surprised me if he had learned about the creatures long before I had. I really needed to move up the ranks.

I began to swing at him, before Rohesia pulled my arm back, instead dowsing Casimar's head with a spray of water. He sputtered and spat as he ran away from us.

"You can stone them," she breathed, looking at me expectantly. I could see the wheels in her mind turning, only they were too fast for me.

"Too bad it doesn't last."

"But it could give us enough time to kill them. Trust me."

Yanking me forward, we fought side by side, making our way from one side of the foyer to the double doors that lead to the garden. Shattered glass crunched under our boots as we went to work.

We soon got into a rhythm: I would stone the creatures, temporarily stopping them, which allowed Rohesia enough time to turn them to ash. If she was preoccupied, then I would decapitate the monsters in one, final swoop.

I had to look at the golems as monsters that wanted to harm us and the citizens of Iydara. That was the only way I would be able to get through this night. There was no use trying to talk them down, they only craved violence and destruction.

Stone. Fire.

Stone. Slash. Repeat.

Sweat drenched our clothes as we exited the foyer and entered the lavish and expansive garden. Rows of maze-like rose bushes made it difficult to see where we were going.

"Usa!" Rohesia shouted at me, seconds too late.

I grunted in pain as I landed in a particularly thorny bed of blooming white roses. Snapping teeth grazed my face, as I came face to face with Samara Aineans.

She was a lonesome real estate agent that had stolen thousands of doubloons from The Collectress by falsifying financial documents. I hadn't thought about her in years.

It had been my first mission with Rohesia, though not my first mission in Iydara. The Collectress had tagged along on my first ten missions, showing me what to do and what her expectations were.

As Samara Aineans continued to snap her stony teeth at me, I became overwhelmed with memories of her stoning.

We had been holed up in a hotel in the Western Boundary for days, with no sighting of the real estate agent on the run. It had been by absolute luck, and lust, that we had found her.

Rohesia and I had been taking shots when Samara sauntered up to the bar and invited Rohesia to her bed, the latter concealed as a human with bulging muscles, windswept hair, and plush, pillow-like lips. It had been quick work after Rohesia had followed Samara to her bedchambers.

The Collectress had been impressed by how well we worked together and had deemed us partners for the foreseeable future.

Most workers that were employed for The Collectress operated alone. And for good reason. With each mage trying to climb the ranks, it was cutthroat and competitive. But Rohesia was already at the top, and at the time I had no desire to climb the ranks, I was only focused on staying alive and saving up enough money to leave Iydara for good.

I struggled to hold Samara off, her stony shoulders ramming me further and further into the rose bush. Dozens of sharp thorns poked into my sides, tearing through my layers of clothing with ease.

I sucked in a sharp breath as the thorns slashed into my skin, stabbing me with spite. It felt as though a hundred needles were being yanked across my skin.

As leaves and petals fell onto my face, I lifted my sword up and stabbed her through the gut. The weapon only went in a few inches before the tip snapped, falling to the ground.

My broken broadsword fell from my hands as Samara stepped on my wrist and I watched it bend at an impossible angle. I hissed in agony as fiery pain crawled up my arm. She shifted her entire body weight onto me, forcing the air out of my body with a forearm pressed into my throat.

Panic rose within me as I struggled to move out from under her towering form. My knee connected with her torso, which only caused me more pain and ripped my pants.

A loud screech filled my ears and heat licked my cheeks as Samara went up in flames. Rohesia had made sure that the flames didn't touch a single hair on my head. We watched as she turned to ash, our breathing ragged as we turned to face our next opponents.

Only there weren't any.

I scrunched my face as Rohesia gently placed her warm hands on my wrist. With a single spell, she quickly and wholly mended my shattered bones. It was only slightly stiff and sore when she was done.

We walked through the maze of statues, finding that around half of them had been transformed from mere stone to living, fighting golems.

The other half were still unmoving figurines.

Rohesia and I gulped as we looked around the property.

The devastation the creatures had caused was immeasurable.

Soft flames blackened the immaculate lawn, threatening to lick the sides of a wooden gazebo at the center of the garden. Broken glass sparkled like shining stars in the early morning light, opposing the destruction across the property.

The land smelled of death. It was a rather rank and metallic odor: one that reminded me of the essence of the god who took my innocence. As flashbacks of that night threatened to surface, I fought to push the thoughts away. Bile filled my mouth as his image appeared in my mind despite my best efforts. Once again, I fought to stay in control of my emotions.

I sucked in a sharp breath, my hands shaking. I held in the lungful of oxygen until we reached clean, untampered air.

Then, we began to count our dead.

Five humans and three mages had perished in the battle. We had killed close to seventy of the creatures in return, but it hadn't been enough. There were almost fifty golems still unaccounted for, suggesting they had escaped and were running loose in Iydara.

The outside of the mansion had sustained the brunt of the major damage. Rose bushes had been trampled and burned alongside the gazebo and the lawn. Flames had attempted to enter the building but had been fended off with protection spells.

Rohesia and I, along with a handful of carefully chosen mages, sat in The Collectress's chambers, awaiting her arrival. The rest of the residents remained outside the room, either fixing the garden and the foyer, or attending to the wounded.

I kept my head down. This was partially my fault. Those statues had been created by me. And brought back to life, no, cursed by someone else. I still couldn't wrap my head around the revelation.

Dark thoughts roamed freely in my mind, calling me a murderer. Rohesia and I had killed at least a dozen of the stony creatures. I frowned as I remembered their rather violent deaths.

I peeked out from under the curtain of my curly hair, seeing Rohesia chewing on her nails. If she was showing signs of anxiety, then this situation was even worse than I had originally thought.

No one dared to steal from The Collectress. It was like a fly playing a game of cat and mouse with a deadly black widow.

Because of this, there was little to no security in the gardens. No cameras. No guards. Not even dogs.

The Collectress was at the very top of the food chain. She had a devilish reputation for murder, mayhem, and revenge. No one breathed in her mansion without her permission.

It was rumored that she had an otherworldly ability to sense others, thanks to her dunamis. Security was pointless when The Collectress was so attuned to the presence of others. But someone had managed to find a flaw in her abilities.

More importantly, the same someone had managed to transform almost one hundred and fifty statues into golems. They had done it fast, and right under The Collectress's nose. This attack was personal. The only question was, who had done it?

And I suspected that the answer was a rather big and ugly one. The Collectress had more enemies than she did hairs on her head. But were any of them part of a secret new species of gorgon?

I still didn't believe that the species existed. I had been a gorgon for all twenty years of my life, and so had my mother, and her mother, and so on and so forth. Surely there would have at least been rumors of a more powerful type of gorgon over the years.

The only place I could get those kinds of answers was buried deep in the snow-covered Anghor Peaks, and I refused to ever go back there.

Rohesia and the others stopped talking, hearing something that only their ears could pick up. My hearing was better than mortals, but not nearly as good as a mage's.

Hurried but gentle footsteps echoed in the open chamber. I knew without looking up that it was The Collectress. She walked as softly as a whisper in the wind.

Those around me began to sit, their chairs scraping against the floors. Many were hunched over, about to sit when The Collectress's command rang through the air.

"Stand. This won't take long."

Her voice was cut steel.

Someone to the right of me took a rather large gulp of air and I silently laughed as I saw that it was Casimar. I would have thought that The Collectress's third in command wouldn't be afraid of her.

It seemed that I was wrong.

Perhaps he had more brains than I gave him credit for.

"Today, tragedy occurred." Her eyes seemed solemn as she looked at each individual, sympathetically meeting their eyes, even mine. "Today, we lost so much."

Heads bowed and sniffles came from the back corner. I hadn't known any of the mages that had passed today, most of them having lived here for under six months.

"Most of all, we lost," she took a steadying breath, "the garden."

I couldn't help myself, I snickered.

Of course, her precious garden was more important than the lives that had been lost. A few of her most loyal followers shot livid glowers at me, but I caught Rohesia's eye, and she looked pleased.

Even though she was The Collectress's second in command, Rohesia had always found the garden to be rather abhorrent and unnatural. Though she never let anyone but me hear those words.

"Security is of the utmost importance here at the mansion. Starting today, everyone, and I do mean everyone," her eyes met mine, "will begin pulling security rounds."

A collective groan filled the room.

"Your shifts will last twelve hours each, being split between the front of the property and the garden. Those on shift tonight are Kirke, Tanith, Lutes, Jaedi…"

I zoned out as she began listing off twenty or so names. We would each have a shift every three days unless we were on a mission. Suddenly, missions just got a lot more enjoyable.

"You're dismissed."

Finally.

I pushed off the wall, walking over to Rohesia and linking her arm in mine. We were about to walk out of the door unnoticed when The Collectress stopped us.

"Not you two."

No, of course not.

I took a steadying breath and turned on my heel, tempted to run out of the room regardless of what The Collectress needed or wanted. There were no flames blazing in the fireplace, meaning there would not be a branding tonight.

I was relieved.

I wasn't sure my back could take another one for at least a few more months. Rohesia had only received one branding since arriving at The Collectress's mansion.

It hadn't been for misbehavior, though. A single, dainty marigold was branded on her right shoulder, naming her as the second in command. Casimar had a similar brand, though the marigold on his shoulder had been removed via magic and he now had an upside-down rose on his left shoulder.

An uncomfortable silence filled the room as Rohesia and I took our seats, waiting for whatever The Collectress had to say. But instead, she simply poured three glasses of red wine and waited.

I resisted the urge to squirm in my seat, instead focusing on the wine. Sipping slowly, I tried, and failed not to choke on the putrid alcohol.

Wine was okay. Not my go to, but as long as it was a nice Moscato and chilled, I didn't mind it.

But this. This was an abomination.

The liquid was unusually bitter and warm to the touch. I cringed as I set the glass down on The Collectress's desk, not bothering to grab a coaster. Rohesia sipped on hers lightly, while The Collectress poured herself a second glass.

"Drusilla Deeine. Dear! What are you doing to those poor girls? Warm wine is not appropriate for such gatherings," a nasal voice echoed from behind me.

I immediately knew he was a mage, his essence hitting me like a charging horse. The man was short and round, his black hair gelled down and parted in the middle. Oval glasses framed his brown eyes, resting on pink tinged cheeks. His beige complexion paled at the numerous bottles of wine littered around the desk.

In his hands was a plate of rich desserts, including mini muffins, crème puffs, peanut butter cookies, and bowls of pudding.

I liked this guest already.

As if sensing my gaze, the man walked over, barely taller than me as I sat in my chair, and took my hand in his. He offered me a crème puff and I snatched it greedily with my empty hand.

I hadn't eaten since the previous morning and was beginning to feel the effects of battling golems on an empty stomach. A moan became caught in my throat as I devoured the dessert and reached for a mini muffin.

Don't mind if I do.

"Eusebius Erast, but you, my dear, can call me E.E." His lips brushed mine and I frowned, liking him slightly less. He did the same to Rohesia and we shared a weighted look.

"What brings you here, E.E.?" Rohesia asked, seeming upset that The Collectress had not bothered to inform her about this little meeting.

E.E. tilted his head, taking in the mood of the room, as if he was tempted to use it to his advantage.

"Pray tell, didn't Drusilla tell you?"

Drusilla sat behind her desk, shooting daggers at E.E. for using her real name. A servant had once used The Collectress's real name and the next day he had joined her garden.

"No, she failed to mention that little detail," Rohesia responded sharply, not bothering to hide the hurt and distrust in her tone.

"Well, look at that. Silly ol' me putting a rift between Iydara's finest leaders," he chuckled, rubbing an imaginary beard on his double chin.

"Get to the point, Eusebius. Now."

The Collectress sounded slightly less annoyed, and more bored. She was working on her third glass of wine, and it seemed like the alcohol did nothing to help her foul mood.

"Ah. Yes. Of course." E.E. cleared his throat and ran a hand over his black hair, only for it to come back shiny. "As you know, these golem creatures have been popping up for months now. Tonight was different. It was planned. Meticulous. Devious."

Rohesia and I nodded, not quite sure where he was going with this. Or what his purpose served.

"I haven't seen such planning since the disappearance of Albion de Keldd, back in the year of 807. Of course, you two were not even conceived back then. It was a different time and place. I remember the day like it was yesterday. Such a wealthy and prestigious, not to mention generous, human going missing like that, well—"

He was immediately cut off as The Collectress slammed down her drink, E.E. jumping out of the way as to avoid a splash of wine that threatened to ruin his white suit. I had the feeling that their friendship was one created out of business rather than similar personalities.

"Yes, well, anyway. The golem creatures were only mildly worrisome, but after tonight, the wardens and I believe that they pose an immediate threat to mortals everywhere."

A warden?

I wouldn't have expected E.E. to be a warden. But stranger things had happened.

"Without knowing who is transforming the statues into something more sinister, we are at a roadblock. This is where you two come in." E.E. glanced at us, sweat dripping down his face as he took a swig of amber-colored liquor.

"Our investigation regarding the golems has come to a standstill. And you, dear Medusa, are needed. Being a gorgon, you can perhaps provide some insight into what breed of gorgon is creating these monsters. And you, dear Rohesia, will play the role of the overseer. Drusilla has too much on her plate to currently handle this situation."

Of course, The Collectress couldn't be bothered. But at least I didn't have to worry about her breathing down my neck.

Lightbulbs went off in my head as I realized what this man was. He wasn't a warden. No, he was something better.

"You're a detective?"

"Ah. The gorgon has finally figured it out."

I glowered at him, defensively crossing my arms.

"If you think that I am going to play detective with you, then you have another thing coming." My skin was still crawling where he had pressed his thin lips to mine.

"You will do this, Usa," The Collectress voiced.

"While embarking on this investigation, neither of you will have security duty," I immediately straightened in my chair, "and you will be staying at the detective's headquarters instead of here, located in the south end of the Western Boundary. I expect you both to be on your best behavior."

She tossed a heated look my way.

I would always much rather play detective than deal with security detail and The Collectress's missions. Maybe it would be like a mini vacation, minus the beach, sunshine, and umbrella cocktails.

But still, a vacation nonetheless.

"Before I forget, I will unfortunately be working on another case."

I breathed a sigh of satisfaction.

Sure the man had given me gooey, mouth-watering desserts but I drew the line at personal boundaries. Something he did not seem to have nor respect.

E.E. must have mistaken the look of relief on my face for one of sadness, because he stood behind me, grasping my shoulders in his small hands.

"Do not fret, dear Medusa. I have my best man on this."

Dread undulated in my belly as I imagined working with an overweight balding man. I pictured the detective would favor cigars and find the opinions of women to be beneath him.

I batted away E.E.'s hands, straightening my shoulders.

"I can handle him."

"I'm sure you can," he smiled, waddling over to the adjacent wall.

I almost fell out of my seat as E.E. opened the door for a man with haunting blue eyes and a cruelly handsome face. I watched in horror as he walked across the room and introduced himself as Brooks de Blasis.

Shit, de Blasis?

Brooks quickly shook Rohesia's hand. "Brooks, but my friends call me Rook."

Rohesia shot him a flirty grin, unabashedly checking out his backside as he walked towards me.

My eyes trailed up his towering form as he stood in front of me. Agitation curled in my stomach.

"Nice to meet you, Usa," Brooks said, amusement glimmering in his cobalt eyes.

"Medusa," I warned, taking his large hand in mine.

"Are we not friends?"

"I don't recall us being friends."

"Funny how I remember things differently. And it's Rook." Brooks smirked, rubbing his thumb slyly across the scar on his throat that I had gifted him.

"Sounds like you will be *lovely* to work with, Brooks," I told him sweetly.

He frowned at me.

Rohesia threw me a questioning and stunned look.

71

There would be many, many questions later.

"Now that introductions are out of the way, be ready to leave in fifteen minutes sharp," Brooks ordered, his baritone voice suddenly resembling sharpened steel.

I no longer saw a hint of amusement in his eyes. Nor any sign of the man I had conversed with, and fought, previously.

Rohesia and I nodded, leaving The Collectress's chambers. Rohesia peppered me with questions about Brooks but I just shrugged in response. She got the hint and instead went on about how she was glad to leave her chambers, not being able to stand The Collectress for another moment.

I tuned her out, fear coiling in my stomach. The man who had witnessed the stoning was a de Blasis. Perhaps it was a coincidence that Beresford and Brooks shared a last name, but something told me that it wasn't.

7

Brooks had given us fifteen minutes to pack. And we were ready in eight. Neither of us had many belongings, so we packed only the essentials: toothpaste, vinyls, and a half-empty bottle of tequila.

"I wonder when we'll be here next," I said, looking around our small but cozy room. The walls were painted a light lavender and had matching curtains. Rohesia had chosen the color before I had moved in.

"Hopefully soon," Rohesia answered, playing a word search game on her phone and popping her gum thoughtfully.

I didn't share her thoughts.

I hoped we didn't have to return for a few weeks or months. Freedom seemed to be at the tips of my fingers, something I hadn't felt in a few years. Sometimes we don't know what it is to miss something until we have it cruelly ripped from our hands.

E.E. escorted us from our room and out of the mansion, not bothering to say goodbye to The Collectress.

My breathing was uneven as we departed, leaving the center of Iydara in a horse drawn buggy, the favorite mode of transportation for E.E., apparently. The Western Boundary was a few hours away.

Rohesia sat by me quietly, her hands tightly clasped on her lap. She pursed her lips as the lights of the mansion faded away into darkness.

I should have comforted her. I know I should have. That's what a good friend would do. But I couldn't bring myself to.

We had been living with the mage that branded me and abused my abilities for too long. I knew Rohesia loved her, in a twisted and confusing way, but I couldn't bring myself to feel an ounce of sadness.

Not now.

Not with this euphoric sense of freedom that was coursing through my veins. My chest felt light. The heavy, continuous sense of impending doom had lessened. I couldn't help the smile that turned the corner of my mouth upright.

Time seemed to go by much faster with freedom at my fingertips. And so, when we stopped at a lonely cottage two hours into our journey, it felt like no more than twenty minutes had passed.

Flickering candlelight and cracked walls warned me to stay inside the relative safety of the carriage while Brooks checked the wheels and E.E. took a call on his cell phone. I took the opportunity to check in with Rohesia.

"At least we won't have to deal with Casimar for a while," I noted cheerfully, plastering a smile on my face.

She echoed my smile half-heartedly and simply nodded, sinking further down into the leather seats. Rohesia continued to wring her hands in her lap, looking outside.

I glanced out of the window and noticed that E.E. wasn't back yet. Brooks was petting the thick neck of one of the paint geldings that pulled the buggy.

Reaching beneath the seat below us, I rifled through my duffle bag. I grinned when the Bluetooth speaker I had packed brushed my fingers.

Without hesitation, I began to play one of our favorite dancing songs at full blast. The music reverberated through the carriage, making my teeth vibrate.

Rohesia groaned, tossing her head back into the seat, her grin growing. I let out a screech as the chorus hit, dragging her out of the carriage. Brooks didn't protest. He only raised his eyebrows questioningly and narrowed his eyes at us.

We began swaying our hips and singing along in the deserted parking lot. The muddy ground that we danced on smelled like rotting sewage, but we didn't care. We had danced in worse places.

E.E. ended his call, watching us with wide eyes, a blush creeping up his cheeks and onto his forehead. Rohesia pulled him into our dance circle, laughing as he began to flap his arms above his head wildly.

Our dance partner roughly cleared his throat as the song ended and I took the opportunity to release myself from my friend's grasp. Rohesia and I landed in the back seat in a pile of sweat and giggles. My head fell onto her shoulder as we continued our journey to the Western Boundary.

"Are you okay?" I asked her, taking a sip of my water.

"Honestly? I'm petrified. I've lived in the mansion for the past few decades. It's my home," she released a heavy sigh, her fingers tracing the tattoos on her arms, "but I'm eager to get to the bottom of this mess. I just need some time to adjust."

I nodded, understanding the nervousness and adjustment period associated with leaving one's home. When I left Kilmarn, I felt utterly lost. Loneliness became my best friend as I journeyed from my home to join the mortal lands of Iydara.

If I returned to Kilmarn, I would be killed on sight.

In that sense, Rohesia was lucky. She could return to her home without fearing for her life.

My heart often ached for the land of glittering snow and towering emerald evergreens. There was no other place like it. Ice and fog covered the ground at all times, protecting the community from curious outsiders. It had been my safe haven.

Up until that fateful night, I had been the joyful youngest daughter of Ceto, our coven's leader. And then, instantaneously, I became the unclean, cursed, and renounced offspring of Ceto.

All because of the lust and cruelty of a licentious god. The only people who knew the details of my curse and what had happened on the night of my sixteenth birthday were Rohesia and The Collectress. And I planned to keep it that way. The less people who knew, the better.

Though The Collectress had more use for me alive than dead, it didn't stop the relentless threats of exposure. I wouldn't be surprised if the number of threats were slowly creeping into the hundreds.

Blowing out a breath, I slowly turned in my seat to find Rohesia sleeping. I didn't need much convincing. Laying my head on her lap, I allowed the exhaustion of the past few days to catch up with me.

8

A chubby black cat with a white patch on its chest lay sprawled across the front desk of the detective's headquarters. I gave him a scratch behind the ear as we walked past the front of the low-lit office. His slow blinking golden eyes warmed my heart as I took in the stainless steel decor and cramped cubicles with overflowing binders and blinking computer screens.

E.E. had referred to their headquarters as The Hub.

Interns carrying stacks of loose paper scurried past us, offering E.E. a small smile, but turning deathly pale at the site of Brooks. I raised my eyebrows at Rohesia, who only shrugged in return.

Turning down a dark corridor, one that reminded me of the living quarters at The Collectress's mansion, we stopped in front of a steel door with the number nineteen scrawled in black paint on it. E.E. opened the door, frowning when he entered.

A single twin sized bed was pushed up against the wall, along with a dresser and desk. Various toiletries and a stack of towels were placed on the small dresser, next to a closed door of what I assumed was the bathroom.

Sighing, E.E. turned to face us. "Because your arrival was so unexpected, this is the best we have for now. One of you can stay here, near the brain of The Hub, and the other can stay with Detective de Blasis in the employee living quarters at the other end of the building."

"I'll stay here, closer to the brain, since I'm the one with the most of them," Rohesia joked, sashaying her hips as she entered the room and slammed the door in my face, but not before throwing me a not so subtle wink. Without a second to protest, I silently followed E.E. and Brooks to the other living quarters.

After a maze of employee corridors, we reached a hallway that had a single door at the end of it. Unlike the others, this one was not marked.

"Forgive me if Rook's living quarters aren't up to your expectations, I only learned of the situation hours ago and had little time to prepare."

Brooks scowled at E.E.'s comment, jamming the key into the door. E.E. gave us a curt nod, off to solve his own investigations, leaving Brooks and I to enter the apartment alone.

The residence was dimly lit with blue fluorescents like the rest of the building. A pair of cracked loveseats sat across from a large flatscreen, with a scuffed coffee table in between.

I walked around the sitting room, noticing no personal belongings or art. A ghost would have more belongings than Detective Brooks did. My new roommate stood far from me, twisting the silver ring on his middle finger.

Connected to the living room, was a joint kitchen and dining room. Out of curiosity, I walked into the kitchen, opening the out-of-date refrigerator and then the pantry. Both were minimally stocked.

"So do you just live off of air and the meager calories from the tormented souls you've killed?" I quipped in disbelief.

The squeak of leather echoed through the apartment as Brooks plopped down into one of the loveseats, turning on the television.

"Pretty certain there's a banana in there."

I stared at the congealed, brown and yellow mass that sat in a clear plastic bag. Wrinkling my nose, I picked up the forgotten food and tried not to gag as the slimy fruit attempted to drip from the bag, promptly tossing it in the empty garbage bin.

"So, tortured souls for dinner it is then," I sighed.

"They're delicious with a side of potato salad," Brooks deadpanned, placing his hands behind his head as he watched a black-and-white movie.

Bottles of whiskey in varying levels of emptiness littered the cupboards, along with three boxes of stale sugar flakes. A coffee mug that said, 'THIS is what a great detective looks like,' sat next to a few bags of chocolate flavored coffee beans.

Exiting the kitchen, I exhaled. Though I had only ever lived in Kilmarn with my mother and sisters, and with Rohesia at the mansion, I imagined living with Brooks would be like living with a disgruntled brother.

Thankfully, like the rest of the apartment, minus the rogue banana, the bathroom was clean and tidy. Attached to the bathroom was a master bedroom. I pinched my eyebrows together as I entered the large bedchamber. A curtain separated the room in half, a queen bed on one side and a twin on the other.

My stomach dropped at the lack of privacy and fear threatened to take hold. I couldn't stay in this room with Brooks. It was out of the question. Pulling at the back of my neck, I slowly sat down on the twin-sized bed, breathing slowly.

Memories of that night began to take hold.

No.

Deep breaths.

In and out.

Out and in.

Flashes of greedy, rough hands.

Silent screams.

The stench of stale sweat.

Tears pricked at my eyes, but I shoved down the terror before it could claw its way out and make a mess of things. The last thing I needed was for Brooks to think my head wasn't in the game and I needed to be taken off of the case.

Take back control.

Five things I can see.

A navy lampshade with gold trim. One running shoe that was missing its partner. A spider plant that could use a little bit more water, given its wilting leaves. The bookshelf was overflowing with well-loved books that had cracked spines. And finally, the flatscreen.

Four things I could touch.

Easy.

The ground. The wall. A burnished doorknob. The strings of my beloved hoodie.

Next, three things I could hear.

Or was it three things I could taste?

Keep breathing. You're almost there.

The muted hush of the television from the living room. Brooks' baritone voice who was currently talking, no, arguing, with someone on the phone. A subtle, almost imperceptible sound of electricity humming throughout the apartment.

Two things I could smell.

Tart raspberries and syrupy vanilla, my perfume. The vague scent of Brooks's essence, warm cinnamon and bitter orange.

And finally, one thing I could taste.

Spongy, strawberry-flavored gum that I had been chewing on for a bit too long. Hours had passed since Rohesia had given it to me, and I needed to spit it out before it gave me a jaw ache.

Slowly, the blossoming terror died, leaving me mentally and emotionally exhausted. Cool beads of sweat were beginning to dry at my temples and my hands were no longer shaking.

Last year, I would have been curled in a ball on the ground, lost in the flashback.

Progress.

That was something, at least.

Slivers of pride and hope mingled in my chest as I took a steadying breath and peeked around the corner, finding Brooks absorbed in the television.

Giving myself a silent pep-talk, I quietly began to drag the twin-size mattress through the doorway of the bedroom.

"What are you doing?"

"Shit," I cursed, placing a hand over my racing heart.

Brooks just raised his eyes in question.

"I like my privacy," I stated simply, shrugging my shoulders.

"That's what the curtain is for."

Clenching my jaw, I glanced around Brooks's form and saw the perfect corner to place my bed in the dining area.

"If it's safety you're worried about, I can take the twin out here and you can take the bedroom," Brooks told me softly, his hand raised in the air, as if to pat me reassuringly on the shoulder.

"No, it's okay. I don't mind, really. It will be like camping," I hurriedly said, tugging at the edge of the mattress with my hands while trying to balance it with my arms.

The damn thing kept buckling in the middle.

Muttering to himself, Brooks grabbed the mattress from the middle and moved it into the living room. With a satisfied look, he landed in the center of the bed.

"I-uh—"

"The bedroom has a lock, lovely."

And like that, all my inhibitions about being a meek houseguest went out the window. A lock meant safety while I slept and I could use some peace of mind while staying here with someone I hardly knew.

"Thank you, Brooks," I said.

And gods did I mean it.

He gave me a silent nod before continuing to watch his movie.

Walking over to the bedroom I plopped down on the queen bed, throwing my bag on the floor. The curtain that split the room in half was to my left, giving me even more privacy from the door.

The panic in my stomach finally dissipated entirely.

Nothing bad was going to happen to me here.

Not like that night.

Brooks's loud groan resonated throughout the apartment as I turned on the television that was in front of the bed. I began watching one of my favorite rom-coms as Brooks marched through the room, pulling the curtain back in annoyance.

"You can only run one television at a time."

"Not a fan of rom-coms?" I teased, tucking a pillow under my chest as a woman with waist long hair sauntered across the television screen.

"I love them. Why don't I watch one with you and I'll braid your hair while I'm at it," he said dryly, eyeing the flatscreen with disdain.

"I'd have better luck with E.E. doing my hair," I countered.

"You'd be surprised, lovely," Brooks said, attempting to grab the remote from the edge of the bed. Swiping it before he could, I tucked it into the pocket of my pants, thanking the gods that it was the pair with deep pockets.

At last, an Iydaraian designer who gave women deep pockets, instead of the industry standard pockets that could hold a singular mint.

"Better luck next time, detective."

I stood, pushing him through the curtain on the other side of the room. Satisfied with my clear message, I plopped down on the bed again.

"Pull back the curtain. We need to discuss this," Brooks griped.

"Your poor choice in movies?"

I could practically hear his eyes roll.

"The case, smartass. Now, pull back the curtain," he repeated.

"Absolutely not."

"Why?"

"Because you can ask your questions just as well from the other side of the room. Ever heard of privacy, detective?"

Privacy was power. And I didn't need a nosey detective digging into my past. Especially not when there was a large bounty dangling over my head. Of course The Collectress knew of the bounty, she was the one who supervised it.

Just another way to keep me in check.

The only silver lining was that the picture of me was when I was in my gorgon form, which no one ever saw unless I was on a mission for The Collectress with Rohesia.

I would be punished harshly if someone cashed in on the bounty. The Collectress would know I had been showing my gorgon to someone that was not stoned or dead.

It left room for betrayal on my part, something she did not tolerate.

Brooks's chuckle skittered across my bones. "You're more than welcome to privacy, lovely, given you have your own room. And I'd love some of my own for the next few weeks, since I was joking about braiding your hair." I snickered as he continued, "Now that we've established that we both have privacy, we've been ordered to figure out who is behind these attacks. And you're the only gorgon in Iydara so, I hate to tell you, lovely, but ignoring me isn't an option at this moment."

The way he said that nickname.

Lovely.

So patronizing and grumpily. It made me want to hold a knife to his throat.

Again.

Rolling off the bed, I walked over to the curtain, yanking it back. "I'm sure you love using your patronizing nicknames to push people around, but *I* was the one E.E. brought in on this case. And unless you can sprout any snakes from that head of yours, that means that you work for me."

"Those measly garter snakes, you mean?" he questioned, a hint of a smile threatening to show on his full lips.

"Oh, I think you mean vipers," I snapped, standing on my tiptoes, surprised to find that the top of my head only reached his chin.

A loud crash echoed through the room as the curtain came toppling down on top of me. Fighting through the material, I glared at Brooks, who was now leaning against the wall.

"Not feeling the curtains anymore?" I said thoughtfully, tapping a finger on my chin. "I like your way of thinking. I found that they closed off the room."

Brooks clenched his jaw, holding up a hand before I could finish protesting. "Neither of us gets a say in this arrangement. So rather than waste your time getting mad at the lack of privacy or so-called patronizing nicknames, why don't you compile a list of suspects that could be behind the golem attacks?"

"Would you like that list emailed or handwritten on rose-scented parchment?"

Ignoring my question, Brooks gave me a humorless smile, moving to sit on the edge of the bed, silently watching the movie with me.

I focused on the television, refusing to show any emotion. Rohesia told me on the ride over that there had been a dozen or so attacks in Iydara over the last year. My fight with Beresford being one of them. Unsure of just how much Brooks knew, I was hesitant to be upfront with him.

The detective obviously knew about magic as well, and deep down, I was afraid that the bounty on my head would prove to be too great of a temptation if he found out about it. Since E.E. was working for The Collectress and Brooks was working for E.E., I would only trust him as far as I could throw him.

Which, looking at the size of him, was maybe a foot.

Standing, Brooks smiles at me as he begins to reassemble the dismantled curtains and curtain rod. "I'm gonna hand you an olive branch, lovely."

"Yay for me."

"If I solve this case, I have the opportunity to be the lead detective on a rather important cold case. So, in other words, I will do anything to solve this. Anything. Even if it means laying you down on that very bed and holding a dagger to your throat as you write down the name of every gorgon in Iydara."

The 'rather important cold case' piqued my interest. What kind of case would be that important to him?

His blue eyes flashed, the pupils dilating strangely.

I blinked and they were once again normal.

The night we met flashed through my mind once again and I dared a glance at his throat. It certainly wasn't knife-play that had caused the dozens of deep scars on his flesh.

Brooks took a deep, steadying breath before continuing.

"You're the only gorgon on this side of the Anghor Peaks, which gives us an advantage. Put those big brains of yours to good use and make me a list. By morning. That's an order."

"I think you forgot the olive branch," I frowned.

"It's more of a twig."

Grumbling to myself about bossy coworkers, I began to unpack.

"Oh, and lovely?"

Slowly stepping towards me, until my thighs were pressing against the mattress and he was towering in front of me, Brooks lowered his lips to my ear.

"Yes, Brooks?"

His breath was hot and caused gooseflesh to appear on my skin. My breathing hitched but not in panic as it did when most men stood close to me. This was a certain...calm.

"I'd prefer lavender scented parchment paper."

Scoffing, I shoved him away, tempted to tell him what he could do with his damned list, but he threw the door shut and left the room before I was able to voice my thoughts out loud.

Anxiety coursed through me once I found myself alone in the bedroom, aware of how difficult and rude I was being.

Brooks didn't realize my uncalled for and childish actions were stemming from the blatant fear of my coven and trauma, rather than the inconvenience of my living quarters.

There were only a handful of gorgons that I knew of who could be behind these attacks. One was my mother and the other two were my sisters. And they were supposed to be in Kilmarn, hundreds of miles away from me.

If they were here, in Iydara, then I was a dead gorgon walking.

9

Brooks de Blasis marched towards me, stepping over a pile of fresh snow. We had agreed to meet outside The Hub over an hour ago. But I had taken a slight detour to Rohesia's room.

I looked down at my shiny new ring, admiring the twinkling sapphire stone in the early morning light. The gold band paired nicely with the glittering nail polish I wore.

"You're late, Brooks."

"Do you mind explaining where you have been for the past hour?" Fury was rolling off his shoulders. Perhaps a walk would cool him off. It was a good thing that we were about to embark on a rather long one.

I fluttered my eyelashes at the detective, motioning for him to follow me. Without any other choice, he did, although begrudgingly. Brooks stuffed his hands in the pockets of his trousers, matching my brisk pace easily because of his long legs.

"Do I get an explanation for this sudden escapade?" Brooks grumped angrily.

I shoved my hand into my pocket, pushing a folded piece of paper into his broad chest. Brooks's navy eyes lightened at it, but then quickly darkened as he opened it and saw that it was blank.

"What is this?"

"My list of suspects."

Brooks spun me around, careful not to slip on the slick sidewalk. "Is this a joke to you?"

I smirked as I remembered asking him the same question a little over a week ago. "Do you trust me, detective?"

"Absolutely not."

"Smart man. Well then, how can we be partners if you don't trust me?"

"Trust is earned, lovely. And you can earn my trust by communicating."

"Okay," I agreed, smiling up at him.

A look of shock appeared on his face, so surprised was he that I was willing to listen to him. He soon recovered, pressing his lips together in a scowl.

"Why is your list of suspects blank?" he asked, releasing his hold on my shoulder. I contemplated my answer as we walked into a small shopping district.

"Because I don't know of any other gorgons," I lied, waving a hand.

I decided late last night that I wasn't going to tell him about my mother and sisters. They weren't behind these attacks on humans. The coven had better things to do, like hunting me down and sacrificing my body, underneath a full moon, to the goddess Athena.

The attacks would only put The Collectress on high alert for other gorgons, whom she knew would want me, only causing her grip on my leash to tighten.

"Seriously?" he questioned, raising a dark eyebrow at me.

"Serious as a golem attack."

He frowned at my reference.

"You haven't met any other gorgons in your twenty years of life? Not even your own mother?" Brooks asked, not believing me. I didn't blame him.

"Have you met any other gorgons in your," I gave him a quick up and down, wrinkling my nose, and only checking him out a little, "thirty years of life, detective?"

Brooks spat out his coffee, choking on the hot liquid.

"Something wrong?" I asked innocently, twirling a white strand of hair around my finger.

"Thirty, my ass. Try twenty-seven, you brat."

"I don't know, I think I see some crow's feet," I said, my face blank as I examined his face.

"To answer your previous question, no, I haven't met any other gorgons. And if they all behave like you, then gods help us all. But you still haven't answered my question about your mother. I'm sure something as lovely as you didn't just fall out of the sky."

"I have another metaphorical list for you, since you love them so much," I replied, dodging his question once again.

"Wonderful," Brooks snapped impatiently.

"For this partnership to work, I have a list of topics that we cannot discuss. My mother is at the very top of said list. Think you can do that, detective?"

He met my eyes, but didn't protest my request.

"Good. Then, you will see why I'm not going to be wasting any of my time on the gorgon theory. Which brings us to our next destination."

We stopped in front of a dazzling storefront, filled with gorgeous diamond necklaces, flashy gold rings, and glittering ruby bracelets. The icing on top was the name of the store.

'De Blasis Bijouterie' was printed in curling silver letters atop a satin banner.

"Absolutely not, Usa," Brooks hissed into my ear, looking up at the sign in dismay. He grabbed my shoulder again, pulling me into a quieter corner of the shopping district.

"I figured that the next best place to start would be interviewing the relatives of the deceased. Starting with Beresford de Blasis' widow. Who just happens to be a five-star jeweler."

"And who just happens to be my cousin," Brooks said through clenched teeth, boxing me in with his muscular arms. The detective looked like he was five seconds away from strangling me or having a golem attack of his own.

"Well then, what better time for a family reunion than to introduce your family to your fiancée?"

"My wha—"

I quickly ducked underneath his arms, tsking as he went to grab my waist but missed by mere inches.

Warm air greeted us as we entered the lavish store. Glass display cases were scattered around the room, holding thousands, if not millions of doubloons worth of priceless gems and jewelry. Crystal light fixtures hung from the low ceiling, emphasizing the sparkle of the expensive jewels.

My gaze clicked with that of a woman not much older than myself. She took in our joined hands and her mouth fell open.

"Brooks Ascian-Otis de Blasis, is that you?"

Choked laughter escaped me at the use of his full name as the woman crashed into Brooks. He let out a rough chuckle as she wrapped her arms around him.

A booming voice echoed from the back of the store.

"Nola Bonnie de Blasis! I know you did not just leave your station again, ge—"

A stocky man opened the double doors that lead into the back, only to stop short when he saw Brooks, his lips pulled down in a furious scowl.

He did not have the same joyous reaction as Nola.

"Uncle," Brooks said, giving the man a curt nod.

"Brooks," the man replied.

A course, grey hair that was protruding from a mole on his forehead twitched as he walked up to us, his face seeming stuck in a permanent frown.

"Father, play nice," Nola warned, glaring at her dad with the fierceness of a thousand mother bears.

"I didn't say anything, dear. I don't have much to say to a man that deserted his family and only visits when the time is convenient for him." Brooks's uncle had quite the silver tongue and was not afraid to use it.

"That is not wh—"

"I would have expected you to show your face sooner than this. A lot sooner. Especially in your family's time of need," a glance was thrown at Nola, "but I suppose now is better than not at all."

Brooks and his uncle shared a stiff handshake, before leaving me and Nola alone near one of the glass counters.

"That was inten—" I began.

"Tell me about it," Nola huffed, running a hand over her voluminous hair. "They used to go at it like dogs growing up. Even more so when Rook returned to the mainland."

I silently wondered where Brooks had been previously. Humans were only allowed on Tabrn and Iydara. Surely he hadn't been in the Anghor Peaks, near Kilmarn.

"He trapped you for life, eh?" Nola laughed, nodding at the large emerald cut engagement ring on my hand.

"Something like that," I replied.

Guilt coiled in my gut and my hands became clammy as I put the next part of my plan into place.

"It's just hard to know when they're the one, ya know?" I said, airily, admiring the ring that I had borrowed from Rohesia.

"So hard. I remember the night that Beresford proposed to me. I almost said no," she looked past my shoulder as if gazing into the past, "but then I remembered our first date."

I nodded, not having to feign interest in Nola's story.

"It was in a pizza parlor down the road, and they had served us the wrong kind of pizza, one topped with pineapples instead of mushrooms."

We both crinkled our noses in disgust.

"But Beresford pushed me to try it. Yeah, it was only a silly pizza, but that's what you do when you're in love. You push each other, so you can turn into the best version of yourself."

I didn't voice my thoughts, but it had seemed that Beresford needed to be pushed over a cliff. The file Brooks had taken from The Hub was long and gruesome, even longer than the one The Collectress had on him. He had laid his hands on too many women, including his own wife and daughter. Maybe that's what Brooks had meant when he said that Beresford had it coming.

The Collectress hadn't been able to touch him because of his last name, a last name that controlled ninety percent of Iydara's gemstone and precious metal markets, and I would bet a thousand silver doubloons that was the reason why Beresford took his wife's last name instead of the other way around.

I felt lightheaded as her essence barreled into me. Decaying flesh, rosemary, and something unidentifiable. The same thing I had tasted in Brooks's the night of our first meeting.

It was bitter yet sweet.

Unsure what it was, I placed it in the 'Deal with Later' category in my mind. Which was currently occupied by my mother, the pile of dirty laundry in my duffle bag, and my impending twenty-fifth birthday.

Lost in my own thoughts, I studied Nola's red-rimmed eyes and dark circles that even makeup couldn't hide.

I was the cause of this woman's pain. No matter how much of a jerk her husband had been, I couldn't begin to imagine what it would be like to lose that kind of love. Not that I would know the first thing about love. My own relationships had been short and far-in-between.

"I can't imagine losing a partner," I mumbled sadly, toying with the ring on my finger. I had lost family members before, but never someone as close as a spouse or partner.

"The grief never ends. The pain will never go away. Your breath will catch in your chest when you remember them. It will feel like you are losing them all over again," shaky breaths left her body, causing the jewelry in her hand to quiver, "but, grief isn't a sign of weakness. It is the price of love. That is something to be grateful for. To rejoice in."

I looked at Nola. At the woman who was talking with the gorgon that had murdered her husband. Really looked at her. And I saw only pure, untainted generosity and a sympathetic heart.

I swallowed slowly, regret digging at my throat.

My next words burned as they left my traitorous mouth.

"I only hope that your grief and pain will lessen once they catch the monster who did it."

The wardens had notified the de Blasis family of Beresford's death the day after I stoned him. With stonings, the family was told that the deceased had perished from a hit-and-run, petty theft gone wrong, or medical emergency.

Her brown eyes flashed, and I was afraid that I had pushed her too far. But she looked around the shop, eyeing the customers on the far side of the building, and leaned towards me.

"We know who killed him," Nola said softly, her eyes guarded as she motioned for me to come closer, "The Collectress."

My eyes widened in real surprise. The jeweler knew more than she had originally let on. I wondered if she knew about magic like her cousin.

"Beresford had a gambling problem; we all knew it. But when he borrowed that money from The Collectress, he paid it back days later. He always paid it back."

"Days later, you say?" Confusion zapped through my bones like a strike of lightning. The Collectress had been adamant that Beresford was months late on repayment and that's why I had been ordered to stone him.

Nola pulled a petite pocketbook from her shirt pocket, grabbing a thick piece of pink paper. I recognized those pink slips of receipt paper. I had watched The Collectress write on them countless times.

Sure enough, the receipt for repayment showed that Beresford had paid the bill days after taking out the loan. The Collectress's looping signature was below Beresford's.

I wanted to disappear into the white carpet.

"He did take out a second loan, but it wasn't due until the week after he died." Nola pulled out a blue ticket this time, showing me the payment due dates.

The second loan must have been the one he was referring to before I stoned him. But Beresford had still had over a week left to repay her.

The Collectress had lied. To all of us.

Swallowing the word vomit that was threatening to spill from my mouth, I gasped at the first piece of outlandish jewelry that caught my eye.

"Ohmygosh, I need that necklace! Come look at this, Brooks."

"What is it, lovely?" Brooks asked joyfully, though his eyes were throwing daggers at mine.

"That sapphire necklace would pair perfectly with my ring, don't you think? Would you mind grabbing it, Nola?"

The necklace was in a glass case just beneath the receipts Nola had yet to tuck away. I nudged Brooks towards them as his cousin grabbed the necklace.

A million questions flitted through my mind as Brooks slyly studied the receipts.

Why have an innocent man stoned?

If The Collectress had lied about this, what else was she concealing? How could I even trust that she had no involvement in the golem attacks herself?

"Oh bummer, the clarity isn't as I had hoped. You'll let me know when you get another in, won't you?"

Nola nodded eagerly.

"You're the best. Kisses!" I giggled as we hurriedly left the store with more questions than answers.

We were a block away before either of us spoke.

"Kisses, seriously?" my partner mocked.

My face burned.

"Shut up. I panicked."

"Obviously."

"Oh, because you've gone undercover before?" I questioned.

"I have, actually," he said with pride.

The air quickly turned solemn at my next suggestion.

"Nola needs protection."

"I've already got a detail heading out to their place."

I nodded, relieved.

10

Fluorescent lights hummed through the pristine white hallways of the Eastern Boundary Community Hospital. Steel surgical instruments stared back at me as Brooks and I entered the coroner's office. The smell of cleaning supplies was overwhelming and made my breakfast of coffee turn into a ball of iron in my stomach.

Brooks and I had been on the way to meet up with Rohesia, to inform her about our meeting with Nola de Blasis and the lies that The Collectress had told us, when E.E. had called.

The detective had informed us that the autopsy performed on Beresford de Blasis was complete, and we needed to meet with the medical examiner immediately.

I hated hospitals and anything associated with them. The smell brought back painful memories of the night of my sixteenth birthday, memories that I would rather not relive. Breathing through my mouth helped some as we patiently waited for the medical examiner.

Rows of immaculate, reflective steel drawers distorted our reflections, lining the walls in an orderly fashion. Circular metal drains were scattered about the sterile floor, one appearing every few feet. My stomach clenched as my mind drifted to the reason that they would need multiple drains that large.

"Nervous, lovely?" Brooks asked, his voice lowered. The detective tilted his head at me in question as I fought against the shadows that were crowding the edge of my vision.

"Hardly," I snorted, crossing my arms in defiance.

"It's okay if you can't handle it. I understand. Not everyone is cut out to be a detective."

"Puh-lease. I could do this in my sleep." I stretched my arms above my head, yawning.

"We'll see about that," he chuckled darkly, doubt glimmering in those cobalt eyes of his.

Brooks hadn't bothered to talk to me since the stunt I pulled earlier this morning. I didn't blame him. When we had just arrived back at The Hub's headquarters, he started receiving hourly calls from his mother, begging him to bring his fiancée over for dinner.

The calls had only stopped once Brooks told her that it was a crude joke played by a desperate, lonely stalker of his. I had chucked an empty bottle of soda at him when I overheard this.

But it was oh so worth hearing Mrs. de Blasis ask Brooks if he still had the pepper spray that she had gotten him for his birthday.

I did feel bad, nonetheless.

From what I had seen of Nola de Blasis's online presence, she shied away from the authorities and had refused to talk to them about what happened to her husband. Even if Brooks had been the one to interview her about the death of her husband, I doubted that she would have opened up much to him.

But talking to a soon-to-be-relative that was looking for wedding advice and swooning over her new ring? It had been the perfect distraction.

My shoulders straightened as a woman with mile-long legs sashayed in from the hallway. "Rookie! How are you? It's been ages."

I'm pretty sure my mouth dropped open as I watched the medical examiner hug Brooks, one of her sleek legs wrapping around his. Annoyance reared its ugly head as she gave him a peck on his cheek and he gave her one in return.

"Rookie?" I mouthed at him.

"Shut. Up," he mouthed back through clenched teeth.

She finally seemed to acknowledge me when I snickered back at the detective. I walked over to the pair, waiting for the woman to unlatch herself from Brooks.

"Oh! How rude of me. You didn't tell me you had students shadowing you today, Rookie."

I narrowed my eyes at her and took her dainty hand in mine. Her long nails scraped my fingers as she let go of my hand.

"Eirlys, this is Usa. Usa, meet Eirlys. Usa is my partner on this case. She's an expert in all thing's gorgon. A bit of a fanatic if I must say."

"Aw, how cute. I didn't know the bureau employed students." Eirlys looked me up and down with pity, her bottom lip protruding.

"Actually, I will turn twenty-five pretty soon. Sorry to disappoint," I informed her, causing Eirlys to scrunch her small nose, as if she had eaten something sour.

I fought the urge to roll my eyes as she wrapped her arms around Brooks's shoulders, batting her long eyelashes up at him.

Taking a steadying breath, I gave Eirlys a smile. "E.E. told us to come down here for Beresford de Blasis's autopsy results. They were rather urgent."

Pouting, Eirlys unlatched herself from Brooks's massive form and shuffled some papers in her hands. "Yes. I am so sorry for your loss, Rookie, you must be devastated."

"Terribly," Brooks said, sarcasm coating his voice.

Eirlys didn't seem to catch it, going on and on about how wonderful Beresford had been and how the community would be lost without his guiding presence.

Dread clouded Eirlys' eyes as she opened Beresford's file. She continued to look at Brooks, refusing to acknowledge that I was an investigator on the case.

"Every life, be it a statue, human, or mage, releases an aura when they use a large amount of magic. Some more powerful beings can even taste or smell these auras. If you are around a mage when they use fire magic, or when one creates a spell, et cetera, those aura particles can enter your very own bloodstream. Even if you weren't the one to use a large amount of magic," Eirlys stated matter-of-factly, throwing tresses of platinum hair over a dainty shoulder.

"You're talking about an essence?" I asked.

"Yes," Eirlys said, slowly blinking at me, as if suddenly remembering that I was there. "Mages, humans, and gorgons all have very different essences. Because of this, the essence particles they release when using great quantities of magic are easy to distinguish from one another."

"How do you differentiate between old and new essences in a person's bloodstream? Say, if a person were stoned weeks before being transformed into a golem?" Brooks questioned, writing down notes in a small, tattered Moleskine notebook that he kept in his back pocket.

"It isn't easy." Eirlys smiled, batting her eyelashes at Brooks. "It takes years of training, but lucky for you, I'm an expert in the field."

"Lucky indeed," Brooks said, throwing Eirlys a wink.

"Or the fact that there is scientific, mage-reviewed research which states that an outside essence, one that is not from the host body, cannot live for more than seventy-two hours in the bloodstream," I interjected. "And the sooner you are around a large amount of magic, say, being turned into a golem, the more essence particles there are lingering in your system."

I paced around the room, playing with the ring on my finger, having forgotten to return it to Rohesia. "Having an unknown essence in one's bloodstream for more than seventy-two hours is deadly. Everyone knows that. That's why our bodies release any large amount of essence particles that are not our own within seventy-two hours of coming into contact with them."

Brooks gave me an incredulous look, shocked that I knew that tidbit of information. Even Eirlys seemed surprised.

Rohesia had insisted that she teach me about magic, as a way to protect me from those that wanted to maliciously use it against me.

Ignorance equated to death.

"Beresford was stoned a week before he died. The essence particles given off during his stoning would have been out of his system within three days," I said, turning to Eirlys who looked shell-shocked at my amount of forensic knowledge.

Brooks turned to me. "How many hours was Beresford's statue missing before he attacked you?"

"Less than twelve."

Brooks began pacing, spinning the silver ring on his finger again. "The particles from the stoning would have been out of his system almost a week ago. But if he was transformed into a golem within seventy-two hours of his stoning, the essence particles would have lingered in his system, since not enough time had passed for them to flush out of his body. Correct?"

"Correct," Eirlys stated.

Brooks nodded, following along easily.

Recovering from her dazed state, Eirlys filled in the blanks. "Because Beresford died within twelve hours of his transformation into a golem, it would be safe to assume that he carried around two hundred or more milligrams of essence particles in his system."

"Right." Brooks nodded, giving Eirlys a blank look.

The coroner looked like she was going to explode if she kept her secret any longer.

"Beresford de Blasis's autopsy showed that he had zero milligrams of essence particles in his system at the time of his death. And all the other golems that died within seventy-two hours of being transformed? Not one of them had a trace of a different essence in their bloodstream." Eirlys breathed, her eyes widening with excitement.

Brooks stopped pacing, sharing a befuddled look with me.

Eirlys gave me the papers she was scanning. "Here. Look for yourself, gorgon expert."

I nodded my thanks.

Sure enough, Beresford de Blasis had no trace of essence particles in his system at the time of his death. Neither did any of the other golems.

"I don't understand," Brooks voiced, his brow furrowed as he gazed at the papers from over my shoulder.

"We expected Beresford to have high levels of gorgon essence particles in his system. But he had none. We thought it was a fluke at first, and that the witness's timelines were off. But then we looked at security footage from a neighbor of The Collectress."

Pulling out a smart tablet, Eirlys showed us grainy footage of Beresford in golem form, walking down the sidewalk. The timestamp confirmed it was the night before he attacked me in the alleyway.

"What are you saying?"

"I'm saying that Beresford de Blasis, and all the other golems, weren't created by a gorgon, or any type of magical being."

My head began to spin.

"He was transformed by something that is magic, but doesn't produce an essence," Eirlys hinted, running a manicured hand over her flushed cheeks.

Something that is magic, but isn't?

That didn't make any sense.

Who would be able to transform a statue into a golem, but not release a magical essence when doing so?

"As always, you never cease to amaze me, Eirlys. Thank you so much for your help," Brooks said, giving her a winning smile.

"Of course, Rookie. Anything for you," she crooned, placing a kiss on his cheek, Brooks didn't return it this time. Her slender arms wrapped around his shoulders, embracing him in a seductive hug.

I leaned against the wall of steel drawers, waiting for their long embrace to end.

"You know there are dead bodies in those, right?" Brooks chirped, looking at me over Eirlys's shoulder.

Of course, I did. Everyone knew that. But instead of being the polite and mature partner, my tongue decided to run away from me.

Again.

"No shit, Sherlock."

Eirlys rolled her eyes at my lame joke.

But I managed to wrangle a low chuckle out of Brooks.

I knew that Brooks was making a concerted effort to keep his mouth shut when we finally returned to the apartment an hour later. His skin seemed to be buzzing with excitement from the moment we left the coroner's office.

And he couldn't stop spinning the ring on his finger.

I wasn't sure why.

It seemed to me that we had met a dead end.

"So at least we know that gorgons and any other magical beings are off the list," I said, folding my feet under myself as I sat on one of the cracked, leather loveseats.

Brooks grunted in response, taking a beer from the refrigerator, and taking a long swig.

"Unless you think that Eirlys was lying?"

"You know as well as I do that it is nearly impossible to fake forensic evidence. Especially with the overwhelming number of cases where golems did not have essence particles in their systems at the time of their death," he took another swig of his beer, "and I know Eirlys, especially when she's lying or telling the truth."

"How do you know Eirlys?" I asked, wincing at my clipped tone.

What was that about? Sure, Brooks was attractive. But that didn't warrant the irritation that I felt when I watched Eirlys and Brooks embracing. It sure didn't give me permission to wonder what it would be like to be the one on the receiving end of one of his embraces.

My eyes stay plastered on the television, watching an infomercial about a device that could shred cheese in three different ways.

"We dated in college for a bit, but it was arranged between our parents. Eirlys's family owns a rather large jewelry shop, like mine, and thought it would be best for her and me to date and eventually marry."

Brooks let out a loud sigh, emptying his beer bottle. "But I didn't want an empire. I still don't. So, I broke it off before it could get too serious."

"What *do* you want then, Brooks?"

He threw an all-consuming gaze my way, his dilated pupils trailing up my body. They lingered on my mouth for a second, before eventually reaching my eyes.

"Something I can't have," he murmured, rubbing a hand over his five-o-clock shadow in contemplation.

Butterflies swarmed in my stomach, but I stomped them down before they transformed into something more, something that I wasn't sure I could handle.

"Let's look at this again. Since gorgons and other magical beings are out of the question, maybe it's a human? Or someone who doesn't release an essence when using magic?" I asked.

"But humans can't use magic," Brooks stated.

"Not that we know of. And everyone releases an essence, Brooks. I can sense them," I sighed.

Humans using magic would cause an uproar with the gods, mages, and even me. They were the gods favorites because they couldn't fight back with magic. Allowing them to have access to magic would upset the balance of nature.

"Okay, so definitely not someone," Brooks said, taking out his tattered notebook and flipping through the pages.

I watched as he tore out pages from the notebook, scattering them on the battered coffee table. The detective stood from his own seat, squatting near the loveseat I was resting in.

I observed his methods as his eyes slid over the papers, his mind working fast.

Then he lifted his head.

Brooks clucked his tongue at me but didn't stand from his squatted position. "What if it's a *something?*"

I unfolded my arms, gazing at his transcripts. There were also drawings of odd, twisting figurines. They reminded me of an abstract sculpture made by an artist.

"You're referring to a relic?" I breathed, leaning in closer to see his notes. I had learned from The Collectress that certain relics could possess the abilities of the gods. You just had to know how to access the power.

"Relic, idol, artifact, any object that can act as a conduit for magic."

I had never heard of a relic acting as a conduit for magic.

I wrinkled my brow, crossing my arms over my chest. "You make it sound so straightforward, like these conduit objects actually exist. If that were the case, *anyone* could access magic and wouldn't leave any trace."

"But that's the thing, lovely. You aren't supposed to exist. No human would believe me if I strutted outside and yelled to the heavens that I had a gorgeous gorgon holed up in my apartment."

Before I could respond, Brooks flipped through his notebook once again, looking for something excitedly. "Here."

I squinted my eyes, not quite able to decipher his chicken scratch. It was half cursive and half print. The letters were squished together on the practically transparent and yellowing paper, making it difficult to read.

Brooks surveyed my face with a casual, taunting disinterest that made my pulse pound, going as far to flick one of my braids.

"Come on, Watson. A born detective learns how to decipher crappy handwriting before they can walk. How do you expect to solve this case if you can't even read your own partner's handwriting?"

I leaned back into the chair, concentrating on his horrible handwriting.

"Beresford de Blasis. Illegal activism." I held the paper up to my nose.

"No. Activities."

I raised my eyebrows, shifting the papers in my hand.

"Keep reading."

"Money laundry—laundering, embezzlement, aggravated asses—assault, and relish- relic trafficking."

Relic trafficking.

I only knew of one other person that trafficked stolen antiques.

"You think Beresford was stoned because he was competing against The Collectress?"

The theory made sense. What better way to knock out your competition than killing them? But why would The Collectress send us on a scavenger hunt to find Beresford's killer if she herself was the murderer?

"Possibly. But I think the better theory is that Beresford got his hands on this." He showed me a picture of a sculpture of clear, winding branches. The arms resembled tentacles, though these were smooth in texture, having no suction cups or scales.

"What is it?" I asked, intrigued by the shape.

"A fulgurite."

"A figure-what?"

"A fulgurite," Brooks chuckled, running a hand over his tightly coiled hair, "is a piece of fossilized lightning. When lightning hits sand, it usually transforms into a clump or mass of organic debris."

"Though sometimes when the conditions are just right, the fulgurite turns into a piece of clear, breathtaking glass. Like this," He continued.

He removed the ring on his finger, placing it gently in my palm.

I had thought that the ring was made out of steel or sterling silver, but I was wrong. The ring was made of a dark ashen glass. It weighed nothing; I could barely feel it in my hand as I examined it.

"Beresford was after a fulgurite like this?"

"Not just any fulgurite. Zeus' Fulgurite." He swiped on the tablet, showing me the glass sculpture once again. It was breathtaking, with its twisting, curving branches that were determined to brush the stars and hold the hands of the gods and goddesses that roamed the skies.

"Thousands of years ago, a bolt of Zeus' lightning hit a beach on the island of Raas, creating a magnificent piece of fulgurite. For years, citizens of the island paid no mind to the statue, thinking it was no more than a paperweight. It wasn't until a mage came into contact with the sculpture that people soon realized that the fulgurite could act as a conduit for magic.

"The fulgurite went missing hundreds of years ago. But there are rumors that it is in Iydara, being traded on the black market every few decades. It gives the user unlimited magic power, even mortals."

Including mortals like Beresford.

Or any other mortal that wanted to get ahead of The Collectress or plot her demise.

"And I'm guessing it leaves no trace of a magical essence?"

"Can't leave what you don't have," Brooks murmured, writing down more notes in his torn notebook.

If Beresford had been on the verge of possessing unlimited magic, especially untraceable magic, then The Collectress would have seen him as a threat to her reign. She was the most powerful being in all of Iydara and she wouldn't have wanted to share that title.

She could have stolen the artifact back from Beresford and then used it against him. "But why would The Collectress or Beresford want an army of golems?"

Brooks shrugged. "Why does anyone want anything? Power. Sex. Money. Drugs. The list goes on and on."

I nodded, fear curling in my stomach at the thought of The Collectress having an unstoppable army of golems on top of the mass of mages that were ready to do her bidding.

Though I still couldn't figure out why she would want a golem army, it was our only lead, seeing as how Beresford was dead. But it was clear that she could be using Zeus's Fulgurite to create the monsters of stone.

Without any other tips, we called Rohesia, telling her to inform us of any suspicious movements The Collectress made.

11

It was three days later when Rohesia informed us about The Collectress making an unexpected trip to a centuries-old patch of shadowed trees in Iydara.

The strip known as Marren's Grove was an expansive area of sequoia trees that bordered the Western and Northern Boundaries of Iydara. Humans often spent holiday weekends there, camping and fishing.

We anticipated that The Collectress was meeting up with a seller to buy Zeus' Fulgurite, and not to go camping or fishing.

Our leading theory was that The Collectress had had me stone Beresford not because of an unpaid loan, but because he possessed the fulgurite. She could have stolen it and then was using it to transform statues into golems. And if the relic was being used to transform statues into golems, then we needed to destroy it.

We still weren't sure why she would be wanting to sell the seemingly priceless relic after killing a man just to get it. But that's what we were hoping to figure out today.

Brooks and I left The Hub as the sun started to sink. The Collectress loved to meet with her buyers in the cover of darkness, and if a deal was going to go down in Marren's Grove, then we needed to be the first ones to know.

Gravel crunched under the tires as Rohesia, Brooks and I pulled into the parking lot of the grove. Dozens of other cars and vehicles were crammed into the small lot. Though it was the middle of winter, many humans took advantage of the large lake in the middle of the grove for ice fishing or skating.

"The autopsy results for Beresford came back," I said to Rohesia. We were a few paces behind Brooks as he led us to a side of the lake with underground caves.

"What did it say?" she whispered loudly, catching the gaze of a curious human couple. I waited until they had passed us before informing her about the results, since she had been unexpectedly forced to return to the mansion for a couple of nights to help The Collectress with the aftermath of yet another stoning.

We were hesitant to discuss details of the case over the phone, in case they were being monitored.

I slowly explained what Eirlys had told us. Mentioning that the autopsy had proven that Beresford, along with the other golems, had not been transformed by a gorgon.

I was relieved that the new gorgon species theory had been put to rest. Primarily because I didn't want to risk a run in with my mother or sisters. Or any other members of my coven.

"How do we know that it's the fulgurite that is being used as a conduit?"

"We don't," I sighed, "but it's our only lead for now. Especially since whatever is creating the golems isn't leaving an essence behind."

Though we couldn't see far ahead of us, Brooks seemed to know exactly where we were going. Our pace held steady as we maneuvered over crumbling banks covered with rust-colored, decomposing leaves.

The leather straps of my satchel bit into the back of my frostbitten neck. The pain was irritating enough that it kept me awake and alert through the journey.

After a few moments of careful examination, Brooks stepped through a cluster of creaking snow-heavy branches. Though snow had fallen just the night before, sharp thorns still poked out through the frost covered branches. Layers of thick wool clothing prevented the thorns from impaling me.

109

Rohesia had pulled rose bush thorns out of my body for over ten minutes when I had battled Samara, the real estate agent, and I didn't want to experience that again.

A narrow, deserted pathway appeared before us, leading the way to a labyrinth of caves. Packed snow seemed to be the only obstacle on the road.

Rohesia and I sighed in relief.

The muscles in my legs began to ache from the cold wind and I had to stop a few times to rub my hands on my thighs to keep the blood flowing.

We were just short of one of the cave entrances when my knees instinctively gave way, my gorgon sensing the presence of a group of off-duty wardens around the corner. I hid behind a group of bare bushes, holding my breath in case anyone saw me. The wardens would easily recognize me and I was afraid they would notify The Collectress of my presence, forcing the meeting to be rescheduled.

Strong arms wrapped around my waist, pulling me off the snow-covered ground.

"Easy there, Watson, no need for any of that," Brooks teased, his breath warm and uneven on my neck. Delicious shivers raced up my spine, heat from his body seeping into my cold one.

Pushing myself from his embrace, I caught up to Rohesia, who was exploring the cave entrance. She eyed Brooks with casual interest.

Rohesia had informed us that The Collectress was previously seen in one of the south tunnels. But this was one of a dozen that we needed to explore.

"You and Brooks, hmm?"

Though the shadows were too thick in the cave to clearly see Rohesia's face, I knew by her tone that she was grinning.

"Brooks? Gods no. I'd sooner date Rennyn again."

"It just seemed like you were getting a little comfortable back there." The teasing in her voice seemed to grow with each syllable. I could practically feel her eyebrows waggling on her forehead.

"I misread the situation. Brooks was just helping me get on my feet before someone saw me hiding behind the bushes. Thankfully before I made a total fool out of myself."

"Hmm," she sighed, the sound echoing throughout the cave system.

Stalactites hung from the ceiling, glistening in the low light. Cloudy drops of water fell from the pointed forms, bouncing off our water-resistant jackets. Groups of the calcite deposits became more and more dense as we stumbled upon a fork in the cave system.

"Where's Brooks?" Rohesia asked, concern blanketing her voice. I could have sworn that he was right behind us, but he was nowhere to be seen.

I shrugged. "Probably off doing detective things."

The tunnel on the left was a quarter of the size of the one on the right. It also gave off a rank sulfur smell that seeped into our layers of clothing. Sounds of running water echoed through the tunnel, hinting that there was a spring at the end of it.

The one on the right was fairly inviting and open, emitting a soft white glow. There were no stalactites hanging from the ceiling in the tunnel on the right. Because of this, I pushed Rohesia towards it, remembering her fear of small, dark spaces.

"Meet back here in an hour?" she asked, her hand lingering on the mouth of the entrance.

"Okay."

I watched Rohesia disappear into the tunnel, her shadow becoming bigger and bigger as she ventured further into the cave.

My body thrummed with nervous energy as I stepped into the dark tunnel on the left.

I reached out my arms, my fingertips grazing the walls on either side of me. Stale water and rough rocks grazed my hands as I steadied myself on the walls. This type of darkness, the kind that was all consuming and thick, made my soul weary.

The chances of The Collectress being at the end of this tunnel were at best one in a dozen.

There were hundreds of pitch-black tunnels in Marren's Grove, and if Rohesia was wrong, and The Collectress wasn't in one of the southern tunnels, then we would be chasing ourselves in circles.

The smell of sulfur overwhelmed me as I continued to trip and stumble in the darkness.

I reluctantly realized that I wouldn't be able to cover much ground if I couldn't see. I just hoped there were no humans at the end of the tunnel as I pushed my inner gorgon forward, relying on her night vision to guide me to the end of the passageway.

The tunnel had to be no more than a hundred yards long, and perhaps five feet wide, but the same could not be said for the chamber I entered.

Warm air caressed my cheeks as I tiptoed into the roomy cavern of sulfur and midnight. The soft glow of the moon entered the cave through a massive hole in the ceiling, reflecting on the pale blue lake as I explored the cave further.

Shades of plum, emerald and caerulean were scattered across the floor, gathering on the edges of flat, round stepping stones next to the enchanting lake. Though there was a giant hole in the ceiling, the air was not cold.

Gooseflesh appeared on my skin as the air grew hotter and denser the closer I walked to the lake.

Pillars of rising rocks jutted out from the sparkling lake, disappearing into the center of the water.

Climbing the smooth rocks to peer into the center of the lake was possibly the worst idea I'd had all month, besides the time I ate two pints of chocolate cherry ice cream while on my cycle, but I couldn't shake the feeling that I was being guided to the pillars of stone.

The first step was the most difficult. My boots were made for traipsing through feet of snow, not carefully climbing slippery, wet rocks. Without giving it a second thought, I discarded my winter boots and socks, chucking them onto the rocks that hugged the perimeter of the lake.

I discarded a few layers of clothing as well.

Standing in the open, warm cavern in jeans and a cozy, threadbare sweater, I walked along the rocks, finding it easier to maneuver along the pillars with bare feet.

Where the pillars ended, glowing white water splashed against the dark stone. I looked into the depths of the water, surprised to find a swirling whirlpool at the center of the lake.

"They say that if you look into Marren's Eye for too long, you'll be sucked in, never to see the light of day again."

I whirled around to find Brooks standing behind me, gazing into the water apprehensively. He had shed his heavy jacket and shoes as well.

"Marren's Eye," I chuckled dryly, the laugh scathing my throat. "Well, that's perfect, I was running out of nightmare fuel."

He motioned to the whirlpool with a jerk of his sharp chin.

"When the gods still roamed the earth, one of them became obsessed with a common girl named Marren, for she was as stunning as fresh snow on the Anghor Peaks, and as untamable as the winds of a hurricane." Brooks's gaze shifted towards me before once again looking into the water. "She had fiery red hair, curly and as reckless as yours, and memorizing icy eyes, eyes that were so light blue that they sometimes looked white."

I looked at the aqua and white water with newfound fear.

"But the god who fell in love with her was fanatical. Marren turned him down day after day, she was in love with another man. When the god who was after her heart found out that she had already given it to a mere mortal, it greatly angered him."

My heart thumped in my throat and the edge of my vision darkened. Marren's story was too similar to mine. I would bet my life that the god he mentioned was Poseidon.

"If the god couldn't have Marren, then no one could. So, he lured her here, into this lonely cavern. It is said that he drowned her in these waters, her soul forever trapped in this lake, for only the god to have access to," Brooks finished solemnly.

"It seems like the gods can't handle being told no," I whispered, looking at the treacherous turquoise waters with great sadness.

"No, they can't." He grew stiff, looking at me with crippling pity.

A sad smile emerged on my face. "Being told no is a sign of rejection. It's humiliating. It hurts. And the gods don't often respond well to that kind of thing."

If only I could tell Brooks about my past.

But no. I couldn't. Not without opening myself up and being horrifically hurt and betrayed again. I wouldn't allow myself to trust him. Not after being wounded by my own family and ex. Those types of betrayal cut deep and left scars that festered for years.

"Who hurt you?" Brooks asked, as if reading my mind.

"I'll tell you mine, when you tell me yours," I said wearily, eyeing the scars on his throat.

Brooks nodded. "Fair enough."

Dropping his gaze, I stared at my feet.

The glittery black polish on my toenails was chipping and in need of a new coat. I wiggled my toes against the heated stone, focusing on the physical sensations rather than the turmoil in my heart.

The tips of Brooks's fingers grazed my hand. I felt his questions lingering on his lips, as consuming and greedy as the heated flames of a raging fire.

But he didn't push.

And neither did I.

I got the sense that we were both grateful for our silent understanding.

Brooks picked me up with his muscular arms, a wild laugh escaping me as we peered over the edge of the cliff.

"What in gods' names are you doing?" I asked.

"Preparing to jump into the eye."

My heart skidded to a stop.

"That's insane."

"There are a handful of passageways that go underneath Marren's Eye, and this is one way to those tunnels. The other entrances are on the north side of Marren's Grove and would take us all night to reach. This way is more efficient."

"This way is going to get us killed."

Pain radiated through my clenched teeth and jaw as I began to shiver in fear. I took a steadying breath, focusing on the warmth of Brooks's skin on mine.

I attempted to get down from his arms, but before I could, Brooks whispered into my ear, "I dare you to."

He looked at me. His eyes were wild, and in the low light he looked more handsome and human than I'd ever seen him. The night we first met flashed to the forefront of my mind, when he had dared me to stone him.

"What are you waiting for then?" I said, my voice shaking, but not from nervousness. I squeezed my eyes shut and pinched my nose shut for good measure.

I wouldn't back down from any more of his dares.

Brooks's rough laughter echoed throughout the chamber.

Wind rustled my hair as Brooks stepped off the cliff, a scream tearing through my throat as we crashed into the dark waters.

12

My eyes had only been closed for a matter of seconds when we hit the water and I realized that my clothing was dry.

Rushing water flowed all around us, as I clung to Brooks for dear life, but it never directly touched us. A bubble of air surrounded us as the whirlpool took us down, down, down.

The bubble we traveled in reminded me of a waterpark that Rohesia had taken me to once. A fluorescent orange tube had launched us into cold, chlorine filled water. It was one of the rare days that we hadn't had work for The Collectress while she had been in Tabrn. And we had taken advantage of it by interacting with the world as though we were simply teenage girls on summer break.

The sound of a chattering crowd and edgy music enveloped us as we shot into a cave of black, shiny stone. Though a mere mortal, Brooks landed on his feet, only stumbling a bit before putting me on the ground.

We weren't the only ones in the cavern.

About one hundred others, a mix of mages, elves, mortals, and other magical creatures, chatted around a lowered hole in the ground. Railing separated them from whatever was in the cavity.

"Number?"

I spun on my heel, finding a mage handing out bidding numbers to different patrons. The book she held in her hands was thick and teeming with numbered cards.

"Yes, thank you," Brooks murmured, stuffing the bidder's number into the pocket of his shirt.

Along with the hole in the center of the cave, there were different vendors and booths along the walls. Each one was selling something different. Candles, leather goods, knives, soap, jewelry, fried meat, and even blown glass figurines.

"Remember to take your seat in fifteen minutes when the auction begins," the worker said, raising her voice to be heard above the fuss of the crowd.

I pulled Brooks into a semi-secluded corner, dropping my voice to a low whisper, "You didn't mention that we were going to stumble upon the freaking black market."

Rumors floated around Iydara about the black market. But I had never believed them. Not when The Collectress threatened to expose those involved in the illegal selling and trading of goods.

"Didn't think you'd go if you knew."

"How did you even know that it was here?"

"A good detective knows everything, lovely." He booped the tip of my nose before venturing to a booth that was selling fried pickles.

Murdering Brooks would only add to my to-do list, which had only grown since getting out of bed:

1. *Find Zeus's Fulgurite*
2. *Find out who/what was creating golems*
3. *Suffocate Brooks with his pillow*
4. *Buy toothpaste*

Breathing deeply in an attempt to remain calm, I began to look around.

I had heard horror stories about the black market from Rohesia. About terrible fights, unmentionable goods being sold, like organs and skin, and crooked criminals that would sell their own child to make a quick doubloon.

A booth selling glass figurines caught my eye. The man behind the booth gave me a slight nod before returning to the book he was reading.

He was human.

And I couldn't decide if that made me feel better or worse.

Delicate, handmade forest creatures had been crafted out of heated, pulled glass and I was entranced by them. Specifically, a cat with a gorgeous black coat and silver ears.

The cat was about the size of my hand, if not a tad bit smaller. It seemed to watch me curiously with its silver eyes.

I had forgotten my wallet in the coat pocket of my jacket, and sadly studied it in my hand as Brooks appeared at my side, munching on a giant, greasy turkey leg.

"Wann-a bi-te?" he asked, chewing through mouthfuls of delicious meat.

I placed the figurine back on the table and immediately took the leg from him, my stomach clenching from hunger. Grease covered my lips as I took a massive bite. A soft groan escaped my lips as the gloriously flavorful meat hit my tastebuds.

"Right?" Brooks grinned, wiping a trail of grease from my chin with a quick swipe of his thumb.

"So good." I grinned back, licking my lips.

We followed the crowd as everyone began to take their seats, passing the turkey leg back and forth in comfortable silence.

Surrounding the pit, stone benches had been carved from the obsidian walls. Our reflections stared back at us as we waited for the auction to begin.

"What makes you think she's here?"

I hadn't spotted The Collectress yet and was beginning to doubt that she was really here. But I pushed those feelings to the back of my mind. I needed to be able to trust Brooks if I wanted him to trust me.

"I had a knack for going to places I wasn't supposed to as a kid. Including the black market. I met The Collectress long ago at an auction similar to this."

Surprise flitted through me.

"Your poor mother must've had a head full of gray hair by the time you were five."

"Trust me, I was an extremely well-behaved child as far as she knew."

A soft snort escaped me as I looked around the room. The cavern was packed, some buyers being forced to stand, and others being denied entrance because of the lack of open seats.

A man in a black suit entered the pit, a quiet hush falling over the crowd as he raised his hands in the air. He was as gorgeous as Brooks, but cleaner cut and less rugged.

Black tights with slithering snakes adorned the long legs of a woman who carried a large golden mask on a tray. The piece drew gasps from the waiting crowd and the bidding started at five hundred thousand doubloons.

"Mask of Agamemnon," Brooks whispered into my ear.

We watched as the mask was shown to all the buyers, the metal reflecting brilliantly in the light. The bidding was closed at seven million three hundred and fifty thousand doubloons. Jealous curses were thrown in the direction of the winning bid.

The next item was a decorated amphora, according to Brooks, and though less intriguing as the golden mask, it still sold for a whopping ninety-four thousand doubloons.

With each new item, a different seller came from a secret door in the side of the pit. And with each new item, the crowd grew more unruly and wild.

Mugs of beer were being passed through the lines of seats when the last item for auction was announced. Brooks had just returned with a second turkey leg and a plate of fried pickles when someone hushed the crowd.

My heart stopped beating as The Collectress and Brooks's uncle walked into the pit, hand in hand, holding Zeus's Fulgurite.

13

Brooks and I slid down in our seats, calculating the amount of time it would take to get out of here unnoticed. Brooks's face had tightened, his lips pressed into a thin line, while the crinkles around his eyes creased deeply.

"Let's get out of here."

"Not yet," I protested. There was a ten-minute intermission before selling Zeus's Fulgurite, and we needed to use it to gather more information.

Brooks titled his head towards me, listening openly.

"Why is she selling that thing when she killed an innocent man just to possess it?" I hissed into my partner's ear.

It didn't add up. Why go through all that trouble just to pawn it off to someone else?

"Unless there's something more valuable she wants."

"Like what?" I asked.

Brooks shrugged. "I'm not sure."

"Let's go find out," I suggested, nodding towards an opening and closing door that houses other relics and artifacts.

Taking Brooks's large hand in mine, we wound our way through the crowd. A particularly rowdy group of bidders ahead formed a disorderly barricade, blocking our path and forcing us to stop far too close to the pit. My hair only hid so much of my features and Brooks was too familiar to be missed by his uncle. The hair on my neck stood on end as his uncle's stare locked on us

"Sit," Brooks commanded.

I arched my brows, peeking over my shoulder to find Brooks's uncle and one of his goons starting to walk our way. The room held some shadows, but it wasn't dark enough to hide us entirely. We should be making our getaway, not waiting for the show to start.

"Sitting will get us killed," I hissed.

"Not when they're expecting us to flee." Brooks jerked his chin towards the door, where my boss's goons were now carefully watching who entered and exited the room. I recognized two of them from the golem attack on the mansion. They were friends with Casimar and hated me almost as much as he did.

Brooks sat on a crowded bench, squished between a human wearing a snakeskin tracksuit and a mage with boyish looks who seemed to be ten years younger than myself.

Before I could decide whether I should sit at Brooks's feet or find a bench with more room, Brooks's hands gently grasped my hips, pulling me into his lap.

"What are you doing, dear?" I asked through clenched teeth, well aware of the human who seemed too interested in our interaction.

"Just making room for our friends, lovely," he hissed back, motioning towards his uncle's employee who was walking our way.

I buried my face in Brooks's shoulder, covering it with clumps of my wild hair, stiffening as Brooks turned his face towards mine, his breath warm and steady.

Through the curtain of hair, I could still make out the silhouette coming towards us. The man wasn't slowing down.

"How long have you two lovebirds been together?" asked the older woman wearing the tracksuit.

"One ye-five months," Brooks and I said simultaneously.

"One year and five months," I said sweetly.

Brooks harrumphed in agreement.

The woman began talking about her husband, and I would usually happily chat with the widow, encouraging her to share stories of her great love with empathetic interest, and might even shed a tear or two, but that was before we were being tracked down by vengeful employees of Brooks's uncle.

And that was also before I was being held into place by Brooks's rough hands. His hands grasped the curves of my hips firmly, his thumbs mindlessly tracing circles on the slivers of flesh that were peeking out from beneath my shirt.

"Can't have you falling into the pit full of criminals now can we, lovely?" Brooks gazed at me with a lazy, casual delight that I felt all the way down to my toes.

All I could manage was a curt nod, a groan trapped in my throat.

My breath hitched as his hands squeezed my waist, holding onto me tighter as the lighting in the arena grew darker. Surprisingly, in the darkness surrounded by strangers, I was content and comfortable sitting on Brooks's muscular thighs.

"Snake got your tongue?"

Before I could reply, a hand clamped down on my shoulder.

Turning on Brooks's lap, I faced the person who had dared to put their hand on me without permission.

I looked up to only be staring into a pair of angry, all too familiar eyes. "If it isn't Deucey Usy."

Regret coursed through me as I thought about the day the mage overheard me complaining to Rohesia about the pet name my ex-boyfriend had bestowed upon me.

"Hello, Casi. And here I thought my good luck was beginning to run out," I said dryly.

I wasn't sure why he was here. Casimar wasn't an investigator on this case, but had shown keen interest in the disappearances and golems. It was more likely that he was helping The Collectress with the auction. Before I could question the mage further, his other hand clamped down on my other shoulder.

Big mistake.

"I'd remove your hands from her shoulders. Unless you want me to cut them off and throw them into Marren's Eye," Brooks growled, his cobalt eyes flashed, the pupils dilating into thin slits, before returning to normal.

The lighting was throwing uneasy shadows everywhere.

Casi chuckled darkly. "Back off. This is between me and the gorgon. Why don't you go off and die somewhere. You pesky mortals are pretty good at that kind of thing."

Brooks stiffened beneath my legs as I watched his jaw clench in my peripheral vision.

I had a strange feeling that this wasn't the first time these two had exchanged words. That strange feeling was followed up by the undeniable fact that their words were going to turn into blows really fast.

People were beginning to stare and we did not need to draw any more attention to ourselves. The mage next to us slowly began to back off but a flash of light informed me he was pulling out his phone to begin recording.

"Then again, maybe it would be better to cut off your feet. At least if I left your hands, Casimar, you wouldn't be lonely at night. As I'm guessing that's the only company you've had, in well, ever," Brooks taunted through clenched teeth, his voice so dangerously low that I could barely hear him over the pounding of my own heart.

I heard someone choke on a laugh, before quickly disguising it as a cough as Casimar threw daggers in their direction.

"These hands?" Casimar asked, feigning innocence, squeezing my shoulders harder as if to emphasize my point.

It was suddenly growing very warm in the room; Brooks's skin was radiating blistering heat as he stared at Casimar.

Normally, I would have already put Casimar on his ass, laughing as he stared up at the ceiling, but I didn't have the power here. And he knew it. If I caused a scene, we would only garner more attention.

Brooks gently grabbed my thighs, lifting me up and placing me on my feet. Within seconds, he had Casimar's neck digging into the rough edge of the obsidian bench.

"That was the last time you will ever lay your roaming hands on someone who doesn't blatantly ask you to. Especially Usa. Got it?"

The mage just laughed.

A cracking sound followed by a squawk of pain echoed in the space.

Blinking, I stared at Brooks with wide eyes.

Casimar's hand dangled limply from his wrist, now clearly broken. He cried out when Brooks applied more pressure to the shattered bones.

"If you even *think* about touching Usa again, I'll break the other one."

Not used to being put in his place, Casimar screeched empty threats at Brooks. "I'll kill you for this."

"Doubtful," Brooks rumbled.

Cheeks flaming red, Casimar started to stand, only to be pushed into the bench further by Brooks, causing blood to begin dripping from his neck.

The waiting crowd began to take notice of Casimar's squeaky pleas and Brooks's towering form, causing too much attention to be thrown our way.

"As much as I would like to watch Casimar bleed out," I whispered to Brooks gently, placing a hand on his back, "we have a case to work."

Brooks nodded, dropping a gasping Casimar.

Crouching down, Brooks whispered in the mage's ear, causing him to pale with terror. A satisfied smile pulled at the edge of Brooks's mouth.

A bell signified the end of the auction's intermission.

"What did you tell him?" I asked when we are out of earshot

"I described to him, in great detail, how a certain appendage, one located below the belt, is as easy to snap in half as a carrot."

"Probably a baby one in his case," I snorted, as Brooks gave me a satisfied smirk.

We were almost out the doors when Brooks's uncle's words made me stop dead in my tracks. Brooks attempted to yank me from the room, but he soon stopped as his uncle rambled on.

"My dear son-in-law, may his soul rest in peace, didn't know what a treasure he had when he stole Zeus's Fulgurite from a rival dealer. If only the boy had known not to play with the big kids, maybe he wouldn't have gotten himself killed."

The Collectress laughed, all but admitting to the crime.

"Able to give any soul the power of magic, yes, even you pesky mortals," a rowdy laugh filled the auditorium, "create spells, wield elemental magic, and even create monsters straight out of your very own nightmares."

The Collectress's blonde hair gleamed in the light as she walked around the pit, holding the relic above her head. 'Oh's and 'Ah's rang against my ears.

Create monsters straight out of your very own nightmares.

I unlocked my grip from Brooks's arm, racing to the front of the crowd, anger gripping me to my very core. Beresford de Blasis hadn't been late on his payments.

No, the only crime he had committed was having something she wanted but couldn't have.

Elbows jabbed into my side as I reached the railing, looking down into the pit. The Collectress was still oblivious to my presence.

But she wouldn't be for long.

Perhaps I should have thought before jumping down into the pit, but I never did seem to think these things through.

The Collectress's eyes widened in shock as I landed in front of her and took Zeus's Fulgurite off the tray she was carrying.

Mud squished underneath my feet, the ground giving way and causing me to lose my balance. Dark specks of mud flecked the smooth surface of Zeus's Fulgurite as it fell to the ground.

The arena quickly transformed into a sea of quicksand, the ground falling up and down in gigantic waves. I wasn't sure who was behind the magic creating the rolling waves, but that wasn't important.

What was important was leaving the grove with the relic and destroying it.

A large figure landed beside me. As I got ready to shove them into the mud, I recognized the ring on the man's hand.

"What in gods' name was that?" he grunted angrily, his face contorted in a mixture of fury and disbelief.

"Didn't I tell you that we're the halftime entertainment?"

A snarl ripped from Brooks's mouth as he punched a mage in the stomach who had his grubby hands on the fulgurite.

He screeched, dropping the statue.

Chaos ensued.

Dozens of spectators began climbing over the railing, dropping into the arena to get in on the action. Thick mud and debris covered our bodies as we tumbled in the muck, desperate to find a way out and to get hold of Zeus's Fulgurite.

A roaring sound filled my ears as a wall of mud rolled towards me like a raging tsunami, propelled faster by magic. Not surprisingly, The Collectress and Brooks's uncle were nowhere to be seen.

At the last second, I rolled out of the path of the mud wave. My tongue was covered in a layer of gritty, foul-tasting dirt and I gagged as a clump of the mud connected with my face.

With Brooks still fighting the growing crowd, I spotted the fulgurite, held like a precious newborn in the arms of a burly man with fiery hair and a dozen or more facial piercings. I made it my mission to follow him.

The exit was at the south wall, and the fulgurite thief was having a hard time fighting through the crowd. Another wave of mud was beginning to form at the opposite wall. As it grew, I braced myself in the middle of the arena, waiting for the earth to shift below my feet.

"Usa!"

I turned to find Brooks motioning me towards him, his hand gripping a ladder, and in that second, I knew what he wanted.

The wave of mud and rolling earth gave me enough height to grab Brooks's hand, and with the momentum and our combined strength, I was launched into the air, landing smoothly on the ground outside of the arena.

Without wasting a second, I ran to the railing above the exit, watching as the wave took the man with orange hair and piercings by surprise. It caused him to lose his grip on the fulgurite.

The wave was bringing the man towards me.

But I was too far away to grab the idol.

Solid arms wrapped around my waist. I turned to find Brooks behind me. "Trust me?"

I nodded.

Grunting, Brooks lifted me up into his arms, putting me on his shoulders. For a second, I was afraid that my thick thighs would suffocate or squish him, but he didn't seem to be struggling.

With his hips and stomach pressing into the railing, Brooks leaned over the railing, with me on his shoulders. Though his hands gripped my hips firmly, I felt his muscles quivering in time with mine.

I would have only one shot at this.

The man holding Zeus's Fulgurite neared.

The crowd shouted.

My stomach clenched in fear and anticipation as I was held over the railing, the fulgurite within inches of my fingertips. The cool branches of the statue grazed my hands, and I pulled up, one of the man's hands holding onto the base of the fulgurite with impressive strength.

The wave shifted, hitting the wall, and causing the man to loosen his hold on the relic. It was just what I needed to pull the prized fulgurite safely into my awaiting arms.

Before I could celebrate, the force of the undulation threatened to pull me back into the arena. A scream tore its way through my throat.

My balance was off.

I was going to fall in.

But before I could fall headfirst into the pit, Brooks grabbed my arm, pulling me up onto stable ground by my bicep. With only a second to collect ourselves, we shared a grateful look, and I handed the fulgurite to Brooks.

A snarly curse filled the air, which I was fairly certain came from the man I had snatched the fulgurite from, as we ran from the pit and into the maze-like tunnels beneath Marren's Eye.

Vendors were scrambling, packing up their tents and tables. But a few of them had a hungry, greedy look in their eyes. A few sellers began to surround us, drawing weapons of flashing steel and sharpened bone.

I started to pull out my daggers, only to find them missing. They must have been taken during the struggle in the pit. Brooks had only brought a small pocketknife, insisting that we could trust the people here.

"Not a community of violence you said?" I raised my eyebrows at him, hissing.

"Not. Helping," he retorted through clenched teeth.

I held the fulgurite in my hands. The crowd was determined to press our backs into the wall, and we were already too close to them. If they succeeded, we would be trapped.

The obsidian walls contorted our reflections, making it seem as though we had two heads and eight limbs each.

"What ya got there, girly?" a man with a missing eye growled. Though his one remaining eye had grown cloudy with disease, it still flashed with a need for evil. The vendor stood in front of Brooks, who attempted to hold him back, but the detective's pocketknife was nothing compared to the lethal machete in the merchant's hands.

"Glasses. Not that you would get any use out of them." I smiled, snapping my teeth at him.

The man hissed at me, swiping at the air in front of us.

I swallowed loudly, looking at the wall behind us that was growing closer and closer with each step. Taking a chance, I grabbed Brooks's hand, pulling him towards the water tunnel that had taken us from Marren's Eye and spat us out into this cavern.

The tunnel was looking like our only exit. Impulsively, I pushed Brooks into it and held the fulgurite tightly to my chest.

A mob of vendors rushed me as I was propelled into the dark and swirling tunnel of water. There was no magical air bubble this time. And I guessed that was why the vendors had looked so surprised when I pushed Brooks into it and followed after him.

I could only hope that Brooks knew how to swim and could hold his breath longer than most mortals. My lungs burned as the tunnel turned sharply and seemed to travel deep under Marren's Grove.

A split in the tunnel appeared and the raging waters pulled me into the left channel. I reassured myself that Brooks was barreling down the same one.

Though roughly ten seconds had passed, it felt as though I had been tumbling through the bubbling water for minutes. It became harder to hold my breath as more time passed.

The cold water seeped into my very bones, causing tremors to attack my muscles. My grip on the statue lessened as my fingers grew numb.

The torrent soon slowed, and I shot out into a deeper body of water. Rays of light streamed through the inky water, and I almost cried at the sight of the outside world. By some miracle I had managed to keep hold of the fulgurite.

I kicked my feet rapidly, swimming hard and fast towards the glowing light source with one arm pulling me towards the surface. Bubbles frantically escaped from my nose as I fought the waves and ripples on the surface.

Finally breaking free, I gasped for air.

It tasted sweet, despite the sulfur scent in the cave. Panicking, I turned around, finding myself alone in the cavern that held Marren's Eye. As I splashed around to stay afloat, my heart stopped in my chest.

"Brooks!" I shouted into the endless cavern, only to be greeted by never-ending, dark silence.

Perhaps a hundred yards from shore, I started to swim, hoping that the detective was already safe and dry on land. As I paddled, dark thoughts threatened to take over. Thoughts of Brooks's body floating down, down, down to the bottom of the lake.

Something grazed my leg.

I let out a hair-raising shriek.

A clamorous splash broke the turbulent surface of the aqua water to my right, and I held Zeus' Fulgurite above my head, ready to use the statue as a weapon. My grip tightened as the sloshes of water grew larger and louder.

Something grazed my leg a second time, but this time I was ready and kicked out, meeting hard flesh and bone.

"Shit!" I watched in disbelief as Brooks shot out of the depths of the water, clutching his nose as it gushed blood.

"Brooks! Wh- How-You—" I shouted at him, rage painting my face red. My words didn't make sense, but I didn't care. I thought he had drowned, and he was pulling pranks and hooting as though he was a co-medic genius, despite having a bloodied and possibly broken nose.

I started my journey towards shore once again, watching as Brooks swam easily towards the land, practically choking on his own guffawing.

"I know there's a lovely remark somewhere in that pretty head of yours, just dying to break free," Brooks said.

"You're a sick bastard!"

"Ah, there it is."

"Why in gods' name did you do that?"

He shrugged, treading water. "Payback for throwing me into the tunnel of freezing, dark water."

At that moment, I was incredibly tempted to throw the fulgurite at his head. Or maybe I would do it when we got to shore, when he would least expect it.

Brooks's arm grazed my leg again and I laughed darkly. "You really can't leave well enough alone, can you?"

"What do you mean?" Brooks looked perplexed, and I turned around to find him almost ten feet away from me.

"Brooks! Stop moving."

He stilled, recognizing the fervor in my eyes.

Holding the fulgurite close to my chest, I sank below the water, hoping that it had been the same stray kelp leaf or cattail that had skimmed my leg moments ago.

I couldn't see anything in the water, only darkness creeping into the cavern. As I summoned my gorgon, she gazed into the water, her heightened eyesight cutting through the waves of murky water.

My eyes caught movement and I froze.

Slowly, I put my head above the water.

I motioned for Brooks to slowly swim towards me. With every ripple and splash of the water, my heart turned to ice.

"Afraid of the water?" he asked, though I knew he was only cracking a joke to calm himself.

"No," I swallowed, "I'm afraid of what's in it."

My face paled as I climbed on Brooks's back, hoping that one splashing body wouldn't be enough to entice the lurking beast back to the surface.

Silence fell throughout the cavern.

Splash.

Splash.

Splash.

We were fifty yards from shore when Brooks finally spoke, even though I had told him not to. "Usa. What exactly is below the water?"

"You sure you want to know?"

He nodded.

A bigger splash filled the cavern, and I grew deathly still as Brooks peaked over his shoulder. His eyes widened.

"That." I pointed behind us with a shaking finger.

Behind us was a giant, reeking charybdis.

Deadly tentacles protruded from the length of the beast's cylindrical body. Its mouth was surrounded with dozens of glowing crimson eyes. The mouth itself was a large, gaping circle, filled with razor sharp teeth that were covered with bits of dulse and sludge. I wasn't sure there was a floss pick big enough to clean the monster's repugnant ivories. Thick, blue-green skin covered the beast, making it perfectly camouflaged in Marren's Eye.

I had only heard rumors of these monsters, told to us by a priestess in Kilmarn. We had learned about every monster the gods and goddesses had created, including the beastly charybdis.

Half of its mouth sat above the water, as if it was taste testing the water we had just swum through.

The varmint's mouth acted as a huge straw, and the powerful suction would draw us closer until it swallowed us whole. It would be similar to jumping into Marren's Eye, except we would turn into this animal's midnight snack.

My snakes hissed at the beast, and I quickly switched to my mortal form. "Easy now, Brooks. Gentle and quick steps."

Right foot. Left foot.

With every step, the charybdis grew closer. Sweat beaded at both of our temples and Brooks began to shake the closer we got to shore. We were almost in the clear. Maybe twenty yards away.

The charybdis was another thirty yards behind us.

Though we were nearly at the bank, the water was still deep enough for the monster to closely follow us. Every miniscule twitch that Brooks's exhausted muscles made was monitored by the charybdis.

"That's it, Brooks. You got this."

I kept my voice low, terrified that it would set off the beast that was prowling behind us.

A loud laugh suddenly echoed in the cavern, coming from a group of humans that sat near a cluster of pillars on the opposite side of the lake.

The monster lifted its head, causing waves to push into our backs. Its large red eyes locked into mine. They narrowed.

"Run!" I cried.

Brooks did as I said.

The human's laughter died down as quickly as it had started. A rough growling filled the air as we stumbled onto the beach. I watched in horror as the monster barreled towards us, not seeming too concerned about the shallow water depths.

The creature smashed into the soil behind us, causing rocks and boulders to crash down onto the sandy beach. The mountain shook, as if the creature had woken the land from a deep slumber. It released a panicked, nightmarish screech as we ran away.

I could hear its yellow teeth snapping behind us as we sprinted down the length of the beach, but I didn't dare turn around. The creature was able to travel on land, though not as fast as in water, and it writhed towards us like an earthworm.

Brooks grabbed my hand, pulling me faster and faster.

Rocks and debris bit into my feet, but I didn't care.

The creature bellowed into the air once more, a lonesome cry, like it was angry at us for leaving. I dared a glance over my shoulder, slowing. The charybdis was slithering back into the water, its face slowly turning away from us.

Breathless, I turned and tossed Brooks the relic.

My skin grew warm and began to pulsate, as though I was being watched.

A secondary splashing sound filled the air, and I turned towards the lake once more, to find myself face to teeth with the charybdis. Its mouth was double my height and it smelled of rotten fish and death.

"Brooks," I whispered, "walk slowly towards the entrance."

He seemed to hesitate, at war with his differing thoughts. I didn't stop to see which thought won the battle, instead focusing on the charybdis in front of me.

The creature didn't move as I reached out to touch it. Its skin was glossy and smooth but it was also pockmarked and indented. I continued to pet the creature, admiring its skin.

Maybe the charybdis was friendly and misunderstood?

During my first few months in Iydara, I lived in an abandoned house with a grumpy old cat. I had called her Mildred and she had lived with me until a few months ago when she became sick.

She had been a beast to tame, and it had taken me weeks to convince her to let me pet her and take her under my wing. That cat was part of the reason why I didn't end it all.

My hand continued to tremble as my hand skimmed its slimy hide.

A low snarl filled the air.

With only a second to spare, my gorgon took over, anticipating the attack before I could. Without her protection, I would be sliding down the esophagus and into the stomach of a very hungry charybdis.

"Not friendly! I repeat, not friendly!" I exclaimed to myself, shuffling backwards on my hands. My snakes hissed and spat, reaching out to bite the charybdis but falling short.

Brooks started banging on the wall, attempting to draw its attention from me. But his attempts failed. He began cursing to himself.

I gulped loudly.

The creature grew closer, its many eyes glowing. I closed my eyes, not wanting to see the beast's gaping jaw as it swallowed me whole.

I waited.

And waited.

Only its edged teeth didn't pierce my flesh.

Inhaling deeply, I mustered up the courage to open my eyes. Once I did, I wished I had kept them closed for all of eternity.

I saw the back of a terrifying beast that had emerged from the water. It stood shorter than the charybdis, perching on reptilian feet that were decorated with scattered umber scales and pointed, inky talons. The glittering scales traveled up robust legs that sprung from its muscular humanoid torso. Beads of water dripped from burnished, flexible wings that shined brightly in the cavern's dim light. They reminded me of aged and oiled leather.

I took that as my cue to leave.

Wet sand squashed between my toes as I ran towards the exit. Dirt and pointed spikes of dirt continued to rain down on me as the beasts battled on the black sand.

Just as I reached my freedom, a bark of pain caught my attention. The creature with scales was pinned beneath the charybdis, losing the battle as its opponents' tentacles began to snake around its body. The creature's wings shut beneath the excess weight. It was going to die an excruciating death, smothered by wet sand or constricted by formidable tentacles.

The same one I would have faced had it not intervened.

Swearing to myself, I made my dumbest decision that day. And that was saying a lot. Sprinting to the fight, I wedged myself between the two monsters.

The charybdis's rank breath caused my hair to flutter around my shoulders as I met a dozen red, glowing eyes.

I only needed one.

With my hands in front of me, I met the eye of the charybdis, compelling the beast to turn into stone. The creature looked confused at first, as though sensing its end was near.

Pulling myself up, I watched as every eye on the charybdis' head turned to stone. It froze in time. And so I ran.

Because of the size of the charybdis, the curse broke as I raced through the door to safety.

I couldn't stone a living, breathing animal as big as a charybdis without incurring huge physical and magical repercussions. And it was almost impossible to stone the creature when it had multiple eyes. The frustrated wail of the monster shook the stalagmites once more in the tunnel I was in, running for my life.

Footsteps echoed around me, and it was hard to decipher where they were coming from. They seemed to be coming from above and below me. My gorgon sensed the presence of another person as I started to jog down the tunnel. I expected to sense or taste The Collectress's essence.

Only, this person's essence tasted of warm cinnamon and bitter orange.

Brooks crashed into me, his eyes frantically searching my face. "Where in the gods' names did you go?"

"Just saving my own skin," I snapped.

He'd left me to save the fulgurite, I remembered bitterly. I guess that promotion was really something. My partner's eyes flashed with undiluted rage as he threw my clothes and shoes in my face. Apparently he hadn't been too busy to grab our extra clothes and shoes from the cliff above Marren's Eye when I had been sparring with the charybdis. We quickly discarded the wet clothing, the material hitting the ground in a squelch.

I shivered as warm clothing hugged my skin. Brooks handed me the fulgurite as he tugged on his boots.

Zeus's Fulgurite was surprisingly light and sturdy for a piece of glass. My reflection became distorted as I studied it. My hands were clammy from where the glass met my skin.

We had made it out.

Turning the statue over in my hands, I studied its strange branches and details. The Collectress had it in her possession around the time Beresford was transformed into a golem. We knew that she had stoned Beresford de Blasis without reason, because of the receipts from Nola.

I wouldn't have thought that The Collectress was behind the making of the golems, but when she told the crowd the fulgurite could create monsters from their own nightmares... It seemed like too much of a co-incidence.

Brooks and I hadn't talked about what we had done to come into possession of the relic. Brashly stealing the fulgurite and brawling in the cavern where The Collectress held her auctions was grounds to have us thrown in jail.

I was sure they were looking for us and we would be punished for damaging The Collectress's reputation and publicly humiliating her. But we had Zeus's Fulgurite. We just needed to hide it before they found us.

Turning my head, I braced as another presence filled the cavern. Peppermint and cocoa filled my nostrils.

Rohesia skidded to a halt in front of us, sweat and mud covered her trousers. Her eyes widened as she eyed the fulgurite warily. "I thought you had died! It's been over an hour since you were supposed to meet me back at the cave entrance."

"Let me exp—"

Brooks looked on warily as Rohesia grabbed the fulgurite from my hands. We had informed her about the relic, and she had warned us against finding it, talking about vengeful gods and avaricious humans.

Rohesia held her hand up, pausing me mid-sentence, answering a call on her cell phone. And there was only one person's call that she would answer regardless of the time or place.

"I'll bring her back," she murmured into the phone after a few minutes of The Collectress screaming at her.

My heart sank.

I thought about running from Rohesia as well, but I couldn't bring myself to. She didn't deserve to be punished for my foolish behavior. Neither did Brooks.

"To the mansion?" I asked solemnly.

"To the mansion," she replied, sighing heavily, and wrapping her arms around me.

The mansion was just as dull and dreary as it had been a few weeks ago when I had left. Only this time, I was walking in as the enemy instead of an ally.

E.E., The Collectress, and Casimar were waiting for us as we entered the foyer. I expected there to be workers lingering about, but when I saw the look on The Collectress's face, I knew she didn't want any witnesses.

Casimar gave me a cruel and wicked grin, fixing the tie that was wrapped around his neck. He looked dressed for a funeral.

"Ussie."

"How's the wrist?" I sneered, watching in satisfaction as spots of pink stained his cheeks.

We silently fell in step behind the three. Brooks gave me a worried glance, not knowing what was to come. Perhaps E.E.'s presence would prevent Brooks from being hurt.

Heavy silence filled the room as Brooks and I sat in front of The Collectress's desk. The chair squeaked underneath me, filling the void with signs of my nervous energy.

E.E., Rohesia, and The Collectress stood behind her desk, staring at us with varying expressions. E.E. looked one strong wind away from fainting.

Rohesia looked disappointed in me, which felt like being hit with a giant, concrete battering ram. I knew I had let her down.

And The Collectress, she looked pissed.

Casimar stood by the fire, watching it with cruel interest.

Normally I would be staring at my feet, not daring to raise my eyes in fear of punishment from the woman sitting in front of me. But a red-hot zeal was raging in me, from the realization that The Collectress was the one behind the creation of the golems.

So instead of lowering my gaze, I stared ahead, focusing on a photograph of Iydara's skyline at night that was on the wall behind the desk. The buildings glittered and twinkled in the light, reminding me of the mask we saw in Marren's Grove. Though there were towering buildings, they didn't overwhelm the sky, leaving room for the gods' work to shine through.

I expected yelling.

I expected cursing.

What I didn't expect was for Brooks' uncle to come sauntering into the room, Zeus's Fulgurite tucked beneath his arm. I glared at the man, wishing he would drop dead.

It was enough to make Brooks sit straighter in his seat.

"Why do you have Beresford de Blasis's property?" I asked no one in particular, looking at the relic with profound hatred. Before leaving The Hub, Brooks had traced the relic back to Beresford's personal antique collection. Beresford had filed a stolen property report with E.E. days before his death.

"I could have asked you the same thing. Especially with the little show you put on back in Marren's Grove," The Collectress answered, holding the fulgurite in her hands.

"I'm not the one that murdered an innocent man and is creating an army of golems," I barked, my hands clenching the arms of my chair. Brooks's seat creaked as he leaned forward, seeming concerned that I would jump out of mine and attack my boss.

Brooks's uncle laughed sharply. He walked around the desk, standing directly in front of me. I didn't back down when he held my gaze.

"My son-in-law was far from innocent. And as I remember, Drusilla wasn't the one to murder him, now, was she?"

Shame burned my face. He wasn't wrong. I had killed Beresford de Blasis. While The Collectress might have ordered the hit, I was the one to execute it. I had sealed his fate the day I decided to turn him into a living statue.

I was the one that caused Beresford de Blasis to stop breathing. I made his wife a widow and took a father away from his daughter. I stoned Brooks's cousin-in-law without mercy.

And that made me no better than the criminals sitting in front of me.

"Answer her question," Brooks said, his voice low as he directed his question towards the pair.

The Collectress tilted her head at Brooks, seeming unable to believe that he had challenged her like that. Instead of throwing him out like I expected, she simply shook her head and gave him a seductive smile. She made sure to lean forward, pushing her arms under her breasts to accentuate her cleavage.

"Now, now, Brooks. No need for that. I was simply reminding Usa of the truth," my boss purred.

"Answer her," he repeated, leaning forward in his chair.

"Watch yourself," his uncle growled.

Brooks's gaze locked with his uncle's. "No."

With a wave of her hand, The Collectress prevented the fight that was about to occur. "Beresford de Blasis stole my property. I was only claiming what was rightfully mine. Killing him was a necessity."

"What would you need Zeus's Fulgurite for, Collectress?" I asked, my eyebrows raised.

"What do you think I would need it for, dear Usa?"

I scoffed, "For making your army of golems, of course."

A high-pitched laugh escaped her mouth as she grinned wickedly. And Brooks's uncle chuckled darkly.

"One of the key selling points of the fulgurite is that it is capable of making creatures from the owner's nightmares. I imagine golems are from one of yours," I said.

The Collectress seemed to consider my words for a long moment, pouring herself a glass of red wine and lazily swirling it in her hand as she looked between me and Brooks.

I should've poisoned her bottles of wine when I had the chance. It would have prevented this entire situation.

"You have no evidence of such a crime. Even if I was the one to commit it, why would I? I have everything I want or need. I have my own city with workers that bow to only me."

My response lodged in my throat as she stopped in front of me, drawing a lazy finger under my chin and resting it on my lips. She taunted me, piercing the fleshy skin of my lip with a pointed fingernail until I tasted blood.

"But you, Usa. You have everything to lose, and everything to gain."

Another swallow of wine. Another insult.

"Who's to say that you aren't the one behind the golems? After all, what wouldn't a banished gorgon do to rise to power? And think of the protection this golem army could offer you from your dear, dear mother."

Terror latched its sharp and horrid claws deep into my heart. She couldn't possibly think I was the one behind the golems. Turning them would only draw attention to myself, allowing my mother to find me.

She knew I wasn't behind their creation.

I started to speak but was cut off by her lazy tone.

"Yes. I do think it would be best if you and I have another meeting. Perhaps we should finish the spelling lesson we have been working on."

"No, I—"

She placed a finger on my lips, stopping me. "Shh, dear. I forgive you for your confusion. But this will be your one and only warning to never pull something like this again. If you do, I'll feed you to my charybdis."

Without warning, Brooks exploded out of his chair, grabbing The Collectress by her hair and pressing her face into the desk.

"It was you?" Brooks's eyes grew dark, and his voice was sharpened steel.

She let out a chuckle.

"What was me?" The Collectress looked up at Brooks from underneath her thick eyelashes, widening her eyes as though he could possibly believe her words.

I realized with great horror that The Collectress had used dunamis, the dark magic tied to the blood of the gods, to summon and attack us with the charybdis in Marren's Grove.

"While I do favor a good tug of the hair, I'd release your grasp, Brooks. How I love that fiery personality of yours."

A power struggle appeared to be happening between the two while I sat there puzzled, afraid, and weary.

Brooks held her there for a moment, before releasing her and letting out a breath of frustration. The Collectress looked at us with a winning expression, her canines showing as she smiled.

At that moment, I knew I would never be free of her.

Not with her level of power and influence.

Brooks's uncle chuckled in the background as Rohesia and his nephew were led out by wardens. Rohesia shot glaring daggers at The Collectress but didn't fight.

"Rook, I'll be okay," I breathed.

Brooks's eyes met mine, unwavering.

He was reluctant to leave, his jaw clenching as two wardens were forced to haul him out of the room. The detective fought them every step of the way.

I silently wished that Brooks wouldn't make a scene. But it was too late, she had noticed his concern for me.

The Collectress suddenly called out, her eyes glittering with deceit and pure evil. "Wait. Bring Brooks back. I want him to witness this."

Her full lips pulled up into a vicious smile. She motioned for him to stand next to the desk as I bared my back to The Collectress and Brooks's uncle.

"You know where to go."

From my peripheral vision, I watched in horror as The Collectress placed the brand in Brooks's hands. His hands shook as understanding crossed his face.

"No," Brooks told her, his voice rough.

Even though she was shorter than the detective, she grabbed his chin, using magic to force his gaze to meet hers.

"You will," she stated simply, examining her manicure as if we were conversing about the weather or fashion. There would be no arguing with her.

He placed the branding iron on the table.

"Let me rephrase that," The Collectress sighed, "you will. Or else it will be your sweet little niece in this chair next time. What's her name again?"

"Lilith," Brooks's uncle chuckled. Bile swept over my tongue as he hinted at branding his own granddaughter.

The Collectress snapped her fingers. "Ah, yes. Lilith."

I met Brooks's eyes once more, their depths filled with regret and wrath. He needed to do this.

And I knew with undying certainty that The Collectress was not bluffing. She would do anything to remind Iydarians of her power, even hurting an innocent child.

"It's okay. I trust you," I told Brooks, my voice cracking.

A silent understanding passed between us.

Brooks studied my face, as if searching for a lie. When he didn't find one, he nodded, taking a step towards me and ran a hand over my hair. The motion calmed me. Steadied me.

Brooks's face was a blank mask as he placed the first iron brand into the fire. Orange flames hungrily licked the iron, as if the metal was ravenous for burning flesh.

"This might kill you, Usa," The Collectress said, seeming saddened by the possibility.

"Get on with it then," I barked back.

14

"Shh, it's alright," The Collectress said, "you're doing beautifully. I am so proud of you."

The room was spinning and tilting. And we were only on the third letter. The stench of my own burning skin had become familiar to me. It no longer smelled any different than the skin on a roasted pig.

Brooks, his uncle, and The Collectress took turns branding me, the second taking his time and pressing the iron harshly into my skin. I was grateful when Brooks told him to stop, threatening to brand him too. His uncle chuckled but took his nephew's threat seriously.

Though I was in my mortal form, the faster healing abilities of my gorgon still shone through. At that moment, I was going to die or come as close to death as possible for a gorgon. My skin healed faster than mortals, but I still felt pain the same as they did.

Every nerve ending in my back was on fire as the fourth letter was placed on my back. I knew the pain would only grow worse with every letter. I begged for the darkness to take me.

I was ablaze.

I was burnt.

I was a pile of cinders in the wind.

My chest constricted as my sweat-drenched body threatened to collapse into a shivering heap on the floor. Leather straps were placed around my wrists and ankles, along with a heavy metal chain that bound my legs to the chair. I clenched my jaw, attempting to keep my teeth from chattering as the smoke grew thick and the all-consuming fire raged in the fireplace. Tendrils of smoke seeped from my back, caressing my face. The Collectress placed the fifth letter on my back.

My screams were met with deafening silence as broken rays of sunlight peeked through the curtains.

My dreams were filled with flickers of golems commanding fire-breathing monsters, chasing me through Marren's Grove. I screamed for Rohesia, begging her to wake up and save me. Brooks's lifeless body swayed in the wind, hanging from a frayed noose on a blackened mulloway tree.

His eyes were glazed over, staring into the distant forest. Purple and yellow bruises marred the delicate skin on his face, as clotted blood streamed from his nostrils. His neck was turned at an unnatural angle.

Marching under his body were dozens of golems, fresh blood gleaming on their rotted teeth. Crimson liquid streamed from the steel weapons and sharpened swords that were fastened to their backs. I had to help him.

I needed to save him.

This was my fault.

I could not reach Brooks in time.

A thin hand yanked me forward and smothered me into the ground, forcing my lungs to inhale chunks of frozen snow. I fought, attempting to squirm free from their fortifying grasp. But I could not. They were too strong.

Out of my peripheral vision, I watched as Brooks's body was thrown to the ground and set on fire.

My assailant grinned at me with pristine white teeth and perfect cheekbones. The ends of her blonde hair were painted red with the lifeblood of Brooks de Blasis.

The Collectress and her army of blood-spattered golems pursued me relentlessly, halting only when I was violently propelled into the rampant fire alongside Brooks's burning body.

Her cackling laugh seeped into my mind like a ravenous parasite, crawling into every corner and hidden crevice. Her wild giggles took over my mind, until it was all that I could hear.

Blood.

I could taste blood in my mouth, as foreign and wrong as every other agonizing sensation in my body. The sodden fabric in my mouth forced my breath to come out in rapid, short bursts, my tongue fighting whatever rag had been shoved into my mouth.

I flinched as I felt someone near me, causing my heart to beat erratically in my chest. Soft hands caught either side of my face. As I attempted to wrench free of their iron grip, the hands tightened.

The grip held for a passing second, and then two. Firm but not unkind, the hands moved up, letting the stained fabric droop around my neck. Sputtering, I gulped down breaths of hot, burning air, while fighting the urge to cough.

I opened my eyes. Wincing, I touched the tender skin below my eyes, which was swollen and bruised.

My remaining senses slowly returned to me, each one more confusing than the last. The smell of smoldering ash coming from somewhere in the room, then a strange metallic taste glazing my mouth. There was no saliva in my mouth. Oh gods, I needed something to drink to wash away the bitter taste of rotten fruit.

Had they drugged me?

My back ached—it ached worse than anything. Worse than when I broke my wrist. Worse than being stabbed. Each breath was like razor blades being drawn across my back. I couldn't breathe.

"No! Don't—don't touch me!" I screamed, the air in my lungs on fire. I flinched away from my captor's touch as they placed a cool cloth on my forehead, my emerald eyes wild in the reflection of their dark blue ones.

I hurt. I was on fire.

My breaths came in short, shallow pants, my body trembling in uncontrollable fear as the man stepped towards me. On instinct, my gorgon was released. The black and white snakes on my head began spitting and hissing at his advances.

"I'm not going to hurt you, Usa," the man reassured me lightly, grasping my hand and holding it firmly. His eyes met mine. "Listen to me. You're safe now."

I wanted to yank my hand away in panic but didn't. He didn't flinch. He didn't look away from my hissing and spitting snakes.

Tears formed in my eyes, and I let out a shaky breath. "I…"

"It's okay."

Memories came flooding back.

My snakes stopped hissing, exhausted from the pain that was radiating through my mind and body. They soon grew limp.

"We're going to the apartment, Usa. Just hold on," Rohesia said, running her hand over my sweaty hair.

We were moving. Brooks gently lifted me, and stars invaded my vision. I screamed as he walked me out of The Collectress's mansion.

With every step he took, my breathing grew heavier, and my vision blurred. I heard the vague sound of laughing. A louder male leading the chorus of giggling, and hurling insults at me.

I was too tired to see who it was.

Blackness greeted me.

15

Muffled voices whispered around my ears. The voices were familiar, but I couldn't place them. One was deeper, and the other melodious tone scratched at the forefront of my brain, sounding so familiar.

Soft cotton grazed my cheeks as I lay on my stomach, chilly air caressing my burning back. The muscles in my back quivered, and I was afraid they would never still.

"—to tell her."

Anger and dismay seemed to coat the voice of the woman who replied, "No. She's off the case."

The statement was final. Hard. Definite.

"Usa deserves to know that it wa—"

"You don't know her, Brooks. I do. I know what's best."

Something slammed into the wall in the hallway.

Ceramic shattered. I heard the scuffle of feet.

"She needs this case." His voice was taunt, heavy with emotion and unspoken words.

Instead of responding, the bedroom door opened. I quickly closed my eyes. I wasn't ready to face anyone, not after what The Collectress had done to me.

A cooling ointment was placed on the stinging brands on my back. It helped, but was causing me to become sleepy again. Memories were tugging at my mind, and I tried to fight them off.

A soft humming filled the room.

Today was the night of my sixteenth birthday. I watched as my mother placed a string of black and silver shining pearls around my neck. The choker accented the snakes that curled around my face and neck.

Tonight, I would become a blessed Daughter of Athena. For the first and only time in a gorgon's life, all other sixteen-year-olds and I would be blessed by the goddess herself, in the flesh, as she traveled from the heavens to sanctify our coven.

I had never seen a goddess or god in the flesh before, only in the grand paintings and murals that lined the castle walls, in the middle of the snowy Anghor Mountains.

Athena was the most beautiful of all. And she was the gentlest. I hadn't been able to sleep the previous night. I was too excited about meeting my goddess. I prayed that she approved of me.

Excitement and nervousness squirmed in my belly as I rubbed the shimmering white material of the gown I was wearing between my fingers.

The satin material mimicked the ripples of a powerful, flowing stream as it hugged my skin. A sleeve of snowy, armor-like scales accentuated my right arm. My other arm remained bare. The scales ventured up my neck, but didn't cover the necklace my mother had given me.

The scales cupped my right breast and spread to my left hip, sparkling and glittering like tall evergreens with fresh snow. They resembled the scales that were on my own face and body.

A separate satin material clung to the left side of my breast plate and formed an A-line skirt as it ventured down my body. The heavy skirt swished with each step. I stepped into a pair of matching white heels and was paired with a black velvet coin purse.

"Stunning, Medusa. Goddess Athena will surely be pleased."

I smiled in the reflection of the long mirror, my nervous gaze meeting my mother's satisfied one. She looked at me with pride and love. My older sisters, Stheno and Euryale, stood behind our mother, their eyes shining with tears.

I giggled lightly as we exchanged a rare but comforting group hug. Stheno and Euryale had already conducted their blessings years before me.

I knew what to expect. And I was ready.

I had been born for this moment.

"Let's not keep the goddess and coven waiting any longer, shall we?"

My sisters and I nodded in unison.

I fell behind my mother, Stheno, and Euryale.

We exited the lavish castle, walking on cobblestone, snowy pathways, surrounded by towering trees. Our breath danced in front of us in white puffs, mixing with the smoke of sweet burning incense.

A clearing in the middle of the forest held ruins of marble and agate. Broken statues littered the ground around the temples, symbols of false gods and goddesses.

My chin was held high as we entered the temple made of white marble and scintillating gold accents. The short heels I wore clicked against the golden stairs as we walked through the doors. Gasps echoed throughout the temple as we entered. Every gorgon bowed deeply before their queen and princesses.

There were no male gorgons in the temples, for no such creature had ever existed. Women of all different shapes and sizes stared at us as we walked down an aisle of scattered white rose petals.

My mother ordered the entire coven to remain standing, as myself and the other daughters took our seats in front of the decorated stage.

I took a seat next to Aspasia, another gorgon who would be receiving her blessing today. She looked at me with raw happiness glowing in her eyes. Her skin was slightly paler than mine, and golden snakes trailed down her back, accenting her athletic frame. The snakes seemed to be made of liquid gold and were some of the longest I had ever seen.

I squeezed Aspasia's hand as a priestess with a white hood stood in front of the growing crowd. One day, I hoped to be a priestess, to forever serve the goddess Athena.

My twin sisters would take over as leaders of the coven once the gods called my mother home. But that wouldn't be for hundreds of years. It was my duty to serve Athena, and I was prepared to do so for the rest of my existence.

"Welcome, blessed and soon to be blessed. Gathered underneath the radiant stars of the goddess Athena, we come together tonight to honor the future Daughters of Athena. Hundreds of years ago, our grandmother Leciee, a high priestess of Athena, was blessed with the honor of becoming the first gorgon. Our snakes protect and empower us from those that wish us harm. They are our biggest miracle. Though some may look upon us and cringe with fear or disgust out of blatant ignorance, we know that our snakes hold our power."

I wouldn't have wanted to be anything other than a gorgon. My snakes were part of who I was. They protected me. They loved me. And they inspired me.

"But I say, let them stare. Let them misunderstand what they cannot comprehend."

Cheers rang out through the temple, and I smiled until my cheeks hurt as the priestess threw back her hood and looked into the crowd. She was the only daughter of Eliana, the first priestess of our coven, who had recently been called home by the gods.

"With our mortal beauty, and our immortal lives, we will forever be blessed and worship our goddess for all of eternity. That is our true duty in this world. To stay here and serve our wonderful Goddess Athena."

I sometimes grew sad that I would never be able to leave our coven. But I could only imagine the looks I would get if I ventured out into the mortal world with hissing snakes attached to my head. Mother said that even if mortals didn't hurt or kill me, that they would still judge me. Because I was different.

"Come to the stage those of sixteen years, it is your time to receive your blessing and become a Daughter of Athena."

Butterflies erupted in my stomach as I stood with a dozen other girls. We walked to the stage in a single file line, with Aspasia and me taking up the back of the line.

We stood in front of the coven as they shouted their goodbyes. Tears pricked my eyes at the love that pulsated throughout the temple. My mother's eyes met mine and I saw unfiltered pride and adoration.

The priestess gave us each a stick of incense, lighting it as we were ushered down a set of stairs, and into a tepid, dark room that sat beneath the temple. A fire pit sat in the middle of the room, casting eerie shadows upon walls of decorated marble and gold.

Placing our burning incense into the fire pit, we each grabbed a candle from the priestess, lighting it and beginning to chant the Hymn of Athena.

Each girl had learned the hymn from the age of ten, and tonight would be the first time we would sing it together. I was nervous about singing in front of others, but I quickly reprimanded myself. Goddess Athena surely wouldn't care how tone deaf I was.

Gooseflesh tickled my skin as we stepped around the burning pit and began to sing to our goddess, calling her down from the heavens.

"Praise Goddess Athena, the
fierce protectress of the world
Clever one, with a generous heart,
modest maiden, protectress of our coven!
Who guides us through hardships, who
takes in the lost and the fray.
It is she who guards our people.
Wherever we go, she is with us.
Praise our goddess, who gifts us pure souls
and blessed favor!"

The raging fire of the pit grew and grew, wildly dancing above our heads in flashes of blue and white. Gasps left our lips as the fire began to take the form of a woman.

No. Not a woman.

A goddess.

16

A warm, golden hue bathed the room I was asleep in.

A soft snoring echoed throughout the space as I lifted my head from a fluffy down pillow. My heart raced with a sudden fear that I was back at the mansion. It took me a second to gather my surroundings and realize where I was.

I turned my head to find Brooks laying on the floor next to my bed, his chest slowly rising and falling. It had to be close to midnight. And I couldn't imagine sleeping on the floor was comfortable.

"Psst," I whispered, his snoring softening.

Brooks's eyes opened, glazed with sleep as he quickly sat up. "You're alive."

Nodding, I gave him a weak grin, my dehydrated lips cracking at the motion.

Brooks got up, raising a glass of water to my lips, as the pain in my back was preventing me from lifting my arms. I gave him a grateful smile and watched him return to his pile of blankets.

"There's a sleeping potion if you need it. It will help your wounds heal faster too. Do you want it?"

I stared at the shot glass filled with a thick, syrupy potion.

The taste of crushed grapes and mint coated my tongue.

"Where's Rohesia?"

"At the mansion, taking care of publicity. Seems a lot of news outlets got wind of The Collectress's methods of punishment. They have questions."

I nodded, afraid of the trouble I had caused. But I was also filled with joy that her methods of torture had made headlines. Perhaps it would prevent future brandings.

A part of me believed that The Collectress was behind the creation of the golems, but the other part was terrified to accept that, out of disbelief and a gut feeling, we were missing something.

"When you're all rested up, I need to talk to you about the case." Brooks didn't look at me, and that's how I knew it was bad.

This time, tears pricked my eyes, and I swallowed loudly. I had more than likely cost Brooks his promotion and the case was done. But I would face the consequences of my actions in due time.

"Okay." I laid my head down, watching Brooks uncomfortably shuffle around his blankets.

I felt bad that I had taken over his room. Once I was healed, I would gladly give it back to him and camp out with Rohesia or in the living room, at the very least.

"I'm sorry, I didn't mean to fall asleep here," Brooks apologized, beginning to gather his blankets in his arms.

A laugh filled with disbelief brushed past my lips.

Brooks raised an eyebrow at me.

Wincing, I stopped laughing as the burns on my back tightened and painfully pulled. "You're taking care of me and you're sorry?"

Brooks opened his mouth, but I raised a hand to stop him.

"Brooks," I started gently, "I will never be able to repay you for taking care of me. I'm grateful and honestly, a little embarrassed. Falling asleep in my room, which may I remind you is actually yours, is more than okay. I trust you."

Brooks swallowed. "I trust you too, lovely."

"Now, go in the other room and sleep on something other than the uncomfortable wood floors. That's an order, detective."

Brooks snorted. "Cute that you think you can boss me around like that."

"Cute that you think that was my bossy side."

"In that case," he threw me a wink, "I can't wait to meet her."

Rolling my eyes, I give him a snort of my own.

Brooks tilted his head at me, eyes dark. "And besides, I'd rather keep a close eye on you." He paused for a second, searching my eyes, picking his words carefully. "Have you had nightmares before?"

I froze, my hand stopping on a thread I had been playing with. I quickly released the frayed string. "No."

"Are you sure?"

"Yes," I lied, my breathing becoming shallow.

My nightmares haven't bothered me for the past six months. Of course, as luck would have it, they would return when I was staying with Brooks.

The detective bobbed his chin, mixing up an ointment to put on the wounds on my back. The medicine smelled like lavender and tea tree oil. He gave me a few pain pills and I hurriedly gulped them down.

I hissed in discomfort and relief as cold ointment was gently placed on my back with fresh bandages. The clean dressings and medication stopped the itching that had woken me from my slumber.

"Thank you."

"No need to thank me. I'm the one who got us into this mess. I'm the one who hurt you."

In that moment, I knew that the hurt and disdain in Brooks's eyes wasn't directed at me. Every negative feeling was exclusively directed at his own broken soul.

"I was the one who jumped into the arena, Brooks. Not you. And last time I checked, we both would rather be branded than have a child be tortured by that mad woman."

His hands froze on my back. "Maybe. But I could have stopped you, fought harder. If I hadn't been so damned distracted by that fuckhead."

Blinking, I begin to remember Casimar's broken wrist and Brooks's threats toward the mage.

156

My own mother hadn't cared that my body had been violated. She had blamed me. Told people that it had been consensual and sometimes, she denied it entirely.

All to save face and her reputation.

Brooks swallowed loudly before placing a different ointment on my back, this one smelled of lemon and sea salt. It felt different than the others, and eased the pain more than the others.

"He'll never touch you against your will again, no one will. I know what it's like to not have a choice in the matter."

Slowly, I met Brooks's broken eyes and his jaw clenched at my grief-stricken face. I choked back a sob, and for a second my mask fell, revealing the aching hurt in my heart.

And in that second, I mourned.

For him.

For me.

For the people we could have been had greedy assailants not taken our innocence and stomped out the fire of our souls.

But here's the thing about fires.

Embers linger beneath their singed surface, waiting for a spark to set them ablaze, to set them free.

All it takes is a slight breeze.

And maybe this was our breeze.

Even if it felt like a hurricane.

I looked up, my eyes drowning in tears, and let out a rough sob. It sent a shiver down my own spine. I looked behind me, my wounds protesting, but I didn't care.

"It wasn't your fault, Brooks."

After a second spent staring into my eyes for a lie, he removed himself from my presence and made a speedy exit from the room, leaving in his wake a sense of misplaced guilt that etched itself through my core.

17

We fell to our knees, skin and fabric scraping against stone as Athena appeared before us, a kind smile forming on her full lips. Our foreheads touched the ground as we bowed to the goddess before us. Flashes of white light surrounded her as two other forms appeared on either side of the goddess.

Ares and Poseidon stood proudly at her side.

Giggles and gasps echoed throughout the chamber as Athena raised her arms and motioned for us to stand. My feet refused to stay still; I danced on my tiptoes to get a better look at the trio.

Athena stood before us in a thin white dress, the material clinging to her figure, a stark contrast against her tanned skin. Glossy, golden locks fell around her heart-shaped face in lush waves. She was even more stunning than I had dreamed of. The paintings around the castle did her an injustice.

Ares was clad in battle armor, looking ready to protect us with his last dying breath. His biceps bulged as he walked around the room, assessing. Dark curls fell on his forehead, bouncing with every step. I couldn't help but notice how the color of his hair matched his eyes.

Poseidon stayed standing next to Athena; his naked chest gleamed with drops of lingering water as if he had just swum in from the ocean. He wore a golden sarong that emphasized the powerful muscles of his torso. White hair fell in his face, almost as long and wavy as Athena's. The god of the sea peered at us from beneath his thick waves of hair, with stunning light cyan eyes.

Blessed we were indeed.

Tonight, we would be blessed by the goddess Athena and we were in the presence of two gods.

I was awestruck.

Ares and Poseidon visited with the priestess, while Athena called each of us back into a separate room, one by one. I fidgeted with the string of pearls on my neck, and I soon found myself alone in the room.

Poseidon came trudging down the stairs, returning from his visit with the priestess. Ares must have remained with her, as Poseidon entered alone.

I kept my gaze lowered as the god of the sea walked around the room, the silence triggering beads of sweat to form on the back of my neck. I was in the presence of a literal god, and I felt like I was going to combust from panicky unease.

I feigned more and more interest in the floor as Poseidon made his way towards me. I had heard the stories of him: a god with too much time on his hands, perhaps, who favored long, extravagant affairs with mortal women.

Worn brown sandals came into my line of sight. The edge of a gold sarong grazed the floor of the temple. My breathing grew more rapid and shallow.

My jaw clenched as I closed my eyes and instead focused on how I would receive my blessing from Athena. I wouldn't become distracted by Ares or Poseidon or my errant thoughts. No, tonight was about us receiving our blessings from our Goddess Athena.

She was the one we served and worshiped.

A harsh hand gripped my chin, forcing me to look into the eyes of Poseidon.

"Sir—er—I mean—"

The god of the sea grazed my cheek with his thumb, tilting his head at me with a predator's gaze. My stomach clenched in discomfort and dread. I couldn't move my head, as he forced it back to examine me some more.

"Medusa, Daughter of Ceto. How great is your beauty. It is quite rare for a gorgon like you." He seemed to purr the words, moving his hand down my throat and over my shoulders.

"Thank you, your greatness," I mumbled, too shocked and afraid to move.

He toyed with the strand of pearls around my neck, rubbing them between his fingers. Poseidon dropped the necklace and reached out to touch one of my snakes. The snake coiled, ready to attack. But quickly fell motionless under his power. He lazily wrapped the limp form around his finger.

I glanced around the room, no help to be found.

Aspasia was still in the other room with Athena, and the ones that had already received their blessings had been taken upstairs. Ares was nowhere to be found, and the other gorgons were forbidden to come down here.

The priestess…she was gone, too.

Breathe, I told myself. He was a god. He was supposed to protect me, not harm me. The rumors were just that: rumors. I took a shaky breath and slid down the bench I was sitting on, removing Poseidon's grasp from my face.

This seemed to displease him.

"Medusa, come. The god of the sea wishes to bless you."

Painful heat pulsated along my skin.

"I wish only to receive my blessing from Athena, your greatness. For she is the one we worship."

A stinging slap was dragged across my face.

I fought back my tears.

"If you worship one, you worship us all," he snapped.

I couldn't refuse the order of a god, it would only bring shame and hurt upon my family and coven.

Standing, I lifted my gaze, focusing on the wall behind Poseidon's head. "Good gorgon. Now, come."

I dragged my feet across the floor, resisting as he yanked me across the room and into a separate space. He closed the heavy door behind us.

There were no windows. There was no way out besides the firmly closed door. The room seemed to be growing smaller and smaller.

Breathe.

In.

Out.

Breathe.

I repeated those words to myself like a chant as Poseidon walked around me, murmuring to himself about my body and beauty. I wanted to crawl into a hole as he ran one hand across the front of my dress, his fingers lingering on my breasts.

"Please, your greatness. I must go meet with the goddess Athena."

"You do what I say, Medusa, daughter of Ceto. And I say sit."

Compelled by a strange and dark sort of magic, I complied to his demand and sat on the floor. He had control over me, I realized in silent abhorrence. I no longer had authority over my own body.

And that was perhaps the most terrifying part.

"Now isn't that better?" Poseidon whispered, yanking my chin, so I was forced to meet his icy aquamarine eyes. The blatant lust and egotism were so distinct that I wanted to scream. But the air was ripped from my lungs before I could make a sound.

He had stolen my voice.

I opened my mouth again, but again, not even a whisper escaped.

I needed to yell.

To screech, to shriek.

To topple the castle walls above and cause the ground to shudder.

To remind the world that I still existed, that I still breathed while catastrophic melancholy, ire, and sadness devoured my soul from the inside out.

I needed to feel hope.

But that was ripped away from me the moment he stole my voice.

"A body such as yours deserves to be worshiped by the gods themselves, Medusa. Not by mortal men, for they are unworthy of such beauty."

My body began to shake, and I wanted to vomit as he slowly began to undress me. Frozen air nipped at my skin as he bared my flesh to the world. I tried to scream.

My snakes were limp and cold, as if their souls had been cruelly ripped from their bodies. I silently cried for them to awaken and help me, but Poseidon's magic was too strong.

I fought against invisible chains as his hands trailed from my neck to my feet, stopping at places he found extra 'beautiful'.

Poseidon roughly bit the delicate skin above my breast. As if he were a wolf dragging my used and bloody carcass around the stained forest ground.

This couldn't be happening.

I had to be having a nightmare.

That's it.

This was a nightmare from stress.

This wasn't real.

But the screaming of my shattering soul informed me otherwise.

I began to pray to Goddess Athena, begging for her to come and rescue me before the worst could happen. But no one came to my rescue.

Not Athena.

Not the priestess.

Not my mother.

Not even myself.

I closed my eyes as he forced himself on top of me. My screams grew softer and softer as he took my innocence. I had no fight left in me as he collapsed on top of me, his sweat covering my body.

I felt…

Used. Dirty. Disgraceful.

As Poseidon was dressing me, the door flew open, and Athena stood there. I ran to her, crying and sobbing. I expected to find a trace of compassion in my heart, but I found none.

Her face was twisted with anger and anguish as she stared at Poseidon, the god who she loved and was romantically involved with.

Athena pushed me down, and the terror and humiliation that tore through me was unbearable. With the same carnivorous gaze Poseidon had given me, she grabbed my arm harshly, hurrying me along with a quick wave of her delicate hand.

"And you, dear Medusa. You will have a blessing unlike any other."

18

I screamed, waking up drenched in my own sweat. Drops of sweat rolled off my elbows and knees, leaving the sheets damp and frigid. Shivering, I attempted to gather my bearings as Brooks jerked out of his pile of blankets on the floor, running a hand over my wet hair.

"Shh, it was just a bad dream. Just a dream, okay? None of it was real."

I cried harder. If only he knew.

It wasn't just Casimar's wandering hands.

It was so much more than that.

My breath came out in heavy pants, and I attempted to sit up, only to fall flat on my face. It was dark again.

How many hours, or days, had passed?

A soft humming filled the room,

Minutes passed and the familiar tune slowed my racing thoughts.

I let out a wry chuckle.

"I remember you singing that the night we met, very badly might I add." My tired laughter filled the room as Brooks settled back down into his makeshift bed.

Brooks snorted, propping himself up on his elbow to look up at me. "And you sing perfectly on pitch?"

"Of course."

A ghost of a smile touched his lips, but not before he sighed heavily. "How long have you been having those nightmares? And please don't lie and tell me you don't have any."

There was no use in lying. He was sharing a room with me and had heard my screams. And maybe I was desperate to tell someone, to ease the ache and burden of carrying them alone.

"Since the night I turned sixteen."

"That's a very specific date," he raised one eyebrow at me.

"It isn't easy to forget the night your entire world came crashing down around you."

Brooks looked like he wanted to question me further, but I rolled over in the bed, closing myself off to him before he could.

I heard him grind his teeth and shift in bed.

"My entire world came crashing down when I was just a child."

I was surprised that he was opening up to me. Maybe it was a ploy to get me to spill my secrets to him, since he was a detective and naturally curious, but somehow I didn't think it was.

"I had three older sisters. Triplets. Pains in my ass, those three. But we loved each other fiercely, and entirely. Even though we drove my parents crazy, we were happy. And that was all that mattered."

I didn't miss his use of the past tense.

"What happened?"

"They went on a mountain expedition to the Anghor Peaks with my uncle, right before they were supposed to leave for college. One last 'hoorah' before adulthood.

"My uncle was the only one who came back. The bastard told my parents that he couldn't find them after a supposed mountain lion attack. That he woke up one morning and they were gone, their tents torn to shreds. Gone. In the middle of the Anghor Peaks. I wasn't in Iydara at the time and didn't find out about their disappearance until much, much later."

His voice trembled and became heavy with grief.

"My uncle returned with scraps of their bloody clothing, without a scratch on him. My parents believed him, even sold the family business

to him. I never bought into his story though. They're out there somewhere, I just...I can feel it."

"Brooks..."

Though I had fallen out with my sisters, I couldn't imagine losing
them like that. Not knowing where they were, or if they were hungry, or
lonely. But deep down, I knew they didn't feel the same way about me.

At least, not anymore.

"I like to think that the reason I became a detective is to find them
one day. To bring them home to my mother and father. They were my
best friends, and I can't believe my uncle's story. Not with his known
past."

"You think he had something to do with their disappearance?"

"I do."

His uncle seemed like the kind of man that could get away with anything and everything, including murder. In all honesty, I wouldn't have
been surprised if he had staged the attack and left the poor girls stranded.

I silently wondered what would prompt their uncle to cover up their
disappearances, and why he would want his nieces to disappear in the first
place.

"I have nightmares about them a lot. Often, they're running away
from me and I barely touch their hands before they are taken away from
me again. I wake up sweating and without a clue as to where I am. Other
times, they chase me, with ice clinging to their eyelashes and hair, their
lips blue from the cold. And they yell at me to come and rescue them. To
save them."

"Why are you telling me this?" I asked hesitantly.

"Because I need you to know that it's okay to have a past that still
haunts you, that still wrecks your thoughts, memories, even your day-to-
day life."

His words struck a chord.

I contemplated them for a minute.

My mind and body were still healing from trauma and would be for years, and perhaps that was entirely okay. Rohesia had reassured me that everyone had some form of trauma, and repressing certain memories and sensations had helped her to move forward.

But what if that wasn't how healing occurred?

All those years of ignoring my past had done nothing to heal my festering wounds. If anything, it had made them worse.

In terms of healing from a traumatic past, Brooks and I seemed to have very different methods of coping. He was able to talk about his past, and it made him seem stronger and more resilient, not weaker.

Suddenly, I wanted to tell Brooks about my mother and sisters, and what had occurred the night of my sixteenth birthday, but the words got stuck in my throat, fear overcoming me.

I rolled over to face him, my eyes shut.

Did he know about the bounty above my head?

I realized that I couldn't trust him. Not yet at least.

A frustrated sigh tore through my throat as Brooks's mattress shifted again.

I flinched as Brooks's hand grazed my back. Squirming from his reach, I mumbled something about my injuries stinging if they were touched.

"I'm just braiding your hair to keep it off your wounds. My sisters joined forces and taught me so I would always be at their disposal," he says, reminiscing.

Oh.

That was…nice.

In and out of bouts of unconsciousness, I had wondered who had braided my hair so skillfully. Rohesia could only braid her own hair and she got confused when it was somebody other than herself. Normally I plaited it myself, but had a limited range of motion with my current wounds.

I slowly began to doze as Brooks's hands dexterously placed my hair into a braided bun. He did it tight enough that it wouldn't fall out, but also loose enough that it wouldn't give me a raging headache.

"The fulgurite that The Collectress had was a fake," he suddenly stated, "I thought you should know."

It was a fake?

If the fulgurite was fake, then...

"Then whoever or whatever is creating golems is still out there. And The Collectress couldn't have used it to make the golems. Why did she have a damned fake?"

"Precisely. Rohesia and E.E. want us to close the case, but I asked them to give us another week, after you're healed, of course."

He paused as he began mixing up another medicinal potion for me to drink.

"As for your question, your boss and my uncle had gone rogue without telling us. They wanted to draw out a buyer, in hopes that it would lead them to whoever was making the golems, hoping they could cash in on the sale as well."

Greed. Stupid, stupid greed.

There was still such a small amount of time. We were faced with so many unanswered questions. There was a gigantic piece of the puzzle missing, and I couldn't rest until we found it.

I had a feeling that Brooks felt the same way, and there was a reason E.E. had trusted him with such an important case.

"Where is Zeus's real fulgurite then?"

Brooks handed me my tea, sighing.

"We aren't sure. I didn't even know it was a fake until I tried breaking it."

I sputtered, choking on the tea I had started sipping. Brooks handed me a cloth, smirking as the amber-colored water dribbled down my chin.

"You—What?"

"I tried breaking it after The Collectress placed the last brand on your back; they were both so distracted that they didn't notice when I grabbed it. But when I tried to shatter it, it bounced against the ground. A real fulgurite breaks when dropped."

I snorted softly at the picture.

"You're saying I fought a damn charybdis for a fake?"

Brooks stiffened as his eyes met mine, but then grinned easily.

"At least you'll have a good drinking story," he said tightly.

I rolled my eyes.

"Then what could be creating the golems? Could Zeus's Fulgurite still be out there?"

He sighed loudly, placing more bandages on my back as he added some of the sleeping aid to my tea.

"That's another dead end. E.E. still thinks it could be another species of gorgon, but I don't buy that theory. There's no hard evidence of another species, or even another gorgon."

Eirlys's words came back into my mind.

Something that is magic but isn't.

I glanced at the overflowing counter of ointments and potions. My heart stopped in my chest.

Something that is magic but isn't.

I had to tell Brooks.

19

Athena's grasp marred the delicate skin of my arm as we stumbled through the temple. Her grip only tightened when we raced through the ruins outside the place of worship.

Her golden hair glistened under a full moon that was peeking out through wispy clouds, and I wondered if it had borne witness to a god taking my innocence.

Racing up the snow packed stairs and into the castle foyer, where celebrating families and Daughters of Athena stood, I tried to control my breathing. I had a feeling my blessing wasn't going to be as I had always dreamed.

I tried to explain to the goddess that Poseidon had violated me, that he had hurt me. But my words and pleas had fallen on deaf ears. I didn't understand. Why didn't she believe me? Why didn't she seem to want to help me?

Maybe she was going to warn the others, then she would perform my blessing. At least, that's the thought I tried to reassure myself with.

Gasps surrounded us as the goddess casually strode through the castle, some of the families covering their younger daughter's eyes, afraid that they would be cursed if they laid their eyes on Goddess Athena before their sixteenth birthday.

"Goddess Athena! What are you doing with Daughter Medusa?" My mother came running with my sisters, their faces in different states of disarray and fear.

"Why, giving your daughter the ultimate blessing, of course."

Unwilling to defy or question a goddess, my mother and sisters nodded their heads, watching as Athena hauled me to the top of the stairs, above everyone else.

"Gorgons have been unable to go into the mortal lands for centuries. Without the gift of mortality, you are forced to stay in the Anghor Peaks, never to see another face besides the ones standing next to you."

The crowd murmured. But we had been taught that that was a good thing. That mortals were evil, horrible creatures. We were safe here.

The Anghor Peaks were the closest landmark to the gods, which meant they could reach us quicker than anywhere else.

"I have decided to bless you all with the ability to change forms. Yes, you heard me correctly. Tonight, you will be able to change from the appearance of a gorgon to a mortal, as easily as you can blink."

Gasps and cheers filled the room. This was all so amazing.

It was a blessing, indeed.

Then why did it feel like I wanted to die?

"How do we know it will work?" yelled a gorgon with pale blue snakes. She held Aspasia's hand, her chin raised proudly.

Athena gave the crowd a feral grin, circling around my kneeling body. "With Medusa being the first gorgon to receive such a blessing, of course."

My mother and sisters looked shocked, but then smugness began to radiate from where they stood at the bottom of the railing.

The goddess Athena placed her hands on my shoulders, speaking in a strange tongue. Wind forced the castle doors to open violently, causing a few bystanders to jump in shock. The bizarre winds caused my snakes to disappear, leaving in their wake a head full of luxurious curls.

I gasped, feeling the immediate change in my body.

"Change," Athena commanded me, and so I did.

I transformed from my gorgon form and into my mortal form a handful of times, in disbelief. Whenever I changed, it became easier and easier, just like blinking.

"Does it hurt?"

"Your hair looks so soft!"

"Me next!"

"Change me, oh greatness!"

Athena raised her hands, silencing the crowd. She helped me to my feet, showing me off as though I was a prized cow.

"There is a balance when it comes to the magic of the gods and goddesses. I cannot, unfortunately, turn all of you." Groans and cries rang out through the castle at her words.

"But do not fret, Daughters. For there is always a solution for this balance. To be able to change forms like Medusa, the answer is really simple. Sacrifice her to me beneath a full moon, and all the gorgons of your coven, future and past, will have the ability to transform.

"And wouldn't you know, there is a full moon tonight," Athena finished smugly.

My mother paled and my sisters looked greener than usual.

They had to sacrifice me in order to gain my power. That hardly seemed right or fair. And Athena was talking about it as though it was a great bargain. Not as though one of the coven's youngest daughters needed to die.

What if I didn't want to die?

A soft buzzing filled the room and the atmosphere changed dramatically. I cried out in fear as Goddess Athena disappeared.

My mother was the first to attack.

And the others soon followed.

I ran up the stairs, chucking the small clutch I carried at the gorgon behind me. The black velvet purse hit my wannabe attacker in her bulbous nose.

My dress tore as someone pulled at my skirt. I spun on my heel, dipping down, and kicking my leg out. A gorgon cried out in frustration as I knocked on her back.

Sweat covered my brow, dripping into my eyes as I raced through the castle hallways. Mother had relentlessly trained us, forcing us to not to rely on our stoning powers. Especially since gorgons couldn't stone one another. But my tight dress was making it almost impossible to fight my coven.

I stumbled through a servant's elevator that had been left ajar, climbing into it rather noisily. I saw a dozen gorgons race through the kitchen before continuing to another room.

I took that as my cue to take the elevator down to the lower levels. Peeking through the cracks, I carefully opened the elevator, tiptoeing through the library. When the marble floors turned into shabby cement, I made a hard-right turn towards a massive set of doors with rusted handles. My hand wrapped around the knob, giving the heavy door a steady tug.

What greeted me was like something out of a fairytale.

Even as I was in the middle of a nightmare.

Rows and rows of rising plants surrounded me.

The towering greenhouse held a plentiful variety of flowers, succulents, fruit, saplings, and vegetables. Varying scents of saccharine, pungent, and woodsy plants combated my nostrils. The teeming rows of plants were laid out with no clear order or methodology.

My heartbeat steadied as I disappeared into the thick rows of vegetation. A sense of tranquility washed over me. Nature had always been home to me, never simply a place just to visit.

I was in the last row of colorful fruits when the sound of soft footsteps caught my attention. The light steps seemed to be approaching from the row of flora behind mine. My breath quickened as I ran for a door that led to a thick, dark forest.

I suddenly crashed into one of my sisters.

"Hello, sister," she sneered, throwing me into a row of plants by my hair. My head slammed back into a potted plant, ceramic pieces scattering on the ground.

White spots filled my vision and my head spun as Stheno grabbed my choker, pressing me into shards of broken ceramic and clay pots. Bile built up in my throat as she squeezed and twisted the choker around my throat. Beads of blood started to leak from my skin. Her eyes were distant and crazed, possessed by something other than her own rage.

I punctured the back of her hand with my long nails, causing her to hiss in pain. Rolling away from her grasp, I landed on my feet.

Remembering my training, I tightened my core, kept my chin low, and threw a punch at Stheno's unsuspecting form. She blocked me rather quickly with a solid forearm, and I stumbled back, looking for a hole in her defense.

I shifted my form as if to kick her thigh, causing her arms to drop a fraction of an inch. An opening appeared, and I swung, slamming my fist into Stheno's stomach.

My oldest sister grunted in shock.

I blocked her knee as she attempted to kick me in the ribs. Spinning out of her reach, I kicked out my legs, sweeping her long legs out from under her.

Desperately, I grabbed a piece of shattered ceramic pot, clenching it in my palm as I darted into a thicket of trees with pure terror rushing through my veins.

But my sister had always been faster than me.

Stheno came up behind me, tackling me and shoving my head into a pile of melting snow. I choked on the layer of fresh pine needles that blanketed the thawing snow.

My elbow was freed from her stronghold, and I threw it back into her face, satisfied as her nose crunched from the blow. She landed on her back, and I pounced.

With Stheno now looking up at the sky, I placed the sharpened shard of ceramic on her throat. Surprise contorted her face as she watched me.

Though I was the youngest, our mother had been the hardest on me during training. I was never more grateful for that than in this moment.

"Do it," she hissed, her golden snakes snapping and biting at mine.

I contemplated it, slashing her throat. Not that it would kill her, but it would knock her out and injure her greatly. The scar would be a hideous one.

But Stheno was my sister, my blood.

I couldn't do that to her.

Instead, I pushed myself back from her.

"Coward." she spat at my feet.

Stheno circled me, drawing a hidden knife from her thigh, watching me with lethal eyes. It was only a matter of time before the others discovered us. I flung the shard at her chest, ripping the material of her dress but barely grazing her skin before sprinting away from her.

It would be a miracle if I made it up the mountain.

Skilled footsteps trailed behind me as I crashed through the underbrush of the massive trees that surrounded our property.

I ran for what felt like miles.

When I could no longer continue, I eased into a more comfortable stance and calmed my breathing. My mind strained to examine the forest over the howling of the winter wind.

The snow kept a steady pace and curled around me like a shimmering, silver coat. Despite the desperation and annoyance that surged through me, and despite the wind rubbing my frozen skin raw, I savored the feeling of fresh snow landing on my mud-covered body.

Fragmented rays of moonlight shone through the trees, creating a path of light and shadows as I hurtled through the forest. Away from my home.

When my heel caught on a fallen branch, I let out a curse. Bitter, damp snow clung to my body as I tried to desperately dust myself off. Without proper clothing, I wouldn't make it through the night. Nor to Iydara.

The large city was perhaps a two-day ride by carriage and horses. By foot, it would take me at least four, if not five, days to reach. And that was only if it didn't snow any more.

In spite of the odds, I refused to slow down.

A sharp cracking noise stopped me in my tracks, sending sharp waves of suspicion through my tired body. I held my breath.

A large silhouette crashed into me.

Stheno.

Strong arms pinned me on my back.

"Should have slit my throat when you had the chance, little sis." Her snakes attempted to bite my face, their forked tongues craving the taste of blood. Although the snakes weren't poisonous, their bite was certainly painful.

I struggled below her tall form, kicking and kneeing her in the gut to no avail. Sharp, burning pain seeped from my forearm; a deep gash was beginning to form where Stheno was holding her weapon.

"Isn't the full moon absolutely breathtaking tonight? Oh, how the gods have blessed us. I'll make it quick, Usa," Stheno crooned.

She had always hated the fact that we were forbidden to leave the Anghor Peaks. And my death had suddenly become the key to her freedom. This was doubtless the motivation behind her relentless pursuit of me.

I closed my eyes, praying to the gods that still listened that Stheno kept her word, and it would indeed be a quick and painless death. Sparkling trees circled above my head, having a calming effect as she placed a sharpened dagger beneath my ear, beginning to slash my throat from ear to ear.

Only milliseconds had passed before I heard a thud and groan.

I peeked out from under my snow-covered lashes, finding my other sister Euryale standing above Stheno's unmoving form.

"I didn't kill her. Though I kind of wish I could."

I scrambled back, freezing ice and snow biting into my hands as I got to my feet. My hands clenched the knife that Stheno had been about to use on me.

Instead of attacking me, Euryale looked at me solemnly.

"Run, Usa. And never look back."

She tossed me a heavy cloak and didn't say anything else.

I could only nod as my older sister began to drag her twin's unconscious body to Kilmarn, and I scampered the other way, to the human lands of Iydara.

The frayed edges of my heavy dress caught on deep snow drifts, pulling me down into piles of wet, freezing snow. Humiliating pain radiated throughout my body.

I was a mortal.

I was human.

I would die.

My immortality had been ripped from me by an unforgiving goddess who was supposed to protect me and love me. Athena had to be mistaken.

She had to.

I prayed that she would change her mind, but I didn't think she would. The gods never made mistakes.

They never apologized.

Even when they were wrong.

Moisture seeped in through the layers of my dress as I looked around the thick forest. I swiftly changed into my gorgon form, grateful that I still had my night vision.

It felt wrong.

Unnatural.

Being a mortal gorgon should not have been possible.

My gorgon seemed to scream at me that something was wrong. That she was afraid. My blessing wasn't supposed to have been like this. I had been looking forward to it since I was a little girl, and now I was running for my life.

In horror, I realized that I would never be able to return to Kilmarn. Not if I wanted to stay alive.

I could still hear Athena's giggle, her mocking tone.

Dread rippled through my body, the last few hours starting to sink in. She couldn't find me. None of them could.

Blood was seeping from my forearm, and I was scrubbing my skin in the snow, desperate to wash away the trail of blood that followed me. The trail of blood only grew as I ripped a scrap of material from my dress and hastily wrapped it around my arm.

I let out a frustrated scream, relishing in the sound of it echoing throughout the trees. Suddenly, I didn't care who or what heard me. Let them come. My rounded nails raked into my shoulders, creating paths of stinging pain, as I enfolded my arms around myself, falling to the ground in a sobbing heap of anguish and despair.

I wasn't sure how long I sat there, in the cold loneliness. Long enough that my clothes turned damp and my fingertips grew numb.

Everything hurt.

*It hurt to breathe. It hurt to think. It hurt to simply **exist.***

Surviving is ugly.

It's not some noble thing that makes your life richer.

It's a saddening madness that constantly berates your mind, while you try not to feel, try not to think. It's numbing the agony and despair while trying to hold on to a scrap of shredded humanity as it slid through your fingers. It's a bitter dream of what I could have been had my skin not been harmed by the greed of someone else's chaos.

Oh, how I wished the chaos would have ignored me.

Would have chosen to destroy someone else.

But wishful thinking never changed a damn thing.

I pushed the dreams of an untainted soul to the very back of my mind, surprised to find that the pain receded as I ran away from my home.

From my friends. From my sisters and mother. From my goddess.

My mind was torn.

My mother and sisters had always been loving and kind. They were fierce but gentle, and had taught me how to be the same. But the moment the goddess offered them a different life, their feelings for me had seemed to disappear.

Had it been Stheno or Euryale, I was sure that they would gladly be sacrificed to Athena without a second thought, if it meant a better life for our coven.

Was I selfish for choosing my own life over the bettering of the coven's? Perhaps.

But I felt no remorse as I trudged through the mountains of snow and lonely, bitter cold, heading for Iydara.

I wasn't sure what their civilization looked like. We were forbidden to step foot into the human lands, told by my mother that we would be killed if we did.

Running to Iydara gave me a small sense of comfort. I doubted that my sisters or other coven members would risk discovery just to kill me. Maybe being partially mortal had its benefits.

I had never seen my coven that frenzied. Of course, we had, in a sense, murdered people before. But our statues never truly died. And we only stoned people out of self-defense.

I was sixteen and had never stoned anyone before.

And I had never met a human.

Mother said they looked like gorgons, except without snakes and scales, and they were weaker and more evil.

But what could be more evil than attempting to kill your own daughter? To murder your own blood for personal gain...

I raised my eyes from the snow-covered ground, stopping on a narrow trail in the forest. Red mud peaked out through clumps of ice, suggesting that I was at the end of the Anghor Peaks and was entering the mysterious edges of the humans' territory.

There were rumors of wild human and mage civilizations that roamed these mountains, living off the land and the provisions of nature. I fought off images of monsters with gnashing teeth as I walked around the open land.

Squinting in the harsh darkness, a ruddy wall with deserted guard towers came into view. Metal spirals of gold jutted out from domed roofs of the watchtowers and into the star-painted sky. The disintegrating towers cast eerie shadows into the stark land. Despite their abandoned state, a sense of dread washed over me as I observed the structures.

Flakes of chipped green paint and the shattered windows slowly reassured me that this part of the forest was deserted.

Trudging alongside the buildings, I carefully peeked in through broken windows and splintered doors. Fresh bunches of wet snow crunched under the weight of my shoes. Though my feet ached, I didn't dare take the heels off. Frostbite was no joke, and I would rather have blisters than lose my toes. I stuffed my hands into the pockets, thankful that Euryale had given me the cloak.

Though Stheno and Euryale were twins, they were nothing alike. Stheno was nine minutes older than Euryale and held those minutes over her head like precious gold.

Because of their differences, Euryale and I had grown close. She tried to please our mother, but like me, seemed to wilt under Stheno's shadow.

Euryale and I were content to live our lives in Kilmarn, hidden from the rest of the world. But Stheno was too similar to our mother.

They wanted control and destruction.

To make humans and mages fall at our feet.

I walked parallel to the gargantuan brick barricade and ran my fingers along the rough surface of the wall. My fingers eventually met up with five grooves that had been slowly engraved into the brick by another's callused fingertips.

Tracing the charred cement with my fingernail, I collected a layer of fine ash under a now ripped nail. I found it strange that there was ash on the bricks in the middle of winter.

Heavier snowflakes began to fall, reminding me that I needed to find shelter soon. The agony in my arm had lessened, but I knew that I needed to find clean water and herbs before infection set in.

If the wound became septic, I would be dead before I ever made it to Iydara. My gashes and cuts usually healed within minutes, but now that I was mortal, the wound showed no signs of healing anytime soon.

A stairwell landing in one of the guard towers seemed the most promising place of shelter. The ceiling was mostly intact and discarded bags of garden soil provided me with a semi-cosy bed.

My mind and body had started to doze when a strange clicking sound filled the area. It seemed to be coming from a closet by my feet.

I tilted my head to the left, closed my eyes, and held my breath, searching for any sound or energy that did not belong in the abandoned towers and surrounding mountains.

The magical creatures of the forest grew quiet.

The bitter air grew warm.

Even the snow stopped falling.

I turned the handle of the door, the cold metal biting into my hand.

A large raven burst out through the closet, skimming my hair with its gleaming beak. I let out a low, nervous chuckle.

"Just a bird, Medusa. Just a bird."

"I wouldn't be too sure about that."

I whirled around to find a woman standing behind me. She seemed to be in her mid-twenties. Her deep brown skin was hidden under layers of clothing. But what stood out to me were her eyes.

Even in the darkness, I could make out the stunning cobalt color with flecks of gold.

"Ravens are thought to be incredibly intelligent and cunning. They are often drawn to people going through transformations, and ignite the energies of magic allowing them to become one with our intentions and will."

I gulped, backing up from the woman. The raven sat on her shoulder, rubbing its face along the woman's braided top knot.

"My question for you, mortal," she sniffed the air, "is what are your intentions?"

I started to tell her that my only intentions were to survive the night when another woman came running up the stairs.

"Stop with the dramatics, Ophelia! You're scaring the poor girl."

The second woman looked exactly like the first.

Ophelia, the first woman, with the raven perched on her shoulder, looked at me with more disdain. "I get a bad feeling from her."

"Ugh. You say that about everyone, Ophelia. Let Twyla and I help her. We were once like her, remember?" a different voice interjected.

I froze, shocked as I watched another female, identical to the others, appear from the shadows. This one had a nose ring and short coiled hair.

"No, Astraea. You know what Blackleach says about outsiders," the first woman insisted.

"He didn't have any issues with us," Astraea responded, a grin pulling at her full lips.

I took in the three women, triples I realized. Though they were obviously mortals, they dressed and talked like mages. But maybe the times had changed, as I hadn't seen a mage since I was an adolescent gorgon.

The first one, Ophelia, stood furthest from me, a calculating look on her face as she watched me from under the hood of her crimson cloak.

The second woman, Twyla, looked ready to explode from excitement. She could barely contain herself as she grabbed my freezing hands and pulled me towards the group. Round glasses were perched on the tip of her nose, fogging up from the warmth of her breath. Twyla was shorter and rounder than Ophelia, who was all lean muscle and towering height.

The third sister, Astraea, stood next to a stout dire wolf, her hands grasping the railing. Her eyes were also a piercing blue. She had a medical device clipped to her pants with tubing snaking beneath her thermal shirt. The gray dire wolf sat next to her, cocking its head at me with curiosity.

Astraea turned her head towards Ophelia, "Come on, Ophelia. Just for one night?"

"One night, we promise," Twyla chimed in, bouncing on her heels with excitement. They acted like I was a new toy, and I questioned how often they got visitors in this remote part of the woods.

"Fine. But you're telling Blackleach." Ophelia spun on her heel, her raven circling around her as we left the broken guard tower.

It seemed that I wasn't getting a say in the matter.

But I didn't mind, surprisingly.

I would rather take my chances with the three women than freeze to death in the middle of this violent winter. And though these women were human, I had the overwhelming feeling that they belonged to one of Hecate's covens.

If I stayed in my mortal form, I would be okay.

Mages and gorgons were mortal enemies. And I didn't think they would take me home with them if they knew the truth about me. Gorgons were unnatural, and created abnormal creatures with just a gaze into their eyes, going against the instinctive ways of mages.

181

Ophelia skillfully led the way, moving around the piles of snow easily while her cloak floated behind her. Twyla held my arm in hers, singing a mountain song about a meadow. Astraea walked a few paces behind us, her dire wolf close and watchful as he followed her around broken branches and snow drifts.

He was a gorgeous animal with golden eyes, and he stood at Astraea's waist when on all fours. Our gaze met a few times and I picked up on his unconditional love for not only Astraea, but the other two sisters as well.

"What's his name?" I asked Astraea.

"Echo. He's my diabetic alert dog."

Echo barked sharply at his owner, raising his black eyebrows.

Rolling her cobalt eyes, Astraea snickered. "Excuse me. He's my diabetic alert wolf."

Echo looked at Astraea approvingly this time, his tail wagging.

Before I could ask more about him, we came to a standstill. I watched Ophelia walk a few paces from us, searching under a thick brambleberry bush.

"I'm guessing she's the oldest?" I asked Twyla.

She gave a wide grin. "Nope."

"I am," Astraea said.

"By ten lousy minutes," Ophelia snorted, having overheard our conversation.

A purple stone sat in her palm, and we ambled up to a wall of shale stone. It looked like we were at the bottom of a cliff.

"This is the fun part," Astraea whispered. Her body was shaking from either the cold or excitement, I didn't know which.

I watched in quiet awe as Ophelia held the glowing orb in front of her body, while chanting softly to the wall of stone. Blinding bright amethyst started to emit from the side of the mountain. Transforming into a glowing outline, a cave entrance slowly began to form in front of us.

"Told you," Astraea whispered, her dire wolf thumping his fluffy tail.

This was the best part of my day, by far. Going through a hidden, magical door had not been part of my plan, but neither had being assaulted, banished, and hunted by family and the gods and goddesses that I prayed to.

Balmy air weaved itself through my hair, and I took off my shoes, my feet gladly soaking up the warm cave floors. Mages paid us no mind as Ophelia led us through a well-lit passageway.

The cave smelled of medicinal herbs and roasted beef. My stomach growled loudly as I pictured the large feast that the other Daughters of Athena would be currently gorging themselves on.

"Ladies, just what do you think you're doing?"

A mage with white eyes and pale skin held a sack of flour over his shoulders, walking down the passageway we had turned down.

"Just showing our friend from Hecate's Seventh Coven around." Astraea smiled, jabbing me in the ribs as if to tell me to play along.

I happily obliged.

"Yes, sir. They invited me over to practice our magic."

"What exactly will you be practicing?" He raised an eyebrow skeptically at me. The walls seemed to grow closer the longer he looked in my direction.

"She'll be practicing shadow magic. But we're just providing her company and snacks," Twyla shared.

My face was warm from embarrassment, though it could be taken as that I was red from the warmth of the cave and my exposure to the frozen elements. I was thankful that Twyla had covered my mistake. I kept forgetting that the triplets were human and not mages.

"Carry on, but please don't be as rowdy as last time."

"No promises," Twyla smirked, taking her arm in mine once again. I noticed that she had a small birthmark on her arm; it reminded me of a crescent moon.

"What coven is this?" I asked Twyla.

"Hecate's Fifth Coven."

I nodded, the three leading me behind a heavy curtain, where there were three twin-sized beds. The bed frames were built into the wall and were topped with plush mattresses and blankets.

"Blackleach should be here soon," Ophelia said.

The others took off their cloaks, piling them by the entrance, but I didn't remove mine. My forearm ached against the cloth I had wrapped my wound with.

"Why were you in the middle of the freezing forest in heels and a dress like that?" Ophelia asked, placing her fuzzy sock-covered feet under her as she sat in a loveseat, across from the couch where I sat shoulder to shoulder with Astraea and Twyla.

I had anticipated her questions and had my answers ready.

"I was on vacation and got lost."

"Vacationing in the mountains while in that outfit?"

Damn her being so observant.

Okay, maybe I hadn't thought my answer through as well as I thought.

"I like the cold."

"How'd you get lost?"

Ophelia threw another question my way before I could produce an answer to the previous.

"Who were you with?"

"Ophelia. Stop," Twyla snapped, patting my shoulder soothingly. I didn't mind her touch; it was rather comforting after today.

"I'm just trying to make sure we didn't invite an ax murderer into our home."

"If anyone is an ax murderer, it's you," Astraea said dryly.

The dire wolf barked loudly next to Astraea, as if to agree.

Ophelia frowned at him.

The heavy curtain was pulled back slowly. All three girls remained sitting and didn't act afraid. So, I attempted to do the same.

I raised my gaze to see a familiar-looking mage walk into the room. He beamed at the girls as if they were his own children.

And I guess in a sense they were.

If Hecate's Fifth Coven was anything like mine, then I knew they loved each other ferociously and would die for one another.

They protected their loved ones without question.

Blood didn't matter to covens.

When the man caught my gaze, he was a bit taken aback, but he recovered quickly. "Who are you?"

"Usa," I replied, using my nickname from childhood.

I didn't want to risk using my full name in case he had heard about me from my mother or other covens. And I wasn't sure that my full name suited me after tonight.

"Landen Blackleach. But everyone calls me Blackleach."

He didn't offer to shake my hand and I didn't bother to offer mine. Strangely, I didn't mind that he wasn't as willing to welcome me into his arms as the girls had been.

"Where are you from?"

"Ki—" I coughed loudly. "'Scuse me. Iydara. I was on vacation with my family and got lost."

"I see." His lips were pressed together tightly, and I got the feeling that he didn't believe me. If they asked me any more questions about Iydara, then I was screwed.

I knew that the country was broken up into different boundaries and run by mortals, but that was it. My history lessons had been focused on the gods and goddess as well as gorgon ancestry.

"Girls, why don't you go and get some food for Usa. I'm sure she has had a long night and would like dinner before midnight rolls around."

The triplets nodded, pushing back the curtain, leaving Blackleach and me alone.

He took Ophelia's seat and stretched his long legs out in front of him. "Usa. You wouldn't perhaps be Medusa? Daughter of the gorgon queen, Ceto?"

The mage wasted no time.

Lying would only make him even more suspicious and I needed to gain his trust if I wanted a warm bed to sleep in tonight. "Yes, sir."

He nodded. "I thought I recognized you."

"Sir?" *I couldn't remember ever meeting the man in front of me.*

"It was long ago. Before your second birthday, when your grandmother went to rest with the gods and goddesses, and your mother started ruling your coven. How is she by the way?"

I laughed.

And couldn't stop.

Blackleach looked at me as though I was a crazy, wild animal. I felt like one.

"Great. She's great."

He didn't miss my sarcasm.

"I thought gorgons weren't able to shift?"

"Oh, they aren't. I'm just special." *Another bout of manic laughter hit me, and I snorted loudly. Tears fell from my eyes, and I wiped them with my muck covered hands.*

With my crazed laughter, the warmth of the room soon became too much, and I took off my cloak before thinking. Blackleach's eyes widened at the sight of the bloodied cloth wrapped around my arm.

"You—you're human."

"It seems so," *I whispered, hugging myself.*

"May I?" *Blackleach crouched in front of me.*

I nodded.

He gently took my arm in his warm, soft hands. The material was stubbornly clinging to my skin, and the wound was immediately bleeding once he removed it.

I hissed in pain as he applied pressure.

Twyla and Astraea entered the room, placing steaming bowls of stew on the small dinner table, and then went off to find the medical supplies that Blackleach would need to heal my arm.

186

"Gorgons aren't born mortal. And you certainly weren't when I first met you. I distinctly remember you having black snakes, and a few white ones. You were unlike any gorgon I had seen before."

"No, we aren't. I was blessed with mortality today. The first gorgon to be given it, thanks to the goddess Athena."

Tears pricked at my eyes, but not from the pain of Blackleach putting pressure on my wound. Gods, my heart ached.

"I get the impression that it has been more of a curse than a blessing."

Blackleach didn't miss much. His tone was soft and caring, and I understood now why he was the leader of his coven. Unlike my coven, where you were born into leadership, mages often voted in their leaders.

He showed great patience as he waited for me to share my story. I had nothing else to lose, so I told him every horrible, mind-numbing detail of the day. Those who were supposed to protect me had been the very people to hurt me.

Mages worshiped the same gods and goddesses that gorgons did, and I didn't stop to wonder if he would be offended by me cursing his gods. But Blackleach didn't flinch as I spouted off vile cuss words.

At the end of my rant, the tears and bleeding had stopped, and my arm was stitched and bandaged up. Silence wrapped her arms around us, and I got the impression that Blackleach understood what it was like to be thrown out on the curb like forgotten trash.

"Stay the night, Usa. Or as long as you need."

I considered his offer silently, muttering a thanks as he left my room and Ophelia pulled back the curtain. She had been listening.

"I knew you were lying."

I laid on the couch, exhaustion pounding my skull.

"Yes, Ophelia. I'm a liar. And a gorgon. And on the run from my insane mother and coven," I said dryly. The words packed no punch, a sign that the fight was leaving me.

"You're not going to stone us in our sleep, are you?"

I snorted. "I've never stoned anyone. I'm not going to start tonight."

"Is your coven really trying to kill you?"

"Why would I lie about something like that?" I asked.

She shrugged, plopping down on the couch next to me. "Ax murderers lie about everything."

"I guess I need to find an ax, then."

A ghost of a smile appeared on the cautious woman's lips.

"Anything else?" I raised an eyebrow at her, hoping that Twyla and Astraea would be back soon.

"Look," she sighed, her eyes focused on a painting of a yellow meadow, "I know that Blackleach said that you could stay here for a while. But I think it's best if you leave in the morning."

"Way to kick a girl when she's down."

"I'm not trying to be a bitch. Honest. But if your mother and coven are as dead set on finding you and killing you, then I must think about my sisters. If it comes down to it, and your mother attacks us, I won't hesitate to hand you over if it means that my sisters will be safe."

I hadn't known the women for long, but I understood where she was coming from. And I had to respect her wishes.

Twyla and Astraea were kind and had offered me a home with trusting, open arms. If they were harmed because of me... I would never be able to forgive myself.

At last, the other two sisters returned, a stack of vinyl in their hands. I wiped the tears from my eyes and rummaged through piles of discs.

Astraea pulled out a brown vinyl, shoving it into Twyla's hand and telling her to play it.

I waited as the needle began to scratch the record, nervous, as I hadn't been allowed to listen to anything other than hymns and songs that honored Athena.

We listened to two vinyl albums by the end of the night, and I cried at every single song. It was strange listening to music that didn't honor a spiteful goddess.

Piles of food wrappers surrounded us, while soft music continued to play in the background.

Taking the device from her hip, Astraea punched a few buttons and I watched in curiosity as a clear liquid filled the tubing.

My cheeks reddened as Astraea caught my stare, but she met me with warm, kind eyes. "I'm bolusing."

"What does that mean?" I asked hesitantly, not wanting to pry or make her uncomfortable.

"It means that my pancreas doesn't create enough insulin, which makes my blood sugar high. This device allows me to give my body the insulin it needs. Pretty neat, huh?"

"It is."

A few silent moments pass as we ready ourselves for sleep. I lay between Astraea and Twyla, looking up at the ceiling and wishing that my sisters had been like the triplets.

Ophelia was asleep in her bed, softly snoring.

"Usa," Astraea started, "are you going to stay?"

My voice was lodged in my throat.

"Sure."

"Good," she sighed, resting her head on my shoulder.

Sleep came for us all quickly as the last song was played.

20

I was prepared to leave two hours before sunrise, with a bundle of clothes and a week's supply of food and clean water in a sack over my hip.

Late last night, I had made the decision to leave. The risk was too great that my mother would find me. And the risk that she would hurt the coven was even greater, including the sisters I had grown so close to in only a few short hours.

Mages knew of gorgons, but mortals didn't. I would be safer in Iydara, since my mother wouldn't want to expose herself or the coven. At that moment, I was grateful that I could change forms and they could not.

While Twyla and Astraea slept, Ophelia had caught me packing my few belongings and gave me extra clothes, medicine, and food. She said to follow her to Blackleach's room, and that's where we were heading now.

A comfortable silence and understanding fell over us as she gently knocked on the leader's door.

He opened it with sleep still in his eyes. When the mage set his eyes on me, he looked disappointed, but sympathetic.

"Heading to Iydara?" Blackleach asked.

"Yes, sir. Thank you for taking me in for the night."

"Of course."

Ophelia cleared her throat awkwardly.

"Iydara is a few hundred miles from us. Could you transport her to the border? She has only been mortal for a day and would likely die before reaching her destination."

Blackleach contemplated her question.

I hadn't known that Iydara was that far.

Ophelia and I hadn't exactly gotten off on the right foot, but I was thankful that she was asking.

"Give me a minute to prepare and we can leave then."

Ophelia and I nodded in unison.

Less than a minute later, Blackleach emerged in layers of warm clothing and held another sack over his shoulder. I followed the pair as they led me to the front of the hidden cave mouth.

Blackleach held out a hand for each of us.

"Hold on tight and bend your knees when we land."

I didn't have a chance to respond before I was seized by the feeling of being thrown into the middle of a vicious wind tunnel. An endless darkness surrounded us, though flashes of the landscape shone through the ground below us.

I landed clumsily on my face in a pile of snow.

Ophelia chuckled and Blackleach bit his lip in a failed attempt to not join her.

The human and mage stood next to a sign that told us we were entering the Eastern Boundary of Iydara. Though it was winter, the cold was much less frigid here.

"I won't forget your kindness and hospitality," I told Blackleach and Ophelia. If the sisters hadn't found me, I most likely wouldn't have made it through the night.

"I won't forget your selflessness," Ophelia replied, her breath coming out in white puffs.

I had started to walk away from the pair, beginning my journey into a lavish-looking town, when Ophelia stopped me. Her hand squeezed my shoulder roughly. Though I wore layers of thick clothing, it still hurt.

"Wait." She looked around as if someone might overhear us. "Stay away from the woman known as The Collectress."

I raised my eyebrows at her, the snowflakes that gathered in my eyelashes blurring her outline. I could still make out her tight expression, as though she had just encountered death itself.

"*Why?*"

"*She took everything from us.*" Blackleach bowed his head solemnly at her words, and before I could ask Ophelia what she meant, they disappeared into thin air.

21

"He's insane."

We were in a cramped conference room in The Hub. I sat next to Rohesia, with Salem, the black cat who perpetually meandered around the building, on my lap. E.E. and Brooks talked inaudibly, or rather argued, next to a whiteboard in front of us.

It had been two and a half weeks since my arduous torture session with The Collectress. During that time, Rohesia and Brooks had taken shifts to help me heal and recover. While one was watching me, the other was attempting to find Zeus's real fulgurite.

Every effort had come up empty handed.

The rumors of Zeus's Fulgurite being on the black market had seemed somewhat reliable. But we now knew that they were related only to the fake one made of epoxy resin.

It currently sat on the conference table in the room, mocking us. The statue was an exact replica, and I wasn't surprised that it had been confused for the real thing.

"I think Brooks missed a turn at insane, and went straight to Batshit Crazy Boulevard," I whispered to Rohesia, watching as Brooks and E.E. gesture wildly at each other.

Brooks was attempting to clear his travel plans with his boss. He had gotten an unexpected lead, but we were all hesitant to follow through with it.

Brooks's clue about the fulgurite's whereabouts supposedly came from a credible source.

But it would take us to Raas.

As in the monster and demon infested island of Raas.

Part of his reasoning made sense, since Raas was where the fulgurite had originally been discovered. But there were major, life-threatening roadblocks in his plan.

No one had been allowed entrance to the island since the inhabitants were relocated to Iydara and the monsters were transplanted to the sandy island. Dozens of applicants applied to tour the island each year and the gods denied every single one of them. Even if we were allowed, we would need a god or goddess's sweat.

And I was NOT volunteering for sweat collection duty.

Illegal tourist boats sailed the lethal, choppy waters near the island, but they disappeared if they ventured too close. Even if they didn't fall victim to the waters or deadly creatures, there were rumors that the passengers were cursed after just seeing the island.

Rohesia told me one had been maimed by a ravenous bald eagle on his way to work. His liver wasn't the only thing that had been taken from him that day.

Another had lost her ability to speak. Forever. Which was a tragedy given she had been a rising star in Iydara's music scene.

Perhaps the worst, at least in my opinion, was a rumor that a passenger had returned home from the voyage only to be attacked and gnawed on by his own dogs.

The gods were vindictive and creative bastards.

Despite the desperation to find the fulgurite, I was hesitant.

There was a nagging feeling, deep in my soul that had lingered once I had awoken from my semi-comatose state. It was the sense that we were once again barking up the wrong tree. That the fulgurite was not responsible for the creation of the golems.

I just couldn't remember what the real culprit was.

Once I had been thrust back into my torturous memories and flashbacks while my body healed, the thought had slipped out of my fingers like silky strands of rainwater.

To remember the answer to what was creating the golems, I had the undeniable, otherworldly feeling that it would start with me facing my own demons first.

Something I had been avoiding for too long.

Rohesia sighed loudly, putting her head on my shoulder as we watched E.E. and Brooks continue to have it out. It was like watching peacocks fight. All ruffled feathers and squawking sounds.

Now it was my turn to sigh.

It was team Usa, Rohesia, and E.E. against team Brooks. And it was proving to be quite the challenge. While Brooks wanted to travel to Raas, his boss wanted to shut down the investigation entirely.

I understood why, we had screwed up massively by falsely accusing The Collectress. She was a close, personal friend of E.E. and had been furious at him. Details of the case were getting out, mainly on shady conspiracy websites, and humans were beginning to question how safe they were under her reign.

"I can ask my sources in Hecate's First Coven if they know anything. It's a long shot, but they may have some information as to the whereabouts of the fulgurite," Rohesia murmured to me.

It did seem like a long shot.

Even if they did have information on the relic, I wasn't sure they would give it to us. The Collectress had a reputation that could give her almost anything she needed or desired.

Key word being almost.

"Are there any covens that have a vendetta against The Collectress? Maybe her own coven that she left? Could they be behind the golems?"

Abandoning her coven on the bad terms that she did could act as a motive, but mages were normally not so hell-bent on revenge. And it had been years since she left, so why would they act now?

And the golems were abominations of nature, I couldn't picture a coven willingly creating them to take down a former member.

Rohesia contemplated this for a moment, chewing on her bottom lip thoughtfully as E.E. stormed through the room with a phone pressed to his ear.

"I don't think so. Covens are very loyal. Even if a member leaves, they are still considered family. Blood is strong, but the bonds that a coven makes are somehow even stronger," she finally said.

There went that lead.

My stomach clenched at the possibility of the gods being behind the creatures. Could they be punishing her for her recent slip ups while reigning over Iydara?

The Collectress would lose her position in Iydaraian society if it came to light that she wielded magical powers. She might even lose her life. The gods would not stand humans discovering magic, so The Collectress would be dealt with.

Doing so would send a message to all magical beings.

But even gods left an essence when using a large sum of magic, so they would have needed to use the fulgurite as well. And it's not like we could portal up to the heavens and accuse them of such a thing.

The glass door slammed open and a frizzy-haired assistant hurried into the room. She held half a dozen different pagers, remotes, and cell phones in her hands. Each one was buzzing frantically as she turned on the television.

News with Rennyn was broadcasting on Channel 7, and I scrunched my nose with disdain as Rohesia made a gagging noise. Brooks gave us each an incredulous look as E.E. turned up the volume.

"This just in, incredible footage from the Eastern Boundary that finally answers the question, 'are humans really alone?'"

It had always seemed strange to me that Rennyn was a mage but pretended to the world that he was a human.

Then again, I was no better than him.

Screams filled the room as dozens of citizens ran across the screen. The recording was grainy and shaky. Smoke danced in the distance and the sounds of breaking glass resonated in the speakers.

Golems burst through the windows of expensive shops, tackling humans. I could only stare in horror as they left destruction in their wake.

No one could stop them as they trampled dozens of wardens. Mages continued to fight in front of a familiar store with a navy banner and silver script.

Sirens began to screech as Brooks launched himself off his chair. "Is this live?"

The assistant could only nod. Brooks ran across the room with fury written all over his face. Rohesia and I shared a knowing look before following him to the Eastern Boundary.

Once you smelled death, you never forgot it.

It crept into your senses, burrowing into your nostrils and working its way up into your skull, digging its noxious claws into your brain, gouging the organ so you would never forget the smell of rotting flesh.

Death.

That's what Iydara smelled like.

Coppery, foul-smelling blood covered us as we fought our way through the city to De Blasis Bijouterie.

I forced myself to focus on a different sense, to distract myself from the overpowering stench that coated the city like a fine layer of ash.

My wrists were sore from the weight of the sword. Every time I decapitated a golem, my back twinged in pain. Though my broken bones had been healed with magic, my wrist still protested at every slash and stab.

The afternoon sun was still high, causing my skin to prickle and warm, the star refusing to hide as destruction and death reigned in Iydara. Rohesia stayed close to me, burning bodies that I had stoned and decapitated.

We continued to fight, my breath as sharp as a knife being dug into my ribcage. When my physical strength gave out, I tossed the sword to Brooks, who resembled a god with his sweat-covered muscles and honed fighting skills. For a human, he sure didn't act very mortal in battle.

It made me wonder if he had let me tackle him the first night we had met.

My vision wavered as I looked upon the once bustling land. Crimson blood painted the streets, suggesting that there had been more mortal and mage casualties than golem deaths. Glass crunched beneath our feet. I wasn't sure how it could get worse.

Brooks's family store was just beyond reach. Sirens screeched in the air, piercing my eardrums with an eerie lullaby.

Rohesia gathered people into different buildings with her air magic, holding a toddler and baby in her arms as she did so. Brooks was racing towards his cousin, who stood in front of the store, oblivious to the golem that was sneaking up behind her.

Brooks yelled out to her, but she couldn't hear Brooks's pleading over the sounds of death and annihilation.

"Mommy!" her daughter yelled, before being snatched into the arms of the golem. The toddler cried out for Nola, tears cutting paths through a fine layer of dust that had settled on her chubby, round cheeks.

Nola screamed and dropped to her knees but Brooks grabbed her and locked her in the store. Rohesia stayed with the family, defending the storefront with her magic as Brooks and I chased after the golem.

Crowds of golems attacked us, slowing down our pursuit.

I knew we were running out of luck.

And time.

With each street we cleared, our hope seemed to wither as the golem ran further and further away. But still, we ran and ran into the night, desperate to save Nola's daughter.

A golem surged around the corner in front of us, crashing into the monster that was carrying the toddler. The first golem dived in front of the second one, muttering to it in a strange, dark language. They began to wrestle, falling into the street with passing cars and emergency vehicles.

During their struggle, the monster dropped Lilith onto the ground, the child covered in soot and a layer of fine dirt.

Brooks scooped up his cousin in his arms, pressing his mouth to her hair. "Shh…it's okay, Lilith. Everything's okay now."

Her wails quieted as Brooks and I ran away from the golems, our senses running wild. We turned another corner, running past a different jewelry store, when a horrible growl rang through the air.

My skin paled as we were suddenly surrounded by golems.

Brooks placed Lilith in a small and nearly invisible alleyway, telling her to stay there and close her eyes until he or her mother could find her. She pouted but listened to her older cousin anyway.

Brooks and I stood back-to-back, watching as the golems circled us.

"This isn't good," I muttered, watching as the golems crashed into one another to watch our battle.

"Whatever makes you say that?" Brooks asked dryly. Sweat covered our bodies as we attempted to fight off the men and women of stone.

"Oh, nothing really. Just the five golems trying to kill us."

"Actually, it's more like eight," Brooks grunted as he battled with a smaller golem.

"Well, excuse me for not being specific enough," I snapped.

I quickly stoned the golem he was battling and watched as he decapitated the monster in one swift and brutal blow.

Swiping the extra sword from Brooks's back, adrenaline powered my movements as I fought with a massive golem who made Brooks look like a small child.

Running at full speed, I launched myself at the golem, slashing at its head, unleashing weeks of pent-up anger and despair.

After two weeks of being bedridden, the fighting felt good.

The golem easily dodged the blade, pivoting on the ball of his foot. I spun as someone crashed into me. White hot pain flared in my skull as a female golem with rotten teeth knocked me flat on my back. The snow-covered ground did nothing to calm the raging fire in my soul.

The female golem's booted foot kicked out, attempting to pry my sword from my hand. Sweltering pain erupted as she stepped on my hand with the brunt of her body weight, causing my body to jerk.

A tall, gangly golem with stringy blonde hair attacked me from behind, wrapping his forearm around my throat, and the other arm around my waist. I choked and wriggled in his grasp, dropping my sword.

Remembering what my mother had taught me, I stopped struggling and dropped my body weight. I smiled smugly as I slipped through the arm he had wrapped around my waist. The motion caught the golem off guard, allowing me to retrieve my sword.

I saw an opening.

And I took it.

His head landed on the ground and crumbled.

The female golem from earlier sneered at me, having produced a sword of stone out of her own flesh.

Our swords clashed in a deadly exhibition of shining steel and resolve. I let instinct take over and waited until she swung at me. Shooting forward, I raced under her arm, spinning around, and slashing the thin skin of her neck.

She howled in pain. The creature turned, teeth snapping and snarling, murder written on her face. Wardens and mages arrived and fought alongside Brooks and me, slashing and burning every golem in the town.

Swords clashed against one another. Shouts of pain and fury filled the street. Smoke from raging fires and dust from collapsing buildings made it difficult to breathe.

The golems that attacked us were a mix of ones from The Collectress's garden and stone statues that I had not created. This confirmed my worst fears.

There was indeed another gorgon near Iydara.

A heavy arm swung into my gut, launching me into a brick wall. My head smacked against the wall, and I saw stars as the golem advanced on me.

I swung my sword in front of me before it could take another step. But my vision was too blurry to make a clear cut.

"Up and to the left, lovely!" I heard Brooks shout, but he sounded muffled and far away.

I listened to his directions, swinging my sword up, slashing to the left at the final second. I watched with double vision as the golem's body and head dropped to the ground.

Four more stood in front of Brooks.

My ears were ringing, screeching.

No, it wasn't my ears that were screeching.

Crashing down the street was a runaway van. The muffler was scraping across the ground, while a golem manned the vehicle.

I clawed myself up and positioned myself in front of the van, hands shaking and covered in filth and blood as I raised them to the sky. I felt the magic leave the tips of my fingers, encapsulating the van in a tomb of stone as I stared at it. Vines of stone burst through the hood of the van, spreading like a burning wildfire.

Holding my breath, I sent up a silent prayer to the gods.

Maybe they would listen.

Maybe they wouldn't.

Gray stone licked the metal doors and rubber tires in delicious waves. The driver sat motionless as my magic began to trap him in a tomb of stone and pulverized metal. For the first time in years I found comfort in my abilities.

I stood there, entranced by my own magic, as the world burned and froze around me. I had never tried stoning an inorganic object before. As I was unable to stone the golems entirely, I had assumed it would be impossible.

But I was wrong.

Others in my coven hadn't been able to stone inanimate objects, and I wondered if the reason that I was able to was Athena's curse on my soul. Perhaps golems were the exception because they were partially created from my own magic.

Strong arms grasped my waist and pulled.

Brooks and I landed on the ground, grunting as the air was knocked from our lungs. His arms tightened around my waist, pulling me from the path of the vehicle.

We looked on in awe as the van fully became stone, sliding into the other golems and erupting into a jumble of fiery flames and rubble.

Time seemed to still as we watched the fire grow.

"You need to get up, Usa," Brooks murmured into my ear, as the screaming and sobbing slowly came to a halt.

His hands had been tracing circles on my lower stomach, the sensation had distracted me while the fire raged on.

I started to stand, only to be pulled down into his arms once more. "You're holding me down, you idiot."

"So cranky," he teased, his breath hot on my face.

A lingering, crackling tension hung between us.

Things had changed since our midnight conversations while my back healed. There was a certain understanding and warmth that had been previously missing.

And I wasn't sure how to entirely feel about it.

And I wasn't sure if it was from the adrenaline of battle or the fact that we were pressed together, but my breathing became calmer as my back rested flat against Brooks's chest.

We stayed pinned against one another for a few precious moments, borrowing time from the gods that we did not have.

22

The streets were packed with mortals streaming out from half-destroyed buildings, all looking for answers about what had just happened. The world they had known was completely changed.

It was gone, forever drifting on a faraway wind.

Not even The Collectress could contain a disaster as large and deadly as this. Mortals all over Iydara were about to learn that they were indeed not alone. Magic seemed to cling to the air, ready to break free of the confines that had been placed on it for hundreds of years.

I glanced to where my hand was clasped by Lilith's tiny one. She insisted on walking even though Brooks had offered to carry her.

Lilith had the soul of a survivor. Her bottom lip shook but she kept her head held high as we walked down the bloody, burning streets of the Eastern Boundary. She was just like her mother.

Rohesia leapt with joy as we walked around the corner, asking if we were alright and what had happened. I murmured to her that I was fine. That we were all fine.

A crowd had formed outside De Blasis Bijouterie. The saliva dried in my mouth as I noticed a scribbled message on the ground that had been written with crimson blood.

Stop the investigation.

Brooks took a picture of the scrawling message before Rohesia burned the note away with a quick wave of her hand.

"Sure you don't know any other gorgons, lovely?" Brooks asked me, crossing his arms, and raising an eyebrow at me.

At that moment, I regretted lying to him about my past.

Unwilling to lie to him again, I instead focused on my blood- and mud-spattered shoes. Tears welled in my eyes, but I forced them back. I would not let them see me cry.

The detective grabbed my upper arm, pulling me into the bathroom of his family's store. I turned on the sink to drown out the bombshell I was going to drop.

I looked away, dread curling in my gut like sour milk. "Promise me you won't be mad."

The thick clothing I wore was destroyed, covered in rips and tears and blood. My body was aching, but I relished in it. The pain was more pleasant than being stuck in a bed for days.

Brooks had grabbed an ice pack from the freezer and was placing it on a blossoming bruise on his cheek bone. He stared at me as I cleaned a nasty gash on his shoulder.

I started at his neck, wiping specks of blood, his or another's, away with a wet cloth. The wound was deep, with shards of stone embedded deep into his skin.

While I patched him up, he listened to my story and drank liquor out of the bottle. The stoic look on his face only broke when he passed me the clear liquid, and I began pouring the alcohol on his shoulder. He would need stitches, or for Rohesia to heal him with her magic. She and other mages, were tending to others who were more seriously wounded.

I moved onto the back of Brooks's head, where he had been thrown onto the ground by a golem. He hissed in pain as I pulled a chunk of glass out.

I had started at the very beginning: what it had been like to grow up with a loving mother and sisters, how I grew up in a lavish castle with servants and anything I could wish for. My coven had loved me, and I them. I had planned to grow old there and serve the goddess Athena in our temples as a priestess, until the gods called me home to rest.

The conversation had taken a turn when I told him about the curse Athena had placed on me, though she called it a blessing. My voice became mechanical and dull as I told him why she had cursed me, about who had taken my innocence. Brooks promised to put a sword through his chest if he ever laid eyes on the god.

I appreciated the sentiment, but gods couldn't be killed. Especially not by wronged mortals with a thirst for vengeance.

Brooks had been surprised to learn that I was in fact not immortal. Though I was able to change forms, unlike the rest of my coven, there had been a price to pay to achieve a natural balance.

My immortality had been ripped from me.

Gorgons were born immortal and were never supposed to die. We eventually were called home by the gods, but our souls truly never died.

Until me.

I could be killed as easily as any human walking down the street. Even something as mundane as a car crash could take me out.

The vodka burned extra hot when I mentioned that little tidbit. He pulled out an amber liquid, whiskey I realized. Brooks took a swig before handing the bottle to me.

"No wonder you have nightmares. I would too if my family was trying to kill me." He took another swig of whiskey, reminding me of the night we first met.

The liquid tasted pungent and awful as it slowly glided down my throat. It was precisely what I needed. I took another swig, wondering why the gods had cursed me when I had been the perfect devotee. I had never missed a single worship at the temple and prayed eight times a day, like the goddess Athena had said to.

My spiraling thoughts came to a halt as the weight of today began crashing down around me.

This was personal. Someone, most likely another gorgon, had left a bloody note for me.

The bathroom began to spin as I recounted the day's events.

The golems had attacked innocents now. Women, children, men. Their blood spilled because of me. Because I simply existed. Because I didn't have the courage to die for my coven.

I was a coward.

I started to chug the bottle Brooks had given me. He gave me a strange look but didn't seem to be judging me too harshly.

Brooks drank the last of the whiskey, filling up the flask with water from the sink. "If you need to get blackout drunk to process today, even the past few weeks, that's understandable. But there are much better ways to deal with the darkness you're feeling. Methods that aren't self-destructive and harmful to your organs."

He was beginning to sound like my mother.

Ha.

I must be losing it if I was making jokes about my mother.

Narrowing my eyes at him, I crossed my arms in defiance, raising my eyebrows up at him in doubt.

"I mean what I said," Brooks said.

I leaned my head against the wall, eyeing another bottle of whiskey Brooks had pulled out from the cabinet.

"All these attacks, all these deaths, have been because of me. All because I'm a selfish gorgon who refuses to be sacrificed to Athena," I choked back my emotions, "even if it means a better life for my coven. Even if it means my sisters can live the lives they have always dreamed of."

God, I had dreamed of becoming a priestess for Athena. For my coven. I would have dedicated my life to the task. Wasn't dying for my coven the same thing? A task to devote my life to, even if it ended sooner rather than later.

I held onto the liquor bottle, testing the weight of it in my hands.

I loathed Poseidon.

Hated.

And somehow that five letter word wasn't enough to describe the agony and disgust that snaked beneath my skin. It could never describe the utter brokenness.

Iydara had just been on the receiving end of another major attack and somehow, the collapsing and bleeding civilization was not as ruined as I was.

"It was my fault a selfish god couldn't take no for an answer. And trust me, Brooks, I said no. It's my fault for trusting him. Maybe I deserve to die, I am a monster after all." My eyes blurred as I chucked the bottle at the wall, the glass shattering all around the bathroom.

"No."

I raised an eyebrow at him

He tilted his head at me in challenge.

No.

Such a simple, common word.

But in that moment, it made the world tilt on its axis.

"The only real monster is Poseidon," Brooks whispered softly.

Surprisingly, I didn't flinch at his name. Maybe it was the alcohol, maybe it was the bone-chilling numbness that coated my tattered soul. But I didn't begin to question the cause of the reprieve.

"I am just as bad as him. Dozens died today, because of me. How can I keep them safe if I couldn't even save myself?"

There was a long pause.

"Maybe you are a monster," Brooks suggested.

I opened my mouth to agree.

"But maybe we all are."

I knew what he was trying to do, but for some reason, his words infuriated me.

I transformed into my gorgon, snakes spitting.

Backing Brooks into the wall, I placed my hands on either side of his shoulders. "That's where you're wrong, detective. I am *the* monster. I am the one who killed Beresford and all of the others. I am the one who led my coven here. Those who died today, fighting for their lives, while they were just supposed to be out shopping with their families? Their blood is on *my* hands."

He contemplated my words for a second, before brushing a hand across one of my snakes. She gave into his touch and ceased her hissing.

Traitor.

"That's where you're wrong. Their blood is painted on the hands of the criminal behind this mess."

I opened my mouth to argue when my mask finally cracked. Just enough to let Brooks in. Realization dawned on his bruised face.

"What are you so afraid of?"

"Everything!" I yelled, my voice breaking. "Everything, Brooks. I can't breathe, I can't sleep. I can't even walk down the damn street without looking over my shoulder. I'm so afraid that when I fall asleep at night, I'll be back there. And some days, Brooks, some days I wish I would have just let them kill me. It would have saved a lot of lives in the long run."

There.

I had said it. The big and ugly truths that continually weighed me down. I had never said those words out loud. Not to anyone, not even to myself when I was alone in the darkness of my room.

Without saying anything, Brooks enveloped my body in a tight hug. My partner laid his chin on the top of my head, his breathing heavy. I had always craved touch but flinched every time someone offered. In Brooks's arms, I didn't flinch. Instead, I melted into his touch.

"It was never your fault, lovely. Never."

And finally, I broke.

No one had ever said those words to me before. I hadn't realized how much I needed to hear them before today. Poseidon had taken something from me that night, ripped it from me and left me shattered and blood-stained.

"I can't tell you how long it will take to heal. There's no timeline for mending a wound like this, lovely. I know because I have begged for one a million and a half times." Brooks laughed without humor.

"But I will tell you this, take the time you need. Take up space. Scream. Mourn. Laugh. Shout. But never, and I repeat," Brooks gently gripped my chin forcing me to look up at him and meet his simmering blue eyes, "never blame yourself."

And I had always blamed myself.

But in that self-destruction and fear, I had forgotten who I was. I had let the darkness win. Maybe I needed to be broken and bruised to find my strength.

The power I held wasn't one to be taken lightly.

Brooks seemed to sense the shift in me, grinning softly at me. "You feel that power, Usa? Take it. Use it. Become it. And make every person that dared to hurt you fall to their knees."

My breathing steadied and my tears dried.

Brooks began to braid my dirty, bloody hair into two braids.

The motion comforted me, grounded me.

"What do you want, Usa?"

Brooks's question seemed so loaded, but I found myself answering it without hesitation. And most importantly, without shame.

"I want to be a constant reminder that I was not his for the taking. That I belong to no one but myself. Most importantly, I want to go find the bastards behind this and clear my name."

Brooks smiled, flicking the braids over my shoulder. "Then let's go do just that."

23

Here Lies Medusa
Friend, Daughter, and Sister
Cause Of Death: Kraken Bait (Thanks To Her Idiotic Partner, Brooks As-
cian-Otis de Blasis.)
May She Rest in Peace.
Or Pieces (At the Bottom of the Ocean.)

The fabricated photograph of headstone engraving that I had created on my phone, within a matter of minutes, had Rohesia and I in tears. Brooks on the other hand, looked anything other than amused.

Salty sea water sloshed beneath the creaking, algae-covered dock we were standing on, seeming to set the tone for the journey we were beginning.

E.E. had relented after the attack on Iydara, allowing Brooks, Rohesia, and I to follow the lead in Raas. He was feeling more pressure from The Collectress to find the person behind the golems. The Collectress had also been summoned to the heavens by Zeus, which was never a good thing.

If the committee of gods and goddesses found her to be unfit to rule Iydara, she would be kicked from her throne and replaced.

My life had always been hanging by a fraying thread held between her slender hands. With her constant threats to expose my whereabouts to my coven, I often didn't second-guess her commands. But now, her life was on the line and that made me feel a strange sense of giddiness.

Of course there were still the other problems dangling over our heads.

The golems.

If there was indeed another gorgon in Iydara.

The memory I couldn't seem to access.

The trauma caused by a selfish god.

The rioting humans.

Hiding from my coven and escaping Iydara for good.

But, for once, I held a tiny, miniscule sliver of my life in my own hands. And that felt pretty damn great.

Even if I was choosing to venture into monster-infested lands and waters. The realization didn't hit me until we were standing on a sketchy dock in the cover of darkness, waiting for a boat that would take us within swimming distance of Raas's shore.

Brooks and Rohesia reassured me that the beasts that roamed the land and waded beneath the ocean's surface would be sluggish at night, but I couldn't help the flashing images that raced through my mind of a screeching charybdis and fire-breathing dragon-like creature.

"I can't believe we're risking our lives to go to fucking Raas," I muttered beneath my breath.

We could either die from the monsters that lingered on the island and in the surrounding waters or be shot down with a bolt of lightning from Zeus, just to find the real fulgurite that may or may not be there.

Hells, it might not even exist.

It could be a grand fairytale, and we wouldn't know it until we were in the bowels of a bloodthirsty, scaly beast.

Brooks lifted his eyes. "Wouldn't you rather die a glorious, battlefield death at the hands of a magnificent harpy, or die a rather boring one from sitting behind a desk all your life?"

"I'd rather not die at all," I challenged, crossing my arms to fight off the bitter, salty breeze that was assaulting us.

"Then, I dare you to live."

A ghost of a smile tugged at my lips, remembering the night we had met and when he had dared me to stone him. It had been such a random and peculiar statement in the face of death. Brooks's words had taken me off guard that night, and had saved his life in the process.

"If I dare you to take us back to land, will you?" I asked, narrowing my eyes at the detective.

"Not a chance, lovely. Nice try, though," Brooks said, throwing me a wink as we turned around to meet the captain of our ship.

"You've got to be shitting me," Rohesia scoffed, voicing my thoughts as well as hers in one sentence.

Rocking on the choppy waters was a dilapidated dinghy.

The inflatable sides of the vessel were scratched and caked with layers of dried, blackened mud. Discolored patches were scattered across the dinghy's exterior making me question the reliability of the boat.

A far cry from the beautiful ship Brooks had bragged about owning.

I wasn't one for lavish jewelry that glittered in the rays of midafternoon sun nor lavish silks that rivaled the caress of a lover, but I would at least prefer for the walls of my ship to be made out of wood or steel.

Inflatable neoprene plus deadly sea monsters with pointy claws was a recipe for disaster. Much to my surprise, E.E. stepped out of the deathtrap of a boat and handed Brooks four wooden oars. He was drenched in sweat, leading me to believe the motor was unusable.

Sure, I had fought golems and even my own coven and lived to tell the tale, but somehow being a passenger on a questionable-looking dingy and sailing to a forbidden island surrounded by colossal, cruel creatures took the cake.

But I didn't have a choice in the matter.

Not one that meant anything, at least.

It was either chase this lead or face the wrath of my coven, The Collectress, and a handful of angry gods and goddesses.

Monsters in my past.

Monsters in my future.

I couldn't wait for that day that they would all be slayed.

Rohesia and I shared a weighted glance between one another before closing the distance between ourselves and Brooks, who now stood in the boat, offering a hand to E.E. as he joined his employee on the raft.

"Why so glum, lovely?" Brooks asked as he finished helping me into the boat while E.E. helped Rohesia.

"Besides the obvious?" I snorted.

"Yes, besides that," he said, his lip twitching with amusement.

"I've never been on one of these before."

Brooks raised an eyebrow. "A dinghy?"

"A dinghy. Boat. Ship. Raft. All of the above."

E.E. and Rohesia stood on the other side of the vessel, arguing about who would get the oar that didn't have any wooden splinters protruding from the handle.

"Scared?" he asked.

Surprising myself I released a rough laugh, glancing down at my worn black sneakers. "Yeah. Kind of silly of me to be afraid considering all the shit I've been through."

Brooks considered my words and I worried I'd said too much as he continued to busy himself with the dinghy's motor.

That lingering, fiery tension hung between us again.

And I was afraid that every time I showed him a vulnerable, skittish part of me, he would bolt.

But he didn't.

He stayed and gave me an equally vulnerable part in return.

"I think it would be silly not to be afraid. The fear is there for a reason, maybe you should embrace it. Accept it. Thank it. Because it means you're still alive and breathing. It kept you alive for this long, didn't it?"

I pondered his words, considering the possibility of using fear as a tool instead of being hindered by it. The fear from the assault allowed me to be more vigilant and protective of myself. But it also was an obstacle at times.

Fear could be helpful but also a damning hindrance as I still struggled with mistrust and unease around men and my coven. Even from The Collectress and my few friends.

The dismay I felt during my flashbacks often raked down my throat, causing it to bleed and blister, shattering my voice before I could decide what I wanted people to hear.

It robbed me of my voice.

"Sure, the fear reminds me that I am alive. And I'm grateful for that, but I'd rather have it not control me," I responded.

"Losing control and willingly surrendering control are two different things. The second is much more helpful than the first."

"How do you surrender control, then?"

A loud mechanical shrieking sound interrupts Brooks's reply.

"Well, well, she graces us with her presence at last." E.E. clapped, chucking his oar overboard in his barely contained excitement.

"Now what are you going to use to fight off the monsters, E.E.?" I chuckled, wiping my sweaty hands on the front of my jeans.

E.E. paled, watching with great despair and sadness as his oar and weapon slowly drifted away.

Before he could dive into the water, Rohesia used her magic to slowly bring the oar back.

He was practically beaming when Rohesia handed it back to him, algae covered and all. The man even went as far as to offer it to Rohesia, who gladly took it since it was the one without splinters.

"There you go girl," Brooks gently said to the boat, as he set our course to Raas.

"Does she have a name?" I asked.

"No, she doesn't. I was going to name her after my sisters, but…" Brooks swallowed, my heart aching as I recounted the story about his sisters disappearing.

Brooks's face fell for a fraction of a second, before he continued. "But, that felt too final. Too definite that they would never be coming back."

"What about"—I paused for a second, considering how stupid I might sound—"hope. Hope that they will come back one day?"

"Hope?" he said slowly, enunciating the singular syllable in the word as though he was speaking an unfamiliar language.

A second passed between us and I started to redact my statement as a wide grin spreads on his face. "I like the premise of it. But I had something even better in mind."

He's standing behind me now, close enough that the heat from his body was saturating me, warming me up in ways I didn't know were possible.

"What's that?" I asked as his breath tickled my ear.

He placed his hands on my hips and turned me around, a wicked gleam in his eye.

"Kraken Bait."

A raucous laugh bubbled from my lips; my fake cause of death had been death by Kraken.

"So is that how you face your fears? Head on and without an ounce of regret?" I teased him, poking at his chest.

"I think you mean the art of surrendering control," Brooks stated with a knowing smirk.

I shook my head at him, turning away to gaze into the water.

Raas was alluring.

There was no other way to describe it. The island was a growing speck in the distance, one I could thankfully see with my gorgon's night vision, as I gave directions to Brooks, E.E., and Rohesia.

Brooks had killed the motor perhaps thirty minutes ago, not wanting to draw the attention of the monsters that lingered beneath the surface.

The trio had been slowly paddling in weighted silence as we crept upon Raas, as if we were silently trying to prove to the island that we were a predator circling its prey, and not the other way around.

"Stop," I whispered, touching Rohesia's shoulder.

Her jaw clenched, but otherwise she stayed still, her oar completely motionless in the water beside her.

I wasn't sure what I was looking for, but I could *feel* it. Another monster. Maybe even another gorgon. Something was lingering beneath the ocean as we sluggishly paddled our way to Raas.

But without any visual on the monster, we were as good as dead.

I silently nodded my head at the three pairs of eyes staring at me. The soft sound of their paddling surrounded me as I continued to scan the area for potential targets.

The minutes were endless.

The seconds were heavy.

A tortuous cycle; stopping, starting, holding our breath.

But not quite as torturous as making landfall without a singular sighting of a monster. The egging feeling that we were still being hunted didn't go away as we departed the boat.

"Shit," Rohesia groaned, her knees hitting the ground as our feet touched the forbidden black sands of Raas.

My knees collapsed a second after hers, a splitting headache causing my vision to waver. Pressure built in my chest, heavy and terrifying. My breath came out in short, gasping wheezes.

E.E. smartly stayed in the boat, his mouth pressed into a firm line and eyes wide.

Failing to reach Rohesia in my sudden panic, my arms collapsed beneath the weight of my body. Gritty sand crunched between my teeth as I lay face down in the sand.

This was it.

I was going to die at the hands of some pissed off, magical island. And then as soon as the thoughts appeared, I could breathe again.

"What the—" I gasped for air, clawing at my throat.

"Fuck," Rohesia finished for me, eyeing the saltwater with a ferocious thirst.

"That's just a taste of what happens when you step onto the island without some of this in your possession," Brooks stated, holding a vial of one of the gods' sweat in his hand.

Dammit.

I'd been so focused on the beasts beneath the water that I had forgotten about the greedy and prideful ones in the sky.

Patting my jacket pocket, I found my matching vial still there.

"But we had their damn sweat!" Rohesia panted, clutching her own sweat filled vial with ire and disbelief.

"The first visit is always the hardest. The gods do that every time we visit, even if we have the desired extract. Just to remind us of who is in charge and what they could do to us if we disobey," Brooks said rather bitterly, glaring up at the twinkling night stars as if they were the gods themselves.

"You could have warned us," I said, my voice cracking from dry air and panic I had felt moments before.

"Consider it a rite of passage." Brooks shrugged, going to help E.E. to shore as Rohesia and I attempted to calm ourselves.

Noticing that the so-called rite of passage hadn't happened to Brooks, I was tempted to call him out on his bullshit. Though E.E. was dry heaving, it made me wonder how many times Brooks and his boss had been here to not have been attacked as brutally by the wrath of the gods.

Apparently Rohesia had the same thought as me.

"How many times have you been to Raas?" she yelled, angrily stomping to where E.E. was dry heaving.

"A handful or so," E.E., snapped back, wiping the back of his hand across his mouth.

What had they been looking for?

The fulgurite?

Brooks's sisters?

"Then why did you not warn us!" Rohesia said once again, rummaging through her bag in a frenzy.

"Like Brooks sai—"

"E.E., don't even start with that egotistical bullsh—"

Turning around, I cringed at the volume of Rohesia and E.E.'s bickering, trusting that the monsters and beasts of this island would be too sleepy to desire a snack of our flesh and bones.

Though I was jealous and annoyed about the detective's lack of reaction to the potent magic of the island, and the lack of a warning, we were running on borrowed time. The best window of opportunity we had to find the fulgurite would be between the hours of midnight and sunrise, when most of the beasts would be in a restful, and hopefully deep slumber.

"Let's go find Zeus's Fulgurite," I said, checking the straps on my daggers and pack.

"Yes, lead the way." Rohesia motioned towards E.E. and Brooks, the men smartly avoiding her wrathful gaze.

Sand crunched beneath my sneakers as the detectives guided our party into a thicket of brush at the base of rolling black sand dunes. The dark sands glittered beneath the soft moonlight and I could only imagine that the sands would resemble crushed, sparkling diamonds when the sun was at its highest point.

Too bad we wouldn't be here to see it.

Brooks hadn't specified where his source said the fulgurite was located; though the island wasn't vast or grand like Iydara, it would still take us days to search the entire thing if we couldn't pinpoint its location.

And we were desperate to find this relic.

If we didn't, we weren't sure what else was creating the golems. The nagging feeling that we were missing something hadn't gone away since the last branding The Collectress had performed on me. I wasn't sure it was a relic anymore, but I didn't know what else it could be.

Not unless I could access my dreams.

"Did your source say where the fulgurite was? Perhaps near a landmark? I'd rather not have to dig around in this giant sandbox all night long," I told Brooks and E.E., adjusting the straps that were beginning to dig into my shoulders.

The pair shared a weighted look and ignored my questions.

Annoyance flourished in my belly at being so blatantly dismissed. Given Rohesia's deepening frown lines, she wasn't impressed, either.

"Do you guys know where it is?" I asked, this time with more volume and with a harsher tone.

Silence greeted me once again.

Grinding my molars, I rolled the muscles in my neck.

Sure, Brooks and I had a heart to heart, but that didn't give him the right to ignore me. Suddenly, I was overcome with the desire to remind him that I held my own power and was never going to hand it over to someone else ever again.

I was claiming it back and I'd be damned if I let anyone, even a detective with baby blues and a nice ass, treat me like an annoying bug flying around his face.

Snatching a dagger from my thigh, I deftly threw it into the air, aiming for the outside of Brooks's right ear. The blade swiftly careened through the air, only to be grabbed inches from my target by Brooks as he turned around to face me.

My eyebrows raised and my stomach dropped.

That was fast.

"Maybe find a new party trick sometime, lovely? Perhaps a bow and arrow would make this trip much more entertaining," he told me, throwing the blade back at me with a surprising amount of force.

"I bet watching E.E. take that enormous stick out of your ass would be even more entertaining," I snapped, crossing my arms.

Brooks glared at me before turning quickly on his heel.

"Easy there, Rook," E.E. said softly. The latter was now climbing up the sand dunes at an alarmingly quick speed.

Rohesia grabbed my wrist as she lost her footing in the deep sands. But I saw the questions and concerns in her eyes. There were many swirling around my mind as well.

Brooks was acting...strange.

Or was this just a side of him I didn't know about?

"It will be okay," I whispered, "they're probably just stressed about the case."

"Stress doesn't make mortals that fast. If it did, then the barista in the Hub would have my caramel macchiato in my hands before I paid, instead of ten minutes after," she said.

We continued to follow behind the pair cautiously, me watching Brooks and Rohesia watching E.E. They were whispering to one another, looking back at us every thirty seconds or so, and then glancing at the sky after studying us.

For the first time in weeks, I found myself wishing that we were in the safety of The Collectress's mansion.

After about an hour of tense and thigh burning hiking, we made it to the crest of the southernmost dune. It was the smallest out of a dozen or so that formed a semi-circle around a smoldering caldera.

"Why haven't we seen any beasts yet?" I asked Rohesia, as we closed in on the last fifty yards separating our party of four.

"Maybe because we're already with them," she carefully breathed, gesturing towards Brooks and E.E.

Suddenly, I was worried.

We didn't know much about the pair in front of us. Sure we'd been working with them for almost two months, but we didn't really *know* them.

The duo had stopped conversing and were looking up at the stars as if we were on a stargazing expedition during vacation.

As we came to stand by the waiting detectives, a strange humming reverberated through the sands beneath our feet. Piles of sand began to shift precariously, causing our balance to lessen.

Grabbing Rohesia's hand, we started to run.

And then we were falling.

Abrasive grains of sand battered my senses as we plummeted beneath the dunes of Raas. We slid, and slid, and slid, into darkness. Crumbling earth scratched at my already stinging skin. I wouldn't be surprised to find a gathering of fire ants munching on my body.

Air was difficult to come by.

Every breath was paired with a handful of grainy sand, feeling as though I was swallowing hot, burning steel nails.

I refused to let my senses leave me.

Surrender control.

My gorgon easily let go, giving into the frightening sensations instead of flailing my arms and screaming like the human part of me wanted desperately to do.

Tumbling through the dunes reminded me of the tunnels and passageways in Marren's Grove, more specifically the waterway that led to the black market. Except, these passageways were disintegrating and imperfect, riddled with holes that pulled me and Rohesia into different directions.

I wasn't sure where Brooks and E.E. had been pulled to.

The tunnel spat me out rather unceremoniously onto my backside, causing a shooting pain to zap up my spine.

Gagging, my teeth crunched on bits of sand, tasting ash and smoke. Peeling my eyes open, I expected to see darkness and empty tunnels, instead blue glowing lights lined the low-hanging ceiling, creating a perfect map of the constellations.

Unsure of how far I was beneath the dunes, I ran my hands over the mud packed walls, bewildered when my fingertips dug into the dirt and brushed against cold metal.

"Lovely!"

Shit.

Giving the tiny room a cursory glance, I clenched my jaw when I found nowhere to go. I couldn't hide beneath the dunes, not when the room I found myself in was lined with steel.

If I couldn't hide, I would need to be on the offense.

A door was closed to my left, with a small entryway before it, perhaps six feet long. Enough space to open the door and walk a few steps before entering the nine-by-nine room.

Smiling, I knew what to do.

The doorknob started to rattled as someone, I was guessing Brooks by his nonchalant voice and enticing essence, was starting to open the door. I would have seconds to pull this off.

My body warmed as magic pulsated throughout me.

Touching the door, I watched in equal parts joy and despair as it turned to stone and started to fall on Brooks. He gruffly grunted and reached out to catch the falling door out of instinct. Letting gravity do her bidding, the now solid stone door began its descent on his left arm and shoulder.

It would trap him rather effectively and painfully.

Or it would have, had he not bolted backwards and slammed himself against an adjacent wall. Fast yet again.

The stone door crumbled as it crashed against the metal flooring, scattering chunks outwards. One scratched my leg, but I was too furious and mentally wounded to be bothered by the pain.

This was another case of mistrust.

The people that were supposed to help me and protect me were ultimately the ones that hurt me.

My mother, sisters, The Collectress, the gods and goddesses in the sky. And now Brooks and E.E. I wouldn't let him hurt Rohesia and me.

Launching myself at Brooks, I swung my arm back, aiming for his normally attractive face. I usually caught myself stealing glances at the sharp angles of his face.

But now, his good looks just pissed me off.

It seemed that the nastiest snakes wore the prettiest of skins.

Catching my fist, he yanked my arm, twisting it. He did it gently, not causing me pain, which only made me even more angry with him. Brooks's calculating eyes found mine, glittering with a fiery rage.

"I'm going to *murder* you!" I hissed, swinging my leg at him, hoping to connect with flesh.

"Don't threaten me with a good time." Brooks laughed darkly, blocking my kick with his forearm. Grabbing my ankle, he spun me around pulling my leg towards him hard and fast.

His eyes were doing the strange glowing bit that I had seen every so often. In the past, I had thought it had been weird lighting or my eyes playing tricks on me. Now, I knew that Brooks had been the one playing tricks and not my eyes.

I should have trusted my instincts.

Frustrated, I growled, launching myself at him again.

Soon, it became obvious that he had been holding back the night we met, which only infuriated me even more. Every kick or punch I threw at him, he easily redirected or blocked.

Brooks never stopped playing defense, and I wasn't sure if that was a testament to my fighting skills or his.

There was one thing I could do that he couldn't stop.

The thought of it made me sick.

But I had to, my life and Roehsia's were counting on it.

And I needed to find my friend and the fulgurite soon.

After a round of punches and kicks, I threw a knife at him, watching as it cut the delicate skin of a high cheekbone.

The knife embedded itself into the wall behind him.

Brooks leaned against the wall, running his thumb over the carved handle of the dagger. He looked positively indifferent, glowering at the blade as if the inanimate object was at fault for the situation the detective presently found himself in.

He fought off attack after attack, until I was spent.

Currently, I was on my back, staring up at the ceiling of constellations. The lights seemed to be fueled by magic, given the dusty hue and ethereal aura around them, perhaps the makings of a mage or fairy.

Sniffing the air gently, I laughed humorlessly.

Warm cinnamon, bitter orange, a bit of rotting flesh, and something else, something deeper. A scent I noticed before on him and Nola, but had been too careless and occupied to investigate.

It was one I hadn't discovered before encountering him.

The earthiness of the scent reminded me of the sands we currently were trapped beneath. Ashen and burnt.

Could Brooks have ties to Raas? Was that why I had never smelled an essence quite like his before?

An essence could also tell you a lot about a person.

What their personality was like, their fears and desires, where they were from. Silently, I continued to study Brooks's essence, coaxing the magic forward at my own will.

It was like petting a scared, orphaned puppy in the middle of a dank and dark alley. Each one was different and hesitant, I just had to find what calmed them.

My essence reached out to Brooks, curling and dancing around the strange aura. Pain erupted from my temple as my essence brushed up against his.

Okay.

Not physical touch.

Cornering the beast would be of no help to me.

Maybe I had to gain its trust instead.

Lowering my essence to the ground, I hummed as it flattened out, swirling and shimmering, as if to say, 'I'm not going to hurt you. It's okay.'

Glancing at Brooks, I found him still glaring at the dagger, waiting for my next attack. He wasn't aware that he was already ensnared in it.

His essence was hesitant, but curious. It carefully circled mine, leaving a trail of his memories and previous thoughts. My essence picked one up, but not before a wave of memories hit me suddenly, leaving me panting for air.

The bite of cold steel pressed against my neck, over and over again. Drawing my blood for every mistake. Every failure. Until I was deemed not enough and they sent me away.

Nausea rolled through me, forcing me to my side. The room spun and—

Agony. Burning. My veins were on fire.

Sweat dripped down my face, blurring my eyes. Brooks was in front of me, with a concerning amount of panic on his angular face. He was talking to me, shaking me but I didn't hear him.

Magic, dark and inky filled my bones. It felt wrong. All of this. I listened to Yandi, who's comforting words reassured me time and time again. She said I could do this. For them. Even as noxious black smoke poured from my mouth, I believed her.

The rolling nausea came to a grinding halt as my essence scurried back to me, dropping the intense memories with an exhausted hiss.

Brooks was still gripping my arms, concern contorting his features.

I scoffed.

As if he actually cared about my safety.

A thud resonated near the entrance, causing Brooks to push my stumbling form behind his. Multiple individuals walked in, or was it just one?

My vision was still swimming from the attack of Brooks's memories on my essence. Fighting against the tide, I stood next to Brooks, resting a hand on the dagger on my hip.

A defeated sigh left me.

It wasn't Rohesia nor E.E. who stood at the door.

The woman appeared to be my great grandmother's age, with thin, red hair that was peppered with gray, and wrinkles that told stories of youthful innocence and perseverance.

"Brooks! 'Bout time you showed up," the woman cheerfully said, slapping the detective on the back.

So this was the friend that had a connection to Zeus's fulgurite? Why didn't Brooks just tell us that we had to freefall through a sketchy underground, secret tunnel?

I still didn't understand why there were people here, when the gods said there were only monsters and demons on the island. Humans we found, monsters and demons not so much.

Gods, I needed to find Rohesia and get out of here. I had too many questions and not enough answers.

The pair of old friends continued to converse for a few moments, forgetting I was there.

I'd be damned if I was going to be ignored as well as kept out of the loop.

"Hi, I'm Usa. Who are you? Dear Brooks, here, is shit at communicating." I stretched out my hand to the woman who shook it eagerly, the crow's feet at her eyes crinkling.

Brooks looked at me with a clenched jaw.

Good.

"Nice to know that some things never change. The name is Yandi, I'm Brooks's old mentor."

The shock on my face is well hidden as I drop her hand.

Yandi.

227

That was the name in Brooks's memory, the one that made him do something painful and excruciating. The one that marred his neck with cut after cut.

But he seemed willing, I shouldn't forget that.

"Well, let's not keep your friends waiting. Especially the one with the tattoos, she has been quite vocal," Yandi said matter-of-factly, disappearing around the corner and slipping into muted darkness.

A sigh fell from my lips.

Rohesia was okay.

She would be giving whoever was in charge hell, and I had to smile at that.

Brooks followed Yandi, as I fell into step behind him, silent.

"I can only imagine what kind of plans you're creating in that lovely head of yours. I would be sorely disappointed if you weren't coming up with one way or another to stone or kill me," he whispered.

"Bleeding," I say.

He paused for a second, quipping an eyebrow at me, repeating what I said, "Bleeding."

"Stoning you would be the easy way out, and killing you would only give me short, disappointing satisfaction." I looked him up and down for emphasis. "So I'm thinking of all the ways I can make you bleed."

"Is that so?" Brooks asked, his brow rising ever so slightly.

I nodded, watching the different constellations in the ceiling, naming them as we walked past.

Andromeda.

Orion.

Boötes.

"So where's the fulgurite?" I asked Brooks, watching as Yandi took another turn. We had been walking for at least five minutes, turning into a different passageway every hundred yards or so.

"Patience, lovely."

"Patience, seriously? As if I would give you that when you have been so cryptic," I retorted.

"And trust." His throat bobbed as eyes clashed with mine.

"You had my trust once, Brooks. Something as valuable as that should be cherished, but you stomped it into the fucking ground like every other bastard in Iydara."

This time, he didn't see me coming as I pushed him into a pile of sand and held a dagger to his throat, making good on my promise that I would make him bleed.

We were running on borrowed time to find the damned statue. The Collectress would do much worse than scorching our skin if we did not return with the fulgurite.

It was the answer to the golem problem.

But even as I silently told myself that, I knew it was a lie.

Just like the lie I had believed for weeks.

That the man I was straddling cared about me.

Little did Brooks know that I would refuse to be that woman again, the one that fell into trusting traps so easily, with glittering eyes and saccharine smiles.

That woman had once thought that bowing down every morning before a glowing, orange sunrise in the fantastic temples, praying to gods who supposedly heard her, would solve the answers to all of her problems. That same woman had also been convinced that the roughness of life would bury her in the tomb that Poseidon had gouged into the blood-soaked ground for her.

But it hadn't.

She had been born for this.

For the cruelness and hardships of life.

This wasn't the end.

This was a rebirth.

"The way I see it, Brooks," I pressed the knife with greater force, "earning anyone's trust isn't just a singular event. It's a constant push and pull, one you seem to have miraculously failed at. Now, give me one good reason I shouldn't kill you right here, right now?" I lowered my lips to his ear. "Because I think red just happens to be your color."

His low chuckle skittered across the skin of my thighs, snaking its way up my spine and into my ear, as if he were murmuring indecent thoughts to me like a passionate lover.

"Funny, I've thought the same thing about you," he said, dragging his thumb across my lip, smudging my signature crimson lipstick.

This side of him was different.

Rougher around the edges.

It reminded me of when my gorgon came out to play.

My breathing hitched as his thumb continued to drag further south, past my bottom lip and chin.

"As for a legitimate good reason…" He paused to smear the stain of lipstick down my throat, his fingers skittering across my pulse. "I'm trusting you with my life right now, Usa. I won't try to make you understand me or try to justify my reasons, because there are some things that I just can't tell you."

His mysterious words snapped me out of the trance his touch was beginning to place me in. I slapped his hand away.

"That's the thing, Brooks! Justify your reasons. Explain to me what in god's name is going on. You want my trust again? Then earn it. What's with the secrecy? And where are the damned monsters? Why are we here, and don't say it's to find the fulgurite. Don't lie to me again." My eyes burned as I bit down on my lip to keep the tears at bay, ignoring the coldness that came from his hand dropping from my face.

"I never lied to you, lovely, and I certainly never intended to hurt you," Brooks said gently, his eyes filled with a deep hurt and longing that mirrored my own tattered soul.

I scoffed, shaking my head. "Oh, because you lied by omission? Skirting around the truth is worse than lying straight to my damned face. It's like stabbing someone and wiggling the blade around for funsies."

He opened his mouth to speak, but I placed the blade on his mouth, before more lies could spill from his full lips. "And it doesn't matter that you didn't intend to hurt me, Brooks. The point is that you *did*."

"I'm not expecting you to understand, but Usa, I didn't lie to you. Sure, I danced around the truth. But that was to *protect* you," he told me in a hushed voice, "and as far as hurting you, you're right. I might not have intended to hurt you, but I still did, and I am deeply apologetic for that."

"Protect me from what?" I whispered.

"That's what you're going to have to trust me about and I will trust you with my life in return." He stretched an arm to reach an inner pocket of his jacket, pulling out a vial of cloudy liquid.

His way back into Iydara.

He pressed it into my hand, squeezing it so tightly I was surprised it didn't shatter in my palm.

He was trusting me with his life.

Without the vial, he would be trapped on Raas indefinitely.

"Fine," I snapped, "but I need answers soon."

"That's what we came here to get."

I offered my hand to him as I stood. He rubbed his throat, and shame curled in my belly as I watched him smear his blood across his skin.

I added another mark to his already scarred neck.

That thought haunted me as I followed him down the hallway of stars.

24

"And that one's a harpy, kinda unpleasant looking if you ask me. But better dead than chasing us on the island, I suppose," Rohesia informed me cheerfully.

I stood next to Rohesia and E.E. in an elegantly furnished, grand room filled with carved pillars of black sand. The pillars towered above us, spiraling towards the apex of the vaulted ceiling, resembling a chilling thicket of scorched trees.

In a way, the pillars of darkness were eerily breathtaking. The sands they were constructed of glittered beneath the low light of the room, catching my eye with every minute movement. It was like these hidden chambers beneath the sands were created by the stars themself.

Pure and untainted.

The only indication of maliciousness were the dozens of mounted, taxidermy monster and demon heads lining the sparkling walls.

Harpies, chimera, sirens, and many more beasts were hammered to the walls, their grotesque faces stilled by death. It was no wonder we hadn't found any monsters while above ground, most of them seemed to have met their fate at the hands of Yandi and her students.

"And that's when Brooks roundhouse kicked the ghastly Oneiroi while I drove a sword through its mushy brain," Yandi crooned, slapping Brooks on the back while he smiled tightly at his mentor.

There was an air of tension among the pair, an invisible barricade that seemed unscalable. Yandi looked to be forcing a sense of comradery with big smiles and outlandish stories of the past, while Brooks was more reserved and methodical, looking around the room as though he was haunted by the same past that Yandi was jovially conversing about.

Rohesia threw me a weighted look, conveying her thoughts to me in the silent way of hers. Our gazes shifted between one another and the anchored monster heads.

Brooks, Yandi, and the others had killed multiple demons and monsters, all while being human.

It should be impossible.

Unless they weren't human.

Not entirely at least.

Reaching out my essence towards Yandi's, I circled it carefully, a woodsy scent penetrating my nostrils almost simultaneously as the ashen and burned scent.

The latter was the same as the unknown scent that was tied to Brooks's and Nola's essences.

Apparently, Yandi had it too.

They had to be connected to Raas, somehow.

Caressing Yandi's essence with mine, I was surprised to find that hers was a kaleidoscope of deep magenta and bright tangerine. Balmy air wrapped around my shoulders and I soon found myself dropping my shoulders and the creases between my brow unfurrowing. The knots of tension in my neck melted away as I pulled her essence closer towards mine.

Rohesia's voice became muffled as I dug deeper, memories flashing past me in a great blur. Usually, I could grasp them, but I was barreling out of control, spiraling into an abyss. Stumbling, my vision continued to waver and blur before the colors of Yandi's essence enveloped me.

Bile coated my mouth as the world tilted sideways and razor-sharp agony assaulted my knees as they buckled beneath me.

The spinning ceased.

Now, brilliant and dazzling colors were muddied and dull.

Yandi stood in front of me, my vision fracturing, causing three of her to appear in front of me. Her voice scratched at my brain, wrong and unwelcome.

Memories appeared in front of us, projecting against the wall of the desolate room we were in. They flickered with varying shades of light and darkness.

Only they weren't Yandi's memories.

They were mine.

Three girls with snakes for hair jumped on a fluffy bed, hitting one another with down pillows. A singular feather landed near the open, arched window, twirling in the soft autumn light. A knock on the door caused the girls to twitter beneath their breaths while shushing each other as the door creaked open. An adult gorgon appeared, the woman's eyes twinkled with amusement as she assessed the trio, before launching herself at them with her own pillow. Shrieks echoed in the room.

My mind wasn't my own anymore. I could *feel* Yandi's parasitic presence deep in my bones, causing them to ache and burn.

Before I could calm my vision and throw up my mental walls, we were hurled into a different memory.

A handprint burned my cheek. My mother scowled at me from where she was pacing in a tight circle, her lips pressed tight. "Medusa," she demanded, "do better. You will not disappoint this family again."

"Yandi, STOP!" I screeched, yanking at my scalp as we tumbled deeper and deeper into my mind.

Pine needle-encrusted snow soaked my feet, causing them to be numb and burn simultaneously as I ran for my life. Frozen air coated my lungs as I gulped down clean, mountain air.

Dammit!

I needed to stop Yandi before she dove any further, before she uncovered Athena's curse and my coven's need to sacrifice my bloody body beneath a full moon.

Rohesia stood in the arched doorway of the apartment, her lips pursed as she looked at the bed. I lay there, unconscious and flailing about. My friend walked to my side, placing a hand on my forehead, muttering a curse at the blazing heat my body was producing. She gently brushed a curling tendril from my sweat drenched face. Speaking softly, a golden light radiated from her fingertips. I sighed as she drew a symbol on my forehead, becoming still and content beneath her touch. I rested.

We were no longer trapped in my memories. Now, we ripped through my subconscious mind that held dormant thoughts and dreams. Pushing against Yandi's colorful essence, I backed it into a wall, wrapping tendrils of my evergreen aura around hers, forcing it to become smaller and smaller. But not before she yanked one last bit of my mind towards her.

Pungent oils glistened on my branded back in low light, as Brooks stomped out of the room and a tear rolled down my cheek. Leaning closer to my past self, I noted the dark circles beneath her puffy eyes and the anger simmering beneath her skin. She began to fall asleep, but not before mumbling to herself in a dreamy haze.

I stepped closer.

She whispered it again.

Potion.

Gasping, my eyes shot open as I looked up at the constellation lit ceiling, while a rough hand grabbed my shoulder.

I pivoted to find it was Brooks's hand clenched to me. Rohesia stood off to the side, her wide-set eyes brimming with unshed tears.

"What happened?" I croaked.

"You passed out," Rohesia said protectively, placing an arm around my waist and leading me to a velvet chaise. Leaning into the plush seat, I scanned the room searching for the woman who violated my mind just moments ago.

Yandi and E.E. were no longer here.

"Yeah." I blinked, taking a shaky breath.

"Rohesia, could you go get E.E. and Yandi, tell them that we don't need the tonic," Brooks ordered.

Rohesia ignored him, looking at me instead.

I dipped my chin at her and smiled, watching as she hesitantly left the room, searching for Yandi and E.E.

"What really happened there, lovely?" Brooks asked, handing me a glass of water.

"I passed out," I said nonchalantly, sitting straighter while clutching an embroidered pillow tightly to my chest.

"I saw that." He ran a hand over his head, clearly not buying the 'it's not a big deal' act.

"Look, I'm fine," I showed him my palms, "not even a scratch."

The room was still spinning, but I chose to keep that to myself. Gulping down the chilled water, I chewed on my lip, my nervous thoughts a mess.

Yandi delved into my memories and I wasn't strong enough to stop her. Unease settled in me. That had only happened previously with gorgons in my coven.

But she isn't a gorgon, I would sense if she was.

"Usa, there's something you need to kno—"

Yandi, E.E., and Rohesia entered the room, laughing and talking as though nothing was amiss, as though Yandi didn't just invade my mind and being.

What did she want?

"Feeling any better there?" Yandi asked me, her gray eyes squinting with care. But there was a challenge there, too. Daring me to confront her.

She was proud of her actions.

"Just a raging headache, like someone hurled a dagger into my skull. You wouldn't know anything about that, would you?"

Yandi narrowed her eyes for a split second, but it was all I needed to launch my essence into hers and enter her thoughts.

Potion. Potion. Potion. Potionnnn—

"I know nothing of headaches, but I know everything there is about potions," she grunted, "that's what is causing your golem problem."

"It's not the fulgurite?" Rohesia questioned, crossing her arms skeptically.

"No, I saw it in Medusa's mind. When you were healing, your subconscious put the pieces together. You should be thanking me," she accused, her nasally voice defensive.

"You what?" Brooks snapped, his face darkening.

"Relax, Rook, not like I hurt her or anything."

Yet.

Her silent threat was as clear as a cloudless sky.

"The subconscious mind is much more powerful than the conscious mind, capable of solving intricate puzzles that would otherwise stump our cognizant selves." Yandi's gray eyes were as cruel as a winter snow squall as she shrugged.

"Well, thanks for your gracious help, Yandi. We will be in touch," E.E. crooned, forever the peacemaker and voice of reason.

"Nonsense," Yandi waved him off, "we haven't even had breakfast yet."

At her command, bustling servants swarmed in, carrying platters of sizzling cuisine and sloshing glasses of wine. Though I had just got my ass handed to me by Yandi's essence, I reached mine out, searching while we were seated at a wooden table.

I sat between Yandi and Rohesia, while Brooks and E.E. sat across from us. The tension and discomfort in the room only amplified as we were served bloody slabs of meat.

Pivoting in my creaking wooden seat, I caught the eyes of my server, only to be met with black, pupil-less eyes. My essence instinctively reached out, circling him.

But there was nothing, just emptiness.

Expanding my grasp, I checked the other servants, only to find that they too did not have an essence. They were without souls.

Tightening my grip on my knife, I pushed my food around my plate, keeping my defenses up as the soulless servants continued to circle around us.

"It could be her coven," E.E. suggested, waving a bloody knife in the air.

Brooks sat back in his seat with his arms crossed, his food untouched, frowning at whatever turn the conversation had just taken.

"No, The Collectress's coven wouldn't have the resources for those tonics," Rohesia argued, stabbing the grisly meat in front of her with a fork.

The potion.

Like a relic, a potion wouldn't leave an essence when used, and they were more handy and inconspicuous than a treasured fulgurite.

"The Collecress's coven, Hecate's Seventh Coven, lingers at the very top of the Anghor Peaks. While Hecate's First Coven makes tonics and ointments, Hecate's Seventh Coven singularly provides Iydara with a variety of garments, spices, and only a handful of healing tonics," Yandi chimed in, red coating her white teeth.

My heart sank at her words.

"But," she cut a slice of meat, "each of the four covens in Iydara are trained in the world of tonics, potions, and ointments. It could be any coven or mage that The Collectress made angry. Or even a rogue mage."

"Rogue mages?" E.E. asked.

"Mages who have left their covens of their own free will, like The Collectress. Most of them are in search of strength, money, and authority. They call themselves Hecate's Ninth Coven, which is ridiculous given Hecate only has eight covens, with the First, Fifth, and Seventh living in Iydara. Hecate's Ninth Coven is hidden all around Iydara, looking for an opportunity to steal The Collectress's power. Many of them are envious of her position and mad at how she treats them. Or rather, ignores them," Rohesia finished for Yandi, her gaze distant and far-off.

"It would be smart of them. Capture The Collectress's attention by creating a potion that could unstone her precious statues. All the while creating an army that may overtake her and capture the attention of the gods," Brooks agreed reluctantly, earning a bloody, beaming smile from Yandi.

And finding out what the potion was made out of could help us find the source of the materials and then link it back to the supplier and coven.

"What supplies would you need to make a potion like that?"

Rohesia let out a frustrated sigh. "I'm not sure. I haven't made a potion in over four decades. And I've never constructed a potion as heinous as that one."

Mages were very adamant about keeping a natural balance in the lands. Any creation that went against the natural order of life was an abomination. I'm guessing that included the golems.

Rohesia's disgust with whatever mage was creating the golems was clear. My heart ached for my friend.

"We'll find them," I assured her, taking her hand in mine.

"It's not them that I'm worried about." She gave me a measured look.

We had talked about my involvement in the case and what would happen to me if I failed. The Collectress was ready to hand me over to my coven if we couldn't find the person responsible for creating the golems.

"You should be worried, Medusa," Yandi sang, tracing her knife with a fingertip, "very, very worried."

Before I could react, she grabbed her knife with otherworldly speed and thrusted it into the back of my hand, cutting through tendon, flesh, and bone. Vise-like arms wrapped around my neck, cutting off my air supply.

Black and white spots infiltrated my vision as my chair was toppled over and I was thrown into the air. A cracking sound resonated in my ears as my head smacked the wall, Yandi's knife still protruding from the back of my hand. Blood dripped from my skin, forming small craters in the sandy floor.

Clenching my teeth, I hissed in pain and rage as I pulled the knife from my hand, firing it at Yandi's bitter face. My aim was true as the bloody blade embedded itself into her cheek. The woman screeched, launching herself at me.

A familiar, sulfurous odor permeated the air. Without a doubt I knew that Rohesia had sprinkled a grain of sand from Tabrn on the ground and was in the process of burning a lock of her own hair to obtain the light and shadow magic of the gods.

Yandi continued to race towards me, while her servants held down Brooks and E.E. It was just me and Rohesia against Yandi. But little did the woman know that my friend and I were in perfect synchrony.

Close on my heels, my snakes hissed and spat at Yandi's outreached hand.

Just a few more seconds.

Taking a sharp left, I found myself running towards Rohesia, the ground beneath my feet slipping and sliding. Crashing into her, she wrapped her arms around my torso, while she slammed into the ground.

Rohesia propelled bolts of pulsating, inky shadows at my chest, as I flew into the air, now encased by shadows. The ebony clouds curled and twirled across the ground, encasing everyone and everything into shadows within seconds.

With my gorgon and snakes, I was able to discern what was happening within the shadows with ease. Yandi didn't see me coming as I wrapped my arm around her throat and yelled for Rohesia to replace the shadows with light.

Yandi blinked frantically as the shadows dissipated, leaving in their wake a pile of unconscious servants. Rohesia must have scattered a grain of sand from Iydara as well, allowing her to knock the servants unconscious with mind control.

With my arm still wrapped around her throat, I pushed her towards Brooks, ignoring the gooseflesh that arose on my arms from Yandi's touch.

Clouds of dirt invaded the air as Yandi fell to her knees in front of Brooks. Her auburn and gray hair hung around her face, a flimsy curtain protecting her from the past.

"Come on, Brooks. Think about it. What we could do with *her* power," Yandi moaned, rocking back and forth on her knees.

The woman dared a feverish glance towards me, looking between Brooks and I until a shrill giggle escaped her cracked lips.

"Oh, how rich. The huntsman and the gorgon." Yandi rolled to her side, snorting and crying as her manic laughter filled the heated room.

Brooks's head snapped to his former mentor, eyes narrowed and filled with such rage and hatred that chilled me to the bone.

Huntsman.

What the hell? I looked at Brooks, E.E., and Rohesia, and they all shared the same forlorn and shameful look on their faces. I would think that someone was fucking with me, but no one is laughing. I'm once again the outsider with a dumb look on my face.

"I'm sorry, Usa," Rohesia and Brooks said simultaneously.

Mirth bubbled from Yandi's thin lips.

"And poor Medusa. Left out of the loop once again. Strange that the ones said to be your friends would be the ones to betray you so easily," Yandi sang, tilting her head back and forth, back and forth.

"What are you talking about?" I demanded shakily.

Yandi rolled her eyes at me. "Oh, sweetheart, if only you had a brain to go with those looks of yours."

A servant stirred at my feet.

"Dunamis!" Rohesia screeched, holding her head in her hands as the fallen servants began to wake.

Dunamis was the only gift that could overpower the magic of mages and islands. And somehow, Yandi possessed it.

She was hovering above the ground, manically laughing as she continued to raise the unconscious servants.

We needed to leave, we had gotten what we came for.

Once in Iydara, we needed to find a potion that could create the golems. The fulgurite was false news. News that was going to cost us our lives if we didn't flee soon.

E.E. was sprinting out the door, while Rohesia was close behind him, fending off a swarm of bloodthirsty servants with black eyes and crimson pulsating, tangled veins on their cheekbones.

"Go!" I screamed at Rohesia and E.E, the former throwing me a distraught and tearful look that pulled at my heart. Her apology hung in the air between us.

Nodding my head, I ordered them to leave once again.

Someone needed to tell The Collectress about the potion. E.E. knew as much about this case as Brooks, and Rohesia had influence with The Collectress. We needed to use the newfound knowledge to our advantage, especially if we all weren't going to make it out of Raas.

The information could save thousands of lives in Iydara.

Turning my back on my friends, I raced towards Brooks and Yandi, who were engaged in a terrifying battle of life and death on the ground.

He couldn't hold her off for long.

Sliding feet first towards Yandi, I slammed into her, knocking her into the ground. My snakes spit at her, attempting to take a chunk of flesh out of her miserable face.

Rushing air filled my ears as a terrifying bellow echoed throughout the room. Visceral fear gripped my heart like a steel vice as a shadowy figure with towering black wings stood where Yandi once was.

An oneiroi.

A demon that personified dreams. They would invade your mind and make previous dreams, or nightmares, a reality. The beasts were said to stay near the shores.

242

Suddenly growing nauseous, I closed my eyes as the ground beneath my feet swayed and rocked like the sea-foam spattered deck of a ship in a raging winter blizzard.

The overwhelming taste of copper coated my tongue suddenly. My gorgon recognized the beginning of a mental assault, blocking the invasion as I searched for Brooks and Yandi with blurred vision.

The pair was nowhere to be seen.

The oneiroi continued to circle me, cracking its spindly fingers with hunger. My eyes throbbed as the beast continued to move between the ground and ceiling with increasingly dizzying speed.

It stood at least seven feet tall and was rather thin and sickly looking, but I knew better than to underestimate the creature. Black wings were attached to its back with thick, vine-like pieces of bone.

It launched numerous physical attacks while relentlessly stabbing at my mind. A blade slashed through the air, piercing the thin membrane of one of the oneiroi's wings.

Brooks landed next to me, a woosh of air following him.

What the—

Burnished wings that reminded me of aged, oiled leather hung from Brooks's back, his skin now scattered with glittering scales and protruding nubs of bone. He stood on reptilian feet that were decorated with scattered umber scales and pointed, inky talons. The glittering scales traveled up robust legs that sprung from his muscular humanoid torso.

Pointed, serrated horns erupted from a pronounced forehead that was peppered with scales and short, rounded barbs. Vertical, predatory pupils shone from the depths of amber irises. Fangs poked out from a human-like mouth as it released a booming growl, causing stalactites to shudder and quiver in its presence.

Now that I saw the front of the beast, I realized with horror that Brooks was the creature from Marren's grove.

The one that fought the charybdis and saved my life.

Excruciating pain temporarily stabbed my temples, interrupting my train of thought, a sinking feeling that the oneiroi was closer to invading my mind than I had previously thought.

Brooks meets my eyes, his pupils now slit, and yelled at me to run. I shook my head, causing him to mutter beneath his breath and shake my arms with his strong grip.

Buzzing tones danced around my brain, preventing me from hearing him clearly. My mind trembled as I concentrated, desperately attempting to read his lips.

"—her wings!" Brooks yelled, flying behind the creature to attack it from another angle.

Her.

I dodged the first swipe of a razor sharp, black tipped nail from the oneiroi. Managing to duck and miss the second blow, I threw a dagger towards her outstretched wing. But, as my blade left my fingers, I fell to my knees, the oneiroi landing a third and final blow.

This time, in my mind.

My heart stuttered as the room went black.

"Fight her, Usa!" Brooks screamed, sounding distant. He sounded afraid.

Agony flared at the base of my skull, nausea forcing me to dry heave onto the now stone floor. I was somewhere familiar, but my mind refused to put the pieces together.

Stumbling to my feet, I look around the dank room, chains hanging from the wall, swaying gently in the air. A thundering voice echoed through the small space.

"Medusa, how lovely to see you," Poseidon chuckled, appearing in front of me.

Fear, cold and unabashed, slithered down my back, leaving me paralyzed and chilled beneath the intense stare of the god of the sea. Staggering against the wall, I sank down and sat there, rocking as tears cut paths of despair on my cheeks.

"Get up!" Poseidon yelled mockingly, looming over me.

Flinching, I pulled back from his touch, wishing I could disappear into the wall forever. The cool, wet wall sent shivers down my spine, but not nearly as much as the god in front of me did.

"I knew you were weak, Medusa, but never this helpless," the god sneered, spitting in my face as I continued to cower beneath his penetrating, icy eyes.

Weak.

Weak.

Weak.

A shadow hovered near Poseidon and I squinted through the darkness and tears, until a figure stood near the god. My heart fell into my stomach and I vomited over the cracked, cement floors.

My mother.

With hissing snakes she glared at me with such hatred and discontent that it devastated me. Amid the beats of my stuttering heart, my soul crumbled into a pile of ashes.

Saliva dried in my mouth.

I couldn't think.

I couldn't breathe.

So, so weak.

"It wasn't even that bad, Medusa. Just get over it already," my mother chided, shaking her head as Poseidon wrapped an arm around her waist and nuzzled her neck.

"You always had a crush on me, Medusa," Poseidon crooned.

Back and forth they go, scolding and whispering to me.

"It was your fault."

"You didn't fight back."

"Boys will be boys, Medusa. You should know better."

"You know you wanted it."

"Survivor," a third voice encouraged me, so quiet and soft that I almost missed it.

"*Fight,*" the voice said again, this time louder and more persistent.

This time, I watched the door, hoping and praying that someone, anyone would burst into the cell to save me from this purgatory.

But no one did.

Standing, I scurried to the door, pulling and pulling, but it didn't budge. Crying out in desperation, I looked around the room for a key, only to find Poseidon watching me with a familiar hunger that made my stomach turn.

Clawing at my scalp, I pulled my hair. I yanked and twisted it and banged my palms against my head, willing away my haunted memories and tortured thoughts.

So much fear.

So much pain.

My head throbbed while my eyes observed how Poseidon continued to stare and lick his thin lips. He hasn't touched me yet, like something, or someone, was holding him back.

My mother stood by as well, watching.

No one was coming to rescue me, I realized.

I had no choice but to fight for myself with strength.

Staring the pair down with as much courage and resilience as I could muster, I walked towards the door, forgiving myself for the hatred and guilt that I thrust upon my soul at such a young age.

The wide-eyed little girl I had once been was gone forever. There was no bringing her back. She was lost to the monsters that had taken her young soul and transformed it into rippling darkness.

I was no longer innocent.

But in that same heart-wrenching truth, I was no longer powerless.

"Why are you leaving, Medusa? We love you. Don't abandon us," my mother whined, as I make my way towards the door. She sounded so far away and distant now.

"You don't even know what love is," I sneered at her.

My mother was the one person in the world that was supposed to protect me, and instead, she hurt me the worst. Even more so than my assailant had.

Facing Poseidon, I hurled a dagger at his flickering form. "And you never loved me. You just wanted to control me. And I'm done being someone's toy."

Surprise jolted my body as the flying blade sank into the tanned skin of his torso. Dark-black blood pooled around his fingertips, as he attempted to staunch the flow.

My eyes widened.

Gods don't bleed like that.

They can't be killed by my blade.

Crossing the room with newfound purpose, I wrapped my hand around the chilly doorknob, hesitating. This is my chance to rewrite the narrative of what happened that night.

Deciding in a split second, I walked back to the injured god and I dragged my blade across his throat. As he fought to stay standing, a certain type of joy pulsated through my body, one that I relished in.

My mother watched me with disappointed, bloodshot eyes. She looked at me without mercy, like she had all those years ago when I was a terrified and violated sixteen-year-old.

Ignoring my mother, I turned back to Poseidon.

"A friend once told me to bring every person that had dared to cross me, to their knees. And I'm starting with you," I whispered, pressing the tip of my knee into his wound, enjoying the painful gasps that escaped from his mouth.

Sweat beaded at the fallen god's temple, causing his hair to become greasy. It was odd seeing Poseidon in such a state of disarray. His beady eyes refused to leave me as he fought to stay standing.

But even the mighty fall.

When his knees hit the ground, I smiled.

Turning around, I walked out the door.

25

Choking, I opened my eyes, no longer where I had fallen asleep. Cool steel was pressed against my throat.

Again.

This time, it was Yandi holding the blade.

Brooks's cobalt eyes were as cruel as a scorching inferno. "You will find that the moment you cause her any harm is the moment I rip your limbs from their measly sockets and shatter your brittle bones. If you dare hurt her as you say, you will find yourself becoming a charred pile of ashes to be dumped in the churning, bitter ocean."

Dead servants were scattered around the room, their limbs, heads, and hearts ripped from their bodies. Bloody handprints lined the walls as blazing flames danced in the corners of the room.

The oneiroi was gone.

"Think about it, Rook. Think about her power. Going to waste in this pretty head of hers." Yandi tapped the top of my head with her open palm.

A snake managed to connect, and she cursed it.

Brooks tilted his head, seeming to consider her words, an evil grin tugging at the corner of his mouth. "We did have some damned good times."

"We could have more good times, kid," Yandi replied eagerly.

Swaggering towards us, Brooks slapped Yandi on the shoulder, dragging her into a hug. Looking over her shoulder, he winked at me.

Yandi handed him the knife. "You know what to do, Rook."

"Stop struggling," Brooks informed me, his voice deep and commanding, yet calm. I instantly stopped moving. His grip on the knife loosened just slightly.

Brooks said I needed to trust him, and I had the overwhelming feeling I needed to do so more than ever at this moment.

Whimpering, I wrapped my arms around my torso.

"Good, girl." He smiled.

"As long as you listen, you'll be just fine, lovely." I felt something cold touch the skin just below my ribs. It was small but sharp. My eyes widened, Brooks was pressing another dagger to my ribs.

"What's in it for me, Yandi? Her magic? Or are you gonna steal it from me like with the oneiroi?" Brooks sighed, his tone cold and distant, unfamiliar.

"It's yours," Yandi crowed, hopping eagerly.

Brooks trailed his nose in the space between my shoulder and neck, his breath warm and heady as his lips brushed the sensitive spot behind my ear.

"Breathe, lovely," he sighed into my ear, causing my body to hum with nervous and needy energy.

A soft breath escaped my parted lips before I could stop it. Though he seemed perfectly calm, I could feel his tension writhing with mine, curling, teasing, breathless.

The man holding a knife to my neck chuckled deeply, his chest rumbling. "What? Does that feel good?"

"Maybe," I admitted, biting my lip until it grew numb.

"You haven't even begun to feel good yet, Usa," Brooks stated breezily, my knees shaking as his tongue darted to that sensitive spot behind my ear once more.

"Get on with it, Brooks," Yandi snapped, crossing her arms.

"I'm sorry. Just having a little fun with her before I slash her throat and take her magic. Can you blame me?" Brooks murmured appreciatively, dragging the knife in my ribs further up my back, stopping just below my shoulder blades.

"No, can't say that I can," Yandi admitted begrudgingly, tossing her hair over her shoulder.

"So?" Brooks said expectantly, looking towards his former mentor.

Yandi raised her eyebrows in confusion.

I tighten my grip around my torso, focusing on my snakes, on each individual creature. Each breath of every serpent and her position on my head.

My snakes writhed about on my head, creating a distraction in the form of taking turns striking at Brooks's head and shoulders. A longer one slithered down my back, wrapping its body around the hand of Brooks's awaiting dagger.

"The answer to my question, Yandi," Brooks demanded, the words coming out clipped through clenched teeth.

"I already said you could have her powers, Rook." Yandi's eyebrows hit her hairline.

"You know that's not what I'm referring to," he insisted briskly, his voice rising.

Yandi continued to offer him silence, drumming her fingers on her thigh. The shock on her face lingered as she stared at her former student.

"What'd Usa's mother offer you in exchange for Medusa's head?" Brooks thundered with a ringing tone, his face blank and eerily calm.

Shock rippled through my very being. *Ceto?*

Surely I had heard wrong.

His mentor scoffed, looking at the ceiling with an unhinged and radiating anger. But she doesn't deny it.

"Ah. That's it. The Collectress. You're still pissed about her being chosen to rule Iydara, instead of you. Ceto wouldn't have had the authority to give you that power, Yandi, we both know that. Tell me you couldn't have been that naive." Brooks loosened his hold on my neck.

"I deserved it, Rook! You know damn well I could rule Iydara better than her. I've actually killed monsters, what the hell did she do to deserve that power? She took everything from me, boy!"

"Like you took away my only opportunity to find my sisters," he countered with a growl.

"You did that to yourself, huntsman. Shacking up with your target. I taught you better than that. You should have killed Medusa the second you laid eyes on her. If you had, then Ceto would have given you your sisters," Yandi narrowed her eyes, "But like most men, it seems like you were thinking with the wrong head."

I blinked, the wheels in my mind turning.

Brooks was offered his sisters in exchange for my head?

My mother had them?

And it seemed that Yandi was offered sovereignty over Iydara as well as revenge against The Collectress if she could return my head to my mother. With that new information, it wasn't surprising that she attacked me tonight.

But it didn't explain why Brooks hadn't decided to kill me the moment we met.

"Ceto doesn't have my sisters, Yandi," Brooks retorted.

"That's impossible." Yandi's lips pressed into a thin line.

"The Collectress threatened them. She wouldn't do that unless she knew where they were and was keeping an eye on them. We both know she doesn't bluff on her threats." Brooks motioned towards the scar on Yandi's upper arm.

Yandi paled as she rubbed the silvery, jagged scar, looking so young and scared that it took me aback. She was just as broken and messed up as the rest of us.

"And what if Ceto has them and The Collectress is just playing you? The gorgon queen could have them and you would be none the wiser."

"I can *sense* them, Yandi, they're in Iydara. They're not in Kilmarn. You can't fake dunamis." Brooks finally relieved the remaining pressure on my throat.

Brooks had dunamis.

I felt nauseous.

"Now, lovely!" Brooks shouted, pushing me forward, my head turning so fast that my vision swam.

Pushing the torrent of shocking knowledge to the back of my mind, my body struggled to keep up.

Thankfully, my serpents were quicker than me.

They launched the dagger in their grasp, watching as it sailed through the air, sinking into Yandi's awaiting stomach.

"Look at you, Yandi," Brooks taunted, circling Yandi as she fell to her knees, tossing something into the air, "attempting greatness, as if you're a goddess. It's rather pathetic."

The chilled bite in his voice caused Yandi to pale.

Yandi cried out hugging her stomach, watching as Brooks threw a piece of jewelry into the air.

It was a ring.

Similar to the one he worse.

"You don't have to do this, Rook," Yandi wept, kicking her feet like a child having a temper tantrum. "We can act like none of this ever happened," she stammered, her breathing slowing, "just start over."

"Start over?" Brooks questioned, raising an eyebrow at her.

"Come on, huntsman. Think about all the good times we had. All that *I* taught you. You were nothing. And now look at you. That's because of me."

"Maybe," Brooks's gaze softened looking at his former mentor, "but that's still not enough."

A midnight flame engulfed the ring in Brooks's palm within seconds. Silver streams of metal flowed from the crevices of Brooks's hand, dripping onto the sandy floor.

Yandi convulsed, a painful roar escaping from her lips.

Violent tremors shook her body, until black smoke poured from her mouth, ears, and eyes. Her mouth stayed open, frozen by death, as she succumbed to the agony her body had just endured.

"What the hell was that and what the hell are you?" I hissed at Brooks.

"I'm a huntsman, Usa. I hunt and kill." He shrugged, stepping over his former mentor's charred body without a second glance.

"And what do you kill?" I questioned, grabbing his arm.

"Monsters," he whispered, his gaze remorseful.

I dropped his arm as though he burned me.

"Am I one of those?" I asked, our conversation after one of the attacks on Iydara ringing through my mind. I silently wondered if Brooks had lied to me while I poured my heart out to him in the bathroom of his family's business.

"No, lovely, you never were." He reached out to touch my face, but I flinched, deciding to put some distance between us.

"Was that before or after you were going to give my head to my mother?" I snapped, my nails biting into my palms.

Turning on my heel, determined to leave him on this damned island, I stormed off. He deserved to be trapped here forever.

My heart stopped in my chest.

His vial was still in my jacket pocket.

If I concentrated hard enough, I could feel the cool glass pressing up against the thin shirt I wore, along with the intense energy that emulated from it.

"How are you feeling?" Brooks asked carefully as he appeared next to me.

"I don't have enough middle fingers to show you how I'm feeling," I told him, my words not packing as much of a punch as I would have liked them to.

"Someone's cranky," he snickered, prodding me.

"Someone needs to shut their fucking mouth," I bit back.

The constellations above our heads were dying, no longer producing the soft light that they did earlier. Were they tied to Yandi's magic? Or were they simply going out because of the rising sun. I was curious enough that I almost asked Brooks, but my pride wouldn't let me give in.

The stinging of his lies burned like the brands on my back.

Even Rohesia and E.E. hadn't told me the entire truth.

They all knew that Brooks was a huntsman, whatever that was, and had made a point to not tell me.

It hurt.

"Let me tell you a story," Brooks insisted, motioning me forward with his hand to guide me to the surface of Raas.

"Do I get bonus points if I pretend to listen?"

"No," Brooks paused for a second, "but I think it's one you'll want to hear. Then you can decide what to do with that vial in your pocket."

The blood drained from my face at his words, but I didn't deny the obvious truth. I held his life and future in my hands, and that thought only made me feel nauseous.

I wouldn't play with his life like mine had been.

Sand soon merged with gravel as we traveled closer to the surface, as did a lulling melody of running water.

"Do Rohesia and E.E. know this story?" I asked him.

He clenched his jaw, shoving his hands in his pockets, but didn't look away as he answered. "Yes."

I clenched my jaw to prevent myself from cursing and yelling.

"So, what's the story?"

"I'm not the person you thought I was," Brooks informed me carefully.

"Duh."

The detective offered me his hand as we climbed over a steep, ramp-like stone embankment. Ignoring his hand, I pulled myself up with ease, giving him a look that said 'does it look like I need your help?'

254

A wry smile enhanced his full lips, relief seeming to emulate from his wide shoulders. He began to open his mouth to tell me the story, but before he could, I raised my hand to stop him.

"If you lie to me again, Brooks, I won't hesitate to stone you right where you stand. I'm furious for trusting you and for getting myself into this mess. But this is your chance to make it right. Don't screw it up."

I wouldn't tolerate lying anymore, not when Iydaraian's lives were at risk. Not to mention the bounty Brooks and Yandi had been tempted to fill on behalf of my mother.

"I'll do whatever it takes to repair the trust I've foolishly broken, Usa. But I need you to understand that it was to protect you. It was always to protect you," he told me, motioning for me to walk besides him.

"Then prove it. I dare you." I raised my eyebrows at him, but didn't back down from his stare.

Brooks ran a hand over his square jaw, stubble beginning to form. With a deep breath, he told me a story that changed my entire existence.

"I'm not sure how much you are aware of the lore of Iydara, given you haven't lived here as long as most, so I'll start at the beginning. But once you learn this Usa, there's no going back. You'll have an even bigger target on your back. That includes most of the gods and goddesses, and The Collectress, as well as the other rulers of the Enthlos' other islands. The history of Raas and the huntsmen are secrets for a reason."

I nodded. "I need the truth, Brooks."

He bowed his head with understanding.

"What do you know about The Siege of Insanity?" he asked.

I swallowed nervously. "Enthlos, the world we currently live in, began as a world of magic, gods, and mages. The gods wanted their servants, the mages, to be blessed and similar to them in nature. It was a peaceful and historical time."

Looking at Brooks, he nodded at me encouragingly, waiting for me to continue. "Until humans were created by Prometheus and forced to go to battle with them. It was a massacre known as The Siege of Insanity.

Humans lost. And yet, the gods declared the mortal bloodline as the rightful inheritance to Iydara. But, only if humans agreed to have their memories wiped of magic entirely and for their offspring to worship the gods, minus Prometheus of course, without question. The mages and others were forced from Iydara, scattered about the other islands."

Brooks squinted into the darkness in front of us, before shifting his eyes into reptilian slits. "That about sums it up. But, you're missing one crucial part."

"No, I'm not."

"Still having a hard time admitting when you're wrong, lovely?" Brooks taunted as we ventured down a slim tunnel of darkness.

Rolling my eyes at him, I slowed my pace slightly, waiting until the detective was a few feet in front of me. With grace and refinement, I threw my dagger at the back of his head.

He swiveled around and caught it before it could graze his ear, admiring the carved blade in the lowlight, his eyes flaming.

I frowned

Dammit.

Brooks tossed the blade back at me, tsking, stepping towards me. "When are you going to learn a new trick?"

"What's the crucial part that I'm missing about The Siege of Insanity?" I questioned him, instead of dwelling on the fact that he may be quicker than me.

"The gods lied," Brooks continued tonelessly.

"About which part?"

"Most of it."

Blinking slowly, I began to digest what he was implying.

"The eight covens of Hecate grew tired of being beneath their goddess and the other deities. They desired more than to be the playthings and servants of their makers, so they rebelled. That's when Zeus asked Prometheus to create the mortals. To teach the mages a lesson. Zeus and Hecate wanted mages to go to war with humans to stop the rebellion."

I raised my eyebrows at Brooks, my mouth falling open to disagree with him on the history of Iydara, before quickly snapping it shut. Brooks said I needed to trust him. And I also wasn't very knowledgeable about the history of Iydara, given I had lived sheltered in Kilmarn for the majority of my adolescent years.

"I was told that Prometheus was punished for creating the humans," I said, my spine straightening.

Brooks gave me a rueful smile. "Prometheus was indeed punished for his creations. But not the human ones."

Streaks of daylight began to peek through crumbling slits in the ground above our heads, bathing the grainy walls in warm light.

"Once Prometheus became aware that the gods wanted war, he attempted to stop them by creating monsters, demons, and other horrendous beings to wipe out mages *and* humans. Zeus would never allow this. He couldn't stand the idea that all of his followers were going to be killed."

I snorted. "Of course not, who else would wash his gross feet before bed?"

Brooks chuckled at my jab. "I've heard they are quite nasty."

I crinkled my nose at him, not at all curious as to where he learned that bit of information from.

"When the humans lost the war, Zeus offered them a proposition. He did in fact offer the mortals safety and land. But there was a catch. The humans would have to give Zeus a singular human bloodline that would be the god's, to be used for whatever they desired. It was a simple decision. The humans agreed and sacrificed a bloodline to the gods." Brooks said over his shoulder.

"What would the gods want a human bloodline for?" I questioned.

"Well, you see, with the army of monsters and demons running amuck in Enthlos thanks to Prometheus, the already small pool of mages and humans were beginning to die by the dozen. It wouldn't be long before all of their devotees would be dead. And the gods couldn't kill the monsters fabricated by Prometheus, so they decided to fabricate something that could."

"Couldn't or wouldn't?" I seethed, keeping my eyes forward, attempting to ignore the rage taking root in my chest.

"Atta girl," Brooks said approvingly, throwing me a knowing look over his shoulder.

The gods were known for refusing to get their hands dirty, often passing the blame or work onto someone else. Athena had found the perfect scapegoat in me. In her jealousy, she grew blind to the truth, choosing to hand me over to my coven to be viciously murdered for the sake of revenge.

Brooks's words suddenly clicked.

"The gods created the huntsmen with the sacrificed bloodline to kill the monsters that Prometheus made, didn't they?"

My heart skipped a beat and lodged in my throat at the raw torment clouding Brooks's usually vibrant eyes, giving me a glimpse into his story.

My mouth went dry.

Brooks's bloodline was the one used to create huntsmen.

"The gods formulated the plan to create the huntsmen, but mages are the ones that actually created them with the help of Hecate, of course," Brooks corrected me, giving me another piece of an increasingly complex and messy puzzle.

"Why would the mages do that?" I blinked, astounded at the revelation.

Mages would loathe creating such beings. Their magic was a give and take, a balance that despised being used for evil deeds and manipulation tactics. It was unnatural.

"Zeus offered every coven of Hecate's a plot of land in Iydara in exchange for the formation of the huntsmen. A majority of the mages scoffed and turned down the blasphemous offer. But, three covens accepted, thus gaining back their land in Iydara."

My mind spun.

Three out of Hecate's eight covens accepted Zeus's proposition. The First, Fifth, and Seventh.

Almost half.

All for measly plots of land.

I wasn't sure how Hecate's Ninth Coven felt about the huntsmen, since it was created by rogue mages who had left their birth covens.

"How did the mages create them?" I asked hesitantly, accepting Brooks's hand as he led me up a rickety ladder that would take us above ground.

"The gods desired for huntsmen to be more agile and trainable than the monsters and demons threatening Iydara, so the mages proposed mixing a monster bloodline with a human one. With a drop of blood from Zeus, mages were able to take the human bloodline and bind it with a monster bloodline, creating the huntsmen."

"You're half monster? Is Nola? Your sisters?" My eyes bulged out of my head imagining Lilith, his sweet, young niece becoming a half monster.

"Not quite," Brooks sighed mournfully, "a huntsman can only be formed from every other generation or so in the bloodline. Mages said they needed a portion of the original bloodline to stay *untainted* for future huntsmen. As fate would have it, my generation was next in line."

Grunting as he pushed the grate that would lead us to fresh, salty air, Brooks continued his shocking story without missing a beat.

Yandi was related to Brooks, I realized.

"At the age of five, the gods chose me as the next huntsman. My parents were so *proud* to send their youngest child away to turn into a beast that kills other beasts. My great grandmother trained me and accepted me with open arms when I first stepped foot on Raas. I lived with her until the age of twenty, until the gods summoned me to Iydara, to guard the land from any remaining monsters that were not killed by my predecessors."

The charybdis in Marren's Grove came to mind.

259

"Frankly, when I first met Yandi, I disliked her. Loathed her, even. But then I realized it was easier to hate the idea of someone, rather than hating them face to face. Especially when she didn't have a say in our situation, either."

"I'm sorry for your loss, Brooks." I squeezed the hand he still held. I understood what grief felt like, specifically the strange bereavement he was feeling as well.

I was still grieving my coven and sisters and mother.

Though I hadn't killed them, a piece of my soul had withered and perished the day I left Kilmarn.

I dropped Brooks's hand as we reached the surface.

Sunlight, warm and heady pressed on our faces as we emerged from underground. "How does dunamis play into all of this? Yandi had it and was a huntsman. Do huntsmen only have it? If so, is The Collectress a huntsman? How are you even related to her?"

Brooks's eyes went round with awe, a deep, rumbling laughter escaping from his lips at my sudden inquisitiveness.

"Dunamis is a certain side effect, if you will, from creating huntsmen that the gods did not account for. When we kill a monster or demon, their essence combines with our own. In turn, this merging, if you will, grants us some of the beast's magic. Sometimes a minuscule portion, other times all of it. The first huntsmen were obliterated by this factor. To account for this, mages made us these"—Brooks held up his hand to show me his ring glowing in the mid-morning sunlight—"the rings act as conduits for the surge of magic that hits us when we kill something. It pretty much waters down the monster's magic so we don't get killed by the overwhelming release of magic."

Shocked, my mouth fell open. I had been told that dunamis was dark magic from the blood of the gods. But it wasn't.

He cleared his throat as we stepped onto the beach, our dinghy holding two sleeping forms. Relief filled me at the sight of E.E. and Rohesia.

They were safe.

"Because huntsmen absorb the magic of the last creature we slayed, Yandi wanted to kill you so she could *possibly* have the ability to turn people into stone. It's not an exact science. Yandi could have just as easily inherited your snakes but no stoning ability. It's a gamble every time, depending on how the monster's essence blends with a huntsman's essence."

Brooks sighed as he continued.

"Huntsmen refer to the magic we gain from a kill as dunamis. This started when huntsmen were killing multiple monsters a day. It was difficult for them to keep track of which abilities they kept and which ones they had lost at the end of the day. It's much easier to refer to our magic as a singular word than listing off kraken tentacles one day and oneiroi wings the next. If a huntsman were to never kill, then they would never have dunamis."

"So having dunamis is similar to me being mortal and having a gorgon side?" I asked, the dots beginning to connect.

"Exactly. And while my relatives say that being gifted a monster's magic is a well-deserved reward, given everything our bloodline has been through, dunamis is really a curse, Usa."

I knew what it was like to be told I was blessed, but the reality was often a bitter, disconcerting illusion.

My brain felt like it was melting from the wealth of information that Brooks was supplying.

"The oneiroi back there was Yandi. So that was her dunamis?" I questioned rhetorically, dumbfounded.

Brooks grunted in agreement.

"What's your dunamis?" I asked.

"A drakon."

Silently recalling his scales, reptilian eyes, and wings that propelled him around at terrifying speeds, I understood now that his fighting skills were a testament to his arduous upbringing.

"What if you killed the charybdis tomorrow?"

"If I were to kill it, I would lose the drakon's magic. It would be replaced with the charybdis's abilities and that would become my dunamis. Maybe I would have a hundred red eyes or be able to breathe underwater, but I wouldn't know until after I killed it. It just all depends on how their essence reacts to our own."

"And as for The Collectress, we aren't related, thank the gods. She convinced Zeus to let her rule Iydara, instead of Yandi, and likes to tell people she has dunamis. In actuality, Zeus gave her control over the mind of a charybdis. She didn't want the land unguarded when Iydara was between huntsmen while Yandi finished up my training. The Collectress will only ever be a mage because she isn't from my bloodline and her essence cannot merge with her charybdis's, so she does not have dunamis. Thank the gods, for that. But still has the ability to control that damned monster when in Marren's Grove."

That information entangled The Collectress in another web of lies, which was not surprising. Lies expelled out of her mouth every time she opened it.

Which left me to question the merit of her threats.

"Why did Zeus favor The Collectress over Yandi? It sounds like Yandi would have been more qualified."

Brooks clenched his jaw while casting his eyes downward. "She was."

His voice cracked but he continued. "The Collectress believed that Iydara needed a ruler who wasn't so entangled with the beasts and demons and huntsmen of Raas. Because what if Yandi lost control and killed a mortal? The Collectress managed to convince Zeus that it would be safer to let her take over and has ruled Iydara since, only calling on the huntsmen when there was an issue her magic could not solve."

Sensing his grief, I changed the subject.

"That night we met, were you planning to kill me?" I asked him, anxiety forming a tight ball in my stomach.

"If you had asked me that morning, I would have answered yes. Your mother had contacted me, asking me to deliver your head to her in exchange for the whereabouts of my sisters. I jumped at the offer. But, by late that afternoon, I came to the conclusion that she did not have them, nor did she know where they were."

"How?"

"I unfortunately ran into The Collectress while doing recon on you. She threatened the lives of my sisters if I killed her greatest asset. So, in exchange for information on my sisters, E.E. convinced me to take the lead on the golem case and to spare your life. I can *feel* that my sisters are in Iydara, but I can't pinpoint their exact location, just that they are close. The Collectress offered to help me track them down."

Of course my boss would want to protect me so I could create more of her damned statues. Her selfishness never ceased to amaze me. But I was also grateful for that selfishness in that moment; if she hadn't stopped Brooks, I would be dead, and my coven would have invaded Iydara by now.

More questions burst into my mind, and Brooks answered them as rapidly as I asked.

"How many huntsmen are there currently?"

"There were two. Now with Yandi dead, just me. That is, until the next generation comes along and I train the next huntsman."

I expected more for some reason.

"Did you really go to college?"

"Yes."

"Are you immortal?"

"Not quite. My aging process is slower than mortals, but it will pick up once the next huntsman is chosen."

Standing in front of the dinghy, I watched as Rohesia and E.E. woke up, sleepily rubbing their faces. Rohesia caught my gaze and mouthed 'I'm sorry.'

"I understand now," I softly responded, knowing she could catch my answer with her enhanced hearing.

"Any other questions?" Brooks asked, throwing our bags into the boat and starting her up so we could leave this island for good.

"More of a statement, really," I sang, landing in the dinghy with more courage and peace than I'd had in a long time.

Brooks looked at me apprehensively from where he was pushing the dinghy further into the waves. "Why do I get the feeling that I'm going to despise whatever comes out of that pretty mouth of yours?"

Grinning, I reached into my pocket, holding the vial he needed to get into Iydara in front of my face. "I learned a new trick."

And chucked the vial into the ocean.

26

Bringing a date home to the apartment hadn't been what Brooks had in mind when he told me that we should go catch the bastards that were creating the golems when we had landed in Iydara the previous weekend.

But beggars couldn't be choosers.

Rennyn Ormskirk stood awkwardly in the doorway of the living room as Brooks glared at him from his spot on one of the leather loveseats. Brooks hadn't been overly excited about inviting the mage to his apartment, but my ex-boyfriend had information that we desperately needed.

I had convinced E.E. to let me keep Salem, the Hub's cat, in Brooks's apartment, and he was curiously watching me as I placed the last bit of baked risotto into the oven.

My apron skimmed my knees as I set the table, watching the tense staring contest taking place in the other room.

"Fan of baseball, eh?" Rennyn said, wiping his hands on his tweed slacks as he sat down next to Brooks.

Brooks only grunted, taking a swig of his drink as he watched the catcher stumble to snag a foul ball that had been popped up into the cold evening air.

"I played a little in school, but never really could get into it. And I was a lousy pitcher. Never could get my splitter to drop right. But I'll have you know that I did place first at state basketball in middle school," Rennyn said proudly, placing his arm behind the seat. The mage always seemed to bring up that shining star on his record when he was looking to impress someone.

"That's it?"

I choked on my water, watching as Brooks got up from his seat and rummaged through an engraved wooden box sitting on a bookshelf.

He tossed three championship rings at Rennyn. The gold and emerald rings looked to be from the Eastern Boundary Brutes. The Brutes were the top team in Iydara's professional baseball league.

"You played professional ball?" I asked, surprised to learn that tidbit about my partner.

I wanted to ask him if his dunamis gave him an advantage while playing, but was unable to with Rennyn's presence.

"Outfielder for the Brutes for three years while in college," Brooks said humbly, watching as Rennyn put the rings on his own fingers. They seemed to be too big for the mage and slid down his fingers with ease.

I undid my apron, placing it on a barstool as I poured myself a glass of wine. The tension between the two men was both interesting and entertaining.

Rennyn was my ex-boyfriend.

My only ex-boyfriend.

Rohesia had introduced us last year when she insisted that I go out and meet someone. I had decided to indulge her and ended up dating Rennyn for six months before I found him in bed with a mage from the mansion.

It seemed waiting for me to heal from sexual trauma had been too much to ask from Rennyn. What stung the most was that Rennyn had insisted that he would gladly support me in my healing journey and wait patiently until I was ready to take our relationship to the next level, physically.

Obviously that had been a lie.

"Go, go, go, go!" Brooks excitedly told the screen, watching as a man on first base made the break to steal second. He had explained the game to me a few hours ago, and I had to admit that it was fun to watch.

"You humans make no sense to me, why are you yelling at a screen when they obviously can't hear you," Rennyn said dryly.

Brooks snorted and I threw an empty soda can at his head before he could reply. We needed the well-known reporter to cooperate tonight.

Brooks caught the can before it could hit him in the face.

"Lucky catch," I snickered, as he threw the can in the trash by the television as Rennyn gave me a wary look.

Rennyn had a plethora of covert informants and connections, and we needed his help if we were going to solve this case. E.E. and The Collectress had given us a one-month extension to track down a potion that could create the golems.

We were desperate for a lead.

"What did you go to college for?" Rennyn asked, loosening the tie that was around his neck. Brooks was dressed much more casually, in gray sweatpants and an Eastern Boundary Brutes hoodie.

I wore a tight, tea length black dress, the swathes of silk fabric hugging my curves. It was both professional and comfortable.

"Double majored in art history and criminal justice."

"Huh," Rennyn grunted, frowning at the television.

I watched as Brooks took a measured breath, his jaw ticking.

"What about you, Ren?" I asked, even though I knew the answer already.

"Double majored in communications and business. Graduated with honors and landed my news anchor job right out of school." I could have sworn that I saw Rennyn's chest puff up at his dignified statement.

"That's actually how Usa and I met. She was the one who encouraged me to apply for the job." I blushed as Rennyn looked at me with stars in his eyes and Brooks glared at him, twirling his conduit ring around his finger.

Much to my dismay, the ear piercing screech of the oven's timer sliced through the tension as well as a butter knife through wood.

A hand wrapped around my body as I removed the steaming food from the oven.

"Allow me," Rennyn said, grabbing the pans from me.

I was a little annoyed but plastered a smile on my face as we walked over to the table. Brooks raised his eyebrows at me questioningly.

Silence filled the room as we ate our dinner. Brooks sat to the left of me with Rennyn across from me.

"Can you pass the salt?" I asked no one in particular.

Rennyn's hand landed on top of Brooks's.

"Better luck next time," Brooks jabbed, handing me the salt.

I set my fork down rather loudly, earning raised eyebrows from both parties. "Do you guys need to break out the measuring cups for this pissing contest?" I asked sweetly, though my eyes were hurling daggers at both men.

Rennyn paled and Brooks opened his mouth to retort, but I raised my hand, stopping him. His cobalt eyes glittered with delight, but he went back to eating his dinner without further comment.

As soon as I placed the salt in front of my plate, Rennyn placed the pepper shaker in my empty hand.

The one I did not ask for.

"In case you change your mind. You were always so indecisive when it came to dinner," Rennyn said, tossing me a dramatic wink.

A loud snort from Brooks caught my ex's attention.

Rennyn raised a well-manicured eyebrow. "Yes, Detective de Blasis?"

Brooks shrugged. "Strange that you call Usa indecisive when she's the one who caught you balls deep in another woman."

A crimson flush painted Rennyn's pale cheeks. "That thing with Anastasia was an accident. Not like I loved her or whatever."

The sting of Rennyn's betrayal was no longer fresh, but I refused to let him know how irritating it was to hear *her* name.

The girl he told me not to worry about.

The girl who was just a *friend*.

Brooks nodded, appearing to listen to Rennyn's ramble about the accidental affair raptly. "Well, I guess you'll have to show me sometime."

Rennyn frowned hesitantly. "Show you what?"

"How you tripped and fell into a vagina. You said it was an accident. Or did I misunderstand?"

The mage's skin once again turned bright red as he shoved his food around his plate in tense silence.

After a few minutes, Rennyn cleared his throat awkwardly, placing his napkin on his lap. "I can still get the exclusive right?"

Brooks rolled his eyes and muttered something unintelligible under his breath.

"Of course. That's actually what I wanted to talk to you about." I placed my chin in my hand, smiling pleasantly at Rennyn.

He breathed a sigh of relief, pulling out a camera and notebook. Round glasses were perched on his pointed nose, and I silently wondered how I had ever dated the reporter in front of me.

Rennyn's constant need to get a break on a story always came first in our relationship. I had admired his grit and work ethic at first, but that was before he stood me up time after time. And when I had caught him in bed with another mage, his excuse was that he was just chasing a feature. I had tastefully asked him how the story had gotten lost in a woman's vagina.

"When giving me this information about the attacks, golems, and magic in Iydara, you will remain anonymous, as all my sources are. Do you understand?"

I nodded, biting my lower lip anxiously.

In order to get information from the best reporter in Iydara, I would have to give a little information in return.

Just how much information was yet to be decided.

Rohesia and E.E. had encouraged me to be open with Rennyn, but Brooks and I were hesitant for different reasons.

Rennyn cleared his throat, beginning the interview.

"My sources inform me that magic has existed in Iydara for hundreds, if not thousands of years. How is this possible?"

I took a sip of my lemonade. "How is anything possible, Rennyn? How do our bodies know how to breathe? How does the rain fall from the sky and water our crops? The gods. Anything is possible if you just believe."

The words tasted sour and bitter coming out of my mouth, but Brooks had advised me to keep the interview as vague and unclear as possible. That way he couldn't twist my answers. It wasn't beneath Rennyn, either. The mage had done just that and ruined numerous political careers.

Rennyn scribbled in his notebook and fidgeted with the tape recorder he had placed on the table. The blinking red light seemed to be mocking me.

"Yes. Wise words if I do say myself. We know that these creatures, golems as you call them, are made from magic. Have you determined what kind of magic? Or better yet, who is behind their creation?"

"It's an ongoing investigation and I'm not at liberty to say."

Rennyn frowned, tapping his pencil against the dining room table. He seemed annoyed by my answer.

Tap. Pause.

Tap. Tap. Pause.

Tap. Tap. Tap. Tap.

"Surely you know something?" He gave me a fox's grin and leaned in closely.

"I might," I said, flipping my hair over my shoulder.

"And what is that?"

"The Collectress is a mage. She sells ancient artifacts on the black market. One of those items is able to make the golems and she may or may not be in possession of it."

Two truths and a lie.

I wasn't about to tell Rennyn about the potion lead, so I decided to tell him about the relic instead. Even if it was a fake, he didn't need to know that.

"Why would she want to make an army of golems?"

"What better way to keep humans in line when they eventually found out about her being a mage?"

I was betraying The Collectress by selling her out, but Rennyn had information that we desperately needed to solve this case. He had always been a fountain of information when we had dated, and I hoped that was still the case.

"What exactly do these golems look like?" Rennyn asked.

"Oh, I have a video of them," Brooks interjected, pulling up security footage from the attack near his family's store.

Rennyn watched the video with wide, greedy eyes, before suddenly turning green and gasping. Curious, I pulled Brooks's cell phone towards me.

It showed me on camera, decapitating a golem with spewing bodily fluids and brain matter, a furious look on my blood splattered face.

I winced.

"You chopped his head off," Rennyn said dumbfoundedly.

"Better than his balls," I winced, turning the screen off and handing the phone to Brooks who placed the device back in his sweatpants.

"I'm not sure that death is bett—" Rennyn started, attempting to get our interview back on track.

"It is," Brooks argued seriously.

Rennyn's mouth fell open, blinking slowly.

He shook his head, arguing beneath his breath.

"What of these rumors about a new species of gorgon hiding out in Iydara? Could they be the ones behind the attacks as well? Do you have any information on that?" Rennyn questioned, steering our conversation in a much more pleasant direction.

"We don't believe so," I replied, sweat causing hair to stick to the back of my neck. This interview was a reckless gamble.

"And who might I tell the public this information comes from? If it accidentally gets out, that is."

My eyes lit up with humor. And I gave Brooks the honor of telling Rennyn who he should list as the informant in case the information accidentally leaked.

"Arnoul de Blasis, my uncle," Brooks informed Rennyn happily.

Driving a wedge between the pair was the best way to buy us more time to solve the case. It also felt pretty good to be able to get back at The Collectress, especially for Brooks's sisters. A divide between the two could allow for a slip up. And a slip up possibly meant information on his sisters.

"You don't say?" Rennyn whooped, tilting his head at me.

He was perfectly good-looking, in a show business kind of way. Viewers swooned every time the reporter came on screen.

His ginger hair was perfectly combed and gelled back, it contrasted against his light skin and green eyes, making Rennyn Ormskirk easy on the eyes. And perfect for television.

"Yes," I tittered back, leaning in closer as he attempted to push a silver curl behind my ear.

My heart didn't feel any remorse as I flirted with Rennyn. Instead, I felt like a wolf stalking its prey.

He had cheated on me after all.

Rohesia had offered to help me hide the body, but I told her he wasn't worth the energy it would take to kill him.

Rennyn began to stand to leave, and I helped him put on his jacket, giving him a quick and awkward hug.

"Thank you for this, Usa. If there's anything I can do for you, just let me know. You still have my number?"

Hook. Line. And sinker.

"Do you have any information about Hecate's Ninth Coven?" I asked him bluntly. There was no use skipping around an already tough question.

"And why do you think I would know something about that? You know The Collectress has a bounty on most of their heads, not to mention the wrath they incur from the gods." Rennyn straightened his tie, looking down at me.

I huffed a sigh, looking back at Brooks.

"Pay up, lovely." Brooks winked at me, watching us as he leaned up against the wall. His growing smirk caused my stomach to do a series of somersaults.

Shuffling around in my wallet, I sighed overdramatically.

Rennyn's fingers brushed my wrist. "Pay up?"

Pouting, I gave him my best set of puppy dog eyes.

"Brooks said you wouldn't have anything about Hecate's Ninth Coven. But I told him otherwise. We made a bet, and it seems that he won."

I continued to shuffle through my purse, searching for ten doubloons that I didn't have, praying he would fall easily into my trap.

"Wai—wait. You didn't say anything about Hecate's Ninth Coven. I could have sworn you said Hecate's First Coven," Rennyn clarified, taking my hand from my purse, and holding it in his.

My smile could have lit up the entire Eastern Boundary. Shuffling in his bag, Rennyn pulled out a rare black doubloon. It flipped through the air and landed gently in my hand, as if the coin had its own type of magic.

"Ask for Shafira." He gave me a departing smile before leaving the apartment.

The coin he gave me was a deep obsidian, with blood red script and a mage with crimson eyes on the front. On the opposite side was a raging fire with kindling made from destroyed books.

The banging of dishes broke me out of my stupor.

I raised my eyebrows at Brooks as he cleaned up the mess rather loudly. "You good, Sherlock?"

Brooks didn't bother to look at me as he submerged his hands in dirty dishwater. "I prefer it if reporters didn't flirt with my partner in crime. It can be a distraction to this case."

"Jealous, much?" I teased, going over to help dry the dishes and bumping him with my hip.

"No."

"Then why do you have such a grumpy face?"

"I just started to think about how idiotic Rennyn is."

Brooks handed me a damp plate with green swirling vines and luscious monstera leaves. I dried it off as he continued to wash the mountain of dishes.

"It's kind of funny that you're focused on my ex-boyfriend. If The Collectress finds out who it was that ratted her out, then we're in enormous trouble. Even bigger than last time."

"Worth it if I never have to see Rennyn again," he retorted.

"So petty," I mumbled under my breath, wondering why Rennyn had gotten underneath his skin.

"Damn right, I'm pretty."

I snorted, splashing Brooks with sweet smelling bubbles from the sink. "I said petty."

"Not what I heard." Brooks winked at me, placing a messy glob of dish soap bubbles on my hair. I screeched as cold water dribbled down the collar of my dress and down my back.

"You are so dead, de Blasis."

"You've already killed one de Blasis, what's another one?"

Distracted as I choked on my laughter, Brooks placed another pile of bubbles on the top of my head.

A bottle of water on the counter became my weapon of choice as I unscrewed the cap and poured it down his front. I didn't mind the view as his hard muscles became outlined under the wet material.

"Was I not supposed to do that?" I asked innocently, sprinting to the bedroom to take cover.

My breath was knocked out of my chest as Brooks threw me over his shoulder and headed for the bathroom. I was caught in between fits of laughter and shrieking when he ran into the shower, turning the faucet on us.

Warm water splashed on our bodies, causing my dress to hug my body and Brooks's sweats to cling to his thighs. I didn't bother hiding the fact that I was checking him out.

"See something you like, lovely?" Brooks asked, pushing me against the wall. His body pressed against mine, evidence of his desire straining against my lower stomach.

His pupils turned into reptilian slits. Strong emotions seemed to bring out his dunamis.

I chose that moment to turn the water to cold.

I hopped out of the shower, leaving Brooks standing under the icy water. "A cold shower might help your dilemma, Rook. Wouldn't want you to be uncomfortable or anything."

Glancing at his sweatpants, I couldn't stop giggling as he roared in annoyance. I leaned against the door frame, my wet hair hanging in my face as I doubled over.

"You'll pay for this, lovely."

"Seems like a problem for future Usa." I shrugged my shoulders in casual boredom, closing the bathroom door behind me.

27

There had been another golem attack.

Brooks had been holed up in the kitchen for the past twenty minutes, attempting to keep the attack away from the press, promising a future exclusive to Rennyn in return for his help. While I was preparing myself mentally and physically for the crime scene, I had received a hurried and hushed phone call from The Collectress, who sharply informed me of one of the victim's identities.

When Brooks burst through the bedroom door, he stopped in front of where I was standing, as I ended the phone call with my boss, rage painting his normally calm face.

Staring in a round, gold framed mirror, I touched up my lipstick, pressing my lips together. With my back towards Brooks, I touched up my mascara, continuing to stall.

I was having a hard time facing my partner, especially when I knew who we would find brutally murdered when we ventured to the Eastern Boundary.

Without meeting Brooks's gaze, I informed the detective of his direct orders from The Collectress. "You're staying here."

"Not happening," Brooks argued, his voice shocked and tense.

"I wasn't asking and even if I was, it's out of my control," I noted, finally meeting his gaze in the mirror.

"Who is it?" Brooks asked, dark shadows marking the skin beneath his eyes.

"I can't say."

He scoffed, "We're partners. We're in this together."

I contemplated his words, and the risk of disobeying direct orders from The Collectress. Unsure of the disarray of the crime scene, and the state of the body, I battled with my thoughts, wanting to protect Brooks from the hurt he was going to encounter.

But, if it were one of my loved ones, I would want to know. And I was slowly beginning to trust Brooks to tell me the truth, even the difficult ones.

"Okay. But I'm driving," I sighed.

Brooks nodded his thanks, brushing his lips over my cheek while he opened the apartment door for me.

The air on the drive to the crime scene was strained and noticeably raw. Brooks was unusually quiet and fidgety in his leather seat, playing with a palm tree air freshener that hung from the rearview mirror.

"You should try to get some rest," I suggested softly.

"I'm pulling an all-nighter."

I raised my brows skeptically at him, remembering how he hadn't slept while in Raas or on the journey back to Iydara. He needed to rest and I wasn't sure how to convince him otherwise.

"Do you ever sleep?" I questioned with concern.

Brooks often left the apartment in the mornings, with dark circles beneath his eyes and a gallon of coffee in one hand.

"I have a nap scheduled for next Thursday."

I pushed his arm lightly. "I'm serious."

Though I wasn't one to berate his sleeping habits, given I hardly slept most nights, I was concerned about his well-being. And I was unsure of when that had happened exactly. A line began to blur once we returned from Raas, and I wondered just how far we would push each other before giving into the inevitable.

Running a hand over his hair, Brooks's ring shone in the dim lighting. "Truthfully, I haven't had a peaceful night's sleep since my sisters disappeared. I should have protected them. But I failed them instead."

"What were they like?" I asked him gently.

A heavy silence filled the vehicle, and I was afraid that he hadn't heard my question. Or that I had pushed him too far.

"You remind me of them: fierce, determined, and endearingly annoying," Brooks said wistfully.

Turning the corner, I observed Brooks in my peripheral vision as his eyes became glazed over with a strange emotion.

"Tell me about Kilmarn," Brooks rasped, as he absentmindedly wrapped one of my hairs around a finger.

I didn't push him into telling me more about his sisters.

He swallowed loudly, continuing to play with my hair. The action reassured me, but it made a fire burn deep in my stomach that I wasn't sure I wanted to feel.

Clearing my throat, I murmur my response. "It's beautiful. Especially in the spring when the snow is just starting to melt. We believed that the thawing ice held secrets from the previous winter, and we were determined to discover them as the sun beat down on the land."

Clearing my throat, I continued. "The valley our coven resided in was surrounded by towering, snow-covered peaks, with miles upon miles of frosty, emerald trees jutting from craggy rocks. Pine needles constantly covered the ground in every season, the smell sometimes overpowering, but most of the time, especially in fall, the scent of the scattered, fallen needles was refreshing and grounded me."

"Would you have left if you had been given a choice?"

Had Brooks asked me that question a year or two ago, I would have told him no, in an instant. That I wanted to grow old in Kilmarn and follow in the footsteps of my ancestors, worshiping the goddess Athena from sun-up to sun-down.

The first few months I lived in Iydara, I wept and prayed to Athena in the evenings. Every tear-soaked night was answered with deafening silence that shattered my already broken soul. Those somber nights, filled with ghastly nightmares and lost dreams, revealed to me the truth about my future.

"Yes I would have left. I think I needed to be somewhere different. To become someone different," I told him confidently.

He started to ask me another question, but I cut him off.

"My turn."

Brooks sighed loudly, tugging a strand of my hair, but patiently waiting for my question, one I was hoping would melt the nervousness from the cold air.

"Do you know how to unlock handcuffs with a paperclip?"

The detective snorted loudly, tension rolling off of his body in waves. "Of course."

"Can you teach me?"

"Absolutely not."

Pouting, I begin to argue with him. "Wh—"

Brooks pressed a finger to my lips, dragging it down. "Ah, ah. My turn, lovely."

I simpered against his lips.

"Why don't you ever show me your snakes?"

"I do."

"Not unless we're fighting golems or other beasts."

I sighed; he had a point.

"It's not that I'm ashamed of them. I guess I just don't want to make you uncomfortable, especially when I thought you were mortal. Rennyn never liked them and preferred my human side, not that we're together or anything."

Brooks's hand stilled in my hair.

"Do you know what I think?"

"What?" I asked him cautiously.

"Rennyn Ormskirk is a dumbass."

I chuckled. "He definitely wasn't my better half."

"Neither was Eirlys," he admitted.

My stomach did a little somersault at his words.

"I know where we're going," Brooks told me, his voice cracking with grief and repressed pain as we drove the final, familiar blocks to the crime scene.

Brooks breathed slowly as we parked in front of his family's jewelry shop, the banner flapping precariously in tattered strips.

I placed the sedan in park and lifted my gaze to Brooks's.

"Ready?"

It was a silly question. One was never ready for their world to come crashing down, again. But, I needed to hear it from him.

"Thank you for this," Brooks murmured.

"Of course."

The scene was relatively organized for a golem attack, only a few emergency vehicles and wardens stood near the flimsy yellow tape. Thankfully, no reporters were on the scene, meaning Rennyn had done his job perfectly.

A tense arm wrapped around my waist, gripping my skin tightly as we walked towards the scene. "He isn't supposed to be here."

"I can hear you, Rohesia. Dunamis and all," Brooks muttered gruffly.

Rohesia narrowed her eyes at Brooks as he followed a few paces behind us. Ducking beneath the yellow tape, his eyes grew even more solemn. My heart ached for him.

"What are the details of the crime?" I asked, ignoring her complaint. Rohesia tended to tell you the worst news last, blindsiding you in a way, even though she meant well.

But I had a feeling Brooks was similar to me and preferred to be told the bad news before the good news. Saving the best for last and all.

"Classic break-in. But with a twist."

I raised my eyebrows at her.

"It's easier to explain if you see it firsthand," Rohesia informed me conscientiously, aware of Brooks standing behind us.

The detective began to talk, but my friend raised her hand firmly in his face.

"Prepare yourselves," Rohesia commanded, throwing an intense look towards Brooks.

I grabbed his hand, giving it a quick squeeze.

He squeezed my hand in return.

Glass crunched beneath our shoes as we walked through the busted door. Sparkling, expensive jewelry was scattered about the carpeted floor, while some pieces hung haphazardly from their display stands.

The shop was pitch-black, the only light coming from the flashing emergency vehicles that were parked outside. The intervals between flashing lights created creepy shadows that had my heart racing in my chest.

While there was fragmented glass and jewelry covering the floors, there didn't seem to be much else out of place that would classify the crime scene as a break-in with a 'twist' as Rohesia had said.

Rohesia saw the questions in my eyes, but only motioned for us to follow her towards the back of the store, where Brooks's cousins and uncle lived.

I gasped in horror as we rounded the corner, bile coating my mouth and my lunch threatening to expel from my stomach.

Resting against a once pristine, glossy eggshell wall was Brooks's uncle. As we walked closer, I began to breathe through my mouth, the stench of rotten flesh and copper invading my nostrils.

And that's when it hit me.

Brooks's uncle wasn't resting against the wall.

No, he was nailed to it.

Behind Arnoul de Blasis, drawn in his darkened blood, were towering angelic wings, with messily drawn feathers.

A note was nailed to his chest.

"Stop the investigation. Or Lilith is next."

Brooks's face was a blank mask as he studied the scene with great intensity. I recognized what he was doing, distancing himself from the trauma, so it wouldn't overwhelm and destroy you.

I knew that Brooks and Arnoul had never gotten along, but seeing a family member assassinated and exhibited like this was a new, devastating level of sadism.

Crouching down in front of his uncle, Brooks gently closed the man's eyes. "Who found him?"

"Enola."

My shoulders relaxed marginally, glad that Lilith hadn't discovered her grandfather in this state.

"What do you think it means?" Rohesia asked, tilting her head in query.

"A fallen angel?" I supplied, given the angel wings.

Brooks backed up, studying his bloodied uncle as one would study a piece of art in a gallery. He shook his head in disagreement.

"Icarus," he said.

I was familiar with the story of Icarus. A son of a famous craftsman who flew too close to the sun, his wings melted and he tragically perished. Icarus's arrogance and ego caused him to face an untimely and ill-fated death.

"Okay, that tracks. Your uncle was an arrogant bastard, no offense, and my condolences. But why him?" Rohesia asked, crossing her arms skeptically.

"As a warning. It means we're getting close," Brooks said.

"But Arnoul wasn't part of our investigation," I said, confused.

"No, he wasn't," Brooks breathed, blood draining from his face.

Shit.

Frantically grabbing my phone, I opened up my news app.

Turning the volume on my phone, I played an interview that had been posted by Rennyn Ormskirk less than twelve hours ago.

"—and what of these rumors about a new species of gorgons living and hiding out in Iydara? Could they be the ones behind the attacks as well? Do you have any information on that?"

It was Rennyn's voice asking those questions. It was our interview from the other night.

"I might."

My voice giggled through the speaker but was distorted. Like it had been put through an editing software to protect my identity.

"Do you believe that it is a gorgon behind the attacks?"

"Yes."

N—No. The interview was wrong.

Rennyn had somehow cut out the original questions and replaced them with different ones.

I found Rohesia looking at me grimly.

"How is this possible?"

"How is anything possible, Rennyn? How do our bodies know how to breathe? How does the rain fall from the sky and water our crops? The gods. Anything is possible if you just believe."

Brooks's fists were clenched in tight balls at his sides as he watched the interview through my phone screen, looking like he wanted to strangle the mage who had twisted my words.

"And who might I tell the public that this information comes from?"

"Arnoul de Blasis."

"There you have it, folks. Gorgons are creating the monstrous golems that have been attacking our peaceful city. Rest assured that those horrible rumors about The Collectress were just that: rumors. We have set up a hotline for any gorgon sightings, if you see one don't hesitate to ca—"

I drowned out the rest of the interview.

"That bastard," Rohesia hissed, grabbing her phone as it beeped erratically with a dozen or so messages.

"Rennyn must have told The Collectress about our interview. Would she have had your uncle killed?" I asked Brooks.

"I don't think so," Brooks stated, running a hand over his stubble. "Rennyn would have told her that the interview was with you and me. Not Arnoul."

At that moment, it all made sense.

"It wasn't her. It was another gorgon."

Brooks and Rohesia looked at me, surprised.

"Think about it. If the interview was reworked and cut to fit a different agenda, one that makes it seem that the wardens are pursuing a gorgon, then whoever is creating the golems would feel threatened and come after whoever Rennyn got the information from."

"That would make sense if you are right about it being another gorgon. Since The Collectress had been aware of the interview, she wouldn't have been threatened by it, but a gorgon would because they *know* that it is a gorgon behind the attacks."

"Exactly," Brooks agreed. "That explains the note, and why Arnoul was killed and we weren't."

"But gorgons don't know how to make potions," Rohesia reminded me. "It might be a gorgon behind the creation, but someone has to be supplying the gorgon with the potions."

"Okay, so gorgons can't make the potion. But they don't have to," I whispered, tossing the coin from Rennyn into the air, "and I know exactly who to ask about the potion."

It was time to visit Hecate's Ninth Coven.

28

For the second time in my short twenty-four years, I gazed into the aqua depths of Marren's Eye, rubbing my arms as cool air wrapped around my body. The black coin that Rennyn had given me was used to make purchases from Hecate's Ninth Coven on the black market, according to Rohesia.

It was used as life collateral—the coin was laced with a deadly spell that would kill the buyer if they backed out of a deal or gave a seller fake doubloons, or otherwise cheated or ratted them out.

The coin was a death promise that helped to protect the coven from discovery and demise.

I wasn't entirely pleased about venturing into the black market again after last time. But this time, I was prepared.

Brooks wrapped his arms around me, holding me closer than before, and I couldn't help but wonder if it was on account of the flourishing electric tension between us or to keep me from falling on my face.

Swells of white water swirled around us, trapping us in a perfectly round bubble of air as we went crashing through the hidden tunnels beneath Marren's Eye.

Distant laughter brushed my ears as we came around the last curve and shot out of the tunnel. My landing was much more graceful than last time and I murmured thanks to Brooks.

Today, the black market was even more packed than it was when there had been a live auction. Vendors were lined up against every wall, their tables inches from one another, overflowing with trinkets, mouthwatering food, and sharpened weapons that could be used at a moment's notice.

Rohesia had placed a concealment spell on us with grains of sand from Iydara, in case vendors recognized us and decided to take it upon themselves to attack us once again. The spell prevented those around us from recognizing or being interested in us, using a form of mind control that Rohesia didn't use unless absolutely necessary.

"How did you find this place as a teenager?" I asked Brooks, who was paying for two giant turkey legs.

I eagerly looked around the space, intrigued by the close-knit community that broke laws first and asked questions later. As I observed the different patrons, annoyance simmered in my belly, remembering that Rennyn had told us to ask for a woman named Shafira.

Unfortunately I couldn't trust his word anymore.

Not after last night.

Sighing, I was unsurprisingly disappointed that no one was wearing a giant name tag with the name Shafira on it.

Brooks shrugged and handed me the biggest turkey leg, covered with extra barbeque sauce as he contemplated my question. "Yandi allowed me to visit my parents once a year, for an entire twenty-four hours. But when I came to Iydara during that time-frame, I avoided my parents, frustrated and hurt with their actions. So, I explored Iydara in those scarce hours, eventually finding Marren's Grove. One day I found this lake and came across people jumping into the eye. Curiosity got the better of me and I joined them."

I chewed on the meat thoughtfully, eyeing the booth with glass blown animals. "Is that when you met The Collectress?"

"Yes. And I wish I never had run into that mage."

"Why? Other than the obvious reasons."

"She tried to buy me."

I coughed loudly, earning a few glares from sellers.

"What?"

"She wanted to buy me as her own personal plaything, and because she knew I was a huntsman in training. She said I would have a grand future with her if I gave her access to my dunamis. I turned her down, obviously." Brooks winked at me, watching as I looked around the neatly placed animal figurines. The glass animals had caught my eye last time, and I wished I could buy them all.

"Looking for something, miss?"

The human man from our previous visit sat behind a stained folding table, dining on a meal of sizzling, roasted pork and elote.

"This is going to sound silly, but I'm really looking for a black cat with white ears. I could've sworn I saw it here last time," I shyly admitted to the vendor, chewing my lip.

"Sorry miss, but I sold that already."

I sighed in disappointment. "That's okay. Thanks anyway."

"Why not get a different one?" Brooks asked, eyeing the glass sculptures with vague interest.

"Because," I exhaled, "it had white ears and black hair. I dunno, I guess it made me feel less alone. And strange."

I had always been self-conscious of my hair. People often thought I dyed the white, curling strands that fell in front of my face. But I was born that way and had suffered a lot of teasing growing up because of it.

It had started out with just a few strands but had spread as I grew older. The white was constantly spreading, though slower than it had when I was a child.

"What's strange is having reptilian eyes," Brooks said, pointing to himself, "but your hair…"

Brooks shook his head.

Suddenly standing in front of me, Brooks gently grabbed one of my unruly white curls, twirling it around his finger. "Fucking breathtaking."

Blushing at Brooks's statement, I jumped away from his touch as the man behind the booth cleared his throat loudly.

"Do you know where I can find Philemon?" I asked the worker.

287

The day Beresford de Blasis had attacked me, Rohesia and I had been looking for a mage named Philemon Farfose. He had been trading illegal relics, but that's not why I was interested in talking to him.

Philemon was originally from the Hecate's First Coven and had been banned from his coven only recently. That meant he might know about the newer potions that the coven had been working on. Including ones that could turn gorgon statues into golems.

The vendor gave me a toothy grin that was a sign of trouble.

"Only for paying customers."

I fluttered my eyelashes at him in hopes that he would have pity on me. It worked about thirty percent of the time.

"Sorry, girl, but I won't fall prey to those eyes of yours. I'm much more interested in your partner over there." The man leaned towards Brooks with interest, rubbing a hand over his face and licking his lips. The vendor's eyes dragged over every inch of Brooks's body, specifically stopping on his denim covered backside.

Sighing, I stopped to admire his denim clad legs as well.

"How much for the flowers?" Brooks asked, ignoring the man's heated gaze, holding in his hand a dainty glass lily with an intricate bumblebee. The statue seemed to dance in the low light of the caverns.

"Depends on what you're offering," another heated, flirty look was tossed at Brooks.

"Five doubloons," Brooks says bluntly.

"Ten," the vendor counters.

"Six."

"Seven and you got yourself a deal."

The men shook hands after agreeing on seven doubloons for the glass sculpture and we watched as the trinket was carefully wrapped in paper and placed in a black gift bag.

"Now, about Philemon," Brooks started.

The man chuckled. "Oh, yeah. You need to ask Shafira."

I ground my teeth in annoyance.

Rennyn had been right after all.

"And where is Shafira?"

"She isn't in today." The man smirked at us, clearly having tricked us skillfully.

"And just where might we find her on her day off?" I asked sweetly, with as much patience as the gods could grant me.

Which wasn't very much.

The seller handed Brooks a red business card with The Broken Vial Apothecary on the front in black lettering.

The Broken Vial Apothecary was a two-hour drive from Marren's Grove, and close to the edges of the Northern Boundary. It was late in the night, our attempt to find Shafira at Marren's Grove having taken most of the day.

From the information we had gathered, she was a figurehead for Hecate's Ninth Coven, which housed mages from every coven of Hecate. This granted us an unusual opportunity to talk to multiple mages at once, without having to visit each of Hecate's covens individually.

If anyone had information on who or what kind of potion might be transforming The Collectress's statues into golems, it would be Shafira and Hecate's Ninth Coven.

"Hopefully this isn't another dead end," sighed Brooks.

"That's what we'll find out tonight," I said, motioning to the building to our right. Neon signs lit up the otherwise bare exterior of The Broken Vial Apothecary.

I had seen the glow of the shop numerous times. Apothecaries were hard to come by in Iydara because they were seen as taboo. But now that humans were uncovering the truth about magic, the store was bustling with curious buyers.

The black token that Rennyn had given me was burning a hole in my pocket. The coin was to buy rare relics, spells, and even potions from Hecate's Ninth Coven.

"Just trust me," I urged Brooks, watching as he scrunched up his face in disdain at the signs in the window for fortune telling and palm reading. He kept a step behind me, still apprehensive of the store.

Brooks didn't trust Rennyn. Not that I blamed him.

Though Rennyn was a lying, cheating piece of scum, he was good at his job. And I was counting on that to make a break in the case.

I almost gagged from the overwhelming scents of incense and spices that seemed to pour out of every crevice of the store. Strings of colorful beads dangled from the entryway and across a lone door at the back of the store. The walls were painted a deep, rich navy, reminding me of the vastness of the night's sky. Our reflections eerily stared back at us as we gazed up at a ceiling made with an array of mirrors. Each mirror was different in shape and color.

A disgruntled worker was packing boxes of questionable looking liquids and rabbits' feet.

"Welcome to The Broken Vial Apothecary, where we aim to please your every need," the human grumbled, not raising his head as we walked to the counter.

"We were wondering if you could help us find some potions," I said sweetly, removing the coin from my jacket pocket.

He rolled his eyes, muttering to himself about teenagers and their extracurricular activities.

"Why, the last one didn't get you high enough?" the man asked, turning around to move boxes to the back wall. Brooks looked ready to have words with the worker, but the shopkeeper had just spotted the coin between my fingers.

"Yo…you must forgive me. We were not aware that more players would be attending tonight's gathering," he murmured, bowing before us. The worker quickly ran a hand through his greasy comb-over, frantically adjusting his uniform.

"That's quite alright," I quickly glanced at his name tag, "Oliver. If you could just point us in the right direction, we'll be on our way."

Giving him a charming smile, I placed the coin on the counter. It seemed to glow around the curved edges as it landed on the glass workspace.

The worker quickly grabbed it, shoving it into his pocket. He cleared his throat awkwardly and pointed to our clothing. It was beginning to become clear that we had no idea what we were doing.

Shaking his head, he ran to a closet that was adjacent to the counter. Humming lightly, he opened the door, and I saw flashes of fancy suits and glimmering dresses.

"There's a dress code," he told us, matter-of-factly.

Taking a bag with swathes of red fabric tumbling out of the partially opened zipper, I offered Oliver a few extra silver doubloons for his troubles and thanked him.

Walking to the bathroom, I raised my eyebrows in surprise that Brooks was following me in.

"Turn around," I ordered him.

Brooks didn't protest, and only smirked at me as he whirled around to begin to undress himself.

Though simple, the red dress Oliver had picked for me clung to my body like a dream, the V-neck showing off my ample cleavage. Ruching fell across the torso, drawing attention to my hips.

It was stunning.

If only I could reach the damn zipper.

Huffing, I continued to struggle with it until a pair of warm and large hands covered mine. "Got it."

I swallowed loudly, my heart beating out of my chest as Brooks gently swept my hair over one of my shoulders and began to close the zipper.

One of his hands slowly pulled the zipper up, while the other rested on my waist, kneading slow circles into the soft flesh of my hip. I closed my eyes, savoring the feeling of his hands on my body.

"There," Brooks whispered, his breath hot on my neck.

His lips began to trail lazily up my neck and it took all of my self-control not to arch my back into his chest.

Remembering the time-sensitive case we were on, I turned around, glancing at the tie that was draped around his neck. Reaching up to grab the silky material, I began to skillfully knot the tie.

"Got it," I insisted, repeating his own words to him.

Leaning against the sink, Brooks tightly gripped the basin as I nimbly secured his tie. His eyes flickered with longing in between the flashes of constant heartbreak as my fingers skimmed his throat.

Surely, I was imagining the electric air between our bodies.

"There," I breathed.

A loud knock interrupted our heated exchange.

Clearing my throat, I was the first to break the connection.

As we exited the bathroom, Oliver reached under the counter and pressed a hidden button. I whisked around to find a panel of the wall opening.

Brooks was also gone when I turned around. I was no longer surprised that he had managed to walk off without me noticing. From the swaying of the beads at the hidden door, it was safe to guess where he had wandered off to.

"Brooks?" I hesitantly whispered, the hair raising on the back of my neck. The chilled air of the cement building caused an icy chill to twist down my spine.

A bright light greeted me as I walked through to a room filled with pictures of tarot cards, glass orbs, and charms on the wall. Warped mirrors hung from odd angles of the shop, some making me appear ten feet tall or wide and others contorting my body into different shapes. I raised my eyebrows in shock when the last mirror shortened my torso to a quarter of its length and tripled the size of my head.

After leaving the disconcerting hallway of mirrors, I found Brooks in a back corner, in front of a woman with aging hands and fingers adorned with dozens of glowing rings. The stones varied from expensive rubies to translucent, cheap chunks of quartz.

"Come, Usa, let Agnes read your fortune," the mature mage said, her voice cracking from age. She had to be hundreds, if not thousands of years old to show such signs of aging.

Or she was cursed.

Rohesia had told me stories of youthful, alluring mages being transformed into old hags because Hecate had become overwhelmed with jealousy at their beauty.

Because of this resentment, most adolescent mages were forced by their mothers to go before Hecate, who would scar their faces permanently with magic. Sacrificing their beauty to the goddess meant safety and utter devotion. And it also meant most mages had long, gruesome scars on their faces or necks.

Rohesia didn't have one because she had been blessed with being the daughter of Hecate's First Coven's leader.

Agnes's thick gray hair was wrapped in a bun with a bright red scarf. She wore an open-backed dress, revealing swirling tattooed scriptures in varying languages that started at the top of her neck and disappeared below her waist.

The skin on her back was silky and smooth, which led me to believe that she had been cursed by Hecate. If a mage refused to sacrifice her beauty to the goddess, then she would be cursed with everlasting old age.

Sudden horror overcame me as I walked closer. Where her eyes should have been were round empty sockets. The bones of her face protruded against her taut skin, creating a wraithlike effect.

Pink scars ran from the sockets, as if she had clawed out her own eyes.

"How did she know who you were?" Brooks whispered to me, a tinge of awe in his voice. Agnes grabbed Brooks's hand, softly tracing the deep lines in his palm.

"Any supernatural being could hear our conversation from the front, even me," I said softly.

"But no one said your name outside," Brooks quipped.

Leaning back in my seat, I frowned. Fortune tellers constantly spewed mystical riddles to earn a quick living. It was up to the visitor to make heads or tails of their fortune. The predictions were never specific, just jumbled nonsense that anyone with an imagination could create.

"Brooks," Agnes breathed, a whistling noise escaping from her large nostrils, "I sense a great change arising in your life. A terrible yet wonderful surprise will be coming your way. But be wary of the ones with whom you share your blood, for they have betrayed you."

Brooks's forehead puckered, snatching his hand back before Agnes could tell him any more. Pivoting in her rocking chair, Agnes held out her hand towards me expectantly. Her eye sockets moved as she sat in front of us, as if her muscles were trying to see me but could not.

I doubtfully placed my palm in hers and she quickly flipped my hand over, beginning to trace the groves in my hands. Unlike Brooks's reading, mine was more hurried, like Agnes was possessed with a sudden fervor when her dry skin touched mine.

She made a tsking sound with her lips and began to speak to herself in a foreign language. The candles on the table were extinguished by a wandering wind. Probably just a door opening somewhere.

"I see darkness in your future. Inky, deep nothingness. As if your life is hanging in the balance of the gods." Her empty eye sockets looked heavenward.

Agnes finished my fortune, placing a wet cloth on her forehead. Brooks gave her a handsome tip for her time and generosity.

"That was different," I muttered as we walked down a second set of stairs, the darkness merging with warm light as we came closer to a red door that was chipped and deeply scored. The wooden railing that lined the walls ceased a few feet before the door. One step in the wrong direction and we would fall into a never-ending pit.

Brooks knocked on the door, finding it locked as he jiggled the handle. A set of emerald eyes peered out from a sliding peephole.

"Name?"

I froze.

"Rennyn Ormskirk," Brooks said coolly.

Brooks was rather quick on his feet. And it made sense to use my ex-boyfriend's name, since Rennyn had been the one to give us the coin.

A sliding sound made me breathe a sigh of relief.

The underground space had all the markings and tells of being a black market, but unlike the illicit business under Marren's Grove, this one was more prestigious. I was suddenly glad that Oliver had forced us to change.

People dressed in glittering swathes of silk and elegant tuxedos gave us dirty looks, like they knew we didn't belong there. Brooks smiled pleasantly at everyone who threw a glaring look our way.

The sound of casino bells ringing and coins dropping into metal slots echoed throughout the entryway, and I wondered what we were getting ourselves into. As we walked around the corner, the scenery changed drastically.

We were no longer standing in a cramped hallway, but rather a grand, open room. Dozens of slot machines and gambling tables filled the cavernous space.

Waiters walked around discreetly, handing out bubbling flutes of an unfamiliar pink liquid. Grabbing two champagne flutes from a passing waitress, I placed one in Brooks's hand. I looked at the liquid with curiosity but threw it back without much thought.

I sputtered as the sugary, rose-tinted drink coated our throats strangely. The room began to glow vibrantly as I downed a second drink and then started on a third, gluttonously consuming the refreshment until Brooks grabbed my wrist.

His touch burned my skin pleasantly.

"I think you've had enough, lovely," he insisted, the room suddenly spinning. Brooks wasn't as affected by the drink as I was, having only a couple of sips.

"Possibly," I giggled, "but do you know what I haven't had enough of?"

Brooks raised his eyebrows at me skeptically.

"Kicking names and taking ass," I sang.

"I think you mean kicking ass and taking names," Brooks said.

"Nah."

Walking up to a blackjack table, I smiled confidently. It was a simple enough game that I had played many times before. All the player had to do was get as close as possible to a score of twenty-one.

A fifty-two-card deck was used in blackjack, each player given two cards in the first hand, once facing upwards and the other facing down. From there, the goal was to get as close to a score of twenty-one without going over it as well.

What made blackjack most exciting for me was the uncertainty, especially considering the wild card of being dealt an ace, which could be used as one point or eleven.

"Deal me in," Brooks told the dealer, unbuttoning his tuxedo with one hand, moving to sit in the last available chair.

"Me, too," I announced, boldly taking it upon myself to sit on Brooks's lap instead of grabbing a chair from a different table.

Brooks gave me a quizzical look, but didn't protest, instead studying his cards competitively. I recognized some of the vendors that frequented the black market, who sat across from Brooks and me, giving us dirty looks.

Besides me and Brooks, everyone was a mage, their essences similar to Rohesia's and Casimar's. I wondered if everyone in the room was a rogue mage and therefore a member of Hecate's Ninth Coven. If they were, the Ninth Coven was at least double the size of Hecate's other covens in Iydara.

The soft sound of cards being shuffled caused a ball of excitement to form low in my belly. Gambling had always been my vice. And I was adept at it.

Most of the time.

The dealer tossed one card face up towards me, placing the other face down. Before looking at the second card, I placed twenty doubloons into the pot.

A nine of spades sat in front of Brooks, along with his own face-down card. The odds were greater that he would draw lower cards and get close to twenty-one points, but not close enough.

Stealing a glance at my face-down card, I was pleasantly surprised to find an ace of hearts. I could use it as eleven points or one point. The card facing upwards was a seven of spades.

Eighteen points or eight points.

I tapped my hand on the table, motioning for the dealer to give me a third card. Three men didn't ask for another card, content with the hand they were dealt.

Contentment was dangerous when gambling.

The dealer had given me a two-of-hearts.

A sly grin pulled at my lips.

Twenty points.

The odds were against me that I would be dealt another ace, seeing as there were only four of them in a fifty-two-card deck, but still, I took them.

"Getting awfully confident there, lovely," Brooks murmured in my ear, having decided to not add to his original two cards.

While I lounged comfortably on his lap, the cards in my hands shook slightly from Brooks' casually flirtatious tone, his hand gripping my hip gently.

"Confidence is crucial in these *situations*, don't ya think?" I blinked at Brooks, catching my lip between teeth, slowly releasing it. As I watched his eyes flash, reptilian pupils threatening to take over his human ones, I motioned for the dealer to give me a third card.

And I was rewarded with the ace of clubs.

Refusing to show my poker face, I looked at the card with intense boredom, yawning with my spare hand.

Two men tied at nineteen points, another had sixteen, Brooks had twenty, and the last man had twenty as well. But none of them reached twenty-one like I had.

"Read 'em and weep, boys," I bragged airily, flipping my cards over and collecting the pot of winnings in the center of the umber-stained table. Frowns were thrown my way, as were snide comments under the breath.

Humming with glee, I begin to stack the bills and coins in a neat pile. Ignoring the sore losers, I wiggled in my seat excitedly, waiting rather impatiently for the next hand.

A low groan escaped Brooks's parted lips, his jaw clenched.

In my enthusiasm I had momentarily forgotten that my chair was warm and moving.

"I'm sorry, Rook. Is this okay?" I asked him.

Shame filled me.

I should have asked.

"I'm embarrassed to admit just how okay I am having you perched on my lap. Maybe just keep the squirming to a minimum." He moved a hand on the exposed skin of my thigh.

"Is this okay, lovely?" He motioned to where his hands are grazing my thigh and hip

I nodded breathlessly.

The next round, I didn't fare as well. I was given a ten of spades and a nine of hearts. My first thought was to not take a third card, but then remembered that being comfortable and content in gambling wasn't in my blood.

I went out with twenty-four points.

It was difficult to concentrate with Brooks tracing circles along the places of my skin. Groaning complacently, I melted into him.

"Do you like that?" Brooks inquired softly, continuing to knead the taunt muscles of my thigh.

"Eh," I tease, shrugging my shoulders nonchalantly.

A dark chuckle shook Brooks's body. "If you don't like my touch, then why are you panting, lovely?"

Blushing, I readjusted in his lap, purposefully wiggling my ass.

Two could play in this game.

The game went on into the depths of the night, and by the end, it was only a mage named Benedict, Brooks, and myself who had managed not to gamble away our pots.

Brooks's arm was fully wrapped around my waist and I was pulled flush against his chest. We were both stubborn enough to torment and tantalize one another throughout the game.

Brooks brushed his lips against my shoulder, while his fingers near my waist tapped my skin lazily. A moan quietly spilled from my lips, my body too tense and taunt to keep up with tonight's electric push and pull.

"More," I told Brooks, casually leaning forward to move his hand further south.

"Lovely," Brooks hissed his teeth grazing my ear, "as much as I would love that, I can't. Not like this and certainly not with the drinks you had earlier."

His self-control was withering like mine, and I respected and appreciated his boundaries, even if they bruised my fragile heart and ego.

Determined to win this game, I aimed my focus towards the cards, instead of wearing down Brooks's self-control. I surveyed Benedict from the corner of my eye, watching and waiting for the mage to bite his lip. He was a decent card player, but had a rather obvious tell when his hand was less than twenty points.

Brooks asked for one more card.

But I didn't.

As we waited for Benedict to decide his next move, Brooks pulled me even close to his body. "Want to know a secret in exchange for denying you?"

I contemplated this for a second. "Only if it's a good one."

Taking a deep, steadying breath, Brooks whispered so very quietly that I had to strain to hear his rumbling voice. "The first time I heard you moan in Raas, it was like a fucking melody. I haven't been able to get that sound out of my head."

Pink painted my cheek, but I still argued with him, refusing to believe that anyone, especially Brooks, could feel something other than dissatisfaction with me. "I doubt that."

Growling, Brooks suddenly grabbed both of my hips, pressing me further into his lap. "*That* is what you do to me, lovely. Don't you go around deciding what you do or don't do to me."

Swallowing a gasp, I felt his desire, hard and long, pressing into my lower back. My head began to swim at the heat blazing between our bodies.

Benedict sighed loudly, biting his lip, breaking me out of the trance I was falling into. And as I suspected, he didn't ask for another card, content with his hand.

The dealer nodded.

Benedict went first and showed his nineteen points.

I folded over my two cards, revealing twenty-one beautiful points. Reaching over my cards, I started to pull the full pot towards me.

"Not so fast, lovely," Brooks chuckled deeply, folding over his cards, and showing three cards that equaled twenty-one points.

"I think you've met your match, Usa," Benedict chortled, bidding us a good night, and lighting a cigar that smelled of cedar and fresh rain.

I grumbled to myself, begrudgingly splitting the pot with Brooks. He seemed very pleased with himself, even the dealer threw him a congratulatory smile.

"Last round," the dealer said, shuffling the deck of cards one more time. A crowd had grown around our table, and people were taking bets on who would win the game.

Drinks were passed around as the dealer gave us our cards.

Glowering at my cards, I hurriedly rearranged my face into one of indifference.

Seven points.

Brooks had a ten of clubs as his face card; the odds of him being dealt another high card in the same hand were greater than I would have liked.

I tapped the table.

A four of spades.

Eleven points.

Sweat beaded at my temple and I attempted to hide the anticipatory smirk that was threatening to form at my lips. With eleven points, I could easily draw a high card and win the entire game.

I tapped the table a second time.

Brooks didn't tap the table, which made me believe that he had a high card or was lucky enough to draw an ace.

A total of twenty points lay on the table in front of me.

The dealer asked me if I wanted another card, and I started to say no, only to be cut off by a soft challenge from Brooks.

"I dare you to."

Heat flourished in my chest, and I gave him a haughty grin.

Tapping on the table once more, the dealer handed me one more card. Without looking at it, I raised an eyebrow in challenge at Brooks.

Brooks gave me a luscious smile and showed me his twenty points.

"Nice hand," I say teasingly, "but not good enough."

Closing my eyes, I flip over my last card, my heart beating erratically in my chest. Shouts and groans echoed throughout the casino.

Cracking open an eyelid, I hooted in victory.

Twenty-one glorious points.

People began to scatter throughout the chamber, a few of them clapping me on the shoulders while I counted my winnings.

A mage with curling blonde hair, who had gone out within the first few hands, jammed his boney elbow into my ribs. He stopped for a second to meet my confused gaze.

"Probably sleepin' with the dealer," he muttered beneath his cigarette tainted breath

At his words, my gorgon threatened to appear, but I shoved her back. I had been accused of worse, after all. He only wanted a reaction from me, and I wouldn't give him one.

"What did you say to her?" Brooks thundered behind me, annoyance rolling off of his muscled body in waves.

The man who insulted me took a step towards Brooks, unwisely. "Ya heard me. She couldn't have won without givin' him somethin' on the side. Dumbass bitch."

Brooks snatched the man's collar, throwing him onto an occupied poker table and then dragging the man's body across the table with great speed and strength. Cards and chips scattered to the floor.

"Say that again," Brooks taunted, his eyes dangerously close to shifting.

Firmly pressing my hand to Brooks's bicep, I looked at him with gratitude, but mouthed at him 'I got it.'

Brooks released the man and backed up, but kept a large hand on the back of the man's sweaty neck.

The man grumbled beneath Brooks' iron grasp and squirmed beneath my perceptive gaze.

"Bitch," the man spat, a wad of tobacco falling from his mouth.

"Woof," I tell the man, winking at him.

Choked laughter echoed around me.

Even Brooks had a hard time keeping a straight face.

Nodding to Brooks, he released the fuming, red-faced man. The man stomps away angrily, swatting as his friends attempt to help him. They all take one look at Brooks and smartly run in the opposite direction.

"Where'd you learn to play cards like that?" Brooks asked as we continued to explore the casino, with our adversaries being escorted out by security.

"You won't believe me if I tell you."

Looping my arm around his, we searched for Shafira or Philemon. Throughout the night, the crowd had only grown and become rowdier.

"Try me," he said, raising an immaculate eyebrow at me. The other eyebrow had a small scar in the middle, one Brooks said he had gotten from a wrestling match with one of his sisters.

"Mainly my sisters. But also, Casimar."

I had known how to play cards while in Kilmarn but had honed my skill thanks to the mage that I now despised. It was a strange turn of events.

Brooks raised both eyebrows this time, his face shocked.

"I know." I raised my free arm. "But when I first arrived, I tried to make money by frequenting casinos and bars, hoping I could pickpocket some drunken gamblers. It wasn't smart on my part seeing as I had never done it before. And one night, as fate would have it, I pickpocketed the wrong mage."

"Casimar?" Brooks guessed.

I nodded. "He took pity on me, before realizing that I would eventually work for his boss and was a gorgon. He told me that I would get killed if I tried to pickpocket him, or anyone else, because my skills were very lackluster.

"Casimar said that he would teach me a better way to make money, that didn't involve selling my body or getting my hand cut off by someone I was stealing from."

"So, cards became your forte?"

"They did." I beamed, pulling Brooks towards a poker table that had drawn in a large crowd.

"Speak of the devil," Brooks muttered, his face growing unhappy.

We circled around the crowd to find Casimar leaning over the table, whispering into the ear of a player that seemed to be losing. Memories crashed into me, remembering Casimar teaching me how to play cards like a pro.

During the matches, Casimar would tell me how to pick up on other player's tells and how to always go for the big win.

But that was before I learned who he was and what he had done. He had been one of my first friends here, and now he was my enemy.

Lifting his eyes from the player, Casimar met my gaze, throwing me a hungry grin with his yellowing teeth. Stepping away from the table, he walked over towards us.

"I don't remember adding you to the list."

I figured that he was referring to the invite list, but I wasn't going to let him know that we were only here thanks to Rennyn.

"Good thing we aren't here for you, then." I started to spin around, only to be stopped by a tight grasp on my arm.

"Then who are you here for?" Casimar asked, his raised voice drawing unwanted attention.

"Wouldn't you like to know?" I snapped, attempting to break free of his iron clutch. When he refused to let me go, I kicked out, landing a blow to the sensitive area between his legs.

Casimar was suddenly on the ground, and I stood above him. The crowd grew even louder after my attack.

Stepping on the mage's gut with the pointy heel provided by Oliver, I took a bubbling flute of champagne from a waiter, asking him where I could find Shafira.

The waiter was hesitant to meet my gaze but pointed to a long hallway that was tucked in the back of the casino. Crowds of gamblers parted for us, muttering curses and praises as we made our way to the back of the room.

Brooks followed me down the wide hallway to a clean, open sitting room beyond.

"Want to know another secret?" Brooks asked.

"Hmm?"

Pressing me against his chest, Brooks murmured into my ear, his deep voice sending tremors throughout my body, "You are absolutely incredible."

Turning around, I skimmed the silky material of his shirt, my fingers playing with the buttons, teasing him. "I don't know about that."

His breath was on my cheek, so close to mingling with mine.

The toll of a loud clock, announcing the top of the hour, shattered the moment before it could descend into anything more than innocent flirting.

Sighing, Brooks pulled back, looking around the room.

The ticking of a clock filled the space, a steady reminder of each second lost. Each second that someone was continuing to create golems and frame me for it. Each second that we could have used to solve this case.

I paced around the room, anxiously taking in the sparse and bare décor. It reminded me of a gallery showroom, only the pristine white walls were vacant of any expensive art.

A metal door opened, a tall man exiting with a large chunk of raw, red diamonds. Brooks let out a slow whistle as he walked past us. The red diamonds twinkled in the light, the value obvious from their clarity.

A woman with short blonde hair and pale skin sauntered into the room, reading notes from a glittering clipboard, unaware of our presence.

My knife was at her throat before she could take one more step. Brooks stood in front of her, with a gun aimed at the middle of her chest.

She didn't even have the gall to look surprised.

"Collectress," I whispered.

She sighed loudly, removing the glasses from her eyes.

"Oliver, again? Seriously. I thought I told you to put a sign somewhere."

I looked at Brooks, confused as he seemed to be.

And that's when I noticed it.

Burns marred the gentle skin of her neck, crawling underneath her shirt. The warped skin was a pale pink and glossy. The Collectress didn't have those kinds of scars. And this woman's scars didn't invade her face.

I lowered the knife, expecting a fight.

But instead, the woman looked at me with kind eyes and a warm smile. "Pretty dress."

I smiled back, cocking my head at her. "Pretty shoes."

It was a genuine compliment, her glittering black heels twinkled in the bright lights. They were stunning and I would be ordering a pair for myself once we returned to the apartment.

"You can put down the gun, Brooks de Blasis."

Brooks hesitantly did so, confused that she knew his name.

"I recognize you, Brooks, though you may not recognize me. Afterall, we were only toddlers when we met," she said, her lips curving upward.

"But you, darling…" She tapped her lips with a manicured finger. "I do not recognize you."

"Neither do I," I replied.

The woman was a clone of The Collectress, down to the hair and outlandish outfits. The only difference was the jagged scars that covered her neck.

The closer I looked at her, the more I realized how much younger she looked than The Collectress.

"Shafira Deeine. The Collectress's daughter."

29

"My office, if you will," Shafira said, motioning for us to enter the lavish space before us.

The woman slid into a plush chair, interlacing her fingers atop an overscheduled desk calendar. A sleek laptop sat to the right of her, along with sparkly black office supplies that matched her drool-worthy shoes.

Every pen, calculator, and stapler was bedazzled.

Brooks took a seat beside me, looking wildly uncomfortable.

Shafira drank iced water from a rhinestone-covered cup, sipping carefully. "You're here to ask about my birth mother?"

I attempted to keep my face neutral.

Brooks explained carefully, "Yes and no. I'm sure you've heard about the golem situation in Iydara."

"Yes. It is a tragedy indeed." Her voice was weary.

"We believe the golems are being created by a potion of sorts. A source informed us that you may be the leader of Hecate's Ninth Coven, who is known to have a knack for that kind of thing."

"Would your source be Rennyn Ormskirk by chance?"

Her lips closed around her drink, red lipstick marking the straw. The chair she was in spun in circles as she awaited our answer. Shafira was much calmer than I would be if someone had just pulled a gun and knife on me.

Shafira must get mistaken for her mother often.

Brooks avoided her statement, instead trying a different angle. "We were hoping you could point us in the direction of Philemon Farfose."

"You come into my place of work under a false identity to threaten me, and now you expect answers. I have every right to arrest you or throw you out on the streets." She tapped her carefully painted nails on the desk impatiently.

"Except you haven't," I replied.

Shafira contemplated me, looking me up and down all while slurping on her water. She removed the straw from her mouth before answering.

"Philemon is dead."

My heart dropped.

"You wouldn't happen to know how he died, would you?" Brooks asks, jotting in his Moleskine notebook.

"What's that old playground rhyme? Oh yes, 'Snitches get stitches,'" Shafira sang softly.

Apparently, The Collectress had wanted Philemon dead and so had her daughter.

"Hypothetically, why would someone like you have put a hit out on Philemon?"

"Hypothetically." Shafira pauses. "Philemon was Drusilla's pet. He accused me of stealing her clients in front of my workers and longtime buyers. It wasn't good for business."

"Did you steal them?"

"Of course, I did." She shrugged, admiring her sparkling nails.

Brooks snorted at her blatant honesty.

"Drusilla thinks she runs this town, but we both know who really does." A proud smile crossed her face.

"I'm guessing that's you?" I asked.

The Collectress's daughter bobbed her chin.

"Sure, she runs most of the black markets and sells those outdated and dusty artifacts, but I run the important stuff. The things that keep this city running."

"Like what?" Brooks asked, his curiosity piqued.

"Wouldn't you like to know?" She swirled her chair back to me. I could feel Brooks's annoyance invading the air around me.

If only Shafira knew she was talking to one of the few people in Enthlos that had dunamis.

"Do certain potions keep this city running?" I asked.

"If you're suggesting that I'm the one behind the creation of the golems, you would be sorely wrong. Besides, I have more important things to do than to play with my mother's creepy statues."

"If you aren't making this potion, then do you know who would be? Or how they're making it?" I questioned impatiently.

"I've heard rumors of this potion. But that's all that they are, Usa: rumors. No one would be able to make a potion like that. It goes against the basic nature of mages, even rogue ones like myself. Sure, we left our covens, willingly or not, but we are mages at heart. Why do you think we call ourselves Hecate's Ninth Coven?"

"Because one through eight were taken?" Brooks voiced.

Shafira rolls her eyes. "No, smartass. Though we are no longer part of our birth covens, we still worship Hecate and follow her word. Her word is law. It is the air we breathe."

"Clearly one of your mages doesn't believe that," Brooks chimed in, tilting his head in consideration.

Shafira ignored his comment, instead focusing on me. Her holographic nails impatiently tapped on the desk, as she tilted her heart shaped face at me.

Though she was The Collectress's daughter, she could have been her twin. The pair shared the same delicate features and glossy hair. It was like looking at a photograph of The Collectress when she was in her mid-twenties.

Shafira looked at me with grief. "I don't control my brothers and sisters. They do as they please. They answer to no one, especially not The Collectress or her disowned daughter."

Her tone was tinged with hurt.

And for some reason, I believed her. I believed that she wasn't the one behind the potion or golems. I didn't even think she was trying to get back at her mother.

She didn't want revenge.

No, she wanted something that we all craved.

Her mother's approval.

"As much as I wish my mother was behind the golems, so I could take over her position, I know for a fact that she isn't."

"How?" Brooks challenged, a line forming on his forehead as he concentrated on his notes.

She removed a smart tablet from a drawer of her porcelain desk, swiping on the screen. A large monitor appeared in front of us, popping out of a slat on her desk. Shafira swiped through her gallery, finally pulling up a video from the night of the garden attack. The video was timestamped at 0300 hours, minutes before the attack began.

The video showed The Collectress in the casino down the hall, all night, except for when she was called away once the attack began. I had wondered why she hadn't been there at the start of the invasion.

Shafira clicked on a secondary video that had a timestamp of 1500 hours. It was the day and time when golems had stormed the Eastern Boundary square. The footage showed The Collectress and Shafira yelling and screaming at each other for hours.

Another video showed The Collectress at a solo lunch, dining on shrimp scampi. The date was when I had fought Beresford de Blasis in the alleyway.

"You seem to be stalking your mother," Brooks stated.

"Not stalking, detective. Simply keeping an eye on my competition. All of us do it."

Shafira placed the tablet down.

It seemed like The Collectress had an alibi.

"Look, we're just trying to get to the bottom of this, alright? If you hear anything, or see anything at all, give me a call," Brooks asserted, attempting to hand Shafira a business card. She didn't take it from him, only watched as he placed it on her desk.

"I won't need that," Shafira noted.

The art dealer and casino owner stood from her chair, walking us to the door and letting us out.

"One more thing, Usa," Shafira whispered, curling her finger at me.

Stepping towards her, I leaned in.

"If someone is creating such a potion, and I emphasize the word *if*, they will be showing physical symptoms. Coughing, bloodshot eyes, dying fingernails, and sores all over their body. I'm afraid that type of magic comes with a price, even when one thinks they are being careful."

Thanking her, I jogged to meet up with Brooks, who was waiting for me by the hidden entrance, making small talk with the mage who had granted us permission to enter the casino.

The idea of the physical symptoms of creating a potion was helpful, but any one of them could be chalked up to a disease or bout of the flu.

Philemon was dead. He was our only lead into Hecate's First Coven. Being a recent member of the coven that specializes in potions and tonics, he would have had intel that Rohesia did not have.

Maybe we were just chasing ourselves in circles.

Eirlys' words came back to me.

Something that is magic but isn't.

Whatever was changing my statues into golems wasn't a person or magical being. And it didn't leave an essence behind.

"I think we should start looking into abandoned warehouses and buildings. Whoever is making this would need privacy and ventilation," I told Brooks.

He nodded. "That's smart. We can start on it in the morning."

Brooks didn't look as distraught over the dead end as I was.

"Let's take a walk," he suggested, a bounce in his step.

"Now? But what about the case?"

"The case can wait until morning, lovely."

I bit my lip, unsure of what to do.

We would have to wait hours for a warrant to search the buildings that fit our criteria. And it was too late to begin questioning more suspects.

"Fine."

A shriek erupted from my lungs as Brooks pulled me up onto his back. He started running, trampling over discarded trash and candy that had been left in the streets from the start of the winter solstice.

The celebrations would go on for a week, with this morning's parade having kicked off the festivities. Though Rohesia and I had attended the festivals in previous years, we decided we were too busy to attend this year.

I was okay with that. I didn't feel like celebrating with the golems and their creator still on the loose.

But because of the holiday, there were still a number of people out celebrating. Brooks weaved in and out of the crowds skillfully.

The scent of pine needles and mint wafted through the air as we grew closer to the square. People gave us strange looks when Brooks ran past them, with me clinging on for dear life.

The streets bustled with vendors, artists, and shoppers. I hadn't been to the square since the golem attacks, and it looked like the community was almost done with their repairs. Multiple buildings were in the process of replacing storefront windows, and thick sheets of plywood covered the shattered windows.

"Happy Birthday, lovely," Brooks said as we stopped in the middle of the square, handing me a lavender gift bag decorated with sequined balloons.

Removing a dainty box with a black ribbon from the bag, I gasped out loud as I opened the box to find a glass figurine nestled in gold paper. It was the cat that I had seen in the black market, the one with a black coat and white ears.

My eyes ached with the weight of unshed tears.

"How in the gods' names did you find this?"

"A good detective never reveals his sources. And there's something else that might pique your interest in the bottom of that bag."

Reaching down, I pulled out what looked like a tool kit. Confused, I studied it more intently. A squeal erupted from my throat as I realized what it was.

"A lock picking kit?" I exclaimed, wrapping my arms around his torso. He hugged me back tightly, briefly resting his chin on the top of my head.

"Lessons start tonight." Brooks gave me a wink as snow began to softly fall around us.

"What are we waiting for? Let's get back to the apartment. I have some locks to destroy!" I shouted with enthusiasm, earning a few strange looks from passersby.

"Lead the way." Brooks motioned with an arm. "I have to show you a surprise on the way back to The Hub."

I raised my eyebrow at him incredulously. "Another one?"

His response was a smug grin.

Brooks stayed relatively quiet as we walked around the square, watching the snow as it decorated everything in a light blanket of white flakes.

My coven had never celebrated the winter solstice and I didn't know about the celebration until I moved here. It had been rather a nice surprise when Kohesia had taken me out to celebrate on the night of my seventeenth birthday.

"So, what's this big surprise you have for me?" I asked skeptically, walking a few paces in front of Brooks, kicking clumps of snow that were fused to the sidewalk.

"You're practically standing on it."

I stopped walking, confused because I was still standing on the sidewalk. A few vendors selling hot meals and drinks lingered around us, but that was all.

Except for the—

"No way, Brooks. Nice try, but no."

313

I started to walk away towards the direction of The Hub, before Brooks grabbed my arm and pulled me towards him.

He stood behind me, dragged me against his chest. I had a hard time resisting the urge to arch my back against his broad form. Brooks pulled me even closer, pivoting on our heels so he could show me the immense surprise.

"Rohesia told me you hadn't ever been, and I rented out the entire rink for the evening, so yes, you are going."

I apprehensively looked at the ice-skating rink from the corner of my eye. It was a quarter of the size of one of the ponds at Marren's Eye, but much more intimidating.

The rink was empty. Even the attendants had taken the evening off. Frosted lights shone overhead, casting an ethereal glow on the pale blue ice.

I chewed on my lip, trying to figure out a way to politely tell Brooks that I was not setting foot on that thin sheet of ice. The gods would have planned it so that I would fall and break my legs.

"I dare you," Brooks whispered, pulling back some of my hair and whispering into my ear. His warm breath gave me chills that crawled down my spine at a painstakingly slow pace.

And he knew from experience that I wouldn't back down from a dare.

"Alright, Sherlock. Show me what you got," I said, challenging him with a defiant stare. He pulled me towards the rink with child-like excitement and ordered me to sit.

He went into the attendant's box and pulled out two different pairs of skates. I sat on the cold bench as he laced up my boots, my knees wobbling with anxious energy.

The detective laced up his skates quickly and with ease, and I silently wondered where he had learned how to skate. He grabbed my hand, leading me out onto the death trap of slick ice.

I took a shaky step out onto the ice, the hard ground beneath me transforming into something much slipperier and less stable.

My first step was like that of a newborn giraffe, as Brooks did not hesitate to inform me.

"You're laughing now, Brooks. But I'll be skating circles around you wh—"

A sharp pain radiated through my skull as I fell on my back, my breath knocked out of me in one swift motion. Icy cold licked at my clothes as I laid there.

Brooks hooted with laughter, skating circles around me like I had started to promise I would once I got the hang of it.

"Give up?" Brooks asked, spraying me with ice.

"Never."

"Good," he said, his eyes eagerly flashing.

Brooks gave me his hand, pulling me up and helping to keep me steady. "Okay, feet shoulder width apart. There you go. Bend those knees, Watson. Now act like you're pushing a scooter down the street."

I listened to his advice and did what he said. Soon I was able to push off the slippery ice with ease. The only hard part was stopping. I was grateful that no one else was at the ice rink because I would have probably taken them down with me as I fell time and time again.

After one particularly nasty fall, I laid on the ice, looking up at the stars and laughing uncontrollably as Brooks attempted to land a complicated looking spin but fell flat on his face next to me.

"Good thing you're a detective, because you would never make it as a professional ice skater."

"Says the woman who's fallen at least twenty times."

"It hasn't been that many."

He gave me a pointed look, propping himself up to look at me.

"Okay, I'll give you fifteen. But no more than that. I don't think my ego could recover." I giggled, a snort escaping me. His smile only grew.

When my backside grew uncomfortably cold, I stood up, holding out my hand to Brooks.

"One more lap?"

Brooks agreed, taking his hand in mine as we slowly skated around the rink. And before I knew it, one lap turned into two, and two turned into five.

We skated until the attendants came back with a group of young figure skaters and informed us that they needed to use the rink to practice for an upcoming competition.

I started to step off the rink when my foot caught on the rim. Falling back, I tumbled into Brooks, who caught me with ease, pulling me into a tight embrace.

"Easy there." He chuckled, glancing down at my lips.

I flushed and began to hurriedly apologize before he grasped my chin in his hand and tilted my head back. His eyes held a million questions but before I could answer them, he quickly pulled back, panic contorting his handsome features, pushing me away. A crashing sound filled my ears as he was launched backwards into the air.

The blurred creature slammed into Brooks. I knew that he had only been given enough time to either push me out of the way or draw a weapon. And he had chosen me.

My head smacked against the railing that lined the ice rink with a terrifying crack, as the momentum from being pushed caught up to me. Stars crept into my vision when I attempted to stand.

The attendants and other ice skaters ran. Vendors fled into buildings, the doors shutting and locking, yelling for shoppers to clear the square because of a golem attack.

But this was no golem.

I froze at what I saw next.

Gorgon and huntsman battled on the ice, the gorgon pinning Brooks down with a roar that caused the ice to tremble beneath my feet. They struggled for control on the slick ice, slipping around one another in frustration. I screamed at curious pedestrians to go home. They refused to listen and instead began videotaping the incident.

Fear settled in my bones as Brooks fought the monster, attempting to keep his own beast at bay, but I knew by his enraged face that his dunamis was close to surfacing.

I wasn't sure what would happen if mortals found out about him. Would the gods maim him as punishment? Or worse?

Would The Collectress?

Not wanting to find out, I launched myself at the gorgon that was attacking my partner with glee and great skill. I threw a blade that pierced the monster's outstretched leg,

A sharp shriek shook the windows of nearby stores.

Brooks rolled, flipping the gorgon off his body and over the railing. The monster landed in an ice-encrusted pile of snow, dispersing a nearby crowd with its horrifying screech and hissing snakes.

Turning to face me, I saw a head of twirling midnight snakes, and a face with bloodshot emerald eyes and an eager smile. The face was all too similar to mine.

Stheno.

Green blood dripped off the knife in her hand as she yanked the blade from her limb, hissing through clenched teeth. Tossing the weapon in the air, I watched in horror as she threw an orange tipped dagger to my left.

But Brooks didn't see it soon enough.

As he angled himself in front of the gorgon, calling forth his dunamis, the knife sunk into his skin. He shifted quickly, scales and wings erupting from the tuxedo he still wore.

"Call The Hub," Brooks panted, grasping at a gaping wound in his side, it was closing but not fast enough. Stheno now held a glinting sword in her hands, sauntering across the ice as screams of terror rang out through the square.

Brooks dropped to the ground and began writhing in agony.

The sword was perhaps her least powerful weapon.

Why hadn't she stoned him yet?

I hadn't seen her since the night I left Kilmarn. And that night was so fogged with grief and adrenaline and pain that I hadn't recognized my sister until her intense eyes had locked with mine.

"Stheno," I cried out, drawing her attention from Brooks.

"Hello, little gorgon," Stheno cooed, altering her course to me.

My sister was after me, not Brooks.

Relief flitted through me; surely she wouldn't stone him if I was her target.

I raced outside of the rink, chucking my skates off, the ground icy and damp beneath my fuzzy socks. My sword was at the apartment, but I had two daggers sheathed in the lining of my purse. I grabbed my weapons, the carved handles caressing my skin as I turned to face my sister.

Stheno was immortal.

She couldn't die.

But she could be injured. She could bleed.

And so, that is what I would make her do.

Stheno released her grasp on the railing and leaped for me.

I swiped my blades at her. Too slow.

Again, I collapsed on my back as she lunged for me.

My older sister began to fall on top of me, reaching for the daggers in my hand. I lifted my feet, throwing her off with the powerful muscles of my legs, watching as she crashed into a table.

Stheno's head smashed into a vendor's cart of candy canes and chocolate fudge as I dragged her along the end of the table. Green blood splashed onto my face as my knife was embedded into the back of her neck. I didn't let up on the pressure until the hilt was flush with the scales of her skin. Tearing the knife free, Stheno flung me into a pile of filthy gray snow with one graceful movement.

Screw this.

Raw power forced my limbs to shake as my gorgon came forward, ruthless and hungry for violence.

318

"There she is," Stheno cooed, wiping blood from her mouth with the back of her hand. Her face was contorted into a look of surprise, as if she couldn't believe that I had made her bleed.

I was no longer the same gorgon I had been while in Kilmarn.

That was for certain.

"Leave Iydara," I said, pointing my knives at her as we circled around one another.

Brooks was high above us, circling the fight from above, still grasping his side. His jaw was clenched in pain, but he was determined to make my sister pay.

Looking around, I was relieved to find that our former audience had scattered, meaning no one would be recording Brooks's dunamis.

Ducking a blow from my sister, I returned one, causing her lip to split. She roared in anger and I pleasantly smiled at her, as I would rather have Stheno's focus on me instead of Brooks.

I couldn't have another person I cared about die because of me. I wouldn't survive it.

My thoughts didn't stop Brooks from firing his gun into Stheno's back. His shots hit home, but it made no difference. The wounds quickly healed and expelled the bullets.

"You should tell your boyfriend that it's quite rude to shoot his future sister-in-law," Stheno said, watching as her dried blood flaked off her skin. Her clothes were littered with holes and gaping slashes, but she remained uninjured.

"Stop playing human, Usa. We both know who you are. What you are."

Stheno always did have an incredibly short fuse and I knew that her patience did not go far with individuals who were not members of her coven. My sister paced around me, frowning at a broken nail on her hand.

"How does it feel, knowing that I gained what you desired most?" I taunted her, knowing that she would gladly slit my throat to become human.

319

I just hoped my insult would be enough to distract her from Brooks.

An animalistic snarl ripped through her throat as Brooks unloaded another round of bullets into her chest. Some of the bullets became trapped in her chest, her body healing around the foreign object before an exit wound could be formed.

Barreling towards us, Brooks slammed into Stheno, enveloping her with his arms and wings. They tumbled on the ice, until Stheno swiped at one of his wings, slashing it.

Brooks cried out in anguish, falling to his knees as blood flowed from his now ruined wing. His dunamis faded as the pain engulfed him.

Reaching my essence out to Brooks's, I hissed, experiencing the burning agony that was taking over his mind, body, and soul, as if it was my own.

Before I could bridge the physical distance between myself and Stheno, she spun around, bludgeoning Brooks with the hilt of her sword. His head hit the ground with a sickening crack, and his body crumpled, instantly falling still.

My sister turned to face me.

"Don't make this difficult, Medusa." My sister drifted closer, a fanatical gleam in her eyes, as panic began to constrict my thoughts. "You don't belong here. They don't want you here. Look at how many humans and mages have already died because of you. Stop while you're ahead."

Remorse tore at my soul, the memories of the golem attacks flashing in my mind. So many deaths and injuries because I ran to Iydara, to escape my coven.

To escape my fate.

Maybe I was still fated to die at the hands of a gorgon, and my desperate attempts to evade this were only prolonging the inevitable. After all, I was no longer immortal and would die someday.

And I was just one life.

Compared to the hundreds that had perished painfully because of my presence in Iydara, I was a single soul. If I had never escaped from

Kilmarn and traveled to Iydara, magic wouldn't have been exposed. And numerous humans and mages would still be alive.

And maybe The Collectress wouldn't have as much control and power as she currently did. Perhaps Beresford de Blasis would still be alive.

I was only one person.

What right did I have to value my life more highly than those of the people who had died?

Than the children who had died?

As if to get her point across further, Stheno grabbed an unconscious Brooks by his collar, a gentle rasp filling the air as the material of his jacket started to rip. She forced his eyes open, peering into them. I let out a horrifying screech as gray stone began to spread around his eyes.

I couldn't focus on anything—it was as if the world had gone silent, waiting for the decision that I should have made long ago.

I lowered my daggers.

"Where do you want me to meet you?" I breathed to my sister. My time as a human had been fun while it lasted, but I knew it couldn't last forever, for nothing worthwhile ever does.

Stheno grinned. "There's a warehouse behind The Broken Vial Apothecary. Meet me there tomorrow before the sun rises. Don't be late"—she grasped Brooks's chin, who could only feebly fight her off as he gained consciousness—"or he will suffer."

The stone around Brooks's eyes disappeared.

I could only nod as my sister disappeared into the dead of night. Was Stheno the one behind the golems? I supposed I would find out tomorrow morning.

"Usa!" I turned around to find Rohesia racing towards us, her arms overflowing with medical supplies.

Despite the utter destruction to the surrounding buildings, Brooks and I were miraculously the only people that Stheno had harmed.

Rohesia's deft hands worked quickly to seal up the wounds on Brooks. The one on his side was particularly gruesome and deep, orange liquid dripping onto the ground. He fell in and out of consciousness as Rohesia worked on him.

"Poison," Rohesia explained, using magic to expel the liquid from the terrifying wound. Droplets of neon orange liquid hung in the air.

I placed Brooks's head in my lap, stroking his bruised cheek.

"Was that your sister?" Rohesia asked.

I nodded. "Unfortunately."

"Stheno, I'm guessing?"

"The one and only."

How long had she been in Iydara? Long enough to create the golems and organize the attacks?

Why would she want an army of golems?

Stheno had to be the one behind the potions.

My head was spinning at the possibilities. She had to have known that I wouldn't emerge from under The Collectress's wing of protection unless I was working on a case for her.

Stealing and transforming The Collectress's garden statues would have been the perfect ploy to push me into the eye of the public. But after tomorrow, all the death and destruction would come to a halt, I intended to make sure of that.

But what was she doing with the other golems that hadn't been destroyed by the wardens? Were they still in Iydara with her? Perhaps they were in the warehouse where she told me to meet her.

Brooks groaned as he became conscious once again; sweat drenched his face and he looked ashen. A thin scar was visible where Rohesia had healed him. She was now working on a few internal injuries and a nasty gash on the back of his head.

I didn't realize I was bleeding from my thigh until a different mage came up to me and began healing the wound. My head rested against the brick wall of a building as the mages quickly finished working on us.

I looked down to find Brooks grasping my hand with his. The detective's grasp was as strong as his will. He pulled it to his chest as he sat upright.

"Your birthday is cursed, lovely, I think you need to change the day of it," he announced, his fingers absentmindedly rubbing the back of my hand.

I snorted, resting my head on his shoulder as we sat in silence, watching the snow falling around us, cleansing us of dirt and blood and our sins.

Mages and mortals ran around, and loud emergency sirens screeched through the air, piercing my ears.

But at that moment, it was only us.

30

At the apartment, I anxiously waited for Brooks to get out of the shower. I had already taken a quick one, after giving our reports to the wardens and making sure that Brooks was entirely healed from the wound my sister had given him. A faint scar was visible on his torso, but that was it.

That injury wasn't the one I was worried about, though.

Pacing, I waited for him to call upon his dunamis.

Dressed in my sleep shorts and tank top, I anxiously walked around the room, my arms wrapped around myself. Rennyn had made it clear I would owe him a favor, but agreed to wipe any videos or images of Brooks's dunamis if or when they surfaced.

But that was the least of our problems.

I was ninety percent certain that my sister was the one behind the creation of the golems and attacks on Iydara. It was all my fault. My hands were drenched in the lifeblood of innocent citizens of Iydara, and no matter how hard I scrubbed, they would be stained crimson forever.

Seeking a distraction, I sat down on the bed and started to fiddle with the lock picking kit that Brooks had given me. When we had been asking each other questions on the night Arnoul had been killed, I was only half joking about wanting to learn how to pick a lock.

But it seemed like he had picked up on the truth, that I really wanted to learn how to do it. It was badass and useful for cases.

Through the layers of embarrassment and sarcasm that I had concealed the truth with, Brooks had picked up on that. And I wasn't sure how to feel about how well he was beginning to figure me out.

Part of me was excited, but the other was terrified.

Sighing, I crossed my feet on the bed, hearing the steady stream of water in the bathroom came to a halt, replaced by an agonizing groan that rumbled throughout the small apartment.

Bolting from the bed, I knocked on the bathroom door.

"Brooks?"

"Lovely," he gasped, emotion lacing his usually calm, baritone voice.

Deciding against my better judgment, I burst into the bathroom, finding Brooks with his hands propped against a wall. A towel was wrapped around his waist, and my mouth went dry. His tightened muscles glistened with drops of water, and a scatter of hair sat beneath his belly button, trailing under the towel.

His eyes widened at the sight of my shorts and thin shirt. His gaze trailed from the top of my head to my toes, and it was mixed with pain and desire.

His right wing was slumped, the gash from Stheno angry and inflamed. Dried blood scabbed over the wound, providing some help in closing the injury. But I could still see daylight shining through a few inches of the gash.

Wrapping an arm around his waist, I tugged him towards the toilet, making him straddle it so I could investigate further.

"It's not that bad," Brooks insisted, his jaw clenched, attempting to stand.

Before he could, I gently yet forcefully pushed him back down.

"Don't get up, you'll make it worse," I ordered, rummaging through the cabinet beneath the sink, gathering medicine, tonics, and bandages that were left over from my previous injuries.

"I don't need your help."

"Really? It sure looks like you do." I raised an eyebrow at him in stubbornness.

Brooks rests his forehead on his arms, grunting as I begin to clean the wound. "Why didn't Rohesia's magic heal it?"

"Because I wasn't in my dunamis form when she healed me. And the wound will only heal when I am in that form."

I nod. "Want me to go get her?"

A beat of silence.

"No," Brooks croaked, sweat beading at his temple.

A relieved sigh escaped his lips as I poured the lavender and tea tree healing tonic on the wound.

Frowning, I gently place butterfly stitches over the wound, asking Brooks once again if I should go and get Rohesia.

"She won't mind, if you're worried about the time," I pushed.

Rohesia's magic could heal him in minutes, and while the tonics, bandages, and stitches would as well, they would leave a jagged scar.

"No," he told me, more firmly this time.

"Can I ask why?" I

Silence.

"Because I don't deserve help," Brooks finally said, self-hatred flowing from every pore.

"Why do you think you don't deserve help?" I asked him gently, wrapping bandages around his wound. Thin layers of skin were beginning to form around the edges of the gash, attempting to pull itself together.

"Because," Brooks remarked, squeezing the toilet seat with his hands until it began to crack, "I should have protected them."

Understanding barrels into me.

"What do you mean?" I asked for clarification, not wanting to assume I knew his thoughts.

"When we first met, I told you that I wasn't informed of my sisters' disappearances until much later. It was an entire year, Usa. Three-hundred and sixty-five fucking days that I was ignorantly unaware that they were missing. I could have been helping to find them, but I was in fucking Raas playing with swords."

"Turn around, Rook," I whispered, tying up the last of his bandages. The injury from Stheno would heal quickly compared to the one caused by his sisters' disappearance.

It would linger and fester for years to come, painfully reopening and almost closing before succumbing to Brooks's shame, and then being cruelly pried open again.

His mental wound was almost identical to the one my mother had given me. It still festered and bit at me, but it didn't reopen as much after Brooks had given me some much-needed advice.

Brooks met my eyes as I cupped his face softly.

"Remember how you told me to surrender control? Well, I need you to take a deep breath and do that now."

Brooks rested his head entirely in my palms, inhaling a shaky breath. He nodded for me to continue.

"I know your mind is consumed by overwhelming grief and guilt. You're suffocating, anyone can see it. I see it. But, I need you to believe me when I say that your sisters' disappearance was not your fault, Rook. It was out of your control. That guilt you're feeling is misplaced and I hope you one day gain the courage to stare it down and tell it to fuck off. Nothing is permanent in this world. Including your sisters' disappearance. That's the bittersweet thing about life."

Brooks swallowed loudly, turning his head. He pressed a soft kiss to my palm, before lightly biting it. Stifling a groan, I brushed my fingertips over his chiseled cheekbone.

It was going to be a long night for the both of us.

Standing, Brooks wrapped his arms, scattered with shiny scales, around me, holding me tightly as he rested his chin on the top of my head.

"You've gotta stop saying things like that," Brooks murmured into my wild, curly hair.

"Like what?"

"Things that make me want to kiss you."

My heart stutters in my chest. I dared glance up at him, finding him gazing down at me with desire and longing that had my palms sweating and skin tingling with anticipation.

"Why don't you?"

"Because I'd never be able to stop," he admitted.

Brooks would stop though, if I asked him to, with or without words. I know it in my heart. And that's what made this different, him different.

And when he leaned down to kiss me, I let him draw me close. So close that I could smell his enticing minty breath.

Before he could, an errant thought rang through my mind at his words, shattering the spell and causing despair to replace the lust that had been coursing through my veins moments before.

Stheno told me to stop.

To surrender.

And that's what I would be doing tomorrow morning.

At the final second before his lips brushed mine, I turned my cheek with sadness and regret. Brooks deserved better. He needed someone that could give him everything he wanted.

Everything that he deserved.

"Everything okay?" he questioned, frowning at me as I suddenly broke contact with him.

I was already cold and lonely from not touching him.

"Perfect," I told him brightly, "just forgot to ask you about showing me how to use that lock kit you got me."

Brooks nodded, a shadow of hurt crossing his features before he quickly collected himself. Walking into the bedroom, he put on a pair of shorts, not breaking eye contact as I sat on the bed.

He plopped down next to me, taking the kit from my hands and handed me back the padlock from inside. It was cool and heavy in my hands.

"The first thing to know about picking locks is the different types of locks." Brooks handed me a pamphlet as I quickly scanned the list.

"Now, without looking at the list, what type is the one in your hand?"

"A single post shackle padlock," I answered with confidence.

"Correct." Brooks grinned, handing me the tools I would need.

His warm hand lingered on mine and I fought back a shiver.

"Most locks are similar in nature inside and are fairly simple to pick once you get the hang of it. Stand up."

"What about this lock?" I asked, raising my eyebrows at him.

"That's child's play. Once you're used to deadbolts and five-pin tumble locks, you can open any other type in your sleep."

His logic made sense, but still, I was anxious.

Brooks stopped next to the front door. Without a moment's hesitation, he pulled us outside of the apartment and into the hallway of the Hub, locking the door behind us, his wings still on display.

"Hey!" I shouted, wriggling the door handle to no avail.

"Now, pay attention."

I tried to, but it was hard to think with cold air rushing over my skin and Brooks standing next to me wearing nothing but a pair of very worn shorts.

"Locks feature pins that are spring-loaded. When the correctly shaped key is put into a lock, the pins are pushed upward, allowing the lock to be turned."

He motioned to the tools in my hands. "Using a rake pick and a torsion tool, a lock picker can mimic a key."

Nodding, I placed the torsion tool inside the deadbolt first.

"Just like that," Brooks said lazily, looking over my shoulder, his breath hot on my neck.

"Mhmm," I whispered, trying my best not to lean into him.

"Now apply rotational pressure on the torsion tool so the cylinder is under pressure to turn. This will hold unlocked pins in place until all of them are free."

I did as he said, feeling the pressure of the pins release under the torsion tool. This was turning out to be much easier than I originally thought.

"Next," Brooks said, placing his hand on my waist, his fingers meeting the exposed skin of my stomach, "with a rocking motion, use the tip of the rake pick to lift the pins to the shear line, one at a time."

"Like this?" I asked, my voice cracking with desire.

"Yes. And don't forget the rocking motion. That's the most important thing," he purred, his voice deep with need as he pressed his body into mine.

I bit my lip to stop myself from flirting back.

"Listen for a click as the cylinder rotates forward slightly, stopping at the next pin. But don't push in too hard, or—"

I let out a frustrated sigh, the torsion tool dropping from my hand. Having been too focused on Brooks's heated words, I had forgotten about the need to apply pressure to the torsion tool.

"You'll drop the torsion tool." Brooks chuckled, rubbing his finger along the strip of skin at my waist. I fought the urge to lean into his touch, instead picking up my tools once more and trying again.

Only the same thing happened.

Twice.

Irritated, I threw my hands up in the air.

"It seems to me that you need some motivation," Brooks said, a grin beginning to form on his handsome face.

"Wha—"

"WE USED TO LOVE SO WELL. I THOUGHT WE'D BE FOREVER, ME AND MY LADY LOVER. BUT ONE MIDNIGHT, ONE MIDNIGHT WE WALKED TOO MUCH AND DRANK TOO MUCH. SHE GREW COOOOLD. MY LITTLE LADY LOVER..." Brooks crooned at the top of his lungs, shouting down the hall, unconcerned that anyone could see his wings and hear his horrendous singing at a moment's notice.

"AND THEN IT HAPPENEEEED," Brooks sang very off-tune into my ear, "OH NO! OH NO! SHE KISSED A CHICKEN. ALAS, A CHICKEN!"

"MY LITTLE LADY LOVER KISSED A CHICKEN," I shouted, dancing in place as I worked to unlock the door.

It was the song Brooks sang the night we left, one I had heard at random taverns in Iydara. The song was hilarious and crude, but had unique lyrics that made it easy to remember.

I danced on my tiptoes as I successfully unlocked the door to the apartment. Brooks shouted his praise and picked me up in his arms.

A flash of heat passed between us, and I could tell that he wanted to try and kiss me again, but he respected my boundaries. As my heart ached, I asked him to put me down.

We shuffled into the apartment awkwardly, and I thanked him for teaching me how to pick the lock. Brooks gave me a soft smile and said he was going to work in his office for a while.

Finding myself alone in the living room, tears sprung up in the corner of my eyes. Swiping at them, my heart started to break.

I wanted to kiss him.

I needed to.

But I couldn't.

It wouldn't be fair to either of us.

31

The Broken Vial Apothecary was open. The soft flashing light of the 'open' sign radiated in the early morning light. A thick fog covered Iydara, causing the dimness of night to grow darker and deeper.

I was planning to hunt down Stheno and ask her about my future and how she had poisoned the blade that was used on Brooks. She was expecting me to return to Kilmarn with her, and I planned to, but not without answers.

I had awoken with my head on Brooks's chest that morning, his breathing soft and quiet. I realized then that I had made the correct decision to leave, and to do so without having added a physical element to our relationship. The pain that it caused me would be worth it if he could live a life without me in it.

So, I left Brooks there sleeping. The coward in me had refused to tell him where I was going, in fear that he would come after me.

I was armed to the teeth and would not go without a fight.

No one was at the counter as I hesitantly entered the apothecary. There had been no entrance to the warehouse through the land around the store, as they seemed to be connected.

Passing through a labyrinth of colorful beaded curtains, I searched the airy back room for any sign of an employee or Agnes herself.

"Hello?" I called out into the deafening silence.

Nothing.

I turned a sharp corner and a waft of heat assaulted me, a rancid stench permeating the air. My spine straightened and I unleashed my gorgon, holding my sword in front of me, ready to attack.

The smell…Oh, gods.

Death had visited here.

The horrifying scent led me to a storage closet in the back of the store. Shimmering crimson blood was visible from under the closed door, seeping onto the pristine cement flooring.

I held my breath as I opened the door.

In the corner of the closet was Oliver, who I had seen stocking shelves and unpacking boxes just last night. His sickly pale skin was rigid, a knife protruding from the back of his neck. I estimated that he had been dead for less than twelve hours.

Whoever had killed him had made sure he would die quickly. Out of mercy or necessity, I couldn't be sure.

Further into the closet, behind a stack of forgotten crates, was Agnes. She had been dead a few hours longer than Oliver. Her skin was shriveled and beginning to fully decay. Insects and rodents had taken her tongue with them.

I gagged and fought the urge to throw up at the sight of the deceased mage. Sheathing my sword, I covered up her body with an empty sack.

The magic in Agnes's blood would cause her body to decompose faster than Oliver's, since he was human.

The mage had been killed in a more violent manner than Oliver, her head twisted at an unnatural angle. Though she was blind and aging, she had clearly put up one hell of a fight. Defensive scratches marked her arms, and her fingernails were ripped off, dried blood crusting her torn cuticles.

A faint scurrying sound at the front of the room caught my attention and I raised myself from my haunches. I pulled out my sword and tiptoed around a pile of discarded boxes. I tried not to think about the sticky, smelly liquids that were collecting on the bottom of my boots.

My breathing quickened as I walked around the storage room. Row after row of emptied shelves came into view at the back of the store. A set of steel doors were parallel to the empty shelves. My back pressed into their handles as I prepared to open them.

Barrels of a strange purple liquid were littered about the space. The cement of the floor was cracked and warped, as if someone had grown frustrated and punched the ground with great strength.

My footsteps echoed through the warehouse as I looked for my sister. The building was massive; it could have acted as a second headquarters for The Hub. Empty conveyor belts lined the room, with broken glass vials and sculptures crunching beneath my boots as I inspected the room further.

Discarded fast food wrappers were laid across a table, blowing about the floor from the wind of a box fan. I lowered my sword and examined the table, which was scattered with notes and photographs.

There were dozens of photographs of me and Brooks at crime scenes. One of us fighting hordes of golems. One of us at the blackjack table. Perhaps the most eerie photographs of all were the ones of Brooks and me diving into Marren's Eye.

The number of statues I had stoned since living in Iydara was written on a large whiteboard.

Three hundred and eighty-seven.

Under the number was a second, but smaller one, that I guessed was the number of statues that had been turned into golems.

Two hundred and sixty-one.

That was a much larger number than I had expected. How many golems were lurking in the shadows? Waiting for the opportunity to pounce?

Irritation pulsated through me as I realized how close I had been to finding my sister and ending the case, if only I had explored the apothecary more last night.

A secondary whiteboard held a list of ingredients, ranging from witch hazel to arnica. There were irritated scribbles on the board. Broken and empty vials were scattered across the table, suggesting that someone had been here before, either searching for something or haphazardly creating a potion.

Two vials sat in a drawer next to one of the whiteboards. The first potion was purple in color and smelled of rosemary, the adjacent vial was yellow and had bits of dandelion seed floating around in it.

Around half of the purple potions clattered in the drawer, but there was only a single yellow one. The list on the whiteboard did not have dandelion listed as an ingredient, leading me to believe its creator did not want the recipe to be easily accessible.

I didn't dare taste the potions, in concern that they would transform me into a golem, or worse.

Seized by the sudden feeling that I was not alone, I tried to turn around, but found myself pinned to the spot with a knife pressed against the tender flesh of my throat. I stepped back, only to find Brooks the one holding it.

"What are you doing here?" he asked, spinning me around and looking me in the eyes with great annoyance.

"Shopping," I informed him blandly, shoving the potions back into the drawer.

He looked ready to snap at my answer.

"Why were you gone this morning?"

"How did you even find me?"

"A good detective ne—"

"Never reveals his sources, I know," I snapped, my anger displaced.

He tapped his foot, waiting for my answer.

"The apothecary was having an early morning sale and I didn't want to wake you. Stheno and I wanted to do some bonding before she sacrifices me to the Goddess Athena," I informed him dryly, continuing to browse through different notes and ingredients.

"Did she hurt you?" he asked, looking me up and down as if searching for wounds. For good measure, he turned me around and scrutinized me. By some miracle, I hadn't run into my sister yet.

"What does it matter to you? I'm leaving. The case is almost solved, and now you can get more help on your sisters' disappearance," I retorted, untangling myself from his grasp and turning back around to face him.

I silently cursed myself. I had gotten too attached while in Iydara. To Rohesia, to E.E., to the cat that wandered around The Hub, and to Brooks.

He chuckled darkly at my words, pressing me into the edge of the overflowing table. Brooks's hands rested on either side of my hips, and he leaned in close, whispering his next words into my ear.

"You're not leaving, lovely."

"Bite me," I snorted at his arrogance.

"Just tell me where," Brooks told me, delighted.

"You wouldn't even notice if I left Iydara."

As the words spilled from my lips, I knew they were a poorly crafted lie, their only purpose to harm the man in front of me, so he would be safe from my coven. And to save my own heart from any more harm and breakage.

"Do you think I enjoy this tormenting, wild fascination that we have with one another? When I realized that you were gone this morning, I just about lost my damned mind. I fucking notice everything about you, lovely. *Everything*."

I swallowed loudly. I hadn't realized how strongly he felt. This thing between us was pulsating and electric, ever growing and writhing with each heated glance and stolen touch. It was a living, breathing beast that would devour me whole if I let it.

My soul.

My mind.

My heart.

And like most beasts, this one was better off dead. Before it ripped out my bleeding heart with its pearly white teeth.

I needed to leave Iydara and never look back.

Hundreds of lives would be saved if I left.

Including the man in front of me.

Irritation pulsated through me as I fought to break his hold on my wrists. He wouldn't move.

Another push.

The third time, I think I actually lost ground.

I pushed at Brooks's chest relentlessly, grunts of frustration escaping my body as he didn't move, not an inch. "Stop it then! If caring about me only torments you."

Brooks pressed me further into the table, until the cold metal was biting into my lower back. "I can't. My thoughts keep me awake at night, especially the ones about you. How your skin would feel flush against mine, how that smart mouth could be put to good use, or what it would be like to hear you moan my name. And the fact that you have the audacity to demand that I stop caring about you just shows how ignorant you are about the power that you hold over me."

"You are the flames that lick my blood and bring it to a tortuous boil. You are the scathing heat that prickles my skin every time you pin me with your haunting eyes. You are my *torture*."

My control shattered.

"Then do something about it before I leave," I told him, my voice quivering, "I dare you."

"Are you sure that's what you want, Usa?" Brooks questioned, his breathing heavy and shaky.

I could only nod as I fisted his shirt with my hands.

"I'm not playing games, lovely. But I'm not doing anything until you ask me. I need to know for sure that you want this. Want me," Brooks said, pushing himself from the table, and leaving me standing there.

And maybe it was because I would be dead soon, or perhaps it was all the things that were left unsaid between us, but I grabbed his arm before he could turn away.

Brooks's eyes darkened as he glanced at the place where our skin met. This time, I didn't back down from his challenge.

"Kiss me. Kiss me like the oxygen from my lungs is the only thing keeping you alive in this god-forsaken realm." I shoved a finger in his chest.

"No need to beg," he growled, his chuckle skittering across my skin.

"Bast—" My insult was lost in my throat. Brooks slid his hand over my jaw, around my neck, and pulled my body to his.

He started at my collar bone, leaving a trail of soft kisses from my neck to my jaw, finally capturing my lips in an unrestrained moment of passion.

My hands went around Brooks's torso, pulling him closer, pressing myself against him. His hands roamed my neck, soon moving to my hair. He grasped my waist, as if he couldn't touch enough of me at once. The way he fiercely kissed me, with a mixture of his lips and tongue, caused a torrent of soft whimpers to escape me.

He lifted me onto the table as my fingers dug into his shoulders. I couldn't get enough of him. Brooks's hands skimmed over my hips, pulling me against him, as he revived my soul with deep kisses. We kissed each other so desperately that our entire bodies curved into one another.

Brooks let out a low groan as my tongue brushed his. He broke the kiss, pulling away and resting his head on mine, his eyes reptilian slits. His hands rubbed my back, the built-up tension melting away.

"That's it?" I questioned, my breath coming out in shaking pants, slightly disappointed at the change of pace.

"Never."

"Then why di—"

"Because I'm not about to take you in some dingy warehouse that smells like death and chemicals."

I blushed at his words.

As if he could read my mind, Brooks's hand grasped my chin, running his thumb over my bottom lip. "But don't think I won't finish what we just started."

I hopped off the table, my body buzzing with excitement and nervous energy. His hands continued to skim my hips as we searched the piles of papers and notes.

Guilt began to pull at my heart.

Though it had been earth shattering, that kiss hadn't changed anything. I still had to leave Iydara. I wouldn't risk his life or anyone else's. Not anymore.

Brooks released a breath when he found the two vials of potion. The notes we found suggested that the purple one was the potion that was creating the golems. But there were no notes about the yellow potion, and it was the only vial of its kind in the entire warehouse.

Brooks's mind seemed to be going in a hundred different directions as he shoved papers into a bag along with samples of the purple potion. He took out a book from the bag he was carrying, reading highlighted notes and murmuring to himself.

He slowed, looking at the potions with intent.

"Stone me," Brooks said, placing the yellow vial in my hand.

I did a double take, sure that I had heard him wrong.

Releasing a dark laugh, I said, "That's a good one, Brooks, really. But you're insane if you think I'm going to stone you."

He reached out for me.

He looked haunted. Like this case would solve all of his problems. I supposed it would. If Brooks solved it, then he would be that much closer to finding his sisters.

"Why?" I asked him, glancing down at his hand on my arm.

"Because we need to know what is in this vial. If it is what I think it is, then it changes everything. I'm asking you, as my partner, to trust me.

Stone me, then pour the yellow potion into my lips. Just please, don't turn me into a golem."

"What do you think it is?" I asked, though I felt like I already knew the answer.

"I think it's a cure for gorgon statues. Some of the ingredients that I can smell encourage healing and skin regrowth."

"Why don't we just take it to the lab? Have Eirlys take a look at them?" I pleaded, panic beginning to constrict my breathing.

"The analysis would take days. And you and I both know that we don't have that."

I swallowed thickly. My heart raced loudly in my chest.

Was I actually considering stoning him?

"This way, we know for sure," he murmured back, wrapping his arms around my shoulders.

If this vial held a cure for gorgon statues, then it would change everything. Gorgons would no longer be a threat to humans. With this, statues created by dead or unwilling gorgons would be freed.

But what if it was a cure for golems as well as gorgon statues?

Dread curled in my belly.

Would there be side effects for Brooks?

The detective readied himself, using a rusted forklift as support.

I opened myself up to my gorgon, allowing her to take control. Chills skittered down my spine as I let her in, groans of pleasure escaping my mouth before I could stop them.

I kept my eyes on the floor, ashamed of my appearance.

"Lovely," Brooks whispered into the darkness, placing a finger under my chin. I rested my cheek in his hand as he rubbed his thumb against my face.

I met his dark cobalt eyes with my emerald, reptilian ones.

He didn't flinch. Not once.

Rennyn had always cringed when I brought forward my gorgon. He preferred my mortal form and never let me talk about my gorgon, as if she would taint him.

But not Brooks. Never him.

He held my gaze, a strange emotion flickering across his face. I was still shocked that he wasn't terrified of me or my snakes. Most people were disgusted by the slithering creatures, even Rohesia was, but Brooks only looked calm and interested. My snakes seemed to like him, a rather friendly one curling around his hand.

"You don't scare me, Usa. And neither do your garter snakes."

I snorted at his reference, remembering the first time we met, and rested my forehead against his chest. The air around us seemed to grow shallower as I distanced myself from the torrential emotions that were growing in my chest.

"If you use your dunamis will it protect you from any nasty side effects?" I ask, before I continued with this delirious experiment.

"Smart thinking," Brooks agreed, quickly transforming into his dragon-like form. His wing looked better than last night, but was still wrapped up tightly.

"We were both

"See you on the other side."

Those were the last words I heard as I stoned Brooks de Blasis. He readied himself, trust and only slight hesitation beaming in his reptilian eyes.

The process occurred rather quickly. Starting at his eyes and spreading out like a drop of blood on the floor, the stone took over his body. Within a minute, Brooks was completely covered in stone, even his wings bore the evidence of my curse. I could hear his faint, yet strong, heartbeat. I knew he could still hear me, but it felt like I was talking to a ghost.

Though I knew I could unstone Brooks if the potion didn't work, it terrified me that I could possibly be giving him the wrong one. That I could turn him into a golem with one misguided move.

If we were wrong, then Brooks would turn into a horrendous golem, and I would be forced to kil—

No. I shook my head.

I didn't want to think about that possibility.

I quickly grabbed the bottles, smelling them.

We had agreed to give him the yellow potion, but I was terrified that we were wrong. I had to trust Brooks, just like he had trusted me to turn him into stone.

"Breathe, Usa. Breathe."

Unscrewing the cap, I took a deep, steadying breath. Faking the courage I so desperately needed, I raised the container to Brooks's lips and watched in awe as the potion was slowly absorbed into his full lips. The bottle had only been half full, and I prayed that a few drops would be sufficient.

My heart beat frantically as I waited for the potion to work.

Only, nothing happened.

Minutes passed and Brooks stayed trapped in a tomb of stone. Maybe the potion was a fluke. Or perhaps it wasn't being absorbed into his body correctly.

There was only one way to find out.

"I apologize in advance if you can feel this, Brooks. It's gonna hurt like a bitch." I grabbed a large syringe, filling it with the potion.

There was a thinner spot of stone, similar to thick mud, that my mother had told me about on all gorgon statues. In case we needed to suddenly kill a statue, stabbing them in the vulnerable spot would be faster than unstoning and killing them.

Without hesitation, I stabbed it hard and fast into Brooks's neck. And when the needle cut through the tender spot with ease, I sighed in comfort that my mother had been telling the truth.

I pushed the plunger down, watching as the liquid seeped into Brooks's stony skin. Seconds passed, and I was just beginning to think that the potion had failed again when the skin around his neck started to crack and fall to the ground.

Bingo.

I landed in a heap on the floor, with Brooks on top of me, no longer a statue and no longer in his dunamis form.

The potion had worked.

I couldn't believe it.

There was a cure for gorgon statues.

"You...you're crushing my kidney." I inhaled sharply, attempting to move out from under Brooks's large form.

"You don't even know where your kidney is," Brooks stated matter-of-factly, his knee sitting between my legs. He seemed remarkably okay for someone who had been a statue just moments before.

"Fine. Liver, spleen, appendix, any organ at the forefront of my body is now smushed thanks to your massive body."

"Ever so cranky, Usa," Brooks murmured, playing with the snakes in my hair. They wrapped around his hand lovingly.

I was still in my gorgon form, and Brooks still didn't seem to mind. In fact, he appeared to be enjoying the view.

"Aren't you afraid of snakes?" I asked him, watching as he stroked my snakes and they attempted to cuddle with his hand.

"Terrified."

"But you aren't afraid of mine?"

"No, because they're part of you. And I can't exactly be afraid of them when I have dragon scales and can spew fire."

If I hadn't been furiously blushing already, I definitely was when he spoke those words. Brooks placed a gentle kiss on my lips as he stood up, gently hauling me to my feet as we started to explore the rest of the warehouse.

Outside, stained boxes sat around the perimeter of the warehouse, along a towering privacy fence that was topped with spikes and rolls of barbed wire.

Dead grass crunched underneath our boots as we circled the backyard of the property. There was a single toolshed sitting adjacent to the length of fence that led out to the alleyway.

I grabbed the door of the shed, the handle covered in chipped paint and dirt specks. Brooks nodded, unsheathing his sword, and taking a step forward.

The door opened.

And Stheno launched herself at Brooks.

Unlike the other night, Brooks easily blocked my sister, throwing her to the ground quickly. Green blood covered Stheno and I looked at her in horror.

Bewilderment shocked me to my very core.

Stheno was one of the greatest fighters in my coven and now, she was decorated in cuts and slashes, her clothes hanging from her in scraps.

Her scalp was covered in scabs and blood.

The remnants of her snakes were hanging by thin films of skin. Their hearts had been ripped out and taken. It would take weeks for them to heal and grow back. The process would be agonizing and tedious. With her snakes open to infection, they could die.

Stheno wouldn't die from the process, but she could lose the very thing that made her a gorgon.

Brooks stood above my writhing sister, his sword pressed against the thin skin of her neck. Her scales were muted and lifeless, some scattering to the ground as she fought against Brooks' hold.

I moved towards my sister, kneeling in front of her, a vicious smile tugging on the corner of my mouth. "Guess we aren't going to Kilmarn after all?"

She hissed at me, lunging forward, falling short of my boots.

"It's over, Stheno. We found the potion that turns statues into golems. As well as the cure for gorgon statues."

"What is the cure?" she asked, her breathing heavy and strained.

"Don't play dumb. It won't help you, not now," Brooks said, running a finger over the blade of his sword before he sheathed it.

I watched as Brooks placed my sister in a pair of handcuffs, reading her rights as we waited for backup.

We had found the potions. This was all the proof I needed: Stheno was the one behind the creation of the golems. The vile of statue-curing liquid was burning a hole in my pocket and I was impatient to share our findings with Rohesia and The Collectress.

Sirens rang throughout the boundary as Brooks hauled my sister to her feet, her head hung low in defeat.

Despite the good news, there was a growing pit in my stomach. Who had attacked Stheno? Who had ripped the hearts of her snakes out? It had been done rather cruelly.

Was The Collectress acting out of revenge for turning her precious statues into cruel and almost unkillable monsters? We would learn more when we brought her in for questioning.

"I have one more thing I need to do here. You guys leave here the second her ass lands on the cruiser's leather seat," Brooks said, as he handed Stheno off to a different detective

Confused, I followed him to the barrels of golem potion, watching as the final detective departed from the building.

"So, this never ends up in the wrong hands again," he said solemnly, taking a deep breath and spewing flaming maroon and orange flames from his mouth.

We watched in silence as the barrels went up in smoke.

The barrels of purple liquid were the only thing that would be damaged, and we had been sure to grab enough samples to confirm our suspicions.

The glow of the fire illuminated my face, and joy stirred in my heart. Though we still needed to find the why and how of Stheno creating the golems, it felt pretty good to watch all of her hard work burn.

32

The patrol cars departed the warehouse in a show of flashing lights and blaring sirens. Wardens were storming the warehouse and The Broken Vial Apothecary. Every inch of the buildings were being turned over and evidence was being collected now that the noxious barrels of potion were destroyed.

The Collectress said there wouldn't be a public trial and that she would handle the matters personally. I was in favor of this, and she asked me and Brooks to be present during that time. She would be punishing Stheno for the murders of Oliver and Nona as well as the golem attacks.

They must have been in the wrong place at the wrong time. My sister was full of malice and cruelty, and I knew she wouldn't be above killing innocents, especially since she had already murdered hundreds of people by creating the golems.

"Do you think she's guilty?" Iva said from where she sat in the back seat. She was a mage and the Keeper of the Western Boundary.

Brooks glanced at her from the rearview mirror. "Why wouldn't she be?"

She shrugged. "Just want to be sure that this is over."

He gave her a tight smile. "That's hopefully what we'll figure out soon enough."

She nodded, looking out the window while sighing heavily.

"Something you need to get off your chest, Iva?" Brooks asked, his voice tense.

Her eyes shifted to mine. "How do we know she didn't have anything to do with it?"

I stiffened in my seat, uncomfortable as I glared at the Keeper behind us. It had gotten around to mages that I was a gorgon, thanks to working for The Collectress.

The sedan came to a stop.

"Get out," Brooks commanded, his powerful voice holding a dark note. His eyes bore into Iva's, which were widened with shock.

"What?" she said, offended.

"Out."

"But we're over an hour from The Hub."

"Not my problem. You should've thought about that before you insulted my partner."

She continued to sit in the back seat, shellshocked. I couldn't help but stare at Brooks in surprise. Sure, Iva had insulted me, but that didn't warrant her having to walk all the way back.

"Better get a move on if you want to make it back before mid-afternoon, Keeper," Brooks said, tapping his fingers impatiently against the steering wheel.

The slamming of the back passenger door shook the entire vehicle. It was enough to break me out of my stupor, as I watched Iva's athletic form fading into the distance.

"Anything you need to say, Zayd?" Brooks asked the younger Keeper of the Eastern Boundary in the back seat. The Keeper paled and shook his head violently.

"Good," Brooks responded, a wolfish grin on his face.

I rounded on him. "What in gods' name did you do that for?"

He shrugged. "No one insults you and gets away with it."

The vehicle slowed for a second time as we caught up with the rest of the convoy. There were four patrol cars in front of us, and they were all at a standstill.

Brooks and I shared a weighted look. Zayd exited the vehicle first, me and Brooks following behind him. Our weapons were not drawn but our hands were in position in case we needed to use them.

347

The Eastern Boundary's Keeper circled around the driver's side of the first patrol car in front of us. Brooks and I walked to the passenger's side.

"Shit," Brooks cursed.

The driver and wardens in the vehicle had been transformed into statues of stone, their screams forever captured in a layer of gray cement. We drew our weapons and found the same situation in the three other patrol cars.

My hands grasped my daggers, sweat causing the metal to grow slick and sticky. Stheno wasn't able to stone anyone just yet, not with her snakes needing to regrow.

Which meant my coven was closer than I had thought.

"Do not look them in the eyes," I said harshly to Brooks and Zayd. "They have no mercy and will stone you at the first given opportunity."

Zayd gulped loudly but bravely started to scan the area. Brooks gave my hand a squeeze before dropping it and walking into a thicket of trees.

"Ceto!" I shouted into the air.

I was tired of letting fear of my coven control my future. They had taken everything from me, but I wouldn't let them take any more. Today was the day I would start fighting back.

Gravel crunched under my feet as I examined the bodies of the stoned. "Pretty sloppy job for the coven leader. But I doubt the elders would have let you lead the coven after I escaped. Don't be ashamed though, I'm sure you're still the most powerful, well, at least the second most powerful gorgon in all of Iydara."

I continued to spout off offenses, waiting for her to come out. I had already shifted into my gorgon form the moment we found the first wardens stoned in their car.

My skin tingled and tightened, I could sense my sisters in the depths of the forest, watching and waiting. A sharp scream echoed throughout the countryside and caused the hairs on the back of my neck to stand up straight.

Zayd.

Brooks and I found him at the same time, in the iron grasp of my mother. I hadn't seen her in years and time had not been kind to her.

The arms of the Keeper lay limply at his sides, my mother pressing her forearm into his throat.

Brooks and Zayd avoided her eyes, but I stared straight into them, knowing that she couldn't hurt me. Next to her stood Aspasia, another gorgon who had received her blessing on my sixteenth birthday, and Stheno.

I was surprised to see the former, but I reminded myself that I would be doing the exact same thing if it had been Aspasia who Athena had cursed.

"One more step and I'll stone him."

The gravel crunched under my foot. "Go ahead."

Ceto raised an eyebrow at me as I looked at the mage without mercy. The nonchalant look on my face had Zayd shaking.

"The daughter I knew would have wept at an innocent being stoned."

"You lost the right to be her mother when you tried to kill her," Brooks spat next to me, and I winced at his words, wishing he would have stayed quiet instead.

Ceto pushed the Keeper to the ground, her interest suddenly elsewhere. I motioned for Zayd to run, but he paid no attention.

"Stheno didn't tell me you had a lover, and a handsome one at that," she crooned, stepping towards the detective.

I growled, moving in front of him with my knives raised.

"That's no way to treat your mother." Ceto frowned, but didn't take any further steps.

"Would you still mind if I stoned him?" she asked.

I swallowed loudly. "No."

She gave me a predator's grin. "Oh, Medusa. A mother can always tell when her children are lying. And lucky for me, you were always a terrible liar."

Aspasia launched herself at me, all gangly arms and suppressed rage.

349

Her fist connected with my cheekbone, and I was thrown back into Brooks. He attempted to catch me but failed, grunting in discomfort as my head collided with his chin.

The gorgon clawed at my face, her nails digging deep trenches into my skin. I yelled at Brooks to keep his eyes shut, afraid he would open them in an attempt to help me fight.

"Up!" I shouted at him, watching as he swiped at Aspasia blindly. Heading my advice, Brooks aimed higher and his swords cut through one of her snakes. Aspasia bellowed in pain, green blood splattering across the ground.

Ceto and Stheno continued to watch us with boredom.

"Left, down!"

This time Brooks missed, but I took the opportunity to sneak up behind Aspasia and attack her from behind. Brooks quickly shifted into his dunamis form, preparing to spit flames on her.

The air stilled as my back was turned towards Ceto. The sudden quiet was conspicuous and a reminder that I should never turn my back to her.

Silence signified death in my coven.

Metal crunched around us as a semi-truck barreled into the patrol cars. The screeching metal made my ears ring and I fell on my back, reaching for Brooks.

I was thrown back into the path of the moving vehicle. My back collided with the road, and I saw stars as my mother stood in the forest.

"That's our ride. See you on the full moon, darling," she said sweetly, kissing me on my cheek and pulling Stheno and Aspasia behind her.

My head was ringing as I fought to remain conscious.

The ground swayed and oscillated underneath my feet as I hurried to find Brooks. Hadn't he been just beside me?

More sirens were screeching in the background, and I wished they would stop. The sound was only making my pounding headache worse.

A crumpled form lay on the side of the road, and I found Brooks alive. He seemed to be unconscious but was breathing and didn't seem to have any obvious injuries.

The Keeper from earlier lay next to him.

He hadn't been as lucky.

Copious amounts of crimson blood had leaked onto the snow from a gash at Zayd's throat. There would be no coming back from an injury of this magnitude. Regret reared its ugly head as I closed his eyelids over glassy brown eyes.

I turned my attention back to Brooks, realizing that there was blood dripping from one of his wings. I hadn't seen it at first glance but the scarlet liquid was now pooling on the ground.

Looking closer at his wing, panic built in my throat.

But instead of another gastly wound I expected to find, ten numbers stared back at me. My mother or sister had used the fallen Keeper's blood to write on Brooks's skin. My stomach turned as I analyzed the numbers.

Carefully turning over Brooks's uninjured wing, I came across another message.

'Call me ;)' was written haphazardly across the membrane in the same handwriting that had written the message outside De Blasis Bijouterie.

My stomach clenched as I punched the numbers into my cell phone. The area code was from Iydara.

The phone rang.

A familiar voice answered.

I squeezed the phone, watching as it shattered in my hand.

33

Casimar was escorted into the interrogation room just before dark the following day. His hands were cuffed behind his back. The shackles were causing his wrists to turn red and raw, and I was oddly satisfied that he seemed to be in pain.

Brooks pushed him down into his seat and motioned for me to enter. The detective sat across from Casimar, the latter's eyes widening as he caught sight of me.

Anger sparked in my soul as I looked at the mage who was partially to blame for the golems. Though my sister had escaped, The Collectress seemed to be satisfied enough with Casimar's arrest; she'd had it broadcasted across all of Iydara's news channels.

I pulled back a chair, the metal scraping against the ground. Brooks hadn't been seriously injured in the attack, and Ceto hadn't attempted to take me back to Kilmarn. This, and her cryptic departing message, left me wondering if my mother had another attack planned for the night of the full moon.

Once I called the number that had been written on Brooks's wings and realized it was Casimar's, I hurriedly informed The Collectress.

She shockingly discovered that the convoy's location had been leaked to an online chatroom. From there, techs then tracked the leak to Casimar's work laptop.

The wardens that had been stoned were nothing but piles of rock by the time the semi-truck had barreled through the cars. The Keeper that had survived was the one we had dropped off miles down the road.

Brooks was trying not to blame himself. He was convinced that he could have prevented the attack if he hadn't stopped to kick Iva from the vehicle. But I tried to reassure him that no one could stop my mother.

Slamming a folder on the table, I placed pictures of the warehouse and the attacks in front of Casimar. The mage's face was void of any emotion. Rohesia stood with E.E. behind the two-way mirror and had prepared a list of questions for us.

Brooks rolled up his sleeves and rested his chin on his hands. He had been deathly quiet since arriving, and I realized that I would be seeing a different side of him during this interrogation.

"It seems your partner ratted you out the first chance she got. You want to tell us about that?" Brooks asked, tilting his head at Casimar.

Casimar stared at a spot above our heads. He was strapped into the chair by a leather belt and was chained at the hands and ankles. A spell in the interrogation room prevented mage magic from being used, which made me feel a little bit better about being in a cramped space with him.

Brooks stood up, loosening his tie and throwing it on the back of his chair. His eyes were dark, and he looked like death incarnate.

The detective stood behind Casimar, his hands digging into the mage's shoulders. "You want to know what I think?"

Casimar remained silent, shifting his gaze to mine.

"I think that you were Stheno's bitch. That you were the one who did all of her dirty work, and she hid in the shadows, bathing in all of the glory. We're willing to cut you a deal, Casimar. Those gorgons are wicked, evil, and manipulative things.

"Excluding you, lovely." Brooks threw me a wink before his gaze returned to Casimar. "Help us help you."

The mage just continued to stare at me.

Brooks whispered in his ear, "They don't care about you. They're walking free. And where are you? Locked in here."

Casimar's jaw ticked, but still, he only stared at me and ignored Brooks. I didn't back down from his stare, I simply returned it.

"I want to talk to her. Alone."

I stiffened at Casimar's gruff voice. It sounded like he had been deprived of water for days.

"Absolutely not." Brooks chuckled darkly.

Standing up, I pulled Brooks outside the interrogation room. He looked down at me with concern and apprehension.

"If he's willing to talk, let me get it out of him."

"Don't you think it's weird that he only wants you in there? It doesn't make any sense. Especially when we'll be out here listening anyway." He motioned to E.E. and Rohesia who were standing a few feet away.

"I agree with Rook," Rohesia chimed in, rubbing her arms.

Raising my eyebrows at the pair, I looked to E.E. for help.

"Usa has a point," the senior detective sighed. "She's the only chance we have to really get him talking."

Brooks nodded, trusting in my abilities, while Rohesia looked hesitant. Calling on my gorgon, I took a steadying breath and walked into the room with Brooks behind me.

"Touch a single hair, or snake, on her head and I will feed you to the charybdis," Brooks growled, "alive."

Casimar gulped, feeling the weight of this threat.

I wasn't dumb enough to enter the room without any protection, and my gorgons were already spitting and hissing at the criminal seated in front of me.

Casimar seemed to open up immediately without Brooks's lingering presence. "About time you got rid of your boyfriend."

Ignoring his snide comment, I shuffled around the papers and images that were still scattered on the table.

"You need to talk, Casimar. It's the only way for them to cut you a deal," I said slowly.

The mage leaned forward. "Good. I can't wait to see their faces when they find out the reason that I created the golems was you."

I snorted, "Me?"

"Yes, you."

"Why?"

He played with a picture of a decapitated golem in his hands, admiring it with greedy eyes. "I was her favorite before you came along. Before you ruined everything."

Confusion tore through me. He couldn't possibly mean—

"The Collectress?"

A sharp nod.

"She hates me, Casimar. She branded me and beat me any chance that she got. That's not love."

He snickered, greasy hair hanging in his eyes. "That's her love language, Usa. I thought you knew that."

I remained silent.

"I have the same branding as you on my back. Except I'm missing three letters. You know why? Because you showed up." His voice had dropped an octave and his cheeks stained pink with fury.

"You created the golems because she didn't want to brand you anymore?" I laughed without humor.

Casimar grunted with frustration, his hands clutching handfuls of his greasy hair. "You're not understanding. I didn't make the first golems, not Beresford's at least. I was responsible for the ones the night of the garden attack, not the rest. The rest were your sister."

"Interesting," I stated simply.

"You were supposed to die that night," he continued, roaring desperately, "but you and Rohesia were late and ruined my plan."

Realization hit me like a freight train.

The garden attack hadn't been aimed at The Collectress. It had been an attempt on my life. Casimar wanted me dead because I was The Collectress's favorite.

"We found gallons of the golem potion at the warehouse. Do you know who created it?" I asked, switching topics before I leapt across the table and crushed his throat with my hands.

"Stheno called it 'dust.' She didn't trust me enough to tell me who it was from, just that a coven of Hecate's had created it."

"Do you know which coven?" I pressed.

Casimar rolled his eyes. "See, there you go again. Dumb as a rock. I can't believe that The Collectress chose you over me."

"Alright. If Stheno and you weren't making the dust, and one of Hecate's covens was, what about the cure? Did you and Stheno make it? Or was it the coven?"

Casimar furrowed his non-existent eyebrows. "What cure?"

"The cure for gorgon statues. We found a bottle of it in the warehouse."

Casimar shook his head. "That's impossible. Gorgon statues can only be unstoned by the gorgon who created them. Not even dunamis can undo them."

"Stop lying. We found it. We just need to know who made it."

The mage stayed quiet, silently insisting that he had no prior knowledge of the cure.

"What about Agnes and Oliver? Did you kill them? Or was that Stheno?"

Casimar looked sick to his stomach. "They're dead?"

I nodded.

"Shit." He ruffled his thin hair. "I told Stheno about the break-ins, but she called me an idiotic liar. Wonderful sister you have by the way."

"What break-ins?"

He leaned in close. "Someone was using the warehouse when we weren't there. Don't know who. They turned off the cameras and stole some of the barrels of dust."

"Do you have evidence of these break-ins?"

Casimar opened his mouth, only to shut it.

"You don't believe me."

"Of course not. You're exactly the kind of person to lie and pin this on someone else."

"I didn't kill Agnes or Oliver. And I certainly didn't make a cure. Stheno would have castrated me if I did."

Stheno and the rest of the coven would kill or maim anyone they thought had created a cure for gorgon statues. It seemed that they truly hadn't known about it. And neither had Casimar.

"Okay. Say that someone else was breaking in. Why would they take the hearts of Stheno's snakes? Or maybe you were growing tired of being inferior to her? Just like you grew tired of being beneath me."

"They took the hearts?" Casimar let out a low whistle.

"Why does that matter?" I asked.

"Gorgon snake hearts could be used in the making of a cure for statues, I suppose. Nature demands a balance, and the snake hearts could contribute to that balance. A pretty thing like you cou—"

"Enough. Where did Stheno get the dust from?" I snapped at him, growing more and more impatient.

"I already told you, Stheno had it already. From one of Hecate's covens or a rogue witch. She never would tell me."

"How did you convince Stheno to let you borrow some of this dust?"

"I caught her in the garden one night. Convinced her that I wouldn't turn her in if she gave me some of it and let me in on her plans. Stheno didn't seem to mind."

"Why was she creating the golems?"

"To find you, get you at the front of the investigation. And to create an army for your mother."

My heart stopped in my chest.

"Why would Ceto want an army?"

Casimar shrugged. "Stheno never told me."

"Where is the army now?"

"Wouldn't you like to know?" He smiled, his yellow teeth snapping at me. His words taunted me, reminding me of when I had used the same phrase against him at the casino.

"Last question," I mumbled. "How did you alert the gorgons about the convoy's location?"

"Why don't you ask your boyfriend?"

The door slammed open, and Brooks and a warden entered. Brooks looked like the god of wrath and gripped Casimar's upper arm tightly.

"Wait! I'm not done yet."

"Too bad," Brooks muttered, hauling Casimar to his feet.

"Wait, I have something for her!"

"Too bad," Brooks repeated.

"Brooks, wait. What do you have, Casimar?" I asked, curiosity pulling me from my seat.

"A message from the dead."

Mages could sometimes communicate with the dead, and I wasn't going to ignore his claim, even if it was just a ploy to get me close to him.

I nodded at Brooks and the warden.

Stepping close to the mage, I motioned for Brooks and the warden to step back. Casimar got as close to me as he possibly could with his heavy chains.

"Agnes said to guard your heart. That the one you share it with will betray you."

My heart pounded in my chest. I looked up at Casimar, only to be blinded by a wad of spit from his mouth.

Brooks kicked out his legs from underneath him and struck him in the ribs with his steel toe boots. Casimar chortled and coughed as blood leaked from his mouth.

I watched in silent dismay as Brooks led him out of the room, my chest heavy.

Had I shown Brooks my heart when I shouldn't have?

Agnes's words continued to ring throughout my mind as I exited the interrogation room.

34

I couldn't sleep. Too many thoughts and doubts were crawling around in my mind. Brooks was peacefully asleep next to me, his snoring gently echoing throughout the room.

Kicking off the blankets, I sighed.

Agnes's words were still haunting me, three days after Casimar's sentencing. The Collectress had sentenced him to life in prison and put out a large bounty on Stheno's head.

E.E. and The Collectress were building a team to go and find her. Rumors were flowing around The Hub that Brooks and I would be leading the assault team.

Agnes said to guard my heart, and I'd been doing the opposite of that recently. Mine and Brooks's relationship had grown hot and heavy, a burning and raging inferno that took us both by surprise.

I tried to reassure myself that Casimar had only said that to get under my skin. But why had I lied when Brooks asked me what Casimar had said?

Instead of telling him the truth, I had told him that Casimar had only repeated the original fortune that Agnes had given me.

And how had Brooks found me when I had left for the apothecary that morning?

The case was officially closed, but I had the feeling that we were missing crucial details, like why my mother hadn't attempted to kidnap me and bring me back to Kilmarn. The full moon was only a week away, and I doubted my mother would let me fall through her grasp a second time.

She knew where I was and who I was working for.

And who was behind the creation of the cure, and why had they done it? Were they responsible for Oliver's and Agnes's deaths? Did the cure work for golems as well?

Rohesia and E.E. reassured me that Casimar had been lying about not knowing there was a cure for gorgon statues, but I wasn't too sure.

I hadn't told Brooks my concerns because we had hardly seen each other the past few days. He had received a promotion for solving the case and had been busy with interviews and congratulatory brunches and dinners.

I felt the bed shift.

Brooks nuzzled my neck, and the tension in my body seemed to melt away. "Hey, you."

"Hey," I said softly.

"Why can't you sleep?"

I was tempted to lie again, but the pressing questions on my mind were about to drive me crazy. I decided not to tell him about Agnes's fortune, but maybe he could help me answer the other questions.

"Too many thoughts in my head."

"Like what?" Brooks asked, propping himself up on his elbow.

"Why didn't my mom take me?" I questioned.

"Maybe she was feeling generous?"

"That word is not in her vocabulary." I rested my head on a pillow. "I just feel like she's planning something else."

"Why do you think that?"

I shrugged my shoulders, debating on telling him about my mother vowing to see me on the next full moon. Brooks took my questions seriously and I appreciated it.

Perhaps I was wrong for not telling him Agnes's message.

"My mother told me that she would be seeing me on the full moon."

A snake gently wrapped itself around Brooks's hand. I had been shifting into my gorgon form more often as I grew comfortable in his presence.

"Do you think she was telling the truth?" he asks.

"I don't know."

He contemplated my words without judgment.

"Do you feel like you're waiting for the other shoe to drop or that we need to look into the case more?"

"Both," I answered honestly, "and who killed Agnes and Oliver? And who was breaking in to use the warehouse space? Who created the cure? Who attacked Stheno? Is it all the same person?" I sighed. "I guess that's all that's bothering me."

"That's all?" Brooks chuckled, his eyes glittering in the low light of the bedroom. "Questions like that have been swirling around in my head as well, if I'm being honest."

My chest constricted as I looked at him. An unfamiliar emotion threatened to choke me as I ran a finger over his sharp cheekbone.

Casimar was wrong. Brooks wouldn't betray me.

"And I think you're onto something, lovely," Brooks sighed, pressing a kiss into the palm of my hand.

"What do you mean?" My heart was beating rapidly in my chest, whether it was from Brooks's words or his lips pressing light kisses onto my skin, I couldn't be sure.

"I believe The Collectress has more involvement than she says she does. And there are too many loose ends, which she doesn't care to tie up. The golem-making potion is gone and Casimar and Stheno were proven to be behind the crimes. But, I'm worried she's hiding something, especially after Stheno killed my uncle."

"But if The Collectress is the missing piece of the puzzle, then why would she make a cure for the golems?" I questioned.

The questions wouldn't stop forming in my mind, no matter how hard I tried to grab them and stuff them down into the dark crevices of my brain.

Brooks released a heavy sigh. "People do crazy things all the time without a reason. Maybe we're in way over our heads."

Disappointment filled me.

"But if you still want to investigate the case more, chase some more leads, then I fully support you. Just don't let E.E. or Rohesia know."

My grin could have lit up an entire night sky.

Squealing, I wrapped my arms around Brooks and straddled him. "You're the best."

He answered my statement by gripping my waist and inching his hands up the hem of my shirt. The small touch nearly undid me as blood roared in my ears.

We hadn't had a moment alone since the day in the warehouse, and I had replayed our earth-shattering kiss over and over in my head. I wanted more, maybe even needed more.

But I was also petrified.

"You found me, Usa."

"What do you mean?" I asked, lightly tracing the scars that were scattered across his broad chest and neck.

Brooks had told me that Yandi had cut his skin over and over again, every time he failed to kill a monster or stumbled during training. In a way, it reminded me of The Collectress branding my back from my shortcomings.

Brooks looked up at me, his grip on my waist tightening. "You found the parts of me that I didn't know still existed. I thought I had lost those parts when my sisters disappeared. So, thank you."

My cheeks grew warm. "Maybe we found each other."

He trailed his fingers down my back in unhurried, agonizing circles. I pulled the silk shirt over my head, exposing myself to him, wearing nothing but my sleeping shorts. My heart raced in my chest.

A low, breathless sound escaped the back of his throat. Brooks's eyes darkened as he took in my bare shoulders and breasts. His hands trailed from my hips to my stomach, finally cupping my breasts in his hands.

I started to change back into my mortal form, but Brooks stopped me. "What are you doing?"

I frowned. "I didn't want to make you uncomfortable with my snakes. Rennyn ne—"

Suddenly, I was on my back, and Brooks was straddling me.

Swallowing, I waited for the unavoidable fear to come over me.

I waited to hear blood rushing in my ears.

For sweat to coat my hands and back.

And for my chest to constrict as I struggled to breathe.

But the panic never came.

None of it did.

"I wasn't given a choice when I was sent to Raas, nor when I wasn't informed of my sisters' disappearances the moment it happened, so I'm making a choice now. And I choose you."

"And I never want to hear you say that name ever again, understand?" Brooks says, dragging his thumb across my lower lip.

At his words, I shyly changed back into my gorgon form, Brooks letting out a growl of approval at the sight. My hands yanked at his shirt, removing it. My mouth grew dry as he bared his chest to me. Strong muscles rippled beneath my hands as I explored his broad chest and shoulders.

Again, I wanted him to touch me. I needed him to.

"Understood."

It was foolish to keep pretending that we didn't want a relationship. To keep pretending that we didn't crave each other's touch.

"But first, I need to ask you a question?"

I raised my eyebrows at him.

"Do I have your consent to continue?"

Brooks was a pretty amazing man.

Blinking tears away, I dragged a hand over his cheek. "Yes, you do, Brooks. I will tell you to stop if I'm uncomfortable. Do I have yours?"

"Yes, lovely. You always have."

Brooks leaned down, pressing light kisses onto my collarbone. I sighed as he started to apply the kisses lower, and lower. His teeth grazed the sensitive skin between my breasts, and I arched my back.

My shorts slid up my hips as I wrapped my legs around his waist, feeling the extent of his need pressing into me. He groaned as he gently bit my lower lip.

Brooks raised his mouth from my skin, his eyes holding a question that mine answered. Gently, and carefully, he removed my sleeping shorts, leaving me bare.

"My turn." I grinned, pulling his boxers down.

His hand skimmed my cheek and I leaned into his palm.

Brooks's eyes were dilated as he took in my naked body. His hands gripped around my hips. The small circles he continued to trace on my hips were driving me insane.

As I pulled him forward, his chest grazed mine and I gasped.

Our lips met and he released a moan into my mouth as his hands grasped my waist and pulled me towards him, my legs wrapping around his torso.

Locking my arms around his neck, I brushed against him, slowly and deliberately, creating friction that was driving us insane. He met my pace, rubbing up and down.

Before I could stop them, tears threatened to spill from my eyes. At the sight of them, Brooks stopped all of his movement, leaving my body cold in the absence of his touch.

"What's wrong?" he asked me, his voice filled with concern.

"No, don't stop." I sniffled. "These are happy tears, Brooks. Because this time, it is my choice. And I choose you. If I start to get triggered, I'll tell you."

I'd gotten triggered during intimate moments with Rennyn, who had little patience in those moments. He would huff and puff and roll his eyes when I asked him to stop.

But I didn't expect that from Brooks.

Brooks leaned into me, sighing as tears pricked at his own eyes, his voice sounded strangled. "I choose you too, lovely. I need you to remember that if this is the part of your life where you're at now, then that's okay. You won't be there forever. But you'll have me forever."

He began to kiss away my tears.

Gripping his face, I moved his mouth to mine.

His tongue was scorching, demanding. A deep, delightful throbbing was building in my belly, one I had never felt before Brooks.

Flipping me on my stomach, he trailed his lips down my shoulders and neck, causing whimpers of pleasure to escape from my lips. My back arched as his tongue licked my skin, along with the scraping of his teeth.

"More," I cried out.

"So, demanding," Brooks chuckled, but did as I commanded.

I surrendered completely to his touch, never thinking that a single kiss could undo me like Brooks's had. When he flipped me over once more, his mouth needily captured a peaked nipple.

His touch felt good. Right. Not scary or terrifying.

A moan tumbled from my parted lips, pleasure coiling in my core as his fingers tweaked my other nipple.

His touch was electric.

We're electric.

I dug my nails into his bicep, my back arching as his tongue left my breast and went further south. Pleasure unlike anything I had ever felt before caused my thighs to tremble with need.

"Usa," Brooks moaned, licking and lapping at the space between my hip bone and navel, "you are everything. Everything."

His words almost caused me to come undone.

Brooks's stubble scratched the sensitive skin of my thigh, his breath warm and heady as he glided his tongue expertly against my skin. "Remember when I told you that the first time I heard you moan that it was a fucking melody?"

"Uh, huh," I whimpered, my blood boiling with need.

"Well, I'd like to hear that melody right now."

Brooks's words caressed a breathy moan from my lips, as his tongue traced my center. Another moan escaped my mouth as the pleasure started and stopped again.

"Good, girl," he praised me, sinking a finger into my soaked core.

I cried out as his mouth moved to the sensitive nub, sucking and teasing me with every flick of his tongue. Brooks pressed a hand onto my hip, preventing me from bucking and getting the friction I desired.

Groaning in frustration, I threw my head back.

"More," I moaned.

"All you had to do was ask, lovely," Brooks teased, his eyes flaring.

Curling his finger, I gasped in bliss as he added a second.

And then a third.

"You're so gorgeous, lovely," Brooks admired, working my body so tight that I was sure it would explode. At his words, my back arched again, but this time, he didn't hold my hip down.

Grinding against his hungry mouth, he devoured me.

And when my orgasm crashed into me, I screamed his name, stars exploding in my vision. Waves of pleasure rolled through my taunt body and I rode his face and hand until I was wrung out.

My body slumped against the bed, exhausted with pure pleasure, but I needed. Grinning, I reached for Brooks, motioning for him to stand by the edge of the bed.

As I kneeled on the bed, I tugged him closer to me, watching as his thick length twitched in front of me.

"May I?" I asked breathlessly, as I traced the muscles of his stomach, memorizing every line and dip.

A guttural groan fell from his lips as he nodded, making me feel sensual and powerful.

Warm and hard in my eager hand, a moan tumbled out of his mouth, causing gooseflesh to form on my already sensitive skin.

My tongue carefully licked him as I took him in my mouth.

Brooks groaned, thrusting his hip into my mouth.

Wrapping my hand around the base, I licked and sucked his hard length while moving my hand up and down. I was surprised when he fists my snakes, but when a moan escaped my lips, I suddenly realized how good it felt.

Grasping his backside with my hands, I knead the tender flesh with my fingers, gagging on his length as he pressed me further down.

His eyes shifted, as scales and nubs of bone threatened to breakthrough his skin.

I could see the worry in his face, that he is perhaps embarrassed by this side of himself. But I'm not. I love it.

"Let go, Brooks," I ordered him.

"Are you sure?"

His eyes locked with mine and I nodded.

There was no going back.

Brooks released the hold on his dunamis and I was in awe of him.

Popping him out of my mouth, I admired the way his head tilted back in ecstasy. But before I could finish what I started, he dragged my hips to his, lifting my backside for a better angle.

In a single, fluid motion, Brooks buried himself inside of me. I cried out as his entire body jerked forward, as he moved deeper. His hand became tangled in my hair, and I moaned as he started to move.

My mind became a hazy mess of thoughts and desire as he thrusted into me at a maddeningly delicious pace. His breathing hitched as our sizzling skin meets.

I lose myself in him.

In the monstrous sides that we hide from others.

Untangling myself from him, I shifted onto my stomach, needing to take him deeper. Once he claimed me again, I threw my head back in sheer, aching bliss.

The throbbing in my body grew and I gripped the bedsheets, crying out. His hands gripped my hips, nails digging into my delicate skin, desperate to be closer to one another and relieve the building ache.

One desperate hand grabbed my breast, kneading the sensitive skin, taking me further and further to the edge. As I arched my back, Brooks finally filled me entirely.

Everything inside me tensed as a deep thrust pushed me over the edge, pleasure rolling through me like a riptide as I crumpled the bed sheets beneath my grasp.

Brooks follows closely behind me, as I rocked my hips against him. With one last, trembling thrust, he groaned, shuddering within me, my name on his lips.

Collapsing on top of him, I pressed my head to his chest, listening to the ticking of his racing heart. We lay like that for several moments, catching our breath, desire still flowing between us.

"What are you thinking about?" Brooks asked me, pressing a kiss to the top of my head.

"I'm happy," I replied, a sleepy smile blooming on my lips.

"How happy?"

"Very."

Brooks opened his mouth but I interrupt him.

"But I wouldn't say this was the *happiest* moment of my life. Once I found ten doubloons in my coat pocket and used it to buy a slice of chocolate cake. It was ah-mazing."

"Was it 'Better Than Sex Cake'?" he asked, chuckling deeply.

"I think it was," I giggle, "but we can always try again. Wouldn't want you to be outdone by a slice of dessert."

"How thoughtful of you," Brooks quipped, throwing me over his shoulder and slapping my butt as he took me to the living room. A furious blush crept up my neck as I buried my face into his shoulder.

And I realized that I had never been happier.

35

When the front door banged open at dawn, I was barely awake. My night had been filled with power naps and not much quality sleep. Brooks and I had woken up a few times during the night and had made the most of each other's bodies.

I quietly rose from our bed, where Brooks was sleeping under a mountain of tangled blankets. He did not flinch or acknowledge the sound.

Waiting for a clue as to what the unknown noise could be, I yanked on Brooks's discarded shirt and listened.

After a few tense minutes, I decided that it must have been the cleaning crew or the cat. My body relaxed and I laid down to catch some sleep before starting my afternoon investigation into the deaths of Agnes and Oliver.

The creaking of heavy boots on wood quickly caused me to change my mind. A few strained moments passed as I waited for the noises to recede, only they didn't.

Quietly, I tiptoed to Brooks's side of the bed and gently woke him up. He woke with a start, but I placed one hand over his mouth and the other to my lips, motioning for him to be silent. His cobalt eyes widened as he heard the commotion in the living room.

Grabbing his sword from the floor, he quickly and silently dressed. He handed me a small, makeshift shield that I held in my left hand, while palming a dagger in my right. Sweat trickled down my neck as my anxiety grew.

Thick, muffled voices fluttered around the kitchen, faint but audible from our bedroom. Given the layout of the apartment, the intruders would most likely discover the bedroom next.

I found my questions mirrored in Brooks's eyes.

The doorknob rattled and I inhaled a shaky breath through my nose. I braced myself as four wardens burst into the room.

I reacted.

A knife escaped my hand, striking a warden in his broad chest, forcing him to stagger back into the closet doors. He did not get back up. I continued to lash out.

Rohesia had told me horror stories about what happened to the detectives and their families after they arrested criminals. A target was placed on their back that was hard to dodge.

But it didn't make sense that we were fighting wardens instead of gorgons or Casimar's family members.

The other wardens drew hefty shields as we continued to fight for control. I went head-to-head with one as the others attacked Brooks.

Brooks threw a blazing ball of fire at one of his opponents' heads, the flames singeing the warden's hair. The fire hit a curtain and the flames greedily consumed the material.

The warden's eyes glowed with malice in the soft morning light, the flames reflecting in his pupils. A second warden stepped forward, and I threw a vase at his face.

He dodged the improvised weapon.

Panic built up in my chest.

I launched myself at the warden's muscular torso, swinging my wooden shield with all the strength I had. His brown eyes showed a hint of shock, but he hurriedly composed himself and deflected my body with skill.

I crashed into the wooden dresser in front of our bed, the world descending into a wash of pain and red. Using the momentum from crashing into the furniture, I slid across the room on my knees.

One of the wardens grabbed me by my hair and punched me in the face. My eyes watered and I was sure that my nose was broken.

Something dark and tormented exploded in me. Before I knew it, I had stoned the warden, along with two others. I couldn't bring myself to feel too guilty about it, especially since I could easily unstone them.

Confusion and panic swept through me as the person in charge stepped through the splintered door.

"Rohesia?" I asked, bewilderment tearing through my mind as I sat propped against the fractured dresser.

"Hi," she said solemnly.

"What in gods' name are you doing here? With an army of wardens, and an agenda at that?"

Rohesia started to sit next to me, but I stopped her, standing on my own two feet. She quickly healed my broken nose, even though I protested.

Rohesia glanced at Brooks, examining him with a distant look.

"New information has come to light. Information that you need to know about," rumbled a warden with auburn hair, who had followed Rohesia in.

"We don't want to make this hard for you, Usa," Rohesia continued. "Brooks is to go with the wardens. He is going to be interrogated."

My head was spinning. This did not make any sense. What would they want with Brooks? He could never betray me.

Right?

"You can't take him," I said, causing Rohesia to flinch. "He didn't do anything wrong."

Rohesia's brows furrowed with pity. The warden glanced at his stoned companions warily.

"What?" I asked, uncontrolled anger simmering close to the surface of my skin. Disorientation continued to cloud my mind and my judgment as I stood defensively in front of Brooks. My mind was too muddled to make sense of the situation.

"What aren't you telling me?"

I took a step towards Rohesia. The warden noticed the movement and drew his sword. Color slowly drained from her face.

"We have reason to believe that Detective de Blasis was a follower of Stheno's and Casimar's," Rohesia stated.

I recognized the tone she was using. It was one she used when she had a client who wouldn't calm down and was potentially dangerous.

"Do you have a warrant?" I asked.

"They don't need one, lovely. Not since I work for E.E. Isn't that right, Rohesia?"

My best friend nodded.

"Well, do you have any proof?" I demanded, looking at the warden and Rohesia expectantly.

"We do. And we'll show you it when we go to the interrogation room."

I started to protest again, but Brooks stopped me. "It's okay, Usa. They don't have anything on me. Let's just get this over with."

Rohesia looked at me with dark eyes that shimmered with pity and an emotion resembling regret. The warden shifted impatiently.

I quickly dressed in real clothes, and unstoned the wardens, who looked quite sick after returning to the real world.

My bleeding, all too trusting heart screamed at me to not go with them, that they were lying and would hurt Brooks. But my gut weaved a contrasting tale. If they wanted us dead, we would have died within moments of their arrival. And I knew Rohesia, she wouldn't have come here without evidence.

Brooks's kind eyes met mine, a deep understanding gleaming in their cobalt depths. The message from Casimar and Agnes flashed in my mind.

Agnes said to guard your heart. That the one you share it with will betray you.

My legs almost gave out as I crouched in front of the little cat that Brooks had gifted to me, which lay shattered on the floor. It must have fallen off the dresser and shattered during the scuffle.

I hoped it wasn't a premonition.

"Let's go," Brooks announced gruffly, his jaw locked.

Rohesia nodded gratefully, ushering him towards the wardens. They roughly patted him down, searching for any objects that he could use against them or himself.

Brooks hissed in pain as cuffs were placed around his wrists. They were for his own protection, we were told. The cold metal burned his skin, causing raised welts to form. The Collectress often used shackles coated with the sap of oleander flowers on her prisoners, to keep them agreeable.

Outside the apartment, a rowdy crowd had gathered.

Workers of all different shapes and sizes had gathered around the perimeter of the interrogation room. Among the crowd was E.E.

His eyes were glassy with unshed tears as he shouted horrendous insults at us, chanting alongside the crowd.

"LIAR."

"TRAITOR."

"KILLER."

My eyes found E.E.'s as he spewed the worst insult of them all at me. He was supposed to be Brooks's friend, but trials often brought forward one's true intentions and feelings.

"YOU KILLED AGNES!"

I followed closely behind Rohesia, though clearly not close enough because I was pushed into the ground by a spiteful worker.

"Rise and shine, sweetheart," growled a warden with a crimson stain billowing from his chest. It was the one I had thrown into the closet. He grabbed my arm and hauled me to his chest.

"You better get that looked at, sweetheart, lest you forget what a gorgon can do to you," I snapped, smiling at the wound. His face turned as red as the hair on his balding head.

Rohesia yanked me from his grasp before I could finish what I had started. "Let her go, or you'll have garden duty cleaning the statues."

The warden mumbled an apology rather begrudgingly.

"What in the gods' names is happening?" I whispered to Rohesia, panic threatening to cause my light breakfast to spill out onto the floor.

"You'll have to wait and see," she responded, her lips tight as the wardens fought off the growing crowd.

This arrest was public. And it was personal.

Without a word, a dozen highly skilled wardens surrounded Brooks, Rohesia, and me in a tight formation, funneling us through the metal doors. Apprehension built in my chest as I was constricted and pressed against far too many bodies. Someone grabbed my upper arm tightly, as if I would run off as soon as I was given a chance.

I sighed in relief when we passed through the monstrous set of doors, the warden releasing his grasp at a heated look from Rohesia. Instead of going to the interrogation room, we were pushed through some doors with a dozen different locks and passcodes.

We were towed towards an astounding set of polished marble stairs. The enormous staircase seemed to wind up into the ceiling. As we reached the upper levels, the elegantly painted walls were replaced with panes of holographic glass. Shafts of rainbow light glittered on my skin. If Brooks wasn't being led to his interrogation, I could be tempted to dance and sing in their light.

We passed through a set of doors that were identical to the ones guarding the entrance of The Hub. They opened with a heavy creak. The large room was decorated with a palette of deep burgundy and soft black.

Rohesia told me to put my head down. My hands clenched into tight fists in front of me and my teeth ground against one another as I fought my pride.

I felt The Collectress's assessing gaze on me before I saw her. Her presence at The Hub wasn't a good sign.

"Bow," she commanded, her voice cutting through the air like sharpened steel.

Everyone in the room bowed, except for Brooks and me. He was pushed to his knees by a warden but didn't tear his gaze from mine. His eyes were shining with delight at my defiance.

The air shifted around me. I met The Collectress's eyes and did the unthinkable, something that I had daydreamed about doing for years.

I stoned her.

Harsh gasps filled the room as she began to turn. Her eyes widened but it was too late for her to react. She was a step from me when she became completely encased in a tomb of stone.

Rohesia stood by me, her eyes wide, but she didn't make a move to arrest me. Part of me knew that she had been waiting for the day when I would finally stone her. Numerous times I had told Rohesia how I dreamed of doing so, but I didn't have the courage until now.

"Are you just going to stand there?" demanded a warden.

Rohesia shrugged. "The Collectress will be fine for now."

The wardens looked at her incredulously but didn't protest at The Collectress's second-in-command as we passed through the room and left the leader of Iydara stoned. I couldn't help but take note of a few wardens who chuckled and stopped to take pictures with The Collectress.

I should have mentioned that my statutes could still see.

A tight hallway turned into a larger, more private lobby with dozens of doors. I hadn't known that The Hub expanded this far. This must be where they questioned the high-profile criminals.

That single word stopped me in my tracks.

Criminals.

Was Brooks a criminal?

Was he really behind the creation of the golems, along with Casimar and Stheno? Agnes's fortune threatened to take over my mind, but I pushed it back. I wouldn't get through this interrogation if I let it surface again.

The wardens opened a door, leading Brooks inside. Rohesia and I followed in heavy silence. This would make or break my relationship with Brooks I realized.

I was ordered to watch from the window as Rohesia walked into the interrogation room alone. My heart ached for Brooks, and I hoped that this would be over soon.

"The first mistake you made in this situation was causing my best friend to give you her heart. Because of your mindless actions, I'll be forced to pick up the pieces you so carelessly damaged," Rohesia accused, looking at Brooks with disdain.

My cheeks heated as the wardens looked at me. But I didn't give into their stares. Instead, I stared at Brooks, focusing on his cobalt eyes.

"I don't know what you're talking about. And I want a lawyer."

"Lawyers aren't for people like you." Rohesia laughed without humor.

"People like me?" Brooks let out a dark chuckle, tilting his head at my friend. He leaned back in his chair and crossed his arm over his broad chest.

"People that lie," she said, scrunching her nose at him scornfully.

A crinkling sound filled the speaker as Rohesia reached down to grab a clear evidence bag. I couldn't see what was in it, but Brooks blanched at whatever it was.

"We found this near Casimar's supply of dust at the mansion. Care to explain?" She placed the bag on the table, and I finally saw what it was.

In the bag was Brooks's ring, the one he had worn for years, the one that acted as a conduit for the essences that were released whenever a huntsman killed a monster.

Brooks only stared at the bag.

The detective looked at his finger with confusion. "I...I...hadn't noticed it was missing."

I wracked my brain for a memory of Brooks wearing his ring last night. But I couldn't find one.

Brooks's eyes scanned the mirror, seeming to search for my eyes. And for once, I was glad that he couldn't see me.

"Uh huh," Rohesia said, "and I'm sure you just conveniently forgot to mention that dunamis doesn't leave an essence when used. So essentially, you and other huntsmen have a personal, non-traceable way to kill people and use magic. And isn't it convenient that the only other huntsman is dead."

My hands grew cold and sweaty, and my mouth became dry. Had I heard her correctly? His ring didn't leave an essence when used, so it was as deadly and diabolical as Zeus's Fulgurite or a potion.

As if to prove her point, Rohesia stood up, and emptied the bag on the table. The ring slowly spun in a circle, landing in the middle of the table.

Taking a plant from the evidence box, she placed it in front of Brooks. He raised his eyes in question.

Rohesia roughly grabbed his hand, shoving the ring on Brooks's finger. The material glimmered in the low light, shining like a damning and incriminating beacon.

Brooks looked at Rohesia expectantly.

"Using the ring, I want you to make vines sprout from the leaves of the plant in front of you."

"This is ridiculous. That ring only acts as a conduit for when a monster I kill chooses me to carry on their essence. I can't make a plant grow from it. Drakons are fire-breathing beasts, not fucking gardeners."

"Do it, detective. I do mean it when I say your life depends on it," she snapped back impatiently, motioning for him to do as she asked.

"Just imagine vines growing from the plant, in your mind. And the ring will do the rest."

Brooks hesitated, but pulled the plant closer towards him, frowning at its vascular leaves and thorns. Closing his eyes, Brooks rubbed the ring on his finger.

And growths of leafy, green vines sprouted from the plant.

My heart sank into the pit of my stomach.

The wardens near me began to curse at him.

Brooks attempted to jump back but forgot that he was chained to the chair. "No. You have the wrong ring. Mine has never done that. Please. I only have the abilities given to me by a drakon I slayed, no other magic. Dammit, I don't even inherit all of their power, just some. And certainly none of it was elemental magic."

Rohesia clicked her tongue. "Isn't fire an element? And you can breathe fire, correct?"

Brooks stuttered, rocking back and forth in his chair that was bolted to the cement floor. "That's not what I meant. I misspoke. I can't use earth, air, or water magic. Sure, I breathe fire, but it's a drakon's fire, which is very different from elemental fire."

"Maybe, but we also found your digital footprint on Casimar's work laptop. Care to explain?"

"I don't know what you're talking about," Brooks urged, his panicked gaze continuing to search for mine.

"Not sure I believe you and I doubt The Collectress will either."

The pain in my chest only grew as wardens stormed into the interrogation room and yanked Brooks to his feet.

As they exited the room, I stopped in front of the group. Rohesia nodded and let me say my piece. Brooks's eyes enlarged with an indecipherable emotion as he took in my fuming face.

I choked out, "I guess I really never knew you, Brooks."

"So that's it?" He let out a bitter chuckle. "I'm just a stranger to you now?"

379

Brooks's cobalt eyes snapped to mine as he awaited my answer. Tears threatened to spill, but I wouldn't let him see me cry, not anymore. He lost that privilege the moment he started lying to me.

"Yes. You mean nothing to me." I swallowed thickly, the words like sandpaper against my tongue.

He knew I was being untruthful, and somehow, that only made the pain even more unbearable. I knew that I could never fully hate him, even though my gorgon screamed at me that I should tear him into pieces.

"Don't you believe me?" he asked.

"Maybe I did once, but not anymore."

Brooks hung his head in silent defeat.

How could he betray me like this? How could he hurt me?

Most importantly, why even use the ring if there were barrels of the golem-forming potion in the warehouse? Why would Brooks have needed both to create golems?

Or was Brooks's betrayal entirely separate from that of Casimar and Stheno? I felt sick imagining him turning statues into golems.

Insults were thrown at him as he exited the private room. With a departing glance, Brooks and the wardens turned right, entering a long, dark hallway.

I followed Rohesia to the apartment, watching as wardens tore apart every inch of the space. The bedsheets were stripped and placed into large plastic bags.

They rummaged through the closets and took random pieces of Brooks's clothing. My heart ached as I watched a crime scene technician walk through the bedroom with Brooks's championship rings in a bag.

Rohesia stood next to me, holding my hand the entire time.

I found it odd that they weren't collecting any of my things.

"We know you're innocent, Usa," Rohesia murmured, rubbing her hand across my shoulder.

I could only nod in silence.

36

I knew I shouldn't be here. If I was caught, I would be fined or thrown in jail, but I couldn't stop myself. Two days had passed since Brooks's arrest. Sleep continued to evade me, as his mugshot was plastered across every television station and handed out in flyers on the streets of Iydara.

His family was devastated. Nola refused to believe that he would commit such a heinous crime. And so, for her, I was back at the warehouse behind The Broken Vial Apothecary searching for any small clue that might prove the wardens wrong.

I attempted to tell myself that I was only looking into Brooks's innocence for Nola's and Lilith's sake, but I also had a lot invested in the outcome. I couldn't shake the feelings of betrayal and hopelessness that clung to my heart like an invasive disease.

The simple fact that Brooks's ring didn't leave an essence haunted my mind. The answer to all of my questions had been so close to my grasp.

How could I have been so blind? Had he been transforming statues into golems after he kissed me or made me laugh until my stomach ached?

I wasn't entirely sure what I was looking for as I entered the apothecary. The lock had been fairly simple to break into, and I tried not to think about who had taught me that trick.

DNA evidence had been collected at the scene, matching both Casimar and Stheno. Brooks's DNA hadn't been found at the crime scene, but it still didn't explain his ring being found in Casimar's room, and the powers it possessed. We had all seen the ring cause vines to grow on the plant. And Brooks was a huntsman. He could only use the magic given to him by the essence of a slayed monster, in his case a drakon.

Rohesia was researching different breeds of drakon, to see if one with earth magic had previously been created by Prometheus after The Siege of Insanity. But it was long, arduous work that would take weeks, if not months.

There were only physical records, which were tightly sealed by Iydara's record keepers, and it would take much persuasion on our part to see them.

But I would cross that bridge when I got to it. First, I had to find evidence of Brooks's innocence, if there was any left after the crime team and cleaning crew.

The apothecary was stripped bare, even the mirrors that had been on the ceiling had been removed. A sharp cleaning smell permeated through the room, and I silently wondered if the entrance to Shafira's casino was now blocked off.

Or if it had been discovered at all.

With the authority and power that she seemed to hold over Iydara, and with her mother being The Collectress, I doubted that they would have raided her underground casino and lavish office.

Yellow crime scene tape closed off the back door that led to the warehouse. My boots clicked across the linoleum and the sound sent caused gooseflesh to pepper my arms. The emptied store seemed haunted.

Though the space was relatively clean, there were still signs of life in the building. Discarded boxes. Broken crystals. Scattered receipts.

Ducking beneath the tape, I carefully opened the door, surprised to find it unlocked. It creaked open into the heavy silence. Cold air rushed into the store, causing the hair to stand up on the back of my neck.

The warehouse was as barren and empty as the storefront.

I walked to where I had found the bodies of Agnes and Oliver, half expecting to see them still laying there. Instead, there was no evidence at all that they had taken their last breaths in the small storage closet.

It was chilling how one's existence could be so easily wiped from the world. Lingering in the doorway, I thought once more about Agnes's message from beyond.

Guard your heart. The one you share it with will betray you.

Had she known about Brooks's betrayal when she first met him? Or that I would fall for him so blindly that I would ignore the facts that were blatantly placed in front of me.

Brooks would soon be transferred to a higher security prison near the Eastern Boundary Square, with Casimar. It was rumored that they were sharing a prison cell, and I couldn't help but smirk at the fact.

Leaving the haunted doorway behind, I began to scan the emptied shelves, unsure what I was supposed to be looking for. The cleaning and investigation teams had left the space spotlessly clean.

Outside, in the shed where we had found the injured Stheno, I found no trace of the gorgon's blood. Even the slashes in the side of the shed had been repaired. Squatting, I examined the building carefully, hoping to find something that the cleaning crew had missed.

I sighed, brushing off dirt and grass from my jeans. The cleaning crew had done their job too well. I couldn't even see the stain where Stheno lay bleeding for hours. Gorgon blood was hard to clean, and I was shocked that they had done such a good job at wiping it away.

Inspecting the alleyway, I saw that there were no neighbors or other stores around, meaning that there was a slim possibility of anyone catching evidence on surveillance cameras.

Maybe I was chasing a lead that didn't exist. Brooks could have been involved and didn't use the warehouse to create golems with his dunamis.

What would Brooks's motivation be to create golems in the first place?

He hated his uncle and The Collectress, but I couldn't see him hurting and injuring other people and businesses because of his need for vengeance. Brooks's sisters were too important to him to risk their lives for revenge. But I had only known him for a few months short of a year.

Perhaps I didn't know him as well as I thought I did.

He had once told me that he would do anything to see his sisters again, and to figure out what had happened to them.

Was this what he meant by 'anything'?

Wandering over to the table that Brooks had first kissed me on, I examined it with an all-consuming twinge in my heart. It became hard to breathe as the passionate memories assailed my mind. A fire stirred in my belly, and I looked away, needing to break the connection before I ran off to find him.

Pushing myself off the table, I cringed as my finger became trapped in a wad of sticky chewing gum beneath the table. The pink bubblegum stuck to my finger with a will of its own.

After removing it from my hand, I held the chewed-up gum in my palm. My breath caught in my throat.

Medical supplies shone in the bright lights as I walked into the coroner's office. I hadn't wanted to come back here, but I wasn't left with many other options.

Sniffling filled the air as I stepped into the room full of dead bodies and large drains on the floor.

"Eirlys?"

The clicking of heels walking across the floor echoed against my ears. Whirling around, I found Eirlys exiting her office, mascara running down her face and her hair in need of a brush.

"Usa! What are you doing here?" She didn't look happy to have an unexpected visitor and I couldn't blame her.

"I was wondering if you could test some evidence for me."

Her interest piqued. "Is it about Brooks's case?"

I opened my mouth, unsure if I should tell her the truth.

She rolled her light blue eyes at me, snatching the bag from my hand. "Your face just gave you away."

I frowned. I thought I had more of a poker face than that.

Maybe when it came to cards, but not Brooks.

Sitting in a spinning chair, she motioned for me to sit down next to her. She wrinkled her nose in confusion as she removed the specimen of gum from the bag with gloved hands.

An awkward silence filled the air.

Clearing my throat, I nodded at her glittery pink eyeshadow.

"That's a pretty shade."

"Thanks," she responded tightly.

Exhaling, I leaned back in the chair, spinning and looking up at the ceiling, trying to distract myself from the past few days. I found it rather morbid that the ceiling had mirrors similar that in the apothecary.

"Why did he pick you?" Eirlys asked, not looking up from where she was placing the gum into a clear solution. Her tone was blunt, but not unkind.

I stopped spinning, raising my eyebrow at her.

"Brooks?"

Another eye roll. "No, Santa Claus."

Ignoring her sarcasm, I turned to face her, realizing that she had been crying because of Brooks's arrest.

"Honestly, I wish he hadn't."

She scoffed, examining the vial. "You don't mean that."

I didn't. But I didn't say anything to confirm her thoughts.

"Even if he did choose me, it doesn't matter now. He's in jail. He killed hundreds of people with the golems."

"You can't honestly believe that, can you? Otherwise, you wouldn't be here."

Again, I didn't respond.

Her shoulders sagged. "Look, I know that you and I didn't start off on the best terms. I'm a jealous person, and I always will be."

I admired her honesty, nodding as she continued to talk and work on extracting DNA from the piece of pink bubblegum.

"But you and I both know that while Brooks is capable of many, many things, murdering innocents is not one of them."

"I know," I admitted, resting my cheek in my hand as I watched her work.

"What evidence did they have against him?" she asked, furrowing her brow as she dropped a different liquid into the vial with the gum.

I quickly explained the ring and dunamis to her.

"Those ding-a-lings." She blushed. "Excuse my language."

I raised my eyebrow at her but laughed at her insult, starting to like her a little bit more than when I came in.

Removing her glove, Eirlys takes off a ring on her middle finger that is scarily similar to the one Brooks wears.

"I knew of Brooks's dunamis, since we were engaged to be married. The mages that created the rings wanted something that would blend in and not be easily detectable by the rest of Hecate's covens. That's why the mages made dupes of the rings. In case a huntsman was in danger of discovery, then a monster wouldn't be able to pinpoint the real huntsman's conduit from the fakes. Thus protecting the huntsman's identity."

"How many of these are there?"

"Probably dozens scattered throughout different generations of the bloodlines, including those marrying into the family."

Holding it in my hand, I noticed how it felt and looked exactly like Brooks's.

"But I watched the ring glow and use elemental earth magic."

She shrugged, taking the ring back.

"People can fool you into believing anything. Make you see what they want you to, then call you crazy if you contradict it. Most individuals in power aren't above rewriting history to forgo any kind of responsibility."

Eirlys' words struck a chord.

Standing, she walked over to a machine that had been flashing and whirling. Stopping the machine, she removed the liquid as a report was printed.

Her head hung low as she handed me the report. My stomach clenched as I read it.

The machine hadn't been able to extract any DNA from the gum. The report informed us that the sample had been compromised.

Tears formed in Eirlys eyes, and she stomped her foot in frustration. "Now he will never get out of there."

"I wouldn't be too sure of that," I said, running a hand over my mess of tangled curls. I took a steadying breath.

I only knew of one person who never left home without bright pink bubblegum. A back-up plan was quickly forming in my mind.

Once I had informed Eirlys of my plan, she nodded with excitement, telling me to call her if I needed any help.

We quickly exchanged cell phone numbers and she embraced me in a tight hug.

"Don't let Brooks get away, Usa. Don't make the same mistake that I did. You'll regret it for your whole life if you do," she asserted, removing herself from the hug and pressing her lips into a thin line.

"I won't," I vowed.

With the evidence and report stuffed into my purse, I found my cell phone, beginning the first step of my plan to prove Brooks's innocence.

37

"You're doing the right thing," Rohesia soothingly said into my hair, brushing it out of my snot-covered face, while snapping her bright pink gum.

"Then why does it feel so wrong?" I cried out, covering my face with my hands.

We were at the apartment I had shared with Brooks, boxing up the last of my personal items as I prepared to move back into the mansion with Rohesia.

I had spilled my guts to her, letting her see me as the broken, devastated girl that I knew she thought I was. But what she didn't know was that I wasn't giving up on Brooks.

Rohesia placed a glass of wine in my hand, her lips pulled downward. I sniffled a thanks and looked around the room, the area seeming bare without any of Brooks's personal touches.

"Don't you go doing that," my friend chided, grabbing a carton of ice cream from the freezer.

"What?" I asked, my bottom lip quivering.

"Wanting him back."

Sighing, I pulled a blanket over myself and grabbed a spoon from Rohesia, starting to dig into the chocolate and marshmallow dessert.

Rohesia grabbed the remote and put on one of my favorite romantic comedy movies, and rested her head on my shoulder.

My heart raced at what I needed to do next.

She had always thought of me as weak and in need of rescue. But I hadn't needed saving for years. And I was no longer weak.

"Don't be mad, but I need to know where you found his ring in Casimar's room. I need more closure." I sobbed, stuffing my mouth with a spoonful of ice cream.

The sugary food sat in my stomach heavily as I fought off waves of nausea.

Without missing a beat, Rohesia responded, "It was in Casimar's gym bag."

I wiped a tear from my eye.

"Oh. I guess that makes sense."

Rohesia nodded, watching the movie while keeping one nervous eye on me. I was walking on thin ice, and I hoped she wouldn't catch on.

"Brooks always wore one of his college championship rings with his conduit ring, did you guys find that one as well?" I asked.

I felt her stiffen on my shoulder.

"Yes, it was right next to the other ring. It was placed in evidence as well. Why are you so curious all of a sudden?"

"I just can't believe it, I guess. I have the worst luck with guys. First Rennyn then Brooks. What's wrong with me?"

Again, I covered my face with my hands, but this time, it was to hide the flush of anger. Brooks only had three championship rings, all of which had been taken from the apartment by the crime scene technician team.

When I had asked Brooks if he ever wore them, he had said that he never did because he was planning on giving one to each of his sisters when they returned. And by wearing them out, he risked losing or damaging them.

Falling for my trap, Rohesia fed me sweet words about how it wasn't my fault, but Brooks's. That I was perfect. But he was flawed. A huntsman who was trained to kill monsters and manipulate them.

Rohesia's crop top rode up as she stretched her arms, and her tattoo caught my eye. The thin outline of a heart was tattooed on her ribs. I had the exact same one on my foot. We always joked that we were two bodies with one heart.

My breath caught in my chest.

The world stopped on its axis.

I realized with horror that I should have believed Brooks.

Guard your heart. The one who you share it with will betray you.

Standing up, I excused myself, blaming my sudden departure on my monthly cycle and hormones. Heaving in the toilet, the weight of Rohesia's betrayal slammed into me.

The matching heart tattoo on top of my foot stared back at me mockingly, and I wished I could scrub it off.

Rohesia had been my friend for years, and I considered her a soulmate of sorts. A platonic soulmate. A friend soulmate. My best friend and the sister I had always dreamed about having.

And she had deceived me.

I wouldn't truly believe it until I had evidence.

The individuals who had access to the apartment were me, Brooks, E.E., and Rohesia. Since Brooks and I hadn't planted the ring in Casimar's room, and E.E. was obviously shocked and heartbroken at Brooks's arrest, that only left one person.

In front of the mirror, I took a deep, steadying breath. Transforming into my gorgon, I admired her strength and resilience. Without her, I would never have made it.

I would never have been able to endure this harsh world.

And for once, I was thankful for the curse Athena had placed on me. Without it, I would have never found my own strength. I would have forever been a compliant and zealous people pleaser.

The heaviness of the last years had buried into my weary bones. But that heaviness had formed a resilience that I had not known was possible. Burrowed in the trauma was bravery to find happiness in the agony.

I was no longer a victim.

No. I was a survivor.

And I would take back what was mine.

Looking at my reflection with determination, I decided that I would free Brooks.

Shuffling in the bathroom cabinet, I pressed a button behind a stack of towels, which opened a hidden compartment. The slot held a loaded gun, which Brooks had told Rohesia and I about in case of emergencies. My hand touched something. But it wasn't a gun.

I chuckled darkly as my hand pulled out an unopened pack of pink, strawberry flavored bubblegum.

Carefully opening the bathroom door, I walked out into the hallway, finding that Rohesia was no longer sitting on the loveseat. The kitchen was empty as well.

Opening a drawer, I rummaged around for a knife, only to find all of them gone. Instead, all I was left to face Rohesia with was a plastic spoon.

I grumbled to myself but remembered the power and strength I had in myself. With my gorgon, I could easily stone her.

Entering the bedroom, I found Rohesia standing by the window, looking out into the streets of Iydara. She shifted her gaze as I walked in.

"Feeling better? If you need me to get you a tonic, just say the word," Rohesia insisted, keeping her hands behind her back.

"Actually, I have almost everything that I need, but not a tonic." I popped an obnoxiously loud and large bubble, causing her to grin wildly.

"What else could you possibly need?"

"Well, first a best friend who doesn't lie to me," I snapped.

"We all can't have what we want," she told me, looking out the window wistfully.

I gave her a loaded look. "And what exactly do you want?"

"Wouldn't you like to know," she said, waving the missing gun at me.

Sitting on the bed, I leaned back on my arms, watching her.

"Safe to say you're the one that planted the ring?"

"I'm not at liberty to say."

I choked on a bitter laugh, spitting the gum out. The wad landed in front of her, and she stepped over it with a frown.

Without hesitation, I called on my power, putting all my strength into meeting her eyes and stoning her. I felt the power leave me, only to be snapped back at me like a rubber band.

What in the gods' names?

Rohesia tilted her head.

"What'd you do to me?" I asked, suddenly feeling queasy and groggy. My eyes blurred and I attempted to stand up, only to land in a heap on the floor.

"Just a simple spell to tame that pesky gorgon of yours."

"Why?"

"Because I wanted to."

A sickening crack reverberated in my head, and blood trickled down my face. She had put the gun to good use after all.

38

The sudden honking of a horn jolted me awake as my body tilted and crashed into the lap of someone wearing scratchy wool pants.

My eyes burst open as I attempted to push myself up.

Only, I couldn't.

My body was paralyzed.

A gloved hand propped me up with ease.

I opened my mouth and a squeak came out. My brain was a jumbled, tangled mess, not able to speak coherent sentences or piece together the broken memories that were crashing around my head like an adrift ship at sea.

Memories tried to break the surface of the tidal waves, but I was too exhausted to pull them from the depths of my shattered mind.

And my gorgon refused to come forward.

I tried again to make sense of the memories, but like broken pieces of straw, they disintegrated between my curious hands.

Why was I here?

"I know you're confused, Usa. But I promise it will all make sense soon. You just rest. I'm taking you home."

Home.

To the mansion?

The vehicle lurched again, and as I fell over once again, I could only see the gray sky as the car was parked. I strained my mortal ears, desperate to hear anything.

The driver's door opened and someone dragged my limp body out. They took no care in handling me as I knocked my head against the door of the car. In the process of dragging me out of the vehicle, they slipped on the ground, dropping my paralyzed body and using it as a landing pad of their own.

It was a strange sensation, being numb but still feeling the weight of my clothes as they became drenched with moisture from melted piles of snow.

"Careful with her!" Rohesia yelled, glaring at Iva who had been dragging me through a mound of slushy ice.

I coughed loudly as Rohesia released the silencing spell on my mouth. She and the other Keeper grabbed my arms and carried my lifeless body into a cave.

Dread took over my mind.

I wondered if this is what my statues felt like when they were transformed into stone.

The pair continued to carry me down a flight of stairs and into a rank and gloomy room. No, it wasn't a room. It was a prison, a dungeon.

Heavy metal bars lined the windows, and thick locks barricaded the doors. The ceiling above my cell was exposed to the outside, fresh snow covering the floor of my cage.

I was trapped.

Without anyone to help me.

I closed my eyes and cried.

The moment I smelled the decaying bodies in adjacent cells, and the twisted, white mass of skeletons that were attached to walls, the fight came back to me. I wasn't going to end up like those corpses, nailed to the wall for all of eternity.

The only problem was that I couldn't move. Sensation was slowly returning to my hands, but that was it. My eyes attempted to take in the entire area, but it was impossible as I couldn't move my head more than an inch.

The cells smelled of perished souls.

I refused to die here.

Iva had thrown my limp body onto the ground, informing me that Rohesia and Ceto would be down to see me soon. Moisture continued to seep into my clothing, until it started to freeze to my chapped skin.

I saw no clear way of escape.

Even if I could move, there were steel bars all around me.

And though there was no roof over my cell, the opening was at least thirty feet above my head. There was no way to scale the walls, as there was not enough space to give myself a running head start.

Panic bubbled in my chest.

How had this happened?

I knew the answer.

Rohesia.

My mother.

Yet, the pieces refused to fit together.

My throat and eyes burned.

My best friend had betrayed me. And worse yet, I had believed her over Brooks. And Brooks, he was in prison because of my mistakes and disbelief. I hadn't believed him when he had needed me most. I could have fought for him more, advocated his character in front of The Collectress and E.E., they would have had the power to release him, or at least put off his arrest until other avenues could be searched.

The last words I had uttered to him replayed in my mind like a broken record.

How could I not have seen Rohesia for what she was? Could I really be that foolish?

Rohesia had been good to me. She'd been my best friend and co-worker for almost many years. She held my hand and let me cry on her shoulder. I had trusted her. With my life.

She had gained my friendship, my trust, my love.

A pulsing, pounding anger and sorrow swept through me. I wanted to scream, but the sound couldn't make it past the knot of emotion in my throat.

Had she solely been focused on returning me to my mother all these years?

But why now? There had been years filled with full moons.

Had she been the one to murder Agnes and Oliver?

As hours passed, and more unanswered questions formed in my mind, sensation slowly came back to my body. I gently braided the strands of hair that were tangled and damp from fallen snow.

I thought Brooks had betrayed me, but in reality, I was the one who had betrayed him. He had given himself to me, and I had destroyed him, just like I had been afraid of.

He was in a cell somewhere because of me.

I squeezed my eyes shut as scream threatened to spill from my mouth. I couldn't think about him. His smile made cries echo in my mind. I needed to focus.

What was I going to do?

I needed to leave.

Iydara had two prisons and I knew this wasn't one of them. I had visited both of them while working on cases for The Collectress.

And we had been driving for a while. Which meant that we were somewhere near the Anghor Peaks and Kilmarn. Or we could be closing in on the Northern Boundary, near the ocean, but the bitter cold that leaked through the hole in the ceiling led me to believe that we were in fact near the Anghor Peaks.

I knew that once we crossed the sprawling forest of Kilmarn there would be no coming back for me. The full moon was tomorrow night.

I knew I would be sacrificed if I was still in captivity by then.

But how was I going to get out of it? The prison was deep in the mountains, and I knew my only hope would be to convince Rohesia to help me.

Parts of my loving and nurturing friend had to be in there somewhere, I just had to find them.

Two pairs of footsteps approached me.

I tensed when Rohesia and my mother came into view. If only the cell could lock from the inside as well.

Rohesia looked like she had aged twenty years. As if this entire ordeal had been difficult on her. As if she actually cared.

Ceto looked the same as she did the day of the convoy attack, only now, she looked delighted at the sight of her daughter in an impenetrable jail cell.

The cell door opened with a wave of my mother's hand.

"Mother," I spat, leaning my head against the cement wall.

"Disgrace," she shot back.

Rohesia squatted in front of me, a tray of food in her arms. "Hungry?"

Yes, I was. But I wouldn't eat or drink anything from her.

She had probably poisoned it again.

As if she could read my mind, she took a sip of the water and ate a bite of the soft bread. My stomach clenched with hunger, and my throat burned with thirst, but I could only stare as she placed the tray in front of me.

With most of the sensation back in my arms, I grabbed the edge of the tray, flinging it at her with all my might. I was disappointed when she blocked the food with a shield of air magic.

"It wasn't spelled," she insisted, hurt darkening her eyes.

"You weren't above enchanting me before," I scoffed.

"That was different. I needed you to stay calm until we got to our destination."

"And where exactly might that be?"

Neither party responded.

I had the strangest urge to laugh, but instead I just stared at the skeletons above their heads. I wondered what crimes they had committed to end up as décor in a prison cell.

"Usa," Rohesia started, sitting by me.

"Don't call me that."

"You need to understand why I did what I did."

Fury blasted through my spine. "What, manipulate your best friend and frame two innocent people?"

"Casimar wasn't innocent, he used the dust on the garden that night. And he is guilty of his other crimes. I thought you would be happy to know that he can't hurt anyone anymore."

I was, but I couldn't stop thinking about his innocent cellmate.

My mother took a step towards me. "You have forgotten who you are, Medusa. The world is our enemy. They are evil and wicked and do not know our ways of life. And that man only wanted you for your body, much like the god Poseidon."

I lost it.

I launched myself at her, pushing her to the ground and releasing my gorgon. My snakes hissed and bit at hers, the two groups becoming tangled in one another. It was a sea of black, white, and gold.

Of course, the gods and goddesses would have it that gorgons couldn't stone one another.

"There she is," my mother said in awe, extracting herself from under my body as though I weighed no more than a doll. Exhausted from the energy I had just exerted, I collapsed.

Humiliation tore through me as I realized I had given Ceto exactly what she wanted. She had wanted me to attack her, to see my snakes.

Despite this, I didn't immediately change back into my human form. She might have lured me into showing my snakes, but I left them out for myself.

"Why?" I asked Rohesia, watching as she paced in front of me, wringing her hands behind her back. Her steps were slow and heavy, like the guilt of putting a spell on her friend and kidnapping said friend was physically weighing her down.

One side of my mother's lips curled up. "I can be very convincing."

I ignored her, waiting for Rohesia's answer.

"Twenty-one thousand, three hundred and five days ago, I was banished from my coven. Hecate's First Coven. It happened on a clear, sunny day. I thought nothing could go wrong. I was in the prime of my years, learning and creating so many spells, potions, and pure unfiltered magic."

I could only stare at her with hatred as she continued.

"Including a potion that could revert gorgon statues back to their original forms."

"There is no such cure for statues," I said. "Only the gorgon that stoned them could save them from an eternity of lifelessness. If such a thing existed, it would change everything."

I was sure that this had to be the same cure that I had given Brooks, but I didn't let on that I knew of it. Let alone that I had stashed some of it in the apartment.

She nodded. "It is possible, Usa. There is a sample of it in my pocket as we speak. It completely heals and transforms the person who was turned into a statue against their will. Mentally, physically, emotionally, spiritually. They would be set free from the unnatural ways of the gorgons. You and Brooks were close to finding out the truth. But you had the wrong idea about the golem-making potion. At first, it wasn't a potion to create monstrous golems. Instead, it was a cure for gorgon statues."

Taking a deep breath, she continued her story.

"Hecate's First Coven nearly perfected the cure. And with that kind of cure being developed, rumors swirled. When we were almost done perfecting it, a member of your gorgon coven broke into our facilities. They stole what we had been working on, but they didn't know that the potion they stole was an unsuccessful one. That it created nightmarish monsters." Her eyes flashed and I knew she was referring to golems.

"Once your coven realized the possibilities of having a potion that could create golems, nearly unkillable statues, they set out to find a way to get the rest of the failed potions."

"But how did you get banished because of my coven's discovery of the potions?" I asked.

I had never seen Rohesia this broken. Her eyes were distant and fixated above my head, as if she could reach into the past and fix the moment that her life forever changed.

"I had been tasked with destroying the failed potions. It was a complicated process, one that took place miles away from Hecate's First Coven's residence, to prevent accidents and cross-contamination. Little did I know that your coven was lingering in the shadows."

My mother gave Rohesia a pointed, malicious grin, which she ignored. I detested them both, but I hated my mother the most. Maybe even more than The Collectress.

"Disposing of the failed potions had been the first task that the coven trusted me with after I became a mage. And so, I transported gallons upon gallons of failed potions with me to a field by Kilmarn. There, I met a girl who insisted on trading me a talking snake for the gallons of potion. I was only a young girl then, and no one had informed me that destroying the potions was of the utmost importance. I thought it was like taking out the trash, and I didn't see a problem with trading some of it for a pet snake."

"It was Stheno," my mother interjected, beaming with pride.

No wonder she had been my mother's favorite for years.

"I gave all of the forbidden potions to your sister without a second thought. And when I returned to my coven, I showed off my new talking pet snake, and I told everyone what I did. Rather than the awe I had expected, I was met with anger and admonishment. I was permanently banished from the Hecate's First Coven."

Part of me felt hurt for Rohesia. It had been an honest mistake, but mistakes were deadly in mage covens.

"I wandered the land for years, searching for a new coven. I almost gave up until I came in contact with The Collectress. While I loathed working for her, I hoped that I could one day find a piece of glass that might convince my coven to take me back."

"Zeus's Fulgurite," I supplied.

Rohesia nodded, huffing out a breath.

"When Brooks revealed that the fulgurite was a fake, I needed a new plan. For the first time in decades, I talked to the leader of my coven, asking if there was anything I could do to be welcomed back into the fold. I had learned my lesson and was ready to start anew. And she said there was something I could do."

"Goody," I said dryly, punishing her with my gaze.

"I only needed to return the remainder of the failed golem creating potion to my coven for proper disposal. And I needed to create a cure for gorgon statues. It seemed easy enough, I thought.

"I was able to find Stheno's headquarters after following Casimar night after night. Your sister had barrels of the failed potion and was creating an army of golems to bring to your mother. When I attacked Stheno, I took the hearts of her snakes to create a cure for the statues. Nature calls for a balance, afterall. And it worked.

"When I returned to the warehouse the next day, to destroy the gallons of failed potion, I found that it had been burned down." She raised an eyebrow at me. "With the majority of the potion burned away, I had to find a way to convince your mother to give me the rest of the potion that still lingered in Kilmarn."

"Me," I whispered, fighting back tears of dismay at her disloyalty. I had trusted Rohesia with my biggest secret and she had turned her back on me as soon as it became beneficial to her.

She had traded me like a relic.

"But why frame an innocent man?" I questioned.

"Because Brooks ruined my plan."

"Don't say his name," I growled, snapping my teeth at her.

401

Ignoring me, she continued.

"Brooks was getting too close, asking questions that needed to be buried instead of looked into. And I was hoping that you would leave it alone once you found your bloodied sister and the bodies of Agnes and Oliver.

"I hoped that with the case closed, I could convince you to help me hunt down Zeus' Fulgurite. But when I was given the option of returning you to your mother for the rest of the potion, I took it given I had no other options. Those barrels destroyed at the warehouse were my freedom, Usa, and your boyfriend ignorantly turned them into ash. With the last barrels of dust in Kilmarn, I had to give you to your mom in order to return to my coven. And I need my coven like I need air in my lungs. And I'm sure you'll be happy to hear that my coven is expecting me back within the hour."

"But how did Brooks's ring use earth magic, when his dunamis only allowed him to use fire magic?" I asked, confusion clouding my mind.

"Oh, Usa. You really don't know much about the capabilities of magic," Rohesia sighed. "You forget that I can see into the immediate future. I knew Brooks would imagine exactly what I asked him to, if it would prove his innocence. With some spelled sands from Tabrn, mixed into the soil of the potted plant, it was easy to make it seem like he was the one behind the spell, when in actuality I was."

"He was innocent," I cried out, throwing myself at her, only to be yanked back by magic.

"The fact that Brooks had it out for his uncle and The Collectress was just good luck. It played into my plan beautifully. The wardens are considering executing him, did you know? I'm sure he and Casimar will have the best time taking turns at the guillotine. I wonder who will go first."

The Rohesia I had known, if I had ever really known her, was gone. There was only a brutal, self-serving mage in her place. I saw no remnants of the woman who danced in the rain with me while drinking wine from the bottle.

"This wasn't personal, Usa. It was a business deal. You're still my best friend." She bent down, leaning to brush a kiss on top of my head.

I threw my forehead into hers, hoping I had broken something.

A few teeth, a nose, a facial bone, anything really.

But I didn't have that kind of luck.

"Goodbye, Medusa. I'll always love you."

"You never loved the real me. If anything, you only loved the weak version of me that you conjured up in your mind," I spat at her shoes.

She did not acknowledge my statement.

And that was the last I ever saw of Rohesia.

"Why are you doing this?" I asked Ceto.

"Because we're going to war."

"You can't attack the mortals, they're innocent."

"Oh darling. I'm not going to war with humans." She leaned in close and showed me her perfect teeth. "We're going to war with the gods."

It took me a second to process her words.

The gods?

If she was going to war with the gods, then why attack Iydara? Why terrorize citizens of an innocent city?

Unless she was trying to gain the attention of the deities.

"Better get a good night's rest, darling. For a new dawn begins tomorrow night, starting with your sacrifice to the goddess Athena," Ceto chirped, exiting the cell with light footsteps.

39

It was the morning of the full moon. Cold air flowed through the ceiling of my jail cell. I didn't sleep last night.

My body was stiff and ached from a combination of sitting and laying on the hard floor. Food had been brought into my cell at dawn, but I refused to eat it, afraid that it would be poisoned. Staying in my gorgon form meant I was stronger than I would be as a mortal, so the lack of food was yet to seriously deplete my strength.

My cell opened and I hissed.

Stheno and Euryale entered.

Stheno seemed to be in discomfort, the process of re-growing one's snakes was agonizing. I ignored her hostile stare, instead focusing on my other sister, whose stare was even more deadly.

Euryale glared at me. "Mother said you need to eat. We are leaving in ten minutes. Ready yourself."

She turned to leave, but I couldn't let her.

"What happened to you?" I asked, looking at her with an unfamiliar feeling of distrust.

"What happened to me?" She laughed without humor, running a hand around one of her snakes. "What happened to you, baby sis? Falling in love with someone who kills monsters. I thought you knew better than that."

Stheno snapped her teeth at me, nodding along with Euryale's words.

No.

I wouldn't accept her words.

There was something Euryale wasn't telling me.

I gripped my tray of food, and with my other hand, I put the spoon in the bowl of stew, pretending to sip it. Suddenly, I gasped, looking around my sisters and into the hallway beyond.

Only Stheno fell for it, spinning around to see what had shocked me. The momentary distraction was all I needed.

Flinging the tray into her, I watched with amusement as the cold stew and bread covered her clean clothes.

"Whoops. Sorry, sis. Must be partially numb still," I said, shaking out my arms.

Fuming, Stheno took my tray, food dripping down her front. Departing the cell, she left me and Euryale alone.

Finally.

"Okay. What really happened? I know years have passed since we have talked, and we were so close, but despite those lost years, I can still tell when something is upsetting you. I can tell when you are hurting."

Euryale stayed silent, until rare tears gathered in her eyes.

She looked around, as if my mother or Stheno could be listening in on our conversation.

"Poseidon," my sister whispered.

With one word, my vision was painted crimson with an insatiable wrath. We both knew we couldn't risk Ceto or Stheno hearing us. Euryale didn't deserve to be chained up and killed too.

"He visits me once every few months, if not more. He said he needed to teach me a lesson, so I wouldn't turn out like my sister. Mother knew. So did Stheno. But they let him do it anyway."

Even without her telling me the details, I knew what he had done.

How he had violated her.

Because it was what he had done to me the night of my sixteenth birthday. "Does Athena know?"

"No. I don't think so."

I breathed a sigh of relief.

"Why does that matter?"

I quickly told her the real reason that Athena had banished me. Her hand clamped over her mouth as I told her my story. Our experiences were the same, down to the words that Poseidon had used to manipulate and shame us.

"Please. Euryale. You know how this is going to end. Help me get out of here."

My older sister looked at me, glancing down at my cuffs as she contemplated my request. Swiping her tears away, she took a step towards me.

Only for the cell door to fly open.

"I'm sorry, Usa. I can't," she quickly breathed.

I nodded.

I didn't blame her.

My mother and the gods once scared me as well.

Stheno entered the room, bearing clean clothes, while looking at us with accusatory questions in her emerald eyes. Euryale had turned her face into a perfect mask of boredom, and I was relieved.

Maybe I wouldn't live through the night, but I would make sure that Euryale did.

Stheno handed me a second tray of food. My gaze softened when I met Euryale's, conveying a silent message with as much conviction as I could muster.

With understanding, Euryale rolled her eyes, sighing loudly.

I flung the food into Euryale's face.

Screeching, she ran up to me, slapping my face. Through the specks of food on her face, I could see the gratefulness in her eyes. If Stheno grew suspicious of Euryale, she wouldn't hesitate to tell our mother. And if mother knew how much Euryale and I still cared for one another after all these years, then she would be tortured as well.

A collar had been added to my shackles, and it was hard to breathe with the thick iron suffocating me. Euryale yanked me up by my chains, the metal biting into my neck.

"You ungrateful bit—" Stheno started to swing but was stopped by our mother.

Ceto entered the cell, dressed in a gown of pearls and cream silk. Her snakes framed her face beautifully.

"Enough, daughters. Let's go." She snapped her fingers at us, and Euryale jerked on my chains a second time.

Stumbling onto my knees, I landed in a pile of discarded stew, the broth soaking into my already snow-drench jeans.

My chains scraped against the ground.

Euryale forced my head down and I spat at her feet.

We silently knew that every push, insult, and harsh word was to keep one another safe, but each one still hurt.

As we climbed stairs constructed of dried mud, snow started to fall on my face once again. When it was Euryale's turn to ascend, she handed my chains to Stheno. We rose from the depths of old soil into the fresh air above the ground.

Howling wind looped through my snakes, causing them to shiver and shake against my skull. I watched as my mother's and Euryale's snakes did the same thing.

"How can you still consider yourself a gorgon without your snakes?" I asked Stheno, mockingly widening my eyes at her.

It was stupid of me to ask her that, when she was the one holding my chains, but I didn't care.

"None of that matters. Especially since I know you'll be dead in a few hours," she snapped, gritting her teeth. I knew she was less likely to hit and abuse me with mother around.

"I need to go to the bathroom," I said, looking at Stheno.

"Hold it."

"I can't."

"Hold it, Medusa," Euryale chimed in.

Ceto took my chains from Stheno and yanked them.

Hard.

We walked to an open plot, snow falling around us in glittering, dancing sheets. Ceto tossed me into a covered carriage, the walls and locks made of iron. She slammed the door closed, and I turned around to look out of the barricaded windows.

A sharp howl shattered through the silence.

Whirling around, I looked out the other window, squinting at the tree line. A familiar looking dire wolf sat amongst the greenery, a glossy black raven perched on its shoulder.

Peeking over my shoulder, I quickly looked to see if my mother or sisters had heard it. They stood in a circle in the field, chanting words that I couldn't hear.

As I looked at the tree line once again, the dire wolf and raven were gone. I frowned. They had just been there.

Suddenly, a pin in one of the locks outside the carriage window started to quiver. It created a low tinkling sound that grated against my nerves. As I started to investigate further, I noticed that the entire lock was beginning to shake, violently so.

Tremors vibrated through the carriage.

Peeking through the barred window, my stomach dropped.

The sky had darkened, and the snow had stopped falling.

Wispy clouds whirled around the sky, wanting to escape a whirlwind that was forming in the middle of the field.

Claps of thunder bounced off the mountains.

I could no longer see my mother and sisters.

Frantically scrambling back on my feet, I kicked at the door . The sound was drowned out by the bellowing, lamenting rage of mother nature. Sharp pain radiated through my legs as I struck the solid door again and again.

The metal didn't budge.

With another glance out of the window, I halted my kicking.

I was probably safer in the carriage than out there.

Golems were breaking through the snow-covered layers of ground, crushing mounds of dirt beneath their boulder-like bodies. A manic laugh resounded throughout the field, and I saw my mother practically prancing back to the carriage.

I was launched into the doors as she whipped the horses and we began racing down the side of the mountain at an alarming pace.

Trees and animals passed us in a blur. They screeched and shrieked as the mass of golems crashed into them, tearing everything, and everyone, into shreds.

40

Screams resonated through the once peaceful streets of Iydara.

The streets were soaked in the blood of innocents. I could hear it dripping from the lamp posts and walls of destroyed buildings.

Drip.

Drip.

Drip.

While mages and gorgons tore each other apart, the golems only had a mind for humans. They didn't stand a chance.

My mother had wanted war, and war she got.

Mages battled alongside humans, trying to desperately fend off the hordes of golems. But there were hundreds of the monsters, and so few people with magic.

It was a massacre.

Carnage.

Slaughter.

The number of followers the gods had was dwindling by the hour, it would only be a matter of time before they came down from the heavens.

I sat in the carriage, frantically trying to drown out the sounds of the dying. But I could hear their yells nonetheless. I could feel their suffering. The stench of their blood radiated from the sidewalks.

My mother forced me to stay in the cramped carriage as my people were slaughtered. My cries for someone to let me out were extinguished beneath the agony of an entire city.

Flashes of the night Poseidon assaulted me threatened to take over my mind. The memories often came to the surface when I was under duress, and it was all I could do to fight them off.

I could smell him.

I could taste his sweat.

Bile threatened to spill out of my mouth.

My eyes couldn't focus.

Petrifying tremors circulated through my limbs as the memories threatened to pull me into the depths of oblivion. My mind hysterically searched for something, anything, to keep me tethered to the physical world.

It found eyes the color of lapis lazuli.

Skilled hands that braided my hair.

A nickname that I now craved to hear.

Yanking on that tether, I fought through the flashes of Poseidon's hands on me. I shot out of the endless darkness, my breathing frantic, desperate to hold onto the good.

And my grasp of that goodness eventually tightened and grew stronger and more stable. The world around me became clearer as my eyes adjusted to the pitch black of the carriage as I fought and survived.

When did night fall?

I didn't stop to dwell on this thought as I kicked at the doors once more and attempted to pry them open with brute strength.

This wasn't working. I needed a new strategy. With a newfound purpose and will, I stoned the doors.

The weight became too much for their welded hinges, and they crashed into a pile on the ground, alongside my now stone cuffs and chains. Citizens ran in the opposite direction as I stepped over the mound of dust-covered stone.

I looked up at the stars.

I had found him once.

And gods be damned if I didn't find him again.

411

Racing through the city, I realized that we were near the shopping square of the Eastern Boundary, which was close to the prison that Brooks was in.

Shouts and yelps of pain came from my right, where a golem was terrorizing a crowd of civilians. Brooks would have to wait. He was safest locked in a cell with Casimar.

My city had to come first.

Without a physical weapon, all I could do was throw rocks at the golems, distracting them from the terrified pedestrians. The monsters shifted their course, irked and angered.

As they sprinted towards me, I pivoted on my heel, darting beneath fallen banners and leaping over fallen vendor carts. Scattered candies and flowers crunched beneath my feet. The air in my lungs was crisp and cold.

Roars of annoyance came from behind me. I didn't dare look over my shoulder. The rank breath of the golems was hot on my neck, and I knew I couldn't slow down.

Veering right, I came face to face with a raging, burning inferno. Buildings were in flames. Shattered glass and broken trinkets littered the street.

With a silent prayer and a moment of daring courage, I entered a building with a smoldering roof, the herd of golems close behind. Bellows of exasperation transformed into roars of blistering suffering as licks of flame engulfed the golems.

Thick wafts of smoke made my eyes water and the flames were threatening to take me down, but I crouched low to the ground where the fire couldn't reach me. On my hands and knees, I searched for an exit.

Flames had engulfed the area behind the counter.

I turned towards the front of the store, trying to hold my breath. The golems were burning, just as I had planned, but their massive bulk was blocking the exit. Their bodies were slowly turning into piles of charred stone; soon they would be unable to harm me.

Hot metal grazed my arm and I stifled a scream.

But I was running out of air.

Coughing into the sleeve of my shirt, I ran towards a shattered window, jumping through the broken glass and flames towards the fresh air beyond.

I hit the ground rolling.

Tendrils of smoke billowed from my clothing, leaving sizzling holes and burning marks in their wake. But I was alive.

I didn't have long to celebrate my narrow escape before a hand yanked me up by my snakes.

My back arched, and I kicked out behind me, connecting with the shin of my attacker. The grasp on my head lessened as one of my snakes bit the hand of the person behind me.

Ceto.

"Leaving so fast?"

"I've got places to be," I snapped, putting distance between myself and my mother when she let go of my head.

She walked towards me, kicking clumps of stained snow with her pointed boots. The leather material glistened in the low evening light.

"What are you doing?" I asked her.

"What do you mean?"

"Why are you attacking Iydara? What have these people ever done to you?"

"Besides being a nuisance, not much. But it is not them that I am going to war with."

I raised an eyebrow, continuing to walk backwards.

"I'm going to war with the gods."

"I didn't think you were that dumb."

"I think you mean clever," she replied, gazing up at the night sky.

"You're calling them down. Tonight," I whispered, pieces beginning to click together.

413

The gods and goddesses only came down when there was a blessing to be performed, or if their people were in enough peril to warrant divine intervention.

They couldn't risk another Siege of Insanity and have most of their devotees perish at the hands of beasts.

"I am. Starting with Athena."

Two pairs of hands grabbed my arms.

Stheno and Euryale.

I kicked and screamed, attempting to break free, but it was impossible when it was three gorgons against one. The full moon peaked out behind a canvas of wispy clouds, taunting me with her rays of silver light.

A dais had been erected in the middle of the square, complete with glowing candles, large crystals, and burning herbs. Members of my coven stood around the platform, watching, and waiting.

Cheers broke out and flowers were thrown at me as I was forced onto the stage by my mother and sisters. I searched around frantically for a friendly face in the crowd.

I didn't find one.

"Our day of freedom has come, sisters!" my mother shouted, raising a curved knife into the air.

My sisters held down my arms as two different coven members pinned my legs to the stage. I struggled against their hold, only to be slapped by Stheno.

"Let us remember Daughter Medusa's sacrifice for years to come!"

As the clouds began to part, opening for the full moon, Ceto straddled me, her breath warm in my face.

"Why?" I asked her, tears brimming my eyes, but I wouldn't let them fall.

"Because you failed us."

And I knew that she was referring to the night of my blessing. The night Poseidon assaulted me and changed my fate forever.

"No. You failed me, Ceto. Because when the truth is inconvenient, even those you love will betray you. And when Poseidon raping me didn't fit into your life plan, you betrayed me. You abandoned your own daughter, and that's unforgivable."

With a shaking breath I looked up at the clouds.

The knife began to press into my chest, into my still-beating heart. Pressure and pure, blazing pain, unlike anything I had felt before, exploded throughout my chest.

"Goddess Athena! We summon you!"

I closed my eyes.

The stench of blood permeated my nostrils.

Only it wasn't my own.

A horrifying shriek caused the hair on my neck to stand up.

As I grazed my eyelashes with my fingertips, green blood trickled down their length. My body had yet to catch up with my mind. The weight of my mother was gone.

A strange chomping and crunching sound came from behind me. Lifting my head, I saw a dire wolf chewing on my mother. The animal had her head clenched in its powerful jaws.

Stheno and Euryale attempted to free her, only to be attacked by lustrous ravens. The birds pecked at their eyes, causing them to stumble and fall off the dais.

Blood dripped from my chest, the knife still halfway embedded into my flesh. Grasping the handle of carved bone, I yanked it from the depths of my chest.

I hoped that the knife had pierced the thin skin of my heart. Staggering down the steps of the stage, my legs faltered. The knife had penetrated further into my chest than I initially thought.

Just as I thought I was destined to die here after all, strong and steady arms pulled me into an alleyway.

My heart skipped as my stare met the burning gaze of three pairs of stunning, cobalt eyes.

41

Ophelia, Twyla, and Astraea stood in front of me, with wild grins stretching across their captivating faces. Two ravens were perched on Ophelia's shoulders and the dire wolf from the forest stood next to Astraea with fierce loyalty.

Before I could utter a word, Twyla wrapped her arms around me and hugged me fiercely. Astraea hugged my other side and even Ophelia joined in, however gingerly.

I hadn't seen these women in years, and they had come to my rescue. They had saved me.

Another figure emerged from the shadows, taller and stockier than the sisters. The man walked with steady steps and assurance.

Blackleach appeared, a wry smile on his face.

"Is your entire coven here?" I asked, hope burning in my chest.

"Almost."

"How did you know about the attack?" I asked.

"We saw you and your mother's coven in the woods, well Echo did first," Astraea said, hopping from foot to foot with excitement, nudging her dire wolf with a boot clad foot. I smiled. It was nice to know that some things never changed.

Echo nuzzled my hands, licking me softly.

Gray hair now peppered his chin and eyebrows, but he was every bit of a handsome, fierce wolf as he was when I first met him all those years ago. "Thank you, Echo."

He barked back at me, reminding me of his namesake.

Blackleach stood in front of me.

"You're injured."

I nodded, lifting my shirt. The wound was still bleeding, but it didn't hurt as much as it had. With Blackleach's magic and my gorgon's healing abilities, I was likely to be fully healed within minutes.

A warm tingling sensation flitted across the injury, and I took a deep breath as magic filled my veins. The sensation of Tabrn's healing magic was unlike anything I had felt before.

"Ceto's attempting to summon the gods," I murmured as Blackleach finished healing my wound.

Thick silence fell over our group. The last time the gods and goddesses had come down, war and pestilence had fallen over the land. We couldn't let that happen again.

"I never did like your mother," Blackleach sighed.

"Me neither," I agreed, feeling lighter.

Blackleach unsheathed a sword from his back, handing it to me without hesitation. The broadsword felt like home.

"Can you guys hold them off? I need to go and find someone."

The sisters and Hecate's Fifth Coven's leader all nodded.

I charged down the alleyway. A golem launched itself at me, but I was ready. Quickly and efficiently, I stoned the creature and decapitated it with a sweeping swipe of my sword.

Another golem lumbered towards me, and I stepped back, balancing my weight on my left foot, and threw my right fist out in a curved punch at its temple. Pivoting, the golem brought up its right forearm to counter the blow.

It didn't see my broadsword until it was too late.

Monster after monster fell beneath my sword.

Though my arms ached, I continued to fight.

Unlike my first battles with the golems, I was more confident in my abilities this time. I believed in myself, in my power.

The closer I ran to the prison, the more mages I saw engaged in fights with golems and Ceto's coven.

A hard body crashed into me.

The cloaked figure wrapped their forearm around my collarbone and shoulders, dragging me into a shadowed alleyway, their other hand pressing a knife against my throat.

"You're going to regret th—" I grunted, struggling.

My voice stopped short.

A pair of lapis lazuli eyes stared back at me, as the person pinned me to the brick wall. Gently, I pulled back their hood, heat and emotion building in my chest as I admired glittering drakon scales on their body.

Brooks.

I cried out in joy as he crushed his lips to mine. His hands gripped my waist, warm and strong. Wrapping my arms around his neck, I pulled him closer as my sword fell to the ground.

We were a rampant river.

A sweeping hurricane on land.

A blazing wildfire.

Our passion had never died, even though we had failed each other. Sobs broke through my lips and salty tears at his comforting presence.

"What are these tears for, lovely?" Brooks murmured against my lips, not pulling back as he wiped the moisture from my eyes.

"I—I can't stop. I'm so sorry, Bro—"

"It's okay. You don't have to be sorry for anything. I've got you. I forgive you, lovely."

He pressed a soft kiss on both of my eyelids.

I couldn't be sure when I stopped crying, or how long we held each other in the shadows of that dark alley as the world around us crashed and burned.

"You didn't believe me," Brooks whispered, referring to the last conversation we had before he was imprisoned.

I nodded.

He traced slow, burning circles on my ribs with his fingers, the cold doing nothing to diminish the heat between us.

"I didn't. I told you that you meant nothing to me," I let out a shaky breath, "because if I didn't, if I didn't—"

A beat of silence passed.

"I love you, Brooks," I finally admitted, my heart in my throat.

He rested his forehead against mine. "A questionable decision on your part."

Rolling my eyes, I smacked his chest.

"Truth or dare?" Brooks asks me.

"Uh—"

He pressed a finger to my lips. "Say truth."

"Okay, truth."

"I love you too, lovely."

I place a kiss on his mouth.

"Another truth. It wasn't fair of me to believe Rohesia over you," I sighed.

"Hey," Brooks tilted my head back, "she was your best friend for so long. There's no shame in believing or trusting those that you love."

Maybe he had a point. But it didn't excuse my actions, at least, not in my mind.

"I knew deep down that it wasn't you. But I didn't expect it to be Rohesia. She was the one who made it seem like you leaked the convoy's location to my coven, and put a spell on the ring that you wore. She also brought me to my mother to be sacrificed and was almost successful."

I took a breath.

"Brooks. Ceto wants to go to war with the gods."

His eyes widened at the multitude of revelations.

"We won't let her," he reassured me, and I nodded in agreement. I wasn't sure how many golems and gorgons were left, but I knew our numbers were growing.

419

All of Hecate's covens in Iydara had heard Blackleach's plea for help, and they were continuing to show up. Even the rogue mages in Hecate's Ninth Coven.

"How did you escape?" I asked, as we jogged back to the square, towards my friends.

"You won't believe me if I tell you." He grinned.

"Try me."

My heart soared at our easy conversation. It was like no time at all had passed between us.

"The Collectress."

I almost stopped in my tracks.

"The Collectress?" I repeated, unsure if I had misheard him.

"She's pretty desperate to save Iydara and keep her control. They gave all of the prisoners weapons and tracking devices and let us loose on the city. Said we could reduce our sentences if we killed enough golems."

"We'll prove your innocence, I promise."

"I don't doubt it, Watson," Brooks winked.

Turning the corner, I saw Ophelia, Astraea, and Twyla fighting alongside their familiars. Rogue mages fought with them, burning the bodies of the fallen golems.

Stepping forward, I noticed that Brooks had disappeared from my side. He was kneeling on the ground behind me.

"You brought them back to me," Brooks whispered, tears falling from his eyes onto the ground. He grabbed my hand and didn't let go.

And it was at that moment I finally saw the resemblance between the sisters and Brooks. The same sharp cheekbones and cobalt eyes; they even laughed the same.

Twyla was the first to see her younger brother.

She cried out, running towards us and crashing into Brooks. I retreated from the pair, allowing them a moment of privacy.

Ophelia soon looked over to see what the distraction was, and almost dropped her weapon. She practically threw Astraea over her shoulder in her haste to reach Brooks.

"Ophelia, put me down!" Astraea shrieked, pounding on her triplet's back.

Brooks chuckled. "Hello, Astraea."

Ophelia dropped Astraea, who fell to her knees as she waited her turn to hug her brother.

After Ophelia and Brooks's embrace, Astraea whimpered, holding onto her dire wolf as it led her to her brother. She touched his face and pressed her forehead to his. A strangled laugh escaped her throat.

"What in gods' name happened that day?" Brooks choked out, wrapping his sisters in a hug.

"Arnoul and The Collectress happened," Ophelia sighed, leaning into her brother, tears collecting in her eyes.

"The night of the trip, we overheard Arnoul on the phone with The Collectress. She wanted him to kill us so Mom and Dad would be so grief stricken that they would step down as owners of the store. And with you in Raas, Arnoul would be next in line to take it over. They wanted to use the store as a front to sell black market jewels and relics," Twyla informed us.

"We left that night and were found by Hecate's Fifth Coven. They protected us all these years," Astraea stated, petting her dire wolf.

"Why not return to Iydara and tell us?" Brooks asked. "I would have protected you."

Hurt tinged his voice.

"Arnoul threatened Hecate's Fifth Coven. Said if we returned he would have the coven removed from Iydara. We had to protect them," Ophelia said, trying to get their brother to understand.

Brooks was always the one who did the protecting, and I imagined it was hard for him to allow his sister to do the same thing.

"I never stopped looking for you."

421

"We know," Astraea said, smiling.

"How do you fit into all of this?" Brooks asked me, realizing that I hadn't needed to be introduced to his sisters.

"That," I said, "is another story, for another time."

Breaking free from his sisters, Brooks wrapped his arms around me, kissing me lightly. This kiss was different to all of the ones before. It was gentle. And made my heart ache.

"Save that for the wedding!" Ophelia groaned, while Twyla and Astraea cat-called us. I couldn't help but laugh as we picked up our swords.

There was much fighting left to be done, but I knew one thing for certain: I had found my home.

42

Hundreds of golems littered the streets, staining the ground with their blood. The dais my mother had tried to sacrifice me on was empty. Ceto was nowhere to be seen and other gorgons were long gone, fighting or fleeing Iydara.

I noticed Stheno was leaning against the platform with three swords jutting out from her chest. She didn't seem to have the energy or will to remove them.

We carefully scanned the area, our backs towards one another and our hands heavy with the weight of swords and daggers. Ophelia's ravens patrolled the sky, relaying messages to her with a tilt of their head or look of their yellow eyes.

The hair on my neck started to stand up, as if coerced by the forks of white lighting flashing in the midnight sky. Snow continued to fall in between blinding flares of light and claps of thunder.

Gusts of powerful wind flung specks of dirt into our eyes, pushing our little huddle apart. Our shouts were lost in the sudden currents of the wind.

"Oh, Medusa. How foolish you are."

I tensed.

Warm breath tickled the back of my neck, a knife scraping the thin skin of my throat as I was yanked backwards. My head hit the ground, and I struggled to see my attacker, even in my gorgon form.

The scent of the sea overwhelmed my nostrils.

A grating laugh rang out.

And I realized who it was.

Poseidon.

As the dust cleared, I saw the god in all of his hauntingly destructive glory.

The last time I had seen him, he had been clothed in a sarong, bare chested with his hair hanging in his face. Now, he wore thick plates of battle armor, his face painted with the lifeblood of gorgons and golems. His hair was tied back with a leather cord and he was wielding a broadsword nicknamed The Kiss of Death.

The handle of the blade was made of braided gold, trailing upwards to form a pair of shiny wings. During the forging process, the sword had been embedded with the tears of Thanatos, sealing the weapon with The Kiss of Death.

It didn't matter if you were a human or a god or goddess in a mortal form, one scratch from the blade and you would die. Only the gods were allowed access to such weapons, and it was no wonder that they had come out victorious in every war they were utilized in over eons.

They would even kill golems.

But that didn't stop me from attacking him.

Panting, I swung my sword at his, the clashing metal sending painful vibrations down my arms. Poseidon easily blocked the next swing of my blade.

Brooks was deep in battle with Ceto. His sisters were fighting a group of golems. It was madness, complete and utter madness.

Lightning crashed into a tree nearby.

The ground shook.

Chunks of pavement cracked and launched into the air. I took cover with my hands over my head, knowing that my fight with Poseidon was far from over.

Everything from café tables to entire buildings began to groan, their weight shifting ominously. The street shook beneath our feet, chunks of pavement crumbling.

Shouts of horror rang out through the square.

An enormous fissure began to form in the center of the plaza. It grew and grew, transforming into a giant circular hole. The ground trembled as a charybdis emerged from the depths. Large sewer tunnels ran beneath Iydara, and it seemed that they led right to Marren's Grove, providing the charybdis with easy access to the city.

The Collectress sat on the back of the creature, controlling it with her gifted version of dunamis. With a battle cry, she motioned for the charybdis to violently attack a group of golems near a department store.

With an appalling crunch, the monster decapitated ten golems in a single bite. My mother cried out in defeat as her army began to dwindle.

Leaping off the creature, The Collectress landed on the ground, rolling and slashing at the golems that launched themselves at her.

There shouldn't be this many.

We had killed hundreds already, where were they coming from? Understanding slammed into me as I realized I hadn't seen Euryale in over an hour.

Scrambling from the edges of the growing cavity in the street, I vaulted over fallen debris, rushing towards Brooks. Alongside his sisters and members of their coven, he was fighting against livid gorgons and hungry golems.

"Ceto lied. She has more of the dust. Someone is using it to make more golems as we speak," I grunted, blocking a sloppy throw from a golem.

"Who and where?"

I exhaled. "That's where you come in, detective."

Brooks grinned, decapitating a golem with a show of flashing steel and honed skills. He grabbed my hand, searching the square with a quick glance of his eyes.

Brooks's throat bobbed, and his face dropped solemnly. Without hesitation, he pulled me in the direction of the fallen dais.

425

Stheno was still propped against the stage, daggers protruding from her scale covered chest. Jerking away from us, she feebly struggled to fight us off.

"Where's the rest of the dust?" Brooks asked.

Stheno didn't answer, instead staring over our heads.

Her face became pale as Brooks placed his hand on the knife bulging from her gut. The weight of his hand on the knife caused tears to spring in her eyes.

"Don't," she pleaded, her voice cracking.

His hand didn't hesitate on the knife.

With a skillful and swift motion, he removed the dagger.

Relief flashed in her eyes, a soft groan escaping her lips.

The dagger embedded beneath her collar bone gave little resistance as he removed it, nor did the knife that had pierced the soft skin of her side.

"Why?" my sister asked, confusion knitting her eyebrows together. She seemed thoroughly shocked by Brooks's act of compassion.

"Most of the time, mercy will get you places faster than cruelty," he stated matter-of-factly.

"Now, where's the dust, Stheno?" I asked.

Her eyes met mine.

She lifted her chin, motioning towards a run-down building behind the dais. Brooks offered one more act of kindness towards my sister, even though she had betrayed me and hurt him. Lifting her onto the platform, he ordered a mage from The Hub to protect my sister and to not let her out of their sight until The Collectress could be informed of Stheno's arrest. Taking no chances, Brooks placed handcuffs on my sister before we left.

The building Stheno had motioned towards was less than one hundred yards away from the dais. We walked carefully onto the dilapidated and aged porch. Rickety floorboards creaked under the weight of our bodies and armor. The entryway and first floor were empty, save for a handful of lingering cobwebs and rats.

Walking up the stairs, Brooks tilted his head, motioning me forward. My gorgon sensed multiple presences at the end of the hallway.

Hesitantly, Brooks opened the door.

Statues from The Collectress's garden littered the room, alongside the barrels of dust that hadn't been turned over to Rohesia when she had traded me for the potion.

I recognized every statue, and knew all of their names.

Euryale was nowhere to be found.

"This is my chance to make this right," I told Brooks.

With great understanding, Brooks stood guard while I began the tedious process of unstoning the victims. The first statue took a great amount of effort from me. Sweat drenched my back, and my limbs shook, but with each unstoning, the process went faster.

As I began to work on the final three victims, a sudden crash caught my attention. In my peripheral vision, I saw Brooks and Euryale throwing punches at one another.

The unstoned victims stood around the room, confused and dazed. I motioned for them to leave, but they just blinked at me.

With a frustrated sigh, I hurriedly worked to unstone the final statue from The Collectress's garden. Perspiration dripped into my eyes, clouding my vision.

I whipped around at the sound of shattering glass. Brooks fell out of the broken window in a tangle of limbs, dragging Euryale close behind him. The drop was three stories.

Heart beating rapidly in my chest, I raced to the window. I watched as Brooks reached out to me in slow motion, his face frozen in fear, knowing that his wing was still in the process of healing.

I called out to him, but it was too late.

He closed his eyes and attempted to fly.

But just as he was about to hit the hard, frozen ground, an ethereally solid draught of wind lifted him upwards, gently catching his wings. That was all he needed to launch himself into the air.

A sigh of relief escaped me.

Euryale had landed not far from Brooks, running away when she realized that he was unharmed and still pursuing her.

Brooks raced towards the dais, finding my mother readying herself to flee as well. He crashed straight into her. Ceto's snakes attempted to bite him, only to be cut off by his daggers.

I sprinted down the stairs, ready to face my mother, only to be thrown into a wall by strong arms that seemed to emerge from nowhere.

A dark laugh skittered across my bones. "What do we have here?"

Head spinning, I drew my sword.

Poseidon stood in the entryway of the old building. With a rapid swing of his deadly sword, I was pushed into the porch from the weight of our clashing blades, stumbling out onto the street.

Our fighting moved to the square.

He didn't stop his onslaught against me.

And neither did I.

For every blow from his sword, I returned the favor.

"You took everything from me," I cried out.

"Just your sweet innocence," Poseidon retorted, grunting from the weight of my blow. He gazed at me with a predatory gleam in his eyes and licked his lips, his hefty stare trailing down the entire length of my body.

And my control fractured.

I ducked beneath his arm, our swords clashing together with enormous force. My elbow came into contact with his wrist, knocking his sword out of his iron grasp.

Scrambling for the weapon, I held it aloft.

The Kiss of Death.

"No," I answered, drawing the sword back, "you took my family. My home. My future. My confidence. My ability to trust. My love for life. And so, so much more."

I swung again, backing him into a corner.

"But guess what?" I asked Poseidon.

The god only stumbled backwards, shocked by my wrath.

"I'm taking it all back," I vowed, shoving the tip of the sword deep into the chest of the sea god.

The weapon vibrated in my hands.

Poseidon's eyes grew distant, and his head lolled to the side.

His tanned hands gripped the weapon in desperation, the blade cutting into his calloused palms in a futile attempt to yank it from his chest.

I watched in disbelief as his bloodied hands finally fell to the ground, my heart thumping in my chest. The sword, edged with blood, cracked down the center.

I had slain a god. The world seemed to go quiet.

Everything was still.

Even the battling between the gorgons and gods came to a sudden stop. No one uttered a word.

As rivers of blood leaked from Poseidon's chest, I remembered the night I was forced into the chamber with him.

I thrashed and fought and became a pile of ash beneath his destructive touch, screaming for my innocent soul to be spared.

He meant to destroy me, thinking I wouldn't survive.

Little did he know, I'd *fucking* thrive in the chaos.

Flashes of a lost life as a priestess burned through my mind. Of a life lived with my coven in snowy mountains beneath rays of prismatic sunlight.

So much potential had been ripped from me because of one man's selfish act of greed.

The grief was unbearable.

But I would no longer flinch when I heard his name.

Because he ceased to exist.

Stepping back, I dropped to my knees.

I was free at last.

Brooks lowered the sword that he had poised against my mother's neck, his eyes shining with pride and love and so much more.

I was created to be destroyed. He was created to destroy me. And yet, we collided with moon dust in our lungs, sunlight in our eyes, and killed a ruler of the skies.

We were war and death and everything we shouldn't be.

And yet, here we were.

In the stillness, I forced myself to scan the crowd. My gaze locked on Athena. Her face was twisted with anger and anguish as she stared at the dead god, the one who she had loved. I expected to find a trace of compassion in my heart, but I found none.

Devastation was written in the elegant plains of her face. Agony flooded her round eyes. She seemed to be a breath away from collapsing onto the broken pavement. But as the moment passed, and she stayed standing, her eyes sparked with revulsion.

With revenge.

I adjusted my hold on Poseidon's sword as Athena stalked towards me. Even Zeus and Ares seemed to be holding their breath.

"Please," I begged her, "stop this madness."

Athena looked at me with a hatred so pure and transparent that it sent a shockwave of terror through me. I could see her desperation, the ache of her resolve. With a guttural scream, Athena turned and swung her sword.

It was over before I knew what was happening.

The sickening sound of blood splattering on concrete.

Ceto looked down at her chest, as if in slow motion, where blood blossomed from the wound that Athena had inflicted with her own Kiss of Death broadsword.

My mother crashed to her knees in a heap.

Dead.

Athena turned on her heel, joining the other gods and goddesses. "Leave Iydara, gorgons. Or face the same fate as your leader and Poseidon."

Meeting my eyes for a final time, Athena smiled.

She smiled at me.

But this was not a conciliatory smile. Her saccharine grin promised demise and heartache.

With a spark of blinding light, Zeus threw his lightning bolt into the sky, killing the remaining golems with a final, fatal flash of forked lightning.

Poseidon's body disappeared into the sky, gone forever. The gods and goddesses disappeared into the heavens, leaving smoldering buildings and blood in their wake.

Twyla, Ophelia, and Astraea dropped their weapons.

Brooks pressed a silent kiss to my lips, soft and reassuring.

I pressed my forehead into his chest, shaking.

We had won.

We would be okay.

That was until my face came into contact with something sticky.

Frowning, I touched my skin; my fingertips were coated in thick, crimson blood. Brooks was bleeding heavily.

Too much blood was spilling from the small wound.

I attempted to staunch the bleeding with pressure from my hands, but endless amounts of blood still leaked out. But who had wounded him? He had seemed fine just moments before.

Then the truth hit me like a ton of bricks.

Athena had known that the sword would nick Brooks when she shoved it through my mother's body; he was still holding a knife to her throat from behind.

That's why Athena had smiled at me. She knew I didn't love my mother, given the amount of times I had prayed to her and told her so, and I had found it strange that Athena had killed my mother.

I had thought that maybe Athena was taking my side and choosing to finally end the violence or but of course, her motivation was actually revenge.

But Ceto hadn't been her target.

It had been Brooks.

Brooks leaned into me with the entire weight of his broad form, his eyes glossy. This couldn't be happening.

No. No. No.

It wasn't supposed to end this way. But I couldn't escape it. Everything had gone wrong. The world was in ruins around me. And it was all my fault.

As he crashed to his knees, I ripped open his shirt to find a gash near his sternum. He had been pierced by Athena's deadly sword. He had been kissed by death.

I had ripped Athena's lover from her, and she was going to do the same to me.

I did not care that Iydara was saved.

I did not care that Poseidon and my mother were dead.

I cared that Brooks was dying and there was nothing I could do about it.

"I got you. It's gonna be okay. You're going to be okay."

I laid Brooks down, pure agony tearing through my heart. Sitting on the ground, I placed his head in my lap.

I should have known that nothing good could ever last in this world. But he had fooled me.

"I dare you to stay," I cried out, choking on my ragged breaths, "I dare you to live."

Brooks's sisters came to his side, hanging their heads.

They had just gotten him back.

I refused to believe that we were meant to end like this.

I had to hold onto hope.

A soft smile appeared on his mouth.

"I didn't mean to love you so much," he rasped.

Brooks's cobalt eyes, ones that had steadied me, that had saved me and grounded me, grew distant. His hand grasped one of my snakes. I held his head in my hands, pressing a kiss to his lips, tears mingling with our breath.

I wailed out through the tears. "Please, save him, Zeus."

Pleading, bargaining, I would do anything to save him.

"I can stone you," I gasped desperately.

It would allow him to stay alive while I searched for a cure.

Brooks parted his blood smeared lips. "You have to let me go, lovely. I want to feel human one more time. And what's more human than dying?"

Emotion overcame me. He had no choice in becoming a huntsman. No control over the situation. But this, his death, he had a say in. And I had to honor that, even if it obliterated my soul.

"You found," a choking gasp escaped his lips, a lingering breath, "me."

I sobbed.

"Find me a-again." He swallowed, his voice muffled.

He couldn't leave me. Not now.

Not after everything.

Brooks squeezed my hand, and I knew he needed to hear my promise before the darkness dragged him under.

"I will," I promised, resting my forehead against his.

Brooks Ascian-Otis de Blasis inhaled. Once. Twice.

And then, there was no light left in his eyes.

No life.

And I unleashed my gorgon upon the world, becoming exactly what society had painted me to be.

A monster.

EPILOGUE

I have no love left in my soul.

My soul is made of impenetrable ice, and my heart of stone.

A cold-hearted executioner.

Ruthless. Callous. Spiteful.

I used to be lovely when I smiled.

Now I grin madly with gnashing, bloody teeth.

Wearing a glorious crown that twists and hisses, savoring justice, I know that the sinners of the world will not escape my wrath.

I was coming for them.

For the ones that turned his cobalt eyes into waves of darkness and decay.

The gasping sounds of a potentially glorious life constantly surrounded me, mocked me, the roar of the ocean, the ear-splitting laughter of imaginary children, and time that was cruelly ripped from my hands.

Encased in tombs of stone, the ones that hurt him are preyed upon without pity, jaws eternally pried open in frozen screams.

But it doesn't ease the excruciating agony.

None of it does.

Because now. Now, there is nothing left. Nothing but devastation. Never-ending devastation. A ravaged soul.

And when Perseus came for my head, I let him take it.

Because even the most horrific monsters need love to survive.

ACKNOWLEDGEMENTS

I first want to thank my Lord and Savior, Jesus Christ for this unbelievable journey and life that I am so blessed to live. Without Him, none of this would have ever been possible. I am in constant awe of His graciousness and goodness in my life.

To Nolan, I am so incredibly blessed to be your mom. You inspire me every day and I am unbelievably proud of you. You can do anything you set your mind to, so aim for the stars. This book is proof of that. Not that you're allowed to read this book until you are older than the age of twenty-one haha. I love you.

To Nathan, where do I begin? You believe in me when I don't believe in myself. You complete me. Your dedication to me and our son is heartwarming and makes me feel so blessed to be your wife. Thank you for loving me when I am unlovable. I love you most.

To Hannah, thank you for telling me to chase my dreams and for always believing in me. There aren't enough words to tell you how much you mean to me. I am so blessed to be your person. I appreciate you and our daily calls. Without you, I would still be living to please others, instead of following my dreams. And I love you to the moon and to saturn. You're the best sister ever.

To Amber, thank you. Seriously. Thank you for reading the first very rough draft of this book back in 2021. Your input and excitement for my book helped to grow my confidence. I don't know if this book would have seen the light of day if not for your input and belief in me. Also, thank you for letting me borrow your printer to print off my contract because I didn't have one haha.

To Addie, thank you for your constant love and support. Especially while I figured out how to juggle mom life and work life. You help me keep going when the mom guilt becomes overwhelming. I love you and won't be able to ever put into words how much our friendship means to me.

To Steven and Cat, thank you for all of your constant support and love. Without you guys, I wouldn't be where I am today, writing this book and others in the future. I love you guys.

To Cris, thank you for keeping me sane during this process and for your encouraging words and wisdom. Thank you for helping me heal through therapy and EMDR and for helping me find my inner Wonder Woman. Seriously, thank you.

To my high school English teacher, Sue Shelton. I always loved to write and you constantly complimented my writing. My senior year, you gave me an award that was titled "The Writer With A Future Award", and that award, although some may say unimportant or juvenile, was a major stepping stone for my confidence and my writing career.

To my incredible editors, Rowan Thomas, and Vulpine Press' Publishing Director, Sarah Hembrow. Your belief and comments and input helped make this book what it is today. Thank you for making my childhood dream become a reality. The countless hours you spent polishing and commenting on my work makes my heart warm. Your vision and passion for my work gave me so much confidence, which was MUCH needed during my rough postpartum period. Thank you for your patience and guidance during this incredible process.

To the rest of the team at Vulpine Press and Ockham Publishing Group. Words will never be able to describe the disbelief and gratefulness I still feel when telling people I am a published author. The day I signed my contract in October of 2022 lives in my mind forever. So simply, thank you.

L.A. Riemenschneider is a multi-genre author of all things fantasy and romance, using her books to stand in solidarity with those overcoming PTSD, trauma, endometriosis, and other life physical and mental health matters. *Her Writhing Crown* is her debut novel and focuses on the reality of living with PTSD and the strength of survivors.

If she is not found madly typing on her laptop, she enjoys going on adventures with her husband, son, and herd of dogs and cats. She is a lifelong reader, dinosaur lover, and baseball fanatic.

Find her online:
Facebook: L.A. Riemenschneider
TikTok: l.a.riemenschneider
Instagram: L.A.Riemenschneider
Twitter: authorLAR

Printed in Great Britain
by Amazon